HACKNEY LIBRARY SERVICES H

"I think the sun is in the King's eyes," growled Razi, spit flecking his lips, his teeth bared as he surged against the restraining guards, putting his face up to his father's. "His Majesty mistakes me for my *brother*!"

Father and son faced up to each other for a moment, like territorial wolves. Then gradually Jonathon's expression changed into something darker than rage. He looked at Razi in a new manner: an up and down, speculative manner. Wynter didn't like this new expression. It was remote and calculating, all Jonathon's fury fading in exchange for a carefully scheming assessment of his still furious son.

On the ground, by the tree, Christopher murmured something in Merron and rolled onto his side. The King glanced at him and gestured to his guards.

"Take him," he said casually. "Feed him to The Chair. Le

LIB OF HACK
D0320475

By Celine Kiernan

The Moorehawke Trilogy
The Poison Throne
The Crowded Shadows
The Rebel Prince

The Poison Throne

Celine Kiernan

orbit

www.orbitbooks.net

ORBIT

First published in Ireland in 2008 by The O'Brien Press Ltd.
12 Terenure Road East, Rathgar, Dublin 6, Ireland
This paperback edition published in 2010 by Orbit

Copyright © 2008 by Celine Kiernan

Excerpt of *The Prodigal Mage* by Karen Miller
Copyright © 2009 by Karen Miller

The moral right of the author has been asserted.

*All characters and events in this publication, other than those
clearly in the public domain, are fictitious and any resemblance
to real persons, living or dead, is purely coincidental.*

All rights reserved.
No part of this publication may be reproduced, stored in a
retrieval system, or transmitted, in any form or by any means, without
the prior permission in writing of the publisher, nor be otherwise circulated
in any form of binding or cover other than that in which it is published
and without a similar condition including this condition
being imposed on the subsequent purchaser.

A CIP cataloguye record for this book is
available from the British Library.

ISBN 978-1-84149-821-8

Typeset in Garamond by M Rules
Printed in the UK by CPI Mackays, Chatham ME5 8TD

Papers used by Orbit are natural, renewable and
recyclable products sourced from well-managed forests and certified
in accordance with the rules of the Forest Stewardship Council.

Mixed Sources
Product group from well-managed
forests and other controlled sources
www.fsc.org Cert no. SGS-COC-004081
© 1996 Forest Stewardship Council

Orbit
An imprint of
Little, Brown Book Group
100 Victoria Embankment
London EC4Y 0DY

An Hachette UK Company
www.hachette.co.uk

www.orbitbooks.net

For Mam and Dad, I love you.
To Noel, Emmet and Grace, always and with all my heart.

And also my sincere thanks to Roddy Doyle and Catherine
Dunne, because, though most of us never get a chance to say
it, you made a huge difference to us.
A great teacher is never forgotten.

LONDON BOROUGH OF HACKNEY LIBRARIES	
HK10000639	
Bertrams	14/01/2011
TF	£7.99
DAL	01/04/2010

Acknowledgements

With huge thanks to Svetlana Pironko of Author Rights Agency for her protection and guidance. A wonderful agent and a friend too. Also to my first publishers The O'Brien Press who took a chance on me and have supported and helped me, and held my hand all through this strange new process.

Many, *many* thanks to all at Little, Brown who have thrown themselves so enthusiastically into the Moorehawke experience.

And lastly to Pat Mullan, whose kindness and generosity of spirit opened a door I had begun to think was locked for good. Thanks Pat, I'll never be able to thank you enough.

Contents

The Voiceless Cat

The sentry would not let them pass. Even when Wynter's father showed their papers, and explained that they were expected at court, the guards had remained sneering and unpleasant, and refused to open the gates. Eventually, the sentry door was shut and Wynter and her father were left outside while the watchman went off somewhere to "look see".

They had been waiting there, ignored and bewildered, for an entire quarter of the shadows – two hours on the northern clock – with that heavy sentry door shut in their faces, and Wynter could feel her blood beginning a slow rise to anger.

The men that Shirken had paid to accompany them from the North had gone long ago. She did not blame their guides for leaving. Their job had been to get herself and Lorcan safely from one kingship to another, to get them home, and that they had done. She had no quarrel with them. They had been polite and respectful all through the long journey south, and Wynter did not doubt that they were good and honest men. But they were not friends, they were not loyal, except to Shirken and the job he had paid them to complete.

No doubt Shirken's men had watched from the top of the rise as Wynter and her father had reached the foot of the hill and crossed the thick beams of the moat bridge. And no doubt they had waited until the two of them were safe within the protective shadow of the gate arch before turning back into the dark pines and heading home. Mission accomplished.

Wynter's horse, Ozkar, shifted impatiently beside her. He smelled the warm grass baking in the sun behind them, and the dark clear water of the moat. He was thirsty and hungry, and Wynter couldn't blame him for snorting and stamping his hoof. Still, she tugged his rein to get him to settle and shifted her weight discreetly from one foot to the other. Wynter, too, was tired, saddle-sore and generally weary to her bones of travelling. But, at fifteen years old, she was no stranger to courtly protocol and she remained outwardly stoic, as if undisturbed by this unending wait in the heat.

The well practised remoteness of her expression may have given nothing away, but she was, in truth, barely in command of her impatience. All she really wanted to do was throw off her boots and run up the meadows in her bare feet, fling herself down into the long grass and watch the sky.

They had been so long in the grey cold of the North that this singing heat and the clear sunlight of home were like white wine to her. She longed to revel in it. She longed to get her father out into the sun somewhere and let the summer heat bake some warmth back into his bones. He had wisely remained astride his horse, and now he sat there so quietly that Wynter glanced sideways to check that he was still awake. He was. She could see his eyes gleaming in the shadows beneath the brim of his hat. He looked neither left nor right, his gaze focusing inwards, just sitting, waiting for permission to come home.

His long body had a weary curl to it, though, and the palsy in his hands where they folded patiently against the pommel of his saddle was worse than usual.

Wynter eyed her father's trembling fingers with concern. Old men shook like that, not strong-shouldered craftsmen of thirty-three. *Stop fretting*, she told herself, looking forward again and straightening her back. *A good night's rest is all he needs, a nice dinner and then he'll be right as summer rain.*

She rubbed the tips of her fingers against each other, feeling the reassuring numbness of scar and callus. Worthy hands. That's what the two of them had. Worthy hands, capable of supporting them through anything. Out of habit, she glanced back at the roll of carpenter's tools on her horse's rump and then over at the similar roll on the back of her father's saddle. All present and accounted for.

Imperceptibly, Wynter shifted her aching feet again and, for once in her life, wished she was wearing her women's clothing and not her boys britches and short-coat. It was so much easier to move your feet and legs when they were hidden by a skirt. She sighed again at the misguided enthusiasm that had sent her leaping from her horse. She had flung herself from his back on their arrival, expecting the gates to be swept wide and a boisterous welcome to have been orchestrated. What childish conceit. And now, here she stood, pride and protocol not allowing her to remount, forced to stand here like a lowly pageboy until the sentry returned with their permission to pass.

An orange cat trotted delicately along the base of the wall, glowing like a sinuous ember as it passed out of the shadows. At the sight of it, Wynter forgot to be calm and courtly, and she allowed herself to smile and nod and follow the cat's progress with a turn of her head. The cat paused, one paw raised to its white chest, and regarded Wynter with affronted curiosity. Its very posture said, *Can I believe my eyes? Have you dared to look at me?*

Wynter's smile became a grin at the familiar weight of feline disdain, and she wondered how many generations of cat brothers and cat sisters had been born in the five years that she had been away. Before taking up her apprenticeship, Wynter had been the King's Cat-Keeper and she had known all her charges by name. *Whose great-great-grand-kitten-grown-to-cat is this?* she wondered.

She inclined her head and murmured, "All respects to you this fine day, mouse-bane," fully expecting the usual reply, *All the finer for you, having seen me.* But instead, the cat's green eyes opened in shock and confusion at her greeting, and it flickered suddenly away, a flame in sunlight, flowing across the moat bridge and disappearing down onto the loose gravel of the far bank.

Wynter watched it depart with a puzzled frown. Imagine a cat having such atrocious manners and such easily shattered composure! Something wasn't right.

The rattle of the sentry gate brought Wynter's eyes frontwards and the shadows under the portcullis were sliced by a sharp blade of sunlight as the gate opened a crack. The Sergeant of the Watch stuck his head out. He regarded the two of them without a trace of deference, as if surprised to find them still there. Wynter's court-face slipped smoothly into place.

Without another word to them, the Sergeant pulled his head back in and shut the sentry door with a snap of the lock. Wynter's heart dropped, but rose again instantly as the heavy door chains began to pull backwards with a grinding whine of metal on stone. Somewhere within the wall, the Master of the Entrance was turning the big wheel that wound the chains onto their spools.

Yes! thought Wynter, *We have been granted access!*

Slowly, slowly the shadows under the bridge were eaten up by sunlight as the heavy horse gate swung open to reveal the inner gardens and the King's domain.

Victuallor Heron was striding down the wide gravel path as they passed through the gate, his office robe flapping. He must have been at business to be dressed so formally and, indeed, Wynter saw that his fingers were stained with ink. His wrinkled old face was filled with joy and he was advancing on her father as if he would rise up from the ground, a great amiable bird, and descend upon him, horse and all, to wrap him in a hug that would hide both of them from view.

"Lorcan!" he cried as he swept along the gravel, "Lorcan!" and his immediate informality undid a thousand anxious knots in Wynter's mind. Some things, at least, were still all right.

Her father leaned forward from the height of his saddle and smiled tiredly down at his old friend. They clasped hands, her father's big splay-fingered shovel of a hand wrapped tightly in the long fingered agility of Heron's. Their smiling eye contact lingered and spoke volumes.

"Friend Heron," said Lorcan, his warm, rasping voice an embrace in itself, the feeling going far beyond the words.

Heron's eyes sharpened and he lowered his chin a little, his grip on Lorcan's hand tightening.

"I believe you were kept waiting," he said, his eyes flicking almost imperceptibly to the sentry. Something in the set of his face made Wynter glance at the attending guards and what she saw made her heart do a strange little pitter in her chest. The soldiers were openly staring at this exchange between Heron and her father. In fact, they were almost perceptibly *lounging* in the presence of the Victuallor. She swallowed down a lump of uncertainty and glanced back to where her father and Heron were exchanging a meaningful look.

Suddenly her father straightened in the saddle, drawing himself up so that his full height and the true width of his powerful shoulders became apparent. Wynter saw his face go very still. His eyelids dropped to hood the vibrant cat-green of his eyes, and his generous, curving mouth thinned and curled up on one side.

This was what Wynter thought of as The Mask or sometimes The Cloak. It pained her to see it here, despite its magnificence, and she though wearily, *Oh Dad, even here? Even here must we play the terrible game?* But she couldn't help the familiar surge of pride as she saw him transform, and there was a touch of cruel pleasure in her smile as she watched him turn in the saddle and put the weight of his suddenly imperious stare onto the lounging guards.

Lorcan said nothing for a moment, and for that little

while the guards met his eyes as equals, not yet registering the transformation from mere craftsman to something more dangerous. He sat, regally immobile, in the saddle, and he swivelled his head to take in each man, deliberately examining their faces, one at a time, as if adding them to a list somewhere in a dark closet of his mind.

His long guildsman's plait swung in a heavy pendulum down his back, seventeen years' worth of growth, uncut since the day he'd been pronounced master of his trade. The deep red of it was only recently distinguished with swathes of grey, and it gave him the air of prosecutor, judge, jury and executioner. Wynter saw doubt begin to grow in the soldiers' faces, saw iron begin to creep up their spines. Still Lorcan didn't speak, and as Wynter watched, the sentry crystallised into a military unit. Just like that. A gang of rabblerous louts one minute, a unit of soldiers at respectful attention the next.

"Bring me a mounting block," said her father, purposely addressing one man, leaving no doubt that this was an order. That one man, the Sergeant of the Watch himself, took off as sharp as you like and crossed the lawn, disappearing around the corner into the lesser stable block at a quick trot.

My God, thought Wynter, *He doesn't even know yet who my father is, and there he goes. A carpenter – for all he knows a lowland shepherd's son, a fisherman's bastard, or any such variation on nothing at all – just told him to run fetch a mounting block, and look at him. He's off.* She looked up at her father in absolute awe. *And all with the weight of his stare*, she thought.

The Sergeant returned at a fair clip, a mounting block

held out before him like some precious baby. He placed it carefully beneath her father's horse and stepped back a respectful distance as Lorcan slipped from the stirrups and dismounted. If it caused him pain to step to the ground, he managed to hide it, even from Wynter who was fine-tuned to see it.

"Take our horses to the main stables; leave them in the care of the head boy. Tell him they are the property of Protector Lord Lorcan Moorehawke and his apprentice. Tell him I will be around to check on their comfort later today." If the softly rasped orders came as a blow to his pride, the Sergeant certainly didn't show it, and it was to his credit that he didn't bat an eyelid when this lowly carpenter's powerful title was revealed. Instead, he snapped off a crisp salute and gathered Wynter's father's reins from him without any further antipathy.

Wynter met her father's eyes. He would need to go with Heron now. Things were obviously afoot. "Go with them," he said, gently inclining his head to indicate the horses. "Make sure the tools are safe. Get some food and rest." He put his hand on her shoulder, briefly. She longed to tell him to lie down, to rest, to eat. But The Masks were on, for both of them now. And instead of daughterly concern, she dipped her head as an apprentice in deference to the master, and stood watching as Heron led him away up the broad sweep of gravel, to the King's quarters, no doubt, and the entanglements of state.

Shearing's Ghost

It was so quiet, midday in high summer and everyone was at rest, or cooling themselves by the river at the far end of the estate. Wynter knew that the gardens would not come to life again till late in the evening, when the temperature would return to bearable. For now she had the entire palace complex to herself, a rare blessing in this complicated world.

She left the horses, happy in their dim stalls, and quickly crossed the wavering heat of the redbrick stable yards. Her footsteps rang back at her from the stable buildings. Little swallows sliced the sunshine around her, darting moments of shadow in the shimmering air, and the sound of contented horses and the sweet and dreamy smell of dung soothed her.

Home, home, *home*. It all sang to her, *You're home.*

She swerved left, turned at the yellow dovecote and cut a path between the shady trees, angling through the yew walk, heading for the kitchen garden. The air was so much cooler here and thick with resinous scent. Wynter crossed the sleepy sun-hazed paths and colonnades with an undisguised smile on her face, drinking in all the old familiar turns and corners, taking her own sweet time.

All those years in the grey dampness of the North she had silently longed for home, and every night, in response to that unexpressed longing, her heart had conjured this walk for her. Night after night in honey-soaked dreams, she had taken this exact trip from stable to kitchen. And now here she was, real and certain, treading on older feet the happy path of her childhood. She would have liked Razi and Alberon to be here, or the cats maybe, flowing against her ankles as they used to, like warm smoke keeping her company.

Rounding a corner to the limestone courtyard, she was caught unawares by two girls at the well. Unfamiliar faces, or perhaps just grown beyond her recognition. The easy flow of their voices ceased as she came into sight and they turned to look at her. She hoisted the rolls of tools a little higher on her shoulder and continued her walk without any perceptible change of pace or expression.

The path would take her to within six or seven feet of them before it curved away again and they watched her as she approached. They were her age or perhaps a year or two younger, thirteen, maybe, plump-armed and rounded, their faces shaded under the brims of their wide straw hats. The taller girl was a Maid of the Bucket, out to get water. Her pails rested empty on the lip of the well, her yoke balanced on one shoulder. The other girl, younger than Wynter had first thought, maybe only ten, was a goose-herder and she idly batted her striped skirts with a switch as she looked Wynter up and down.

It wasn't the masculinity of Wynter's clothes that

intrigued the girls. Women often travelled in britches and short-coats, and it was quite obvious that she'd been travelling – the strong smell of horse sweat and campfire off her was evidence of that. It wasn't even so much the fact that she was a stranger; palace life was always full of strangers. No, it was her apprentice garb that really grabbed their interest.

She could see their eyes travelling over the uniform, taking in the tightly bound club of hair at her neck and the red tunic embroidered with the carpenter's crest. Both these things told them that Wynter had been four years an authorised apprentice. They slipped a glance at her boots and their eyebrows shot up at the sight of green laces. Only the most talented of apprentices were granted permission for green. They checked for the guild approval pendant and saw it hanging around her neck. This told them that she had earned the right to wages, and not just the bed and board granted to all apprentices.

When they looked her in the eye again, she saw wariness and speculation. *So here is something new*, that look said, *a woman doing well in a man's apprenticeship.* She could sense the cogs turning in their minds as they decided how they felt about that.

Then the older girl smiled at her, a genuine smile that showed dimples, and nodded her head in respectful greeting. Wynter's heart soared like a bird released. Acceptance! She allowed her face to soften slightly and gave them a fleeting smile and a bob of her head as she passed them by.

As soon as her back was turned, Wynter made a triumphant little whooping sound under her breath. The girls' conversation had already bubbled up behind her as she left the yard and rounded a corner out of sight.

Into blessed shade again, the avenue of chestnut trees this time. She looked around in expectation and her grin deepened as she caught sight of what she'd hoped to see here: Shearing's ghost.

The lanky spirit glimmered in the dappled shadows ahead of her. If anything he was even more ragged than she recalled, his tattered cavalry uniform shredded at shoulder and knee, so worn as to be an affront to his magnificent military record. His head was down in thought as he prowled the trees, and Wynter quickened her pace to catch up to him. He was following the path as he always did, wending his endless journey down the avenue, flickering on and off as he traversed the patches of sunlight.

"Rory!" she called softly, as she trotted towards him, "Rory! It's me, I'm home!"

Shearing's ghost jumped and spun on his heels as she rapidly closed the distance between them. His pale, transparent figure shimmered like heat haze as he took her in, registered the changes, put the older face and body to the voice and realised it was his young pal and playmate. She saw a delighted smile begin on his pale lips and he half-raised a hand in greeting as she jogged down the leafy path. Then his face fell and his delight was replaced with concern. Wynter's grin began to fade as Shearing's ghost backed away, his hand up to stop her progress. He looked quickly around in obvious panic, checking that no one was watching.

Wynter ground to a halt, suddenly cold. Shearing was afraid. He was afraid to be seen with her! Wynter had *never* seen a ghost behave this way, ghosts didn't generally care what the living thought of them, and Shearing in particular had no truck with politicking: you were his friend or

you were not, that was all there was to it. At least, that is
how things had been, before she went away.

She stood, still as a statue, while Shearing made certain
they were alone. Then he turned to her, his fine face a picture of regret, and held his finger to his lips. *Shhhhhhhh*,
that gesture said, *we are not safe*. And then he faded away,
his pitying look an echo in the hazy air.

She wasn't sure how long she stood there, her heart hammering in her chest, but it must have been quite a while,
because the Maid of the Bucket caught up with her on her
way back into the palace. The girl cleared her throat as she
came up the path and it made Wynter startle and turn to
look at her.

She stood aside to let the girl pass. As she came abreast
of her, the swinging buckets spattering droplets on the toes
of her dusty boots, the girl eyed Wynter, obviously puzzled
by the sudden change in her demeanour. Where had the
cool self-collection gone? And what was it that had so ruf-
fled the stranger's calm? Wynter knew she'd be the subject
of even more gossip in the maids' dormitory tonight.

Wynter purposely schooled her face and regulated her
breathing. She nodded to the girl and waited until she was
out of sight before allowing herself relax once more into
agitated thought.

Shearing's ghost had really thrown her. She felt as
though the world had just slipped sideways and she was
sliding towards the edge of it. What had happened here,
that cats wouldn't reply to a civil greeting and ghosts were
afraid to converse with a friend?

In the fifteen years of her life Wynter had come to
understand and accept that most human beings were

unpredictable and untrustworthy, faithful only for as long as the wind fared well. But ghosts? Ghosts and cats had always just gone their own way, and although you could never trust a cat to serve anyone's purpose but its own, you always knew where you stood with them. The orange cat on the bridge had been frightened and confused by Wynter's greeting, as disconcerted by her attention as Shearing's ghost had been. And this flung everything up into the air, all the foundations of Wynter's life undermined suddenly, leaving her shaky and confused.

She glanced around her, no one in sight, safe for the moment. She took a very deep breath and briefly closed her eyes. She let herself feel the reassuring weight of her father's roll of tools on her shoulder. The awls and adzes and planes and chisels, collected and cared for during his twenty-two years as apprentice and master, and her own roll of tools, not so substantial, only five years in the gathering so far. She settled her feet wider, balancing herself and feeling the solidity of the ground beneath her boots. Good boots, solid riding boots, made to last. She felt the stir of the sluggish air against her face. She listened to the sleepy chirp of sparrows waiting out the heat in the chestnut trees, the steady flutter of the leaves.

A slow trickle of sweat rolled down her shoulder blades, the sharp smell of travelling rose up from her clothes.

She used all these things to ground herself, as her father had taught her, to make herself solid and *here*. What her father called, *in the moment*. She grabbed her mind and corralled it. Stopped it flying off into all the possibilities of what might come to pass. She forbade herself any more speculation on what might have happened while she was away. All these things would be revealed in time, but only through careful and calm investigation. She centred her mind on just being there, breathing in, breathing out, feeling the ground beneath, the trees above, the weight of the tools on her shoulder.

She opened her eyes, and immediately there were three things Wynter knew for certain. First, she needed food. Second, she needed to find Razi and Alberon, and third, but not least, she needed a bath. Right, she thought, adjusting the tools and releasing her breath in a steady sigh, first things first and all other things would follow. She turned on her heel and calmly made her way to the kitchen.

Razi

At the rear of the palace, a door fronted by wide stone steps swept down to a gravel path. The path wound away from the castle, through an acre or so of tame woodland, and from there across a guarded moat bridge to the densely packed wild forest outside the bailey. The King used this route when he was in the mood for an informal day's hunting or fishing. He called it "the back door". He'd say, *I'm sick of state, let's go out the back door, lads, and dally the day away like wild boys.*

Wynter had often watched the King and her father head out that way together, their fishing poles or bows slung across their shoulders, a little knot of companions in tow. She stood now, looking up the path and recalled how Razi, Alberon and herself used to loll about on the steps watching the men leave, sulking that they couldn't go along. By the time The Great Changes had begun, Razi had already turned fourteen and she and Alberon were well accustomed to the sight of him disappearing up that path with the hunters. It was one of her most vivid memories: Razi, turning to look back at herself and Alberon, his affectionate smile meant to lift their spirits as he left them alone.

"I'll bring you back a rabbit!" he'd call, and he always did, or a pheasant or a clutch of quail eggs. Always some little thing to alleviate the fact that he had abandoned them. That he'd left Alberon, who haunted Razi like a shadow and felt his absence keenly.

When you're eleven, that's what they were told, *when you're eleven you can join the hunt*. But by the time they had turned eleven, everything had changed. Razi had been sent to the Moroccos with his mother; Alberon had been prisoner to the throne, a constant presence at the King's side; and Lorcan and Wynter had been dispatched North, to the cold and damp that had destroyed her father's health.

A high modulated wail broke into her thoughts, making Wynter jump and then laugh as she realised what it was. She hadn't heard that particular sound for years, and it had taken a moment for her to recognise it. The Musulman boys were kneeling in the shade of the trees, making undulating prayers to their God. Wynter rose onto her tiptoes and searched their bobbing ranks for Razi, but he wasn't there. Perhaps he hadn't been brought home at all? That thought sent such a sharp pang through her that she pushed it away. Razi had never been one for prayers, she reminded herself. He *was* here, just elsewhere in the complex.

The smell of roasting mutton intruded on her and her belly cramped in response. Good God, she was hungry. She dropped her recollections and turned away from them, her desire to be in the kitchen suddenly overwhelming.

At the head of the kitchen steps, the statue of the Cold

Lady stood gazing wistfully up the woodland path. Despite the heat, her stone face was covered in frost and little icicles dripped from her delicately carved fingers. Wynter glanced up at her as she passed, marvelling, as always.

The maids and dairy-men had placed their pitchers of milk and cordial, pots of butter and bowls of cream all along the plinth at the hem of the Cold Lady's dress. It reminded Wynter of the offerings that the Midlanders left to their Virgin. She caught the sharp tang of cheddar as she passed by and she was so hungry that her mouth filled instantly with spit. She almost ran down the dark stairs into the fragrant gloom of the kitchen, the Musulmen's prayers rising musically into the sunlight behind her.

It took a moment for her eyes to adjust. A pot-boy pushed past her with a basket of onions, but no one paid her any attention and she was able to survey the organised chaos from her slightly elevated position at the foot of the stairs.

Oh yes. Here was what she had missed. Here was the true heart of home and the spirit of the kingdom she had longed for.

All the mixes of race and religion that summed up King Jonathon's realm seemed focused in the palace kitchen. All the brown and white and cream and yellow faces, sweating and shouting and running about. A high continuous cacophony of multilingual patois and pigeon-talk, gestures and pantomime, combining into an efficient, if disorderly, unit. And at its steaming hub, Marni, huge, bear-like, her meaty arms, her enormous red hands and absurd bulbous face towering over everyone. She was the centre of the cyclone, the perpetual-motion Goddess of the kitchen.

Wynter lifted her head to look over the produce-laden chopping table and sought out the poultry-spit-boy. When she saw him she smiled and some small thing settled in her chest, calming her.

The poultry-spit-boy was the lowest of the low in any palace kitchen. The little lad who would be employed to turn the lighter chicken and poultry spits, while the older men turned the heavy meat spits. She had seen spit-boys of six or seven, naked because of the heat, matted in grease and soot, being screamed at by the basters for flinching when the scalding fat of the meat had burnt their hands. She remembered watching in horror as a Midlands castle cook had beaten one tiny child with a wooden ladle. It made it all the worse that the little child still kept turning the spit. Even as his eyes swelled up into black puffs, he kept the handle going for fear the meat would burn and his punishment would worsen.

To Wynter, the spit-boy was the ultimate indication of the soul of a palace; most of them were blackened, hollow-eyed things, forgotten and abused.

The spit-boy who sat in Marni's kitchen was laughing while he turned the meat. His tiny hands were gloved and a big metal disc attached to the spit handle shielded him from the worst of the scalding splatter. He was sooty and shiny with grease and sweat, but he was clothed in a proper uniform and he was plump and jolly.

He was leaning forward, talking to someone who appeared to be crouched on the floor out of sight. As Wynter watched, the child took a piece of chalk from the unknown person and, still expertly turning the meat with one hand, he wrote something on the flagstones.

Wynter leant to the side to get a better view. A man was hunkered down beside the child, his dark head bent to look at the chalk marks on the floor. He was clad in the sky blue robes of a doctor, and, though his voice was too low for Wynter to hear the words, he said something to the child that brought a grin of pride to his greasy little face.

A pot-girl set a beaker of frothy milk down by the child and a plate of horse-bread and cheese. The little boy went to grab for it, but the doctor stayed him with one brown hand on his arm. Wynter saw his head tilt up to address the girl and her heart leapt as she recognised his profile. Razi.

"Did you boil the milk like I asked, Sarah?"

The girl nodded, her eyes wide.

"Boiled, not just warmed? Made to bubble, and then skimmed so that the evil humours dispersed?"

The girl nodded again and bobbed a curtsy as if that sealed the question. Razi, his back still turned to Wynter, released the child's hand and stayed crouched for a while, watching him cram food into himself. Even while eating, the little fellow continued to turn the meat at the exact speed necessary to let it cook without burning. It was as natural a movement to him as breathing.

As her friend rose from his crouch and turned, Wynter realised that she was not the only one to have grown. She had expected to come home – in her fifteen-year-old body, with her new length of leg and her new height – and find herself the equal of the fourteen-year-old boy she'd left behind, his counterpart in riding and swimming and climbing.

But Razi too had changed and it was a nineteen-year-old man who now stood before her, rubbing chalk dust from his brown hands. He was much taller. His face more defined somehow, all cheekbones and nose, his dark eyes just as large, but hooded. He was clean-shaven, but his glossy curls were in need of a trim and he kept pushing them back from his forehead with an impatient sigh. His blue doctor's robes suited him, and she felt an almost violent stab of pride in him, that he had finished his studies and graduated, despite the terrible times they'd just survived.

Alberon must be so proud of him, she thought.

Razi pushed his hand through his curls and looked around him absently as if trying to remember what came next. His eyes met Wynter's and she saw them pass her by, then snap back with sharp attention. She quirked an eyebrow at him, a challenging smile rising up in her face. *I dare you not to know me, Razi Kingsson. I dare you not to recognise my face.*

"WYNTER!" He *bellowed* it, his deep voice taking her by surprise and shocking the kitchen into stunned silence. The staff jerked and ducked as though a cannon had been fired. "WYNTER!" he shouted again, spreading his hands as if questioning her.

Wynter was so pleased to hear Razi say her name that she laughed out loud and tears sprang to her eyes.

She had sense enough to put the tools down before he waded through the crowd and snatched her from the bottom step. He swung her in a twirling arc that stole the breath from her and had the kitchen staff laughing and clutching for bits and pieces put in peril by his flying robes.

Good Lord, he's strong! she thought in surprise as he lifted her high. He was all deceptive grace, this new Razi, his powerful strength well hidden, his muscle so close to the bone as to make him look skinny. *You've been working with horses*, she thought, recognising the type of wiry power that the work gave to a body.

He flung her out and held her at arm's length. She hung like a cat in his hands, suspended under the armpits, her feet dangling above the ground, laughing. He looked her in the face and then up and down as if marvelling at her. This close up, she could see the gold flecks in his dark eyes. She noticed that there were fine lines around his eyes and mouth. The harsh African sun and five years of uncertainty must have added them to his young face, and she was suddenly fighting a lump in her throat. Razi. It really was him. Razi. Here and now. Alive.

"Hello, big brother," she said, her voice not quite steady, and he hugged her to him with a strangled laugh. He squeezed her so tightly that she had to knock him on the back to let him know she couldn't breathe.

They parted, breathless and laughing, their eyes shiny, and Razi kept his hand on her shoulder as if to stop her from flying away.

"You're in my way, you tinker's whelps." Marni's gravelly voice boomed behind them and they turned to grin at her, her preposterous face, her cloud of frizzy orange hair. She scowled at them, couldn't keep it up and beamed her gap-toothed smile on them instead, batting them with her huge hands so that they knocked into each other like nine-pins, giggling. "Your dad's still determined to turn you into a man, is he?" she growled, eyeing Wynter's uniform. "Ah well," she said, not quite able to hide her pride in Lorcan's unorthodox parenting. "'Tis a damn site better'n marryin' you off to some musty Lord."

Marni practically carried them, one under each arm, and deposited them in a corner out of the way. She laid the table with bread and cheese and cold chicken, a bowl of salt, a bowl of mustard paste, two knives and a fork. She met Razi's inquiring eye as she set down two beakers of cold milk and rolled her eyes to heaven.

"It's *been* boiled!" she exclaimed impatiently, "God forbid there should be *humours* in it," and she lumbered off, wiping her hands on her apron and scowling at some under-chef who was slicing something too thin. Razi smiled to himself and took a piece of chicken onto his plate while Wynter began to pile bread and chicken and cheese onto her own.

Razi played with his meat, shredding it into a pile of neat strips, then shoving it around with his finger. He eyed the amount of food Wynter was packing away and a slow grin began to creep up his face, making his big dark eyes dance with suppressed laughter. Wynter's mouth was too full to permit any kind of conversation, but their eyes kept meeting as she shovelled yet more food down her. It was just like the old days, when they could make each other dissolve into giggles simply by looking.

"Stop it!" she warned, spraying breadcrumbs from a too full mouth, "I'll choke!"

He grinned wider and contrived an innocent expression that only made her worse. Razi's grin, her full belly and all around them the kitchen doing its work – it was so wonderful, so *right* that Wynter thought she might start to cry if she wasn't careful.

She took a deep breath, saw some similar emotion in Razi's face and the two of them looked away from each other suddenly, taking great interest in the convoluted machinations of the kitchen. Marni glanced over at them, a moment of unguarded tenderness on her face, then she turned away, scolding some poor scuttling man who was in her way.

"Where is Alberon, Razi?" Wynter asked. She kept her voice low and only glanced sideways at him. They had had no contact for the last five years; had, until now, not even been sure if the other had survived. Now, questions, if asked at all, would have to be asked gently, obliquely, for fear of opening old wounds or uncovering secrets best left hidden.

Razi cleared his throat and shook his head. "I don't know where Albi is, little sister. He is not here. Father says . . . Father says that he has sent him to the coast, to inspect the fleet." Their eyes met briefly and Wynter looked away.

Razi's face told her that she doubted the King's story, and Wynter's mind filled with questions and her chest tightened with fear.

Why would Alberon, legitimate son and sole heir to the throne, be sent so far from home after such a long and dangerous period of unrest? On the other hand, why would the King lie to Razi – his eldest boy and bastard son, much loved and trusted by the throne? Wynter had no answers, only fear, sly fear, skittering about in her heart like a secret disease.

She glanced around the kitchen, at the sweating, toiling faces, the familiar domestic scene, and sensed the cold waters of politics running beneath it all. Vast and dark and rushing, ready to sweep any of them away. *We must be careful*, she thought, *we must be careful*.

So much that she wanted to ask, but in court life there are things you cannot ask, not aloud, not in a crowded kitchen, not even of your oldest friend.

Razi was tense as a horse at a starting gate, his dark eyes roaming the room, his agitation almost audible. He rubbed his fingers anxiously against his palms and Wynter longed to lay her hand on his, to stop him betraying himself so obviously.

Behind Razi there was a tray of jam tarts cooling on the rack near the high window and, as Wynter watched, the Hungry Ghost lifted two of them to its invisible mouth and they disappeared into mid-air, a bite at a time. Wynter nudged Razi with a smile and stole a glance at Marni, waiting for her usual stormy response to the pesky spirit. Things would be thrown! Curses would be bellowed! Marni's ongoing feud with the Hungry Ghost had always been good for a laugh.

Razi lifted his eyes to see what Wynter was nudging him for and his dark face lost some of its colour. Wynter just had time to register this, when she saw Marni notice another two tarts float up and disappear in a shower of crumbs. The cook's face clouded over with a moment of pure rage, and her expression stole Wynter's smile from her. This wasn't Marni's usual melodramatic overreaction, this was something deeper rising to the surface, some seething undercurrent, tapped and exposed as if Marni's head had been cut open for a moment and its contents revealed.

Wynter saw the cook's hand tighten around her ladle, her whole body shaking with the ferocity of her emotions. Then the giant woman turned her back, her face still wicked with feeling, and pretended not to see, as the invisible spirit demolished the tray of tarts.

Wynter turned to Razi, her eyes wide. He was sighing with huge relief, his eyes on Marni as she stalked away.

"I met Rory on my way here." Wynter said it quietly, her voice purposely inaudible to anyone but her friend. Still, Razi's reaction was shocking. He turned on her, spinning completely around in his seat to face her, his fists clenched, and she pulled away from him, momentarily frightened by the anger in his eyes.

"Did he speak to you?" he hissed, his voice a deadly whisper.

She shook her head. "No. He wouldn't. I . . ."

All the anger drained from Razi's face in an instant, to be replaced by the same shaky relief he'd shown when Marni had allowed the tarts to be eaten. He slumped against the table and put his hand to his forehead. The breath seemed to be knocked out of him and it was only when he murmured, "Good man, Rory. Decent fellow," that Wynter realised that his anger hadn't been directed at her, but at Rory Shearing and the thought that the spirit might have spoken to her.

"What's going on, Razi?"

He lifted his eyes and scanned the kitchen again, not answering.

"Razi?"

He tilted his head, resting his cheek on his hand, and Wynter realised that he was shielding his mouth from the view of the rest of the room.

"Wynter. There are no ghosts anymore." He locked eyes with her, he was telling her something very, very important here. Life or death important. "Father has decreed it. And so it must be."

Wynter laughed in disbelief, glanced furtively around the room and leaned in closer, searching his face. "What . . .?"

"Listen to me. *Listen.* There are no ghosts, Wyn. Understand? Anyone who says otherwise, anyone who communes . . .? They're *gibbeted,* Wynter."

That made her sit back, with a snort of disgust. "Razi, that's not funny, I can't believe you'd think that was funny—"

He grabbed her hand and pulled her in close. "I'm serious."

She snatched her hand away, rubbing the wrist. "It's rumours. That's all. Razi, have some sense! It's your father's enemies, spreading lies. The King would *never*—"

"What way did you come home? Over the mountains, yes? Through the forests? Nothing but hamlets and wood-cutters and boar, am I right?"

She nodded dubiously, still rubbing her burning wrist.

"I came home via the port road, Wyn. I came up through all the main towns. There are gibbets at every crossroads. There are *cages,* Wynter. Father has re-introduced the cages, and people seem more than willing to use them."

Oh God. Gibbets? Gibbets and cages? Here, where they had been illegal since the very day Jonathon took the throne? No. No, no, no.

Since her journey north Wynter had become accustomed to the sudden scent of rotting flesh on the air, to turning a corner and being confronted with a ragged corpse, caged in iron, swinging in the breeze. But she never thought to find them here, never here.

Even at the beginning of the insurrections, when the Circle of Lords were pressuring the King into an inquisition, Jonathon had not succumbed to temptation.

The easiest way to make a people hate is to torture them into submission, he had said, *Happy people are stable people. One will win more hearts and minds with justice than one will ever do with the whip.*

"Oh Razi," she whispered. "What has happened here?" Something else occurred to her and she looked up at him sharply. He flinched, as if anticipating what she was thinking. She swallowed against a suddenly dry throat and said, "Where are my cats, Razi? I met a stranger kitten on the moat bridge and it didn't even reply to my greeting." Her heart dropped to the soles of her feet at the look in his eyes. Then he couldn't look at her anymore. He turned his head and gazed out into the kitchen for a moment as if trying to find a way to break terrible news.

"No one speaks to cats anymore, sis. Please, *please,* don't mention them to anyone." He looked her in the eye again. "Please."

"Why?" she whispered, but then almost immediately held her hand up to stop his answer. She didn't really want to know. Jonathon's kingdom was the last in all of the Europes where cats still spoke to humans. Everywhere else, fear and superstition had driven a wedge between the species that had ended all but the most basic of communication. Wynter had missed many, many things up North, not least among them her cats and their strange, inhuman conversations. She looked down at the table, her lips compressed, and Razi waited patiently until she said, "What happened?"

He took her hand, gently this time. "I don't know the full story, Wyn. I don't know much, if the truth be told. But Father got it into his head that the castle cats . . . well, that they knew *secrets*. That they knew something specific that he did not want known. I think he was afraid that they would talk, that they would tattle."

Wynter sniffed derisively at the thought of a cat tattling. But Razi's expression was terribly sad, and he squeezed her hand. *Oh Razi, what? Just say it.*

"He had them poisoned, Wyn. All of them."

She gasped, a high lamenting cry, and Marni turned her head sharply to look. Wynter tried to pull her hand from Razi's grip, but he held on and reached over and grabbed her other hand, pulling her arms towards him so that she had to face him.

"Shhh now," he said, very firmly and low. "Shhhh." His look said, *Remember where you are. Remember who we are.*

Overwhelmed with sorrow, she struggled against his strong grip, and turned her head up to the ceiling, tears flowing freely down her face. *Oh no,* she thought, *oh no. Not that.*

"I'm sorry."

"Even GreyMother?" He nodded. "Even ButterTongue? SimonSmoke? Coriolanus?" A nod for each beloved name, and then no more nods, just a tragic, sympathetic tilt of his head as the list went on, her wrists still trapped in his hands, held up before him as if she were his prisoner.

A Blatant Tomcat

"*That* is *enough* now, girl! And you! Boy! Let go her wrists; you look like you're trying to *arrest* her."

Marni's harsh voice was low and commanding as she loomed above them, blocking them from prying eyes. Razi and Wynter leapt to obey her. He released her wrists as if burned and she took a sobbing breath and scrubbed the tears from her eyes. Marni handed Wynter a wet cloth, her face hard, and at the same time she shifted to keep her hidden from view. Wynter was grateful for the privacy while she cooled her burning face with the cloth.

Marni looked from one to the other of them, her face a thundercloud. They had spent their childhood in her care, tottering around her feet like strays. Razi's mother had never been interested in her son, except that he brought her nearer to the throne, and Alberon and Wynter had lost their mothers at birth, their love never known to them at all. Marni had raised the three of them like some kind of maternal bear lumbering through their early years. She had been their comfort and their rock, but she wasn't soft or tender as some might expect a mother to be. She was loving in the hard, protective way that animals are loving. They were her cubs, and her cubs would survive, but to survive they'd have to be tough.

"Oh, Marni, my cats . . . the ghosts . . ."

"There's worse than dead cats and silenced ghosts afoot, child. Remember who you are. Get yourself under control."

The bustle of the kitchen continued unabated behind her broad back, but still Marni spoke so low as to be barely audible to them. She put two wooden beakers onto the table with a sharp smacking sound.

"Drink that," she whispered fiercely, "all of it. Even you, boy!" She jabbed a finger at Razi, "Your Musulman God won't strike you down for the sake of a little white wine cordial."

She glared at the two of them, the question in her eyes unmistakable. *Are we all under control now?* And they nodded their reply. *Yes, Marni.* She snorted like a bull and barged back into the fray.

Alcohol should be avoided when angry or depressed. This was what Wynter's father had taught her about drinking. *Wine is for pleasure, not pain.* Still, Wynter drained her cordial in a few swallows, because her throat was burning with tears and because the drink was cold and sweet and numbing. Razi sipped his obediently and then sat like a stone beside her. The kitchen pretended that nothing had happened.

In the long silence that followed, Wynter felt the drink go to work on her head, and immediately regretted that she'd gulped it down so fast. Thank God she'd just eaten, because she began to suspect that there was a little more wine than cordial mixed into the brew.

The drink, the heat of the kitchen, and Razi's steadfast presence all combined with her long journey and her shock, and she was suddenly drenched in an almost unmanageable tiredness. If she could have laid her head onto the crumby table and drifted off without shaming herself in front of the staff, she would have.

"Razi," she mumbled, dredging up the words with an effort, "Let's go outside. Let's walk down to the river. Razi, let's . . . let's go for a swim."

Yes, they could find a place in the shade, under the willows maybe, and they could kick off their boots. She could strip to her underthings and just sleep like the dead while Razi watched over her, as he had done so many times when they were children.

He shifted beside her, a shrug. There was genuine regret in his voice, but even so, his words gave her an unexpected and terrible pang of jealousy. "I can't, little sister. I'm waiting for someone."

"Who?" she demanded, but Marni's sudden bellow startled the two of them and distracted him so he didn't hear.

"Where the *hell* have you been?" The giant cook's ferocious voice silenced the room for a moment so that everyone turned to see the object of her fury.

A plump little maid was slinking up the basement stairs, cheeks all pink and heated-looking, a guilty expression on her face. She scurried towards the plate board and ducked past Marni, who lifted a meaty hand to her in mock threat. The blushing girl pushed her way in between the other maids and grabbed a cloth and a bottle of sweet oil and commenced to oiling the wooden platters for tonight's meal. There immediately rose up an urgent and giggling whispered conversation between herself and her companions.

Wynter was just turning to repeat her question to Razi when she noticed someone coming down the back stairs. Her immediate impression was that the King had hired a troupe of entertainers and that they'd sent a representative to negotiate with the kitchen for food.

She watched him glide down the stairs, as light as a cat in his soft leather boots. *Acrobat's boots*, she thought. He had that blatant confidence that comes from being part of a clan; the bold look that men only get when they have a gang of brothers backing them up. He'd either charm you or slit your throat, this one, and you'd never know the reason for either. Wynter suspected that you could search him for days and never find all the blades he had hidden behind his smile.

She imagined that this young man's people found him invaluable, but his skills wouldn't be needed here. Unlike most castle kitchens, this one freely supplied the transient trades with food and drink. Still, he wasn't to know that, and it would be interesting to see how he'd deal with the force of nature that was Marni.

Wynter propped her heavy head in her hand and yawned; she was so very tired. She watched the man through bleary eyes, waiting for him to approach the cook. He paused halfway down the stairs and tucked his long hair behind his ear, assessing the room from a position of advantage, and Wynter had a moment to take a better look at him.

He was young enough, eighteen, maybe even nineteen. Slight, with a cat's sly grace. Maybe a head shorter than

Razi. He was pale as milk and his face was narrow, watchful, almost amused, framed by a long curtain of straight black hair. He looked brazenly around him with no pretence at deference.

Blatant, thought Wynter, *and dangerous. Very dangerous, to himself and to others, because this one doesn't know his place.*

She saw his eyes find Marni, who would make short shrift of him indeed if he kept that expression on his face. Wynter waited for the courtier's mask of obsequiousness to slide itself into place, but to her surprise, his eyes moved past the big woman and settled on the pink-cheeked maid who had come in before him.

A cold blade of comprehension slid up Wynter's spine as the maid's companions nudged each other. Wynter saw the girl shoot a quick glance over to where the young man now stood. He grinned at her, and she ducked her smiling head, her cheeks flaming, as the whole gaggle of maids dissolved into giggles. There was no doubt now where the young woman had been, and what had kept her late for work.

Wynter sat up slowly, her distaste sparking to hot anger as the young rake dropped the maids a knowing wink and bit the tip of his tongue between his teeth in a gesture both suggestive and crude.

Oh, you're in for a shock, she thought viciously, *you may be used to different, but this is not a household that makes toys of its women.*

Her hands bunched to fists and she went to say something to Razi, but stopped when the young man spotted them, raised his chin in greeting and began to come their way.

He's seen the doctor's robes, Wynter thought, *and wants a consultation. Some ache or pain, or some fever in the troupe. Well, I'll give him something to need consulting about . . .*

She bristled as the man crossed the room, ready to let rip at him. But, to her amazement, Razi, his face wry, lifted a finger in greeting and murmured to himself, "So that's where you've been, you bloody tomcat. You'll get yourself tarred if you're not careful."

Blissfully ignorant of Razi's comment, the young man slid and sidled his way through the kitchen turmoil, his mouth lifted in a crooked smile as he rapidly approached their table. *My God!* thought Wynter, her face incredulous, *This? This is who Razi was waiting for? This rake? Has the world gone mad?*

Her mouth was actually hanging open when the fellow finally got to them, and she had to make a conscious decision to snap it shut as he sauntered up and lounged against the wall by their table.

"Razi," he said by way of greeting, drawing the name out into something insinuating and sly. At the same time, he looked Wynter up and down with undisguised interest. She'd seen that look before, had become accustomed to it ever since her body had blossomed into all its various curves and roundnesses. She treated it to an even greater measure of shuttered disdain than usual.

"Christopher," murmured Razi, putting a similar sly emphasis on the name, and Wynter was astounded to see that he looked amused.

Christopher, eh? she thought. *Well, I've met people like you before, Christopher.* Wynter said the name in her head, drawing it out as Razi had done, but without the obvious affection that her friend had put into it. She found herself glaring up at this man, her rage such that she made no effort to hide it. *I've met lots of people. Just. Like. You.*

You saw them all the time in palace life, people who *latched on.* People who *used.* They would find someone close to the throne and befriend them, usually separating them from the people who cared about them, before bleeding them dry. Not that Razi was any type of idiot. But Wynter had seen fear, isolation and need make fools of the wisest men. *I'm watching you,* she thought as the young man curled his lip at her in a very speculative smile. *I have your measure.*

She opened her mouth to say something sharp about the maid, but Razi was already talking. He was smiling up at the young man, his slow, spreading, generous smile. The easy tone of his voice and the amused affection on his face filled Wynter with a sudden and childish jealousy and she had to bite down on her bottom lip to stop unreasonable tears from springing to her eyes. It dawned on her that she was really quite drunk.

Step back, step back, she thought urgently, sitting up straighter and breathing deep to clear her head, "*speak not in your cups, lest ye regret when sober*". What had she been thinking, slurping down that cordial when she was already so tired? She forced herself to focus on the conversation and tried to quell the urge to leap up and push this *Christopher* right over on his backside and kick him up the kitchen steps.

Stop looking at my friend like that! she thought, *He's not yours.*

Razi was murmuring low, his head tilted to look up into

Christopher's face. The young man had slanting grey eyes, the eyelashes so thick and black as to seem kohled. He was leaning down, listening to Razi with an indulgent smirk, his hands tucked behind his back.

"If you get one of those girls with child, Marni will march you up the aisle herself and I'll help her tuck you into your marriage bed, you bloody rake."

Wynter expected the young man to affect innocence, to spread his hands, or to play the man of the world, but his face settled for a moment into genuinely hurt inquiry, "You don't think I'd ever ruin a lass, do you, Razi?"

Razi smiled and shook his head slightly and the young man straightened, his tomcat grin back in place. "Anyway," Christopher said, turning his eyes to the maids again, "I only give what's asked of me; never go where I'm not invited, so to speak. And you of all people should know there's ways and means of avoiding *that* kind of trouble, what with being a doctor and all . . . aye . . ." he murmured, his eyes drifting along the row of giggling maids at the plate board. "There's enough bastards in this world without adding to their poxy ranks."

Razi just smiled, but Wynter felt the sting of that remark on his behalf and bristled. "Many of those bastards are more worthy than you," she said sharply, and she was surprised that Christopher didn't just burst into flames at the heat of her glare.

Christopher levelled his grey eyes at her and half-smiled. "I meant no offence, little mankin. There are only bastards standing here." He bent his waist in a little bow.

Oh! He was assuming that she'd been offended on her own behalf, and was telling her that he, too, was the product of an unwed union. Blind indignation rose up in her and she almost said *My parents were wed, thank you very much!* The retort leapt to her lips but she realised, just in time, that the indignant pride in those words did nothing but insult Razi and expose a previously unsuspected prejudice in herself.

Careful, she thought, quickly gathering her wits, *the wine has tied your head in knots.*

"Your little friend looks tired, Razi." Christopher's lilting voice swam through the fog, "Would you not let him to bed?"

"Oh, for heaven's sake!" exclaimed Wynter, slapping the table with one hand, the other pressed to her pounding temple. "You know full well I'm not a boy! Stop acting the jester, you haven't the wit!"

She felt rather than saw the young man draw himself up, and thought, *Ah, here we have it. You suffer from pride, don't you, you dangerous braggart. Pride controls you.*

"I only meant not to insult your disguise, firebrand." His voice was cold. "But you might want to work on it a little harder. You'll never pass for a boy with all those bumps and curves."

She lifted her head and raised her lip in what she hoped was a disparaging sneer. "*I'm* not disguised as anything," she said, "*I'm* exactly what you see."

"A boy who butchers wood for a living?" sarcasm dripped from every word, and Wynter glared at him.

"A fourth-year apprentice, guild approved, chartered for the green." None of it meant a thing to him. She could see him trying to process the meaning behind the words and failing. *Where are you from,* she thought suddenly, *that you don't know guild ranking in something so prevalent as car-pentry?*

Even the lowest dung-haulier, attached to the tiniest principality, would know their ranks and roles off by heart. For a courtier to be so utterly ignorant about the symbols of professional rank would be tantamount to being blind, deaf and dumb.

She straightened slowly and looked at him anew. A new-comer then, a stranger to court life. This made him the most dangerous of idiots, ambitious but ignorant. She had seen people like him cut bloody swathes through a royal household. Intentionally or otherwise, people like this could be a poison that would blacken the body of state, spreading death and corruption in their wake.

He saw the antipathy in her eyes and she saw a steel rise up in his.

Beside her, Razi shifted, but Wynter didn't look at him. She just kept her eyes locked on Christopher's. Then the young man suddenly tilted his head into an unexpected smile, dimples showing at the corners of his mouth. His eyes sparkled with wicked humour and, just like that, she found herself ensnared in a staring contest, unwilling to be the first to look away.

How did this *happen?* she thought desperately, feeling panic building at this ridiculous turn of events. *How have I let this dolt corner me so badly?*

He was, after all, just one of the many flies that buzzed around the dung heap of state. She should be able to brush him off Razi without breaking her stride. But here she was, stuck in a childish staring match, her dander up and too proud to break off.

Razi cleared his throat, "Children, children . . ." he admonished mockingly, but his warm voice sounded troubled.

"When does your troupe move on?" Wynter asked coldly, not breaking her stare.

She saw incomprehension in Christopher's face, and he shook his head and squinted at her, "What do you mean?"

She waved a hand up and down to indicate his clothing. Unconsciously, her eyes followed the gesture. Damn! But Christopher appeared not to notice. "You're an entertainer, aren't you? A tumbler of some ilk, or a musician?"

She heard Razi hiss in a breath beside her, and a strange, cold stillness came over Christopher.

"Christopher Garron is my horse-doctor." Razi's voice was hard and had an odd quality to it. "In the three years and a half that I've known him, he's taught me more than I'd ever hoped to learn about horses and their care."

Three and a half years? They'd known each other that long? And, judging by Razi's body, horses had become his passion, so he and Christopher must spend a great deal of each day together. Over three years of being in each other's company, working together at something they loved. *While I rotted alone in the dank North.* She squashed this thought as viciously as she could, it being unfair to both herself and to Razi. Would she truly have denied him a friend in all those years? Hadn't she longed for a friend herself? *No,* she thought, *I longed for home. For home and for Razi and for Alberon — no other. And anyway, I would have made a better choice than this . . . this dangerous sybarite.*

Even as she thought those harsh things about him, it was already becoming painfully clear to her that the main reason she distrusted this Christopher Garron was the very fact of his friendship with Razi. She was so jealous of him that she could happily have stabbed him in the heart.

Christopher was speaking again, that lilting Northland accent. His eyes were cold, his expression flat as iron. The dimples had disappeared from the corners of his mouth. "You're right. Very observant. I am a musician. I tend to Razi's horses because of my skill and love of them, not because it's my heart's passion. I'm the best musician in all the North Countries. Famed in Hadra, where I'm from, for my skill on the guitar and fiddle."

Later, when she was lying in bed, trying to sleep, she would remember the way he said that, the look in his eyes still eating at her. I *am* a musician. Not *I was,* or *I used to be,* but *I am.* As though the music still burned inside him as a living thing, trapped and scrabbling to get out, but never capable of escaping.

"I'm not in disguise, despite your implications. *I* don't need to dress myself up as something I'm not in order to win some attention." His tone was acidic and he sneered down at her carpenter's outfit. "And though I know there are some men who like *those* kind of games, I don't believe our friend here is one of them."

Razi scraped out another little hiss. "Christopher . . ." he warned softly.

Wynter held her hands out, with all their lumps and scars and calluses.

"It's not my clothes that make me what I am. Nor my proximity to the throne that earns me my bread. I make my own way. These are workman's hands, they speak for themselves." She lifted them up to him, palms out, and that gesture, too, would haunt her in the night. Why that? Why had she chosen that particular gesture with which to prove her worth?

Christopher just stood looking at her, his grey eyes opaque, his face unreadable.

"I see that you think I make use of our mutual friend," he said coldly. "I assure you I do not. Perhaps this prettied up little farce of a life suits you, but I no more want to be in it than a cat wants to dance, I—"

"Oh God, that's *enough*!" Razi kept his voice low and he slapped the table only lightly, but the two of them leapt, startled by his sudden sharpness. "Why don't I just stand up, here and now, and let the two of you mark your territory out on me like dogs! Wynter, you can have my left leg, Christopher, you have my right! Then we'll all know where we stand and this bloody . . . this bloody *prowling* can stop!"

He glared up at them in exasperation. His words cut right to the bone of the matter, shaming them both, and they deflated like pig-bladders after a stick and ball match.

"I just . . . I wanted you to be friends!" he said gently, "I want you to *like* each other. Can we at least give it a try?"

Wynter looked at Christopher. There was uncertainty in his grey eyes and hurt, and she still felt a bitter gall of jealousy in her heart and the not unreasonable fear that he was a destructive influence. He *was* a destructive influence, goddamn him. But for Razi's sake she half-stood and held her hand out to shake Christopher's.

She felt an immediate flash of anger when he hesitated, and she withdrew her hand and glared. Christopher released a grunt of frustration, looked about him in distress and then submitted with a sigh. Reluctantly, without looking at her, he held out his hands, not for her to shake, but for her to see, and Wynter gasped and pulled away slightly.

Even with all her experience of wounds and scars and the terrible disfigurements that war and hard labour brought to men's bodies, she found his hands shocking. They were so out of keeping with his easy, self-confident grace. It was with a sudden pang of admiration for his skill that she realised he'd managed to keep them hidden from view the whole time since his arrival.

He's a thief, she thought with a shock.

"I'm not a criminal," he muttered, as if reading her thoughts, and she could tell that he was used to people jumping to that conclusion. A natural enough one, this being the punishment for theft in the North. But she'd never seen it done so viciously, with such awful scarring, and never to both hands. She gazed at the terrible wounds as if expecting them to speak, or transfigure.

He had fine, strong, white hands, the fingers slim and nimble looking. *Yes,* she thought, without satisfaction, *a musician, God help him, and it's obvious.* But the middle finger of each hand was missing. The one on his right was a relatively clean amputation, the finger chopped from its socket, although the mess of shallow scars and runnels up the back of his hand told her that he must have fought madly. The knife had skipped and slid about, mutilating the surrounding flesh and the other fingers around it as the blade dug out his finger. The wound on his left was truly awful, because it spoke of such tremendous brutality. Only a small, gnarled stump of the finger remained, and that was badly crooked, as though the perpetrator had attempted literally to twist the finger from its socket. A long, pale ribbon of scar ran down the back of his hand and disappeared into his cuff, clean and surgical, as if someone had drawn an infection, releasing the pressure on an abscess.

Wynter couldn't help it – her first thoughts were, *he has the advantage on me now, anything I say will make me look an ignorant brute.* And then, no more to her credit than the first thought, *you seem to have a talent for annoying folk, Christopher Garron. Whoever did this really wanted to hurt you.*

She looked up into his face, expecting triumph, and waited for him to press home his advantage. He had all the weaponry he needed now to make her look small in front of Razi. But there was only a shy kind of apology in his smile, and her heart jolted in her chest like an abrupt bang on a drum: *My God, you really have no idea how to play the game, do you?*

He remained standing there, this slim, pale young man with fine black hair and slanting grey eyes, shyly holding out his mutilated hand, unaware of her ungracious thoughts. She must have stared at him for a long moment because eventually he said, "Do you still want to shake my hand?"

Oh Christopher, she thought, with a sudden surge of sympathy, *this life will eat you up. It may well choke on you in the process, but you won't survive it.* And then, with much colder intent, she thought, *I'm not letting you take Razi down when you go.*

She stood smoothly and smiled and took his hand. He accepted her handshake with no further self-consciousness, looking her in the eye and nodding a smile at her, the dimples back in force. "I'm Wynter," she said, "Well met, Christopher Garron. God bless you and your path."

And Razi grinned with delight.

Under the King's Eye

"How is Lorcan? Does he fare well?" Razi slid his eyes sideways to her, judging her reaction. Here was one of those oblique questions that meant everything or nothing, depending on how you responded to them. The course the conversation took after such an inquiry was up to the one giving the answer. *Does he fare well?* Could be inferred as, *is he alive? Has he maintained his pride? His sanity? His health?* She could deflect all those subtexts with a simple *he's fine*, and with anyone but Razi a simple *he's fine* would be what she'd give.

But this *was* Razi and she said, "My father is unwell, brother. I fear for his life."

Razi turned to her, concern written in broad strokes across his handsome face. The three of them were making their way up the back stairs, Christopher and Razi having decided that they needed to show Wynter their beloved horses. She had indicated her consent with a tired shrug; maybe they would become absorbed and she could lie down on a haystack and close her eyes for a while. Christopher had walked on ahead of them, giving them space. *Not so dense then*, she thought, as he had casually let the distance between them grow.

"Would your father allow me examine him? Or would it be imprudent to bring it up?"

"Oh God," she groaned, "don't bring it up, Razi, please. He's mortal afraid of seeming vulnerable."

"I don't blame him in the least," muttered her friend, his brown eyes darkening. "Where is he now? Maybe I can sneak a look at him, judge his humours from afar."

Wynter sighed and ran her hand over her burning eyes. Razi took her by the elbow and leaned in as they continued up the steps. "Wyn? You need to lie down, you're all worn thin. Why don't we accompany you to your chambers, and let you bathe and rest? I'm being selfish . . ."

She laughed and shook her head and held a hand up to silence him.

"Razi, even had I a chamber to retire to, I couldn't bear the thought of being apart from you so soon. I'll lay my head on a bag of hay and let yourself and that fellow play with the horses, all right?"

He smiled and nodded.

"My father is with Heron," she continued, "I assume they went to the King."

Razi gave a bitter little laugh. "So, the wily old bird got to him first, eh? *There's* no surprise."

Wynter paused, the bitterness in Razi's voice chilling her, and she put out her hand to stay her friend. On the steps above them, Christopher stopped immediately and turned to wait for them, slouching patiently against the wall.

"Razi, is Her—" Wynter glanced up at Christopher who

was listening without even pretending not to. She dropped her voice to a whisper. "Is Heron no longer our friend?"

Razi bit his lip, whether in impatience or uncertainty, Wynter couldn't tell. Then he gave her a very pointed look, and when he spoke, his low voice carried, clear and sure, and intentionally up the stone steps to the pale young man above them. "Little sister, I am only certain of having two friends in this castle, and both of them are standing on these stairs with me now. Do you understand?"

Christopher turned and quietly mounted the steps. Wynter watched him until he rounded the corner out of sight. His expression hadn't changed in the slightest at Razi's words, and she had no idea if he even understood the responsibility that Razi had just lain at his feet. Lain at *our* feet, she reminded herself.

"Court life will kill that fellow," she said, then looked Razi straight in the eye and knew at once that he already understood this. "He's not suited for it, Razi. He's too direct. It will destroy him."

Razi shifted uncomfortably and dropped his gaze. "I don't intend to be here long enough for that to happen, sis. I'm moving on."

She almost buckled when he said that. She had to physically restrain herself from grabbing onto him and screaming his name. She swallowed her heart back down into her chest, where it lay like a brick of lead, leaching poison into her system. She shook her head in denial.

"I intend to leave as soon as I can," he said, looking earnestly down at her. "I'm going to Padua, to teach at the university. They have granted me a fellowship. I will be able to continue my research, is that not wonderful? And,

Wyn, I would very much like to set up a household there. I want Christopher to breed my horses for me and I will be needing to build a house . . . I was going to ask—"

"Razi!" Christopher came running back around the corner, hissing as he raced down the stairs towards them. He jerked to a halt when they turned to him, Razi growling in frustration, Wynter dashing tears from her eyes and gritting her teeth. He held his hand up and retreated a step or two, his face apologetic, but urgent. "The Victuallor is coming, and there's a man with him, a big, red-haired fellow."

"Dad!" Wynter pushed her way past Christopher, and ran up the stairs to her father. Moving fast, making distance, just for something to do with all the violent energy she suddenly had bottled up inside her.

Heron and her father came around the bend at a pace, and drew up short at the sight of the youths scattered on the steps below them. Their three faces must have screamed *tension* because the two older men paused in identical poses of uncertainty, and both said "umm" simultaneously in embarrassed surprise.

Wynter wanted to fling herself into her father's arms. She wanted to scream, *Razi is leaving! He's leaving already!* Instead she came to a decorous halt a few steps below him and bowed stiffly, her tears dry on her face.

"Well met, good Father, Victuallor Heron. How fares the King, good sirs?"

Heron looked past her and jerked his chin at Razi. "His Majesty wishes your presence now, my Lord. He would consult with yourself and the Protector Lord Moorehawke in his chambers."

Razi stalked obediently up the steps, but Wynter made a small sound of protest and exclaimed, "Father! Are you not to eat? Have you not rested at all?"

Lorcan made an impatient shushing gesture at her, but Razi paused, took a good long look at her father's face and then turned to Heron, his expression hard. "You have not been able to find me yet, Victuallor. While you are searching, the Protector Lord shall go to the kitchen and have himself a meal."

Heron stared at Razi for a moment and Wynter saw something dawning in the old man's face. He turned slowly and looked at her father, really scrutinising him, really *inspecting* him. Wynter swallowed.

Lorcan narrowed his eyes at his old friend, his face cold, then he turned imperiously away and addressed Razi, "I am most grateful for my Lord's benevolence, but I do not yet need to pause. Please, if you are ready, let us continue to our Majesty's presence." He gave Wynter a fleeting glance and spoke to her even as he was turning to leave. "I shall return when I am released by the King, child. Go bathe and change and rest; there is to be a banquet tonight at sundown."

Then he was off up the steps without another word, his riding boots clattering on the stone, his plait swinging heavily behind him. The smell of horse and campfire and hard travel lingered long after he'd turned the corner and gone from sight.

Heron raised his eyebrow impatiently at Razi who gave Wynter a helpless look. As he turned to go, Razi glanced at Christopher and tilted his head meaningfully as he did, *look after her.* Christopher nodded, and Wynter fought the urge to push him down the steps. Look after her, indeed! Look after *Christopher* more like. *He* was the one most likely to get his throat slit on his way to the privy.

Heron lingered a moment, already half-turned to go. "Garron," he said, "the Protector Lady Wynter and Protector Lord Moorehawke are quartered next to your master's rooms. Ensure the Protector Lady is settled comfortably."

Christopher lifted his chin in response and Heron's eyes flashed at him. *You're meant to bow, you imbecile*, thought Wynter. But the Victuallor didn't bother to comment, he just sneered and padded up the steps after Razi and her father, disappearing quickly from view and leaving the two of them alone.

Wynter retrieved her tools from Marni's care and stalked to the stables without a word. Christopher strode along beside her, surprisingly quiet. She had expected irritating chatter, attempts to draw her out, flirting. But he just kept pace, his grey eyes thoughtful.

When they got to the stables, he disappeared for a moment and returned with two page boys, organising them with admirable efficiency and good humour so that, fairly soon, Wynter's and her father's things were gathered up and transported to their new chambers and she once again had somewhere permanent to lay her head. As permanent as court life could allow, at any rate.

She stood in the middle of their receiving room and looked around her with a heavy heart. It was an excellent suite, a large receiving room with two big shuttered windows looking down onto the orange trees, brightly painted and with cheery tapestries on loan from the King's collection. Off this was a small retiring room and, off that, two spacious and airy bedrooms, both filled with the glorious light of what was now evening. Wynter was pleased to see that the King had furnished the rooms with all the old furniture of their previous accommodation: her pine bed, with its pretty insect-netting and curtains. The wash stand, her blanket box that her father had carved. All of Lorcan's bedroom furniture was here, and in the receiving room, the four rounded armchairs, filled with the cushions that Wynter's mother had embroidered whilst in her confinement. All so familiar and lovely.

But why here? she thought. Why not in their beloved old cottage in the grounds, under the shade of the walnut trees, down by the trout brook at the foot of the meadow? Where they had been blissfully far away from the intricacy of court, and out from under the eye of the King. Where Wynter had been able to get out of bed in the morning and fish for breakfast in the river, still barefoot and wearing her long johns. Where the smell of her father's workshop had kept the air spicy with wood shavings and resin all day long. Now everything would be protocol, politics and etiquette every minute of every hour of every day. Obviously the King wanted them near, he wanted them *observed*. He didn't trust them.

"Do you not like your rooms?"

She was startled out of her reverie by Christopher's quiet voice, and turned quicker than she should have, staggering a little as her head swam. He was leaning by the hall door, and had the sense to ignore her loss of balance.

"They're beautiful," she said as she found her footing, hoping that she sounded sincere. "Very fine."

He didn't seem that impressed. "Huh," he said, and then, looking very directly at her, "Razi said you would hate them. He said you wouldn't like being confined. He tried very hard to get your cottage back for you, you know. The pretty one? By the stream?"

That was too much – Razi's attempted gesture of love and understanding. Suddenly her eyes were filled with tears that she couldn't contain, and she put her hands to her face with a high breathy sob and began weeping.

Thankfully, Christopher didn't come to her, and she stood and emptied herself of grief until there was nothing but weariness remaining, and a high green pain in her forehead from the tears. Finally she straightened and pushed the wet from her face with an efficient movement, sniffing deeply to clear her nose. The doorway was empty, but there were voices in the hall, a smoothly polished court voice and Christopher's Northland accent, arguing.

". . . it is my *job*," insisted the courtier, "I'm supposed to bring them!"

"Give them to me, you God-cursed flunky, or so help me, I'll skin you alive." Christopher's voice was a low hiss of anger.

"It's *my job*—"

A loud slap and a yelp, followed by a shocked silence. Then Christopher's voice, very calm now, "Are you ready to hand them over, or shall I ensure that you spill them and need go back for more?"

Metal things clattered together to the sound of discontented grumbling, and light footsteps retreated. Then

Christopher came in, carefully carrying three large pitchers of steaming water and avoiding Wynter's eyes.

"Now . . . ." he said, as he skirted round her, then sloshed his way into her bedroom. He set two of the pitchers down by her washstand and poured most of the contents of the last into the metal basin. He took a bar of soap from his pocket and left it on the soap-dish. Then he retreated out the door, returning seconds later with armfuls of big cotton sheets for Wynter to dry herself with.

"Right . . ." he said, still not looking at her. "I'll call you in time to dress for the banquet, unless your father is back by then." And he went out, closing the door quietly behind him.

She was so tired now, her body singing like crickets on a hot day. The evening sunlight streaming through the window was heavy with the scent of oranges and orange blossom, and she closed her eyes for a moment and revelled in the heat and the solitude.

She shuffled into her bedroom, drew the bolt and stripped naked, leaving her stinking clothes in a heap on the floor. There was a sea-sponge on top of the pile of towels, along with a nailbrush, clippers and a comb, all engraved with Razi's seal. Thank God she wouldn't have to root for her own.

Slowly, her arms heavy and numb with fatigue, she unwound the leather straps binding her hair and let it fall to her shoulder blades in thick auburn waves. It was stiff and greasy with dirt, though, thankfully, she'd avoided the lice, and she used almost the entire first pitcher scrubbing it and rinsing it until it squeaked. When she was satisfied, she stuck her head back into the basin and combed her hair out under the clean water. It was always easier to unknot the tangles that way. Then she bent at the waist and let the whole heavy curtain of it hang straight and dripping so that she could wrap the length of it in a towel. Finally she straightened up, and with a flick of her hands flung her wrapped hair behind her, leaving it to hang like a long fat sausage down her back.

She threw the used water out of the window and replenished it from the second pitcher. The smell of roses and oranges and the lemon smell of the soap lulled her senses and the room took on a dreamy air as she methodically scrubbed three month's worth of grime from her body.

She had one clean shift, unused since their departure from Shirken's palace. It was musty and smelled of damp, like everything up North eventually did. But it couldn't overpower the smell of lemons from her still damp hair, which she unwrapped and wove into a long braid to tuck under her night cap.

I'll just lie down for a minute, she thought as she crawled under the insect netting and lay on the cool, lavender scented sheets. *I won't sleep till Dad gets here safe . . .* but she was unconscious before the thought had even registered in her brain.

She was standing in a wide field that stretched all the way to the bright blue horizon. It was filled with red poppies and, as she walked, they stained her feet red, and the hem of her shift. She could hear a high whining cry, as if a sea bird were caught in a net, and she looked around for the source of the noise, because it hurt her heart to hear it. The dye from the poppies began to burn her feet and when she looked down she realised that the flowers weren't red at all, but white, white poppies stained with blood.

The crying was close at hand now, and she ran to the crest of a hill and looked down into a small valley. Wolves were gathered around some poor dead animal, gnawing and snarling and worrying its carcass. There were so many wolves that she couldn't see their prey, but she began to understand that the high wailing was coming from it. Oh. The poor creature, it was still alive.

She picked up a longbow that was at her feet and took aim, hoping to put the animal out of its misery. *I'll never be able to draw this bow. It's too big for me.* But she did draw the bow, pulling back smoothly until the fletch brushed her cheek.

She waited patiently for a glimpse of the poor creature, which still screamed in that horrible, high pitched way as its blood sprayed up and coloured the poppies all around it. The wolves began to fight over some small morsel of the creature's flesh and their ranks parted for a moment. She caught a glimpse of sky blue robes and an arm as it flung upwards, in an attempt to escape, or as a reaction to the movement of the ravaging wolves, she couldn't tell.

Oh, she thought, with an interested detachment, *it's Razi.*

She notched the bow a little tighter, released her breath and let the arrow fly with a high singing whine. It seemed to have a long way to go, this arrow, and she was able to trace its flight every inch of the way, admiring how it twisted and swung gently from side to side as it cut its way through the air.

By the time it reached its target all the wolves had gone

and it was only Razi, alone and bloody, lying among the dripping poppies. The arrow found its mark with a loud knock as if Razi's heart was made of wood, and his body leapt at the impact.

The sound reverberated around the little valley, repeated and repeated in a quick rapping succession. Razi's eyes opened and they were grey and slanting and it wasn't Razi at all, but Christopher Garron. He lifted his head, his hair all bloody, and looked at her in terrible hurt and confusion.

"Wynter," he said, and the knocking continued to echo around the valley as she dropped the bow in horror at his bloody mouth, his accusing eyes.

"Wynter," he said again and his voice was fading, getting farther away as all his blood poured out onto the flowers.

"Wynter."

"*Wynter!*"

She woke with a startled gasp.

The shadows had grown but it was still light outside, she couldn't have been asleep more than two hours. Christopher was calling her name and knocking softly but urgently on her bedroom door. "Wynter, Razi and your father are coming. I don't think your father is well."

The Eternal Engine Failing

Wynter scrambled from beneath the netting and rushed to unbolt the door, pushing Christopher back as she flew past him.

"Where are they?" she demanded, looking about her wildly. "What's wrong with my father?"

Christopher put his finger to his lips and gestured to the receiving room. Wynter followed him unthinkingly across the room, until she realised that the hall door was ajar and their rooms open to the scrutiny of anyone who might pass by. She was immediately aware of her thin shift and her night cap, and she hesitated in the receiving room as Christopher continued out into the hall. He didn't notice her lagging behind, and he went out and stood, openly staring down the corridor, his face grave.

Oh, for goodness sake, had he no sense?

"Christopher," she crossed the receiving room and hissed from behind the door, keeping herself hidden from the corridor. "You *can't* just stand there looking!"

He flicked a glance at her and went back to his blatant staring. "Why not?" he whispered. "No one is paying any heed."

"People here are *always* paying heed," she said, flinging her hands out in exasperation. But he just kept on looking, a small frown creasing his eyebrows. "What is it?" she asked, longing to see. "Can you see my father?"

Christopher glanced at her again, and then back up the corridor. His eyes were troubled, his face uncertain, as if he was unsure how to explain the situation. Finally, he grunted impatiently, grabbed her shoulder and pulled her through the door.

"Look," he murmured.

Lorcan and Razi were standing at the junction of the two corridors, about fifty or sixty feet from Christopher and Wynter. They were deep in heated discussion with Heron and three other black-robed councilmen, and for a moment Wynter wondered what on earth Christopher was talking about. Her father looked fine. He was listening intently while Razi gestured and grunted out some low, angry diatribe to the exasperated men in front of them.

Then Wynter noticed how straight her father's back was, how rigid, how his arms were stiff at his sides, his big hands balled into fists. She saw that he wasn't listening at all, not really, he was just standing there with an expression of grim determination on his face. As she watched, Razi discreetly placed his hand on her father's back, right between his shoulder blades, and she saw the muscles tense along Razi's arm, his shoulder jumping into taut relief as he took her father's weight without the other men realising it.

Wynter made a tiny noise of fear and went to leap forward, but Christopher pinched her shoulder, and she put her hand to her mouth and shut herself up.

Suddenly Razi was imperiously waving his hand at the four men, turning them away. She saw sharp anger harden their faces and Heron's mouth twist up into a bitter sneer. But if Razi ordered it, they had to obey, and so they took their leave with frowns and grudging bows.

Razi and Lorcan stood and watched until the four men were out of sight. Then Razi turned to her father, speaking rapidly and with a concerned tilt of his head. Lorcan brushed him off, breaking away from his supporting arm. He took two or three stiff-legged steps towards Wynter and Christopher, his face grim, but his knees buckled almost immediately and Razi had to catch him. He staggered under Lorcan's weighty frame and called for Christopher, who was already halfway down the hall.

Wynter watched, frozen in mute horror as the two men propped Lorcan up and helped him down the corridor and into his rooms. When they had passed her by, she checked the corridor once more and closed and bolted the door, shutting out any possibility of prying eyes.

Once in their room, Lorcan gave up any pretence at strength and let his legs go from under him, so that the two smaller men had difficulty dragging him across the floor. They heaved him into one of the round chairs, and Razi leant him back, putting a cushion between Lorcan's head and the wall.

"Let in more light," he instructed. "Get some water. Christopher, go get my bag. Wynter, get a stool to prop up his feet, take off his boots. *Christopher*, my bag."

Lorcan was so limp and helpless that Wynter thought her father had passed out, but when she looked up from where she knelt at his feet, his eyes were open and staring glassily about. His mouth was wide, his chest heaving; he seemed to be fighting for air. She took all this in as she undid the lacing on his heavy riding boots and dragged them from his feet, which were freezing cold. She put a cushion on the fire-stool and propped Lorcan's feet on it, then began to chafe them to try to get them warm.

"He's so cold, Razi," she said.

"Mmm," Razi murmured. He had undone her father's shirt to the navel and loosened the stays of his trousers. The big man's face was beaded with huge droplets of sweat, the bright mat of orange hair on his powerful chest and belly drenched and slicked down. Razi pressed his ear to Lorcan's breast and was listening intently. When Wynter tried to speak again, Razi lifted his hand and shushed her, reaching over to stroke her cheek without looking at her, before placing his hand on Lorcan's belly and pressing down hard. Lorcan groaned and tried to pull away.

"All right, good friend. All right," Razi said softly, his ear still to Lorcan's chest. He pressed down again, on a different part of Lorcan's belly, to the same response. "That's all right, Lorcan. That's all right." Razi sat back slowly and ran his hands over his face, looking at Wynter's father over the tops of his fingers for a moment. His big brown eyes were cool and considering. Wynter could see him working things out in his head.

Christopher returned and quickly bolted the door behind him. He put Razi's bag down beside the chair. "I've sent for water," he said quietly.

Razi leant forward over Lorcan and murmured something in the man's ear. Lorcan's eyes rolled in shock, but

Razi levelled a look at him and Lorcan nodded uncertainly. Razi patted his shoulder and then, to Wynter's horror, he thrust his hand down the front of her father's trousers and seemed to press his fingers hard into the other man's groin. Lorcan squeezed his eyes shut and turned his head, whether from pain or mortification Wynter couldn't tell, and she looked away, her cheeks burning.

When she dared to glance back, Razi was feeling along both sides of her father's jaw, his face drawn in concentration. Lorcan was beginning to come to himself a bit more and was attempting to lift his head and shoulders from the cushion. He looked over at Christopher with a kind of bleary resentment and tried to pull his shirt closed. Razi stayed him with a hand on his wrist. "Just a little longer, Lorcan. This will all be over soon." He rummaged in his bag and pulled out a short, polished wooden trumpet. He warmed the mouth of it on his stomach and placed it on Lorcan's chest, listening through the other end, his face intense. "Breathe as deep as you can, good friend. And try to hold the air in your lungs." Lorcan struggled to do as Razi asked, but he seemed incapable of holding his breath and ended up gasping, his head dropping back, his skin breaking out once more into an oily sweat.

Finally Razi sat back on his heels, wiped his hands on a lemon-scented cloth that Christopher handed him and looked very seriously at the big man. "Lorcan," he said, "I would like to consult with you now, if you are willing to talk honestly with me."

Lorcan's eyes flickered between Wynter and Christopher, a hunted look on his face. Razi nodded. "Your daughter and Christopher Garron can wait outside if you wish, Lorcan. This concerns no one but you."

It was obvious that Lorcan gave the matter serious consideration, then he dismissed the idea with a wordless shake of his head. Breathing heavily, his teeth bared, he took his feet from the stool and struggled to sit up straighter in his chair. Razi leapt to help, shifting cushions about until Lorcan pushed his hands away and hunched himself into a reasonably upright position. He grabbed the arms of his chair tightly, a trick he had developed to stop his hands from shaking, and looked at Razi from under his eyebrows.

"Speak," he demanded.

Razi remained sitting on his heels and he gestured Wynter and Christopher away with a tilt of his head. They went and sat, one on either side of the fireplace, doing their best to blend into the tapestries.

"In your years abroad, Lorcan, you perhaps had some fever or a long illness?" Razi's voice was quiet and gentle, yet at the same time he had a command about him, a sense of honest confidence that seemed to relax Lorcan.

The big man nodded. "Over two years ago. A fever, it knocked the feathers from me."

Razi smiled and raised a questioning eyebrow. "Took you a while to recover?"

Lorcan nodded again. Then he looked up, his face creased with concern. "My Lord," he said, "there are more important things we should be discussing."

Razi silenced him with a raised hand. "No, good friend. No. We will not discuss anything but your health. That is my wish."

Lorcan clamped his jaw tight and looked away. Razi tapped his knee to regain his attention. "This fever," he continued, "it left you weak? You tired easily? There was perhaps a loss of balance? You have much pain in your hips? Your shoulders?"

Again Lorcan agreed, and Razi pressed his lips together and put his hand on his friend's knee. "You see, Lorcan, I think that the fever has left its humours in your body's waters. This is what I can feel gathered here," he indicated Lorcan's groin, "and here, and here." He gestured to Lorcan's armpit and jaw.

Lorcan shrugged. "Yes. The doctors in the North told me similar. But they bled me and said it should clear . . ."

Razi gritted his teeth and Wynter saw his hands clench. "And you've been bled regularly since, haven't you?" Lorcan nodded. "I thought so, and purged?" Lorcan's eyes found Wynter, and he blushed red and dipped his head. Razi seemed to take a moment to gather himself. Wynter saw him force his hands to relax. "All right, Lorcan. I want you to promise me that you will not allow any doctor to leech you or purge you again. I really must insist."

Lorcan seemed thoroughly confused. He frowned, his eyes questioning, and licked his lips, which were terribly dry.

Don't offer him any water, thought Wynter, knowing that her father would never betray his shaking hands by trying to bring a beaker to his lips.

"Drink this," Razi ordered, and Wynter winced. To her amazement, Lorcan allowed Razi to hold the beaker for him as he sipped from it.

"The other doctors . . ." Lorcan cleared his throat, "the

other doctors said it was beneficial to my system . . . to release the poisons from my blood."

Razi seemed to consider something, what words to use, perhaps, and in the end he just said, "I think they've drained enough poisons. If that kind of treatment is continued, you . . . it is my opinion that your body will begin to leak its own beneficial humours, to your detriment. So, no more bleeding, no more purges. Are we agreed?"

Lorcan raised his bright green eyes to Razi, and Wynter thought she had never seen him look so open and vulnerable. "Agreed. But, my Lord? What is there to be done?"

"You need to rest."

Her father rolled his eyes to heaven at that, and began to pull away. Razi tugged his sleeve, his voice firm as he said, "Lorcan, I do not say this lightly. You *need* to rest. You need to rest frequently and well. You need to eat well. Lorcan, you need to avoid vexation."

Wynter's father actually laughed at this, a proper, hearty laugh that quickly ran out of breath and left him bent at the waist, but still grinning. His mirth was infectious and Razi and Christopher had to chuckle along with him, the joke not lost on any of them. Even Wynter smiled. Avoid vexation. Hah, some chance.

"Ahhh," wheezed her father, straightening carefully and gripping his chair again. "A laugh is as good as a tonic!"

Razi took a deep breath and looked pointedly into Lorcan's eyes. His next words stole Lorcan's grin from him and blew a whistling hole through Wynter's chest. "The humours have gathered in your heart, good friend. I can hear them in there, interrupting the ebb and flow of your body's tides. Such impediments are not to be trifled with.

You *must* pay heed to my instructions, Lorcan. Your life depends on it."

Her father's heart. His heart. Wynter remembered lying on his chest as a small child, listening to the swish and flow of that engine, working steady and eternal beneath her infant ear. Lulling her to sleep, telling her *all is well, all is well, all is well.*

Lorcan gazed at Razi, then over at Wynter, his green eyes bright. He smiled and shrugged as if to say, *we knew this already, didn't we, darling?* He winked at Wynter and she tried to smile back at him. Ever since she could remember, her father had worked hard to make sure Wynter would be able to take care of herself if he wasn't around. He had done a good job of it, and now at last they were home, and he had finally returned her to the safest place on earth, a place where neither her sex nor commoner birth would stand against her. He wasn't afraid to die. But despite it all, despite the talking, the planning, all the preparation for a life alone, Wynter did not want him to leave. She could not imagine going on without his huge smiling affection in her life.

Razi got to his feet. "Now," he said, "I want you to let Christopher and I help you bathe and get you to bed for a few hours before the banquet." Lorcan opened his mouth to protest, his eyes wide with indignation. "Lorcan!" Razi interrupted before the other man could speak. "You cannot do this alone, not at the moment. Just bite back your pride, man, and let us aid you this once. I'm going to give you a draught and it will help you sleep deeply for a short time. You'll wake much refreshed, and I think, if you take it slow and remain calm, you'll get through this bloody *festivity* without too much strain."

What could he do? With a last, rueful look at Wynter, Lorcan allowed the two men to lead him into his chamber, and, when the water came, they helped him to scrub himself clean of the filth of his long journey, and climb at last into bed.

Wynter sat alone in the round chair for the longest time, listening to the low rumble of the men's voices and watching the light move around the walls as the evening drew down. When her father had fallen asleep, Christopher and Razi took their leave of her. Razi kissed her and promised to return before the banquet.

The scent of oranges gave way to the evening fragrance of woodbine and lilies as the shadows grew in the gardens below. The corridor outside began to fill with sound as the air cooled and people began to rouse themselves, or come in from the river to dress for the big event.

Wynter thought of nothing at all. There was nothing that could be of any use. So she let the time flow through her and it was as though she slept for a while, though she knew she did not.

Razi had promised to call her in time to dress, but she got herself up and out of the chair long before he returned, and wandered into her room to try to find something to wear. She had one light coat, one heavy. Two dress uniforms, one of which still lay in a pestilent heap on the floor. One heavy work uniform, three pair of long johns, three shifts, two night caps, four pair of wool stockings, one pair of cotton stockings, two long knickers and a soft fine-wool dress suitable for informal dining in company. She had no formal clothes whatsoever, nothing suitable to wear in the presence of a king.

Razi had put her mother's camphor chest into Wynter's room, and now she understood the reason why.

One at a time, she took her mother's dresses from their layers of lavender paper and nets of dried roses, gilly-flowers and orange pomanders. She noticed with surprise that they had been aired. Over the years, someone had taken care to regularly shake and hang them. Marni, perhaps? Or some maid who had been terribly fond of her mother?

Comprehension dawned, and Wynter mentally slapped herself for her romantic notions. No one had taken care of these dresses through devotion to her mother! Most likely these had, until recently, been the property of some Lady's maid-in-waiting. Poor girl, made to give up her wardrobe all of a sudden to its previous owner. *I'd better watch for scissors in the dark and pins in my soup*, she thought as she laid each lovely creation on the bed.

She hoped their last owner hadn't altered them too much, as her father had told her she was very like her mother in size and shape, and the dresses should fit her pretty well had they not been fiddled with.

Mamma had good taste, she thought as she ran her hand down the rich fabric of one of the dresses. They were cut to the old style, bold clean lines and simple skirts that hung straight down from just below the bosom. Long wide sleeves with contrasting linings and trim. Each had a tight-fitting, long-sleeved silk shift to wear beneath. She decided that she liked them very much; their beautiful colours and elegant simplicity appealed to her. The new style amongst the courtiers up North was all ribbons and swags and little capes and round hats that perched on the back of the head. She would be considered hopelessly old-fashioned and plain in these. *Not to mention freakishly short*, she thought. She was generally considered to be a small person, but the new fashion for high cork heels and built up soles in both men's and women's shoes would really emphasise her lack of stature.

Wynter giggled at the thought of Razi adding those extra inches to his already ridiculous height, and Christopher, with all his slippery grace, tottering along on heels. She doubted they would be indulging in the fad. And what about Albi, he . . . Wynter cut short her thoughts of Albi, hilarious as he would be in heels, broad, bullish and bounding as he was, or had been. She swallowed and turned her attention back to the dresses.

It didn't take her long to choose, and she slipped into sage green satin, embroidered with sprigs of pale roses, with pale rose lining to the sleeves. The matching shift covered her arms to the wrist and puckered at her bosom above the neckline of the bodice. It was surprisingly easy to move in this outfit and she was comfortably cool in the evening air.

She considered trying to do something with her hair, tucking it into one of her mother's pearl studded nets or coiling it or pinning it somehow, but she was a lost cause when it came to hair and she just brushed it out of its long plait and let it fall around her shoulders and down to her shoulder blades in glossy, cracking waves.

What are you? she thought as she examined herself in the mirror. She looked like a doll; her pale face with its constellations of freckles floating in a wavy sea of hair; her usually busy hands resting against the green of her dress, her arms encased in rose coloured silk. She ran her hands across the fabric of her skirt, feeling the calluses on her palms snag and catch. The familiar weight of the dagger she always carried was missing, but there was no place for a weapon in this formal attire. She lifted the skirts, revealing her scuffed felt indoor-boots and grinned. *That's what you are*, she told herself, you *are work-hardened hands, you are scuffed boots under a satin skirt.* She looked herself in the eyes. *Don't forget it*, she told herself.

Razi and Christopher came knocking just as she was considering rousing her father. She drew the bolt and stood back to let them in. Razi was standing in the door, his hand poised to knock again, and Christopher was lounging against the wall across from them, as if he intended to wait outside. At the sight of her, Razi's mouth dropped open and Christopher pushed himself off the wall and stood looking at her with a puzzled little tilt of his head.

Wynter put her hand up and nervously touched her hair. "Is it not all right?"

Razi shook his head, then nodded, blinked and muttered something. Christopher ran his eyes down to her toes and back again and said, "You'll do."

As the two men came into the room, Lorcan's door opened and he surprised them all by stepping out fully dressed and ready to go. Razi made a move to approach him, his face questioning, but Lorcan stopped him with a hooded glare. Razi spread his hands in defeat and turned away.

Lorcan started back at the sight of his daughter. Pausing in the middle of pulling on a suede glove, he took in her face, her hair, the dress.

"Izzy . . . ?" he whispered. Then his confusion cleared, and he smiled sadly. "Wynter," he said.

His lips are so pale, she thought, frightened.

Then he smiled at her, his full, broad sunshine smile and she felt herself relax. It would be fine. Yes it would. Everything would be fine.

The Danger of Subtlety

"Christopher seems to think he's coming to the banquet."
Wynter kept her voice low and her head turned towards
Razi as they followed the crowd through the long corridors
to the dining hall. Christopher was padding along behind
them, discussing music with her father, who was a keen but
atrocious flautist. Wynter didn't want to cause him any
offence and risk another prickly exchange. If he was of the
belief that all and sundry could attend these things, it would
be up to Razi diplomatically to set him straight.

Razi bent his curly head to hers and, with an amused
grin, whispered confidentially, "That's because he is coming
to the banquet." He drew back to see her reaction, his eyes
dancing. She tried not to show her amazement but could-
n't quite carry it off, and he chuckled in glee. "It really
vexes the lords."

Wynter gasped. "Oh, Razi *no*! Please don't tell me he's
seated at the lords' table! They'll have him poisoned!"

Razi made a little sign at his throat. "Don't even joke,
little sister. No, the last four nights he's been seated at the
commoners' board. A great honour."

"A great honour," she murmured, glancing back at the man in question. He was describing something to her father, waving his hands about without a trace of self-consciousness. Her father laughed at something the young man said. Christopher raised his eyebrows, pausing in mock offence and then continued whatever outlandish rubbish he was weaving. Wynter grimaced. "A great honour, indeed."

"He says it's a royal pain in the arse," said Razi with a sigh. "God, Wyn, I can't help but agree. I hate all this, after so long free of it. Father . . ." he paused to nod at a passing courtier, bowed at a loitering knot of ladies and thought better of saying any more about the King.

"You didn't keep a court in the Moroccos, Razi?"

Again, the generous smile, the rueful quirk of his mouth. "Much to mother's distress, no, I did not." He drifted away for a moment, to somewhere warm, somewhere scented with spices. His smile grew a little sad and he looked down at her. "I kept a *home* there, Wyn. It was lovely. That's what I want in Padua. A proper home, with proper family and real friend . . . I want—"

"We're here, my Lord," Lorcan broke in, coming up behind them and taking them both by surprise.

"Ah." Razi looked at the door that would lead them to the royal quarters, where only the royal family and its highest honoured companions would gather before a feast. Razi and Wynter's father would have to break off from them here, so as to make their entrance with the royal party.

Lorcan bent and kissed Wynter quickly on her cheek, squeezing her shoulder before ushering Razi through the door and then letting it swing shut behind them.

Wynter looked at the closed door for a moment, then

turned and looked about quite aimlessly, only to find Christopher watching her. The dimples showed on either side of his mouth in the briefest of smiles. "I'm going this way," he said, indicating the long corridor that led to the common door. His expression said, *are you all right? Do you need me to stay?*

She took a deep breath and straightened her shoulders. "Enjoy your meal, Christopher, and may the morning find you well."

Those damn dimples again, but he had the good grace to bow properly, and headed off down the hall without a further word. Even his retreating back looked amused.

The hall was already quite crowded. The lords' tables in particular, one on either side of the great hall, already filling rapidly. At the end of the hall furthest from the royal platform was the commoners' board; it would be filled with those servants and lesser courtiers specially favoured by the King. At the top, draped in white and scarlet, was the two-tiered royal platform. The higher tier would be reserved for the King, his queen and his heir; the lower tier comprised a long table for the councilmen, favoured lords and any spare royal children that might be around. It would be a lonely meal for the King, thought Wynter, with his queen dead, his heir missing and Razi relegated by protocol to the lower tier.

A page came over to her and asked if she wished to be shown a seat. It was always put that way, "Do you wish to be shown a seat?" to which you had to answer, "Yes" because otherwise you would not know where the King had decided to put you.

She was placed close to the head of the lords' table on

the left – a very good position. While the bottom halves of the lords' tables on both sides filled rapidly, seating at the top filled more slowly, as those places were reserved for the particularly favoured.

The commoners began to stream in and take their places: no pages or protocol there, just a merry jostling and shuffling around for seats. Everyone must be in and seated before the royal entrance, so that they could all rise in unison and salute the King. If you weren't there before the King, you weren't allowed in at all.

Wynter watched Christopher stroll through the crowded commoners' entrance, nodding and smiling at those few who seemed to know him. He made a beeline for a very pretty, dark-haired woman with snapping eyes and a red mouth. Wynter snorted as he bent and murmured into the woman's ear, flashing his dimples. She shuffled up to make room for him. The man on the other side of Christopher said something, laughing, and Christopher gave him that tomcat grin and adjusted his tunic as he sat down.

The room was almost filled now and getting warm. The fanners began to pull their heavy ropes, and the big fans on the ceiling started their gentle swooshing, instantly cooling the air. Buttle-boys served beakers of iced strawberry cordial. There was still no sign of a grand entrance from the royal rooms.

As Wynter took her first sip of cordial, the musicians in the lesser gallery began to play a soft minnelieder, and she automatically glanced at Christopher. Sure enough, he had turned to look up at them, his face hidden from her sight. Wynter saw the woman beside him notice his hands as though for the first time. The woman started and drew back a little. If she had been seated at the lords' table nothing would have been said, but she would have made it her business very quickly to remove herself from his presence. This was a commoner, though, and Wynter saw her puck Christopher on the arm and gesture to his missing fingers.

Christopher held up his hands as if to say, *What, this?* He gave the woman an easy grin, and launched into something animated and complex that ended with a quirked eyebrow and an expressive pause. The woman beside him looked shocked for a moment and then the two of them burst into simultaneous hilarity. The woman dashed tears from her eyes and commented laughingly to him, taking up her beaker to sip her drink. Christopher leaned in to whisper in her ear and she blushed pink. Wynter saw her grin around the rim of her cup.

Rolling her eyes at their behaviour, Wynter turned her attention to another familiar face, Andrew Pritchard, who was taking a seat one place setting up from her on the right. They nodded politely to each other, before he turned to begin a conversation with the man beside him.

A page exited the royal door to their left, and there was a ripple of tension all down the hall. Was the royal party coming? But the boy closed the door gently behind him and the crowd relaxed and conversations rose up again as he began to make his way down between the tables.

On an errand for some councilman, no doubt, thought Wynter, following his weaving progress down the hall. Her relief didn't last long, though, and a knot formed in the pit of her stomach as it became obvious that the page was heading for the commoners' table.

Oh God.

She wasn't the only person surreptitiously tracking the small figure through the crowd. No one entered or left the royal door without being taken note of, and more than a score of the assembly reacted with varying degrees of interest as the page approached the commoners and touched Christopher Garron on the arm.

Wynter couldn't hear what was being said, but she saw Christopher's patent shock and confusion as the page spoke to him. She swallowed and leaned forward in nervous tension as the page gestured impatiently and ushered the baffled young man to his feet. Obeying the page's gestures, Christopher began to make his way to the lords' table.

No! Oh God, was the King mad? Could he possibly be so crazed as to have ordered Christopher to sit amongst the lords? Did he hate him so much? Did he *want* him torn apart by wolves?

Wynter watched in horror as the page led the mortified man through the wide space of no man's land that lay between the commoner's territory and that of the lords.

Don't abandon him! she thought, *don't just leave him here to find his own seat.*

But she knew, she just knew, that this was exactly what the page was going to do. More than anyone else, the servants would detest this outrageous breaking of rank, this terrible, *terrible*, insult to protocol.

As she suspected, the page accompanied Christopher to the end of the table, gestured vaguely to the bench and walked off, his heels clicking in the now almost totally silent room. Christopher was left standing uncertainly at the end of a very long row of pointedly turned backs, all his brash certainty fled.

There was an empty space, about ten persons up from where he stood, and Christopher gratefully made his way towards it. But as he walked up the narrow corridor between the bench and the wall, the lords and ladies shuffled and rearranged themselves so that, by the time he got to it, the space had vanished like a magic trick. Christopher paused for a moment, looking down at the rigidly turned back where his seat had been. Then he slowly began walking towards the next available space, the knowledge of what was going to happen burning in his cheeks. Sure enough, the space was gone by the time he actually got there.

Once, twice, three more times Christopher tried to find a place, as the lords and ladies played their childish, shuffling game. Then he just stood there, rigid with anger, his flaming cheeks the only colour in his face.

He's going to leave, Wynter thought, *he'll turn on his heel and leave, and that will be the end of his life here. There will be no way to survive that kind of insult to the King.* Of course, that was what the lords wanted. If Christopher left now, it would be seen as throwing the King's generosity in his face, and he would have no hope of remaining at court. *It would be the best thing for all of us if that happened,* Wynter thought, watching the young man fume at the other end of the hall. *Best for Razi, best for Christopher, best for me.*

She closed her eyes and begged herself to just *let him go.* But in the end that would have taken the kind of cruelty that Wynter just didn't have in her. Sighing, she opened her eyes and took the sharp knife from the wooden platter in front of her. Casually she put her hand in the empty space on the bench between herself and Andrew Pritchard and leaned back so that Christopher could see her down the length of ramrod straight backs. She raised her chin to him in invitation.

He saw her immediately, how could he not? Her shock of loose red hair suddenly popping into view like that. And she saw him hesitate, uncertainty in his eyes. *He thinks I'm going to trick him*, she realised with a jolt, *that I'll bring him all the way up here and then close the space on him like all the others.* She let the hurt of that show in her face and saw him make up his mind.

He made his slow way down the bench, his arms stiff at his sides, his face still creased up in furious embarrassment, and as he passed them by, the lords and ladies nudged and wriggled and shuffled to make certain that no space became available for him.

When the time came for Andrew Pritchard to shift into the vacant place, he found his hip on very intimate terms with Wynter's sharp meat knife. A shocked glance in her direction met with Wynter's sparking green eyes. He jerked back in time to allow Christopher vault over the bench and settle himself into one of the best seats in the hall.

The minnelieder continued to play and it filled up the silences until the conversation began to swell and grow again. Eventually, the room returned to a semblance of its former volume, but there was a dark, shifting undercurrent to it now. People whispered, people were nudging each other, people were staring. Christopher and Wynter were as exposed and on show as insects pinned to a board.

Christopher cleared his throat and gestured for cordial. None of the buttle-boys managed to see him. He sighed.

"The air is fierce thin up here," he muttered, "I feel the chill."

"You should have come prepared," answered Wynter coldly, "it doesn't do to swim in strange rivers." She pushed her cordial towards him without looking at him and he took a sip without thanks.

"A friend encouraged me. It would appear he lied when he told me to 'come on in! The water's fine'." He shoved her beaker back with a jab of his finger and cast a longing look at the dark-haired woman with the red mouth. She was pointedly avoiding his gaze, her head turned so far in the other direction as to be ridiculous. Christopher sighed again. "What a shame," he murmured.

Wynter glanced at the woman. "You *were* doing rather well there, weren't you? What exactly did you say to make her laugh like that?"

Christopher looked at her for a moment, seeming to consider his reply, then he shrugged and looked away. "Nothing you would find amusing."

"You seem fond of *amusing* women."

The dimples showed, very briefly, as he scanned the room. People made a point of not meeting his eye. "Well, the women here seem a touch starved of affection."

Wynter snorted, and without meaning to, she muttered, "What are you doing here, Christopher?" She meant *what is it you want? What do you hope to gain?*

"God, I wish I knew . . ."

She turned to look him, thrown by his reply. The unexpected sadness in his voice made her stare into his face.

"This is hell; I don't understand why Razi would put himself through it." He continued in a low, confidential tone, "I'm glad I came with him, though, and I'm glad you finally showed up." He scanned the room. "Is there even a single person here who doesn't want something from him? It's like living in a vulture's nest."

Wynter had no idea how to answer that because it was so far from what she had expected to hear, but Christopher was already distracted by some activity on the far side of the room.

"I know I'm not very used to these things," he said, gesturing with his chin, "but isn't it unusual to serve the food before the royal party are seated?"

The double doors were open and some very disconcerted servers were carrying out huge trays. They held the small fowl that were the traditional start to any banquet. A low hum of concern spread its way through the crowd and people began casting worried glances around them. Someone from the commoners' board said, "Shame! For shame!" loud enough for it to be replied to with "Aye!" by some members of the lords' table.

Wynter stared anxiously at the royal door. What could be keeping the royal party? She tried to conceal the panic that had started to roil in the pit of her stomach. What was everyone to do? Should one accept the food? Or would that insult the King, who had not yet sat down or been saluted? Who was going to be foolish enough to take first choice of the meat, traditionally the sole privilege of the royal table? But then, if the tray was offered and one didn't accept the food, would that be considered an insult to the King's generosity? Would it be worse than accepting? What if one took a small piece of meat onto one's plate, but didn't eat it? Would *that* be acceptable?

She could see the same struggle going on in the faces all around her. Except for Christopher, who was looking under his platter and up and down his section of the table, a puzzled expression on his face.

"Where is my knife?" he wondered.

Wynter frowned; there had been a knife there when she sat down. She glanced across at Andrew Pritchard and saw him give his neighbour a satisfied smile. She leaned further back and saw a discreet flurry of movement ripple its way down the lords' table. Something was passing from person to person until, right at the very end of the table, Simon Pursuant called a buttle-boy to him and handed over a "spare" knife. The boy frowned at it and asked a polite question, to which Pursuant shrugged and gestured negligently, *I must have been given two by mistake.* Wynter gritted her teeth in frustration. Childish, petty, stupid . . .

The royal door opened and everyone's attention turned immediately to the very young page who mounted the second tier of the King's table and announced in a high nervous voice, "His Majesty, the Good King Jonathon, bids you eat, having been delayed momentarily in matters . . . um . . ." The child looked nervously over his shoulder and someone hissed at him from the partially opened royal door, ". . . in matters of state. Not wishing his beloved people to hunger in his absence, he bids you to commence the fowl in . . . in the . . . in the assurance he will join you soon." The child fled the stage and the staff commenced to pass around the room with the enormous trays of steaming fowl.

The matter of who would take the first choice of meat thankfully fell on the shoulders of those at the very head of the lords' tables, Francis Coltumer and Laurence Theobald. As they were sitting right next to the royal platform, the servants felt safest approaching them first. They stood, one pair in front of each old man, and unshouldered the huge trays, holding them down at table level for the gentlemen to take their pick. Old hands at this game, Francis and Laurence glanced at each other across the hall, nodded, and simultaneously speared the smallest fowl that either of them could find on the tray in front of them. A sigh of relief rippled through the crowd as the two old fellows dropped the birds onto their plates and began delicately picking at the meat.

Low, uncertain conversation began once more to underscore the music from the minstrel's gallery and the trays were carried from guest to guest. Christopher was still searching for his missing knife, his head beneath the table now, looking under the bench.

"Christopher . . ." murmured Wynter, eyeing the tray that was heading their way. "Christopher!" She kicked him and he jerked upward, banging his head on the table and cursing in Hadrish.

He sat up, rubbing his head, and smiled appreciatively as the fragrant heap of roast fowl was brought on level with his nose. "Oh my," he breathed, licking his lips.

"Tell me which one you want," whispered Wynter, "and I'll ..."

But before she could finish her sentence, Christopher had reached down to his calf and come up with the longest, wickedest dagger that Wynter had ever seen produced from a boot. He speared a nice fat chicken for himself and then glanced at her. "Can I get you one?" he asked, genuinely oblivious to the mixture of fear and outrage being directed his way from the whole length of the table behind him.

Wynter tore her eyes from the long line of sour faces visible over his shoulder, and managed to keep a straight face when she said, "I'll have that partridge please, Christopher."

Despite his injuries, he seemed to have no difficulty dismembering his chicken, and Wynter watched, fascinated, as he neatly separated the meat from the bones. It was only when he spoke to her again that Wynter realised she'd been staring. "It's a very effective revenge, isn't it?" he said evenly, dipping his fingers in the finger bowl and wiping his mutilated hands on his napkin, "designed to rob me of everything I am, but still leave me capable enough to work." He ate without looking at her, his eyes scanning the room.

This isn't the amusing story he told the other woman, Wynter thought. *He's telling me something here that not everyone knows. Why?* She mulled over his words. Revenge, he had said. Not punishment. Revenge. *Who did you offend that they would hurt you so? Some brother? Some husband, perhaps?* But then she remembered Razi's laughing reference to Christopher getting himself tarred, and thought it unlikely that he would have made such a joke had Christopher already suffered so horribly because of his licentiousness.

The royal door opened again, and both she and Christopher turned to see the small pageboy slipping down between their table and the wall, obviously on his way to the other end of the hall.

Christopher snapped out a hand and grabbed the child by his tunic, jerking him to a halt. Wynter gasped and looked about her in mortification. "Oh, Christopher," she whispered, "that's not done!"

Christopher pulled the child to him and hissed in his startled ear, "What's going on in there, mouse?" His Hadrish accent was suddenly very thick.

The child looked around it in panic and struggled. "I can't tell you, my Lord. You know that.

"I ain't your Lord, mouse. I'm just sitting here. How is my Lord Razi? Does he fare well?"

"Christopher!" Wynter put her hand on his arm, but he ignored her and pulled the struggling child closer. People were staring, straining to hear. The big guards on either side of the hall were beginning to take note. "*Christopher!* You'll end up in the keep!"

"I *can't* sir!" the child's voice had reached bat-like pitch in his panic. "I must take a message, sir! Let me go!"

"Who's the message for?"

The child looked around him in fear, the guards were starting to advance but they must have seemed to be moving very slowly to his panic-stricken eyes. "Freeman Garron, sir. At the commoners' board. It's very important, sir. *Please* let me go."

Christopher relaxed his grip, his eyes wide, and the child tried to bolt, but Wynter snatched the back of his tunic, "This is Christopher Garron, child. Tell him your message."

The child moaned in frustration and terror. "No, Lady! *Freeman* Garron, from the commoners' table. Oh *please*, Lady, *please*, it's so important. My Lord Razi said all speed."

Christopher half-stood, his voice rising, and Wynter saw an awful anger, a real, fierce, terrible rage rising in his face.

It frightened her, and the child cowered before this new, dark threat.

"I *am* Freeman Garron, mouse. Now give me your God-cursed message."

The guards had almost reached them, but before they could react, the little page took a good long look at Christopher. The hair, the slanting grey eyes and finally, the hands. The hands, of course, sealed it, and the child gasped and fell to his knees. "Oh my Lord! Forgive me! I am too late!"

The guards looked confused, and then backed off as it became obvious that the little page had found who he was seeking. Christopher snatched him up from his knees and shook him by the shoulder. "I'm *not* your Lord, child! What's the message? Is my Lord Razi well?"

"Lord Ga . . . Freeman Garron, sir. My Lord Razi sends me . . . tuh . . . sends me to . . ." the child had tears in his eyes and Wynter marvelled at how unmoved Christopher remained. He was glaring at the poor mite, his only focus on getting the message. "To tell you . . . do not . . . oh my Lord! He says do not accept any invitations to the lords' table! He needs your eyes on both sides of the hall!"

Christopher flung the child away from him with a curse and glared up the aisle. Wynter thought for one awful moment that he was going to try and rush his way into the royal rooms. But then he spun back to the boy and grabbed him again and snarled in his ear. "Tell Lord Razi that it's too late! Tell him he's lost his eyes. Ask him what I am to do. Do you heed me, child? Ask him what he will have me do!" With that, he hurled the page up the corridor so that he skidded the first few feet and scampered the rest.

Wynter sat, half-turned out of her seat, looking up at Christopher as he stood watching the pageboy gain access to the royal room. His face was hard; Wynter would even call it brutal. He was utterly concentrated on seeing the child through that door. There was nothing else in the room for him and Wynter realised something very suddenly. It was as though a beam of light abruptly focused on this young man and it changed him utterly in her eyes.

Christopher Garron was not here for what he could get. Christopher was not here for the luxury, for the food, or even for the women. And Wynter knew now why Razi had persuaded him to come. Christopher was Razi's friend. He loved him, and Razi trusted him. Trusted him to watch his back. Trusted him to keep him safe. Trusted him to keep him alive.

Looking at Christopher's face, Wynter recognised herself in his expression. It frightened her and comforted her in equal measure to realise that they would both willingly lay down their lives for Razi.

The Terrible Feast

The page never got a chance to give Lord Razi his message. Immediately after his frightened little figure disappeared into the royal rooms, the door swung open again and the first of the councilmen made their entrance from the royal rooms and into the hall. Wynter could see the page, his little face distraught at not being able to finish his task, forced back against the wall as the black-clad councilmen stalked past him.

Something was terribly wrong, any fool could see that. The six councilmen who came through the door were almost cowering, their faces an odd mixture of fear and rage. The guards behind them weren't so much protecting them as herding them out into the banquet hall. Wynter noticed, with a sudden dryness of mouth, that the soldiers' leather spear-covers were off, the metal speartips exposed.

Slowly, and without looking, she reached for Christopher's arm and pulled steadily downwards. "Sit, Christopher," she said very quietly, "sit down and do not make any sudden moves."

He met her eyes for a moment, his fury colliding with

her well-practised composure. She lifted her chin and held his gaze. *Trust me, Christopher, this is not the time for action.* Slowly, he sat and the two of them turned, powerless to do anything but watch as the events unfolded.

Next out the door was Wynter's father, and now it was Christopher's turn to lay a steadying hand on her arm. The young man said nothing and didn't look at her, but he squeezed down so hard that Wynter winced. He held on until she subsided into watchfulness again, not quite able to hide the distress in her face.

Lorcan was literally pushed out of the royal rooms, the huge guard behind him shoving him between the shoulder blades with the handle of his spear and then crowding him through the door with his formidable weight. As soon as Lorcan was across the threshold, though, he tried to turn back, pushing resolutely against the advancing guard. As the silent struggle between the two men continued, all around the hall Wynter felt and saw people begin to rise to their feet.

The guards around the walls cast sideways glances at each other. The air was suddenly sparking with tension. Wynter could feel it running along her shoulders and up the back of her neck. It crackled off Christopher like summer lightning – hot and dangerous, just over the horizon.

The furious grappling between Lorcan and his opponent stilled abruptly when someone within the royal room spoke. Lorcan strained to see over the guard's massive shoulder, and it was obvious he was listening. His whole posture screamed *tell me what to do*! The banquet hall seemed to hold its breath.

Suddenly Lorcan's shoulders sagged. He made one more frustrated shove at the huge guard, snarling up into his impassive face, but it was just anger, a release of impotent anger, and Lorcan turned immediately and stalked to his seat on the bottom tier.

There was a long moment of inactivity, during which Wynter saw Christopher surreptitiously clean his dagger and slip it back into his boot. Her father sat, staring rigidly at his clenched fists; he didn't lift his eyes to find his daughter.

A flurry of motion brought everyone's attention snapping back to the royal door. The remaining councilmen were entering the hall. Unlike the first six men, these eight were certainly not cowed. They came out as a group, their faces determined and, instead of taking their seats, they gathered in a knot at the lower steps, effectively closing off access to the bottom tier of the royal platform. All eight councilmen kept their eyes on the royal door as they stood shoulder to shoulder, a seamless blackrobed barricade. With their gaunt pale faces and their tight black caps, Wynter thought that they exactly resembled the vultures that Christopher considered them to be.

Razi came through the door. He had taken off his doctor's robes and wore the scarlet long-coat and black britches required of him for formal dining. The two guards behind him were much too close for comfort. They were crowding him forward, forcing him to take one stiff legged-step after another. His eyes roamed about without landing on anything in particular, refusing to look anyone in the eye, refusing to lift his gaze and take in the hall. He was in every sense trying just not to be there. Wynter had seen that expression on men before, usually as they approached the scaffold. She felt Christopher tense beside her.

"What's going on?" he murmured. "He looks like a cornered animal."

Yes. That too. That skittering movement of his eyes, the terrified blankness of expression. As though he were waiting for a chance to break cover and flee. She swallowed hard and kept her face and hands still.

Razi approached the immoveable barricade of councilmen. He pressed against them with his shoulder, not looking into their faces, trying desperately to make his way past and take his seat beside Lorcan, but the soldiers behind him continued their relentless forward pressure and the councilmen did not break ranks. Razi was pushed slowly up the line to the stairs that led to the top tier. He stumbled as his foot hit the first step and Wynter saw his eyes lift and meet those of the last councilman. Victuallor Heron.

The fear, the pain, the fury in Razi's eyes had Wynter rising from her seat in rage, and she felt Christopher surge upwards at the same moment. But their impetuosity was masked by the simultaneous appearance of the King, and at once the crowd leapt to its feet in the traditional salute. King Jonathon, magnificent as ever, swept his way past soldiers, councilmen and bastard son and took the steps to the top tier, two at a time. The relief was palpable around the hall as the people raised their drinks and shouted "HO!"

The King strode to the big throne that dominated the top tier and raised his hand in recognition of his people's love. *Sit, sit*, he gestured and so the crowd did. But they were obviously confused as to why he still stood, and why half his councilmen blocked access to the lower tier, while the other half-sat, still as stone in their appointed places. And why was the Lord Razi loitering about at the foot of the steps when he should have been seated and saluting the King like the rest of them?

Jonathon gestured to the soldiers behind Razi and they pushed forward resolutely. Wynter saw Razi lean back into them, his face a stony mask of resistance, but short of falling to the floor and allowing them to drag him, he had no choice but to yield to the pressure. Gradually he was forced up the steps and onto the royal tier.

Everyone, including Wynter and Christopher, had retaken their seats, and all eyes were now widening in horror at the sight of the King's bastard being herded towards the throne. Even the minstrels had ceased to play, and in the deathly quiet Wynter could hear Razi breathing raggedly through his nose. She heard the scuff of his boots on the platform as he dug his heels in. The guards continued to push, sliding him a little distance until he took another step.

They forced him over to the third throne. Alberon's seat. The seat of the rightful heir to Jonathon's kingdom. Wynter heard Razi release a choking sob as the soldiers put their hands on his shoulders. It was very loud and clear in the stillness, and Jonathon made an abrupt gesture to the minstrel's gallery. They cranked out some terrible off-key discordance, their fingers numbed with shock, no doubt, and Jonathon glared at them and yelled out something angry and inarticulate. A light, bouncing little round started up and Jonathon turned his glower at his son.

Razi was looking at him with such pleading, such hurt,

such terrified desperation, that Wynter thought her heart might actually break for him. But Jonathon was merciless, and when he gestured *down* with his hand, the soldiers pressed, two big hands on each of Razi's shoulders. And there he was, Razi the Bastard, sitting in Alberon's place, the sudden and irrevocable pretender to the throne.

The servers came out with the second remove, huge platters of salmon, baked with garlic and dill and pickled mustard seeds. The smell was wonderful, but there were no murmurs of appreciation from the crowd. They sat, tense and round-eyed as lemurs, as the King took his first choice of the proffered food.

The servers stood on the bottom tier, just behind Wynter's father, the platter held high as Jonathon leaned forward and took the pink flesh onto his plate. When the King had filled his plate, tradition dictated that the servers should move on to the next highest in rank. Since Alberon wasn't here and the Queen was dead, that meant they should move down to the bottom tier and offer Lorcan and Razi their choice. The councilmen should come next, then on down the lords' tables, with the commoners' table coming last. For Razi to be offered his food while sitting in Alberon's chair had a terrible significance that no one wished to acknowledge or compound.

The King gestured them to move on, but the two men stood there uncertainly as Razi's hands tightened into knots on the table in front of him. The King glared and gestured for them to serve Razi next. The two men just blinked, completely overwhelmed by this appalling gesture of disloyalty to the real heir to the throne. Abruptly Jonathon roared at them, half-rising from his seat and lifting his knife hand in a genuine threat of violence. The two men staggered back, almost lost their balance when they bumped into Lorcan, and shuffled sideways until the platter was held up before the miserable Razi. He closed his eyes and turned his head away.

The King muttered something to Razi, not looking at him, already beginning to eat his meal. Whatever Razi murmured back darkened the King's glowering face even more, and he leaned across the space between them and growled something into his son's ear. Razi whipped his head around, his expression a murderous equal to that of his father's, and bared his teeth in a short reply.

Father and son glared at each other for a moment, and then the King reached across and took a dripping handful of fish from the serving platter. He dropped it onto his son's plate and turned away, as if that ended the matter. With a sour jerk of his head to send the servers on their way, Jonathon rinsed his hands in the finger bowl and began once again to devour his food.

And that is how it went on, that terrible feast. At each remove, Jonathon would reach out a hand and slop more food down onto his son's overflowing plate, until the table in front of Razi was stained and splattered with numerous sauces and creams and oils. Razi ended up pressed back into his chair, his head averted in disgust. The King ate all put before him, sourly scanning the anxious crowd. If his eye fell on any person not eating or who appeared in any way miserable, he would call out to them to explain their ill humour. Soon everyone was chewing and swallowing and smiling with grim determination.

Only Lorcan, Wynter, Christopher and three of the

councilmen joined Razi in his refusal to eat, and somehow the King contrived not to notice them.

Finally, the fruit and cheese came out and Razi's noxious plate was taken away, the board in front of him wiped clean and a tall beaker of dessert wine set before both himself and the King. Wynter thought that maybe Razi had fallen into some kind of trance, as he seemed to notice nothing of the changes. He sat as still as a statue, his hands resting on the arms of Alberon's throne, his eyes focused on the newly cleaned table, his face blank.

Christopher and Wynter hadn't exchanged a single word since the second remove. Both of them had waved away any further offers of food, but had drained several beakers of strawberry cordial. Wynter had kept her focus on the royal platform, her eyes jumping anxiously between Razi and her father who had not moved since sitting down. Christopher had spent the whole feast scanning the crowd, judging reactions, noting movements, taking in as much conversation as he could hear.

It's almost over now, Wynter thought, *surely after all this Jonathon would never be so cruel as to inflict dancing on the assembly.*

But her heart fell when the King stood and clapped his hands for the tables to be pushed back and the musicians to strike up a Gar-a-ronde. There was a ripple of thoroughly falsified applause and the assembly took their places for the dance.

Christopher and Wynter got up from their seats and drifted towards the throne as the long tables were pushed back against the wall. They stayed together, hoping that at least one of them might slip through the less than subtle barricade of guards and councilmen surrounding their friend. Razi and the King had remained seated, the King lounging in his throne, drinking and scanning the crowd. Razi kept pretty much the same position he'd maintained all evening.

As Wynter and Christopher wandered about in front of the cordon of guards, Razi lifted his eyes for the briefest of moments and found them. Wynter's heart leapt as she realised that he'd just been biding his time, waiting for them to come into his range. She felt Christopher come to attention beside her as Razi's eyes jumped to him. Razi nodded and mouthed, "*Stay.*" Christopher turned without a change of expression and kept drifting, as if casually observing the crowd. But Wynter knew he would not leave their friend alone.

Then Razi turned his attention to her. They hadn't much time, but he allowed himself one small moment of emotion, nothing more than a softening of his eyes, a sorrowful drawing together of his brow. Then she saw him swallow hard and blink, his expression hardening. "Lorcan . . ." he mouthed and flicked his eyes towards the royal room. The door stood open and unguarded. Wynter glanced at it and back at Razi, but his eyes were down again, and the King was staring at her. She turned smoothly and wandered away through the crowd, taking a circuitous route to the royal rooms.

Lorcan was alone. He must have taken advantage of the shifting crowds at the end of the meal and used the chaos to slip away. Wynter found him, wedged into a corner out of sight, his back to the wall, slumped and hidden like an animal at bay. He lifted his eyes to her as she came into his field of vision and grimaced ruefully. He was desperately heaving for breath, his hand to his chest.

"Darling," he rasped, "I'm . . . in trouble."

She didn't exclaim or create any kind of fuss. She just went to him, put her hands on his shoulders and pushed him up until he was standing to his full height against the wall. "Can you make it to our rooms?" she asked, looking up into his sweating face.

"Lord Razi . . .?"

"Christopher is looking after Razi."

Even through his distress, Lorcan managed to raise a doubtful eyebrow at the idea. Wynter put her hand on his breast and felt his heart racing and skipping beneath the fabric of his longcoat. "Dad," she said, "Razi trusts him. And I trust Razi to know what's best. Now please, Dad, please let's get back to our rooms."

The music from the banquet hall had gained momentum, a reel now, spinning its way into a country jig. The dancers would be twirling about like tops. The heat would be unbearable, the tension deafening. Lorcan laid his arm across her shoulder and her knees buckled for a moment. Together they slipped out into the cool gloom of the back corridor and began slowly to make their way down the hall. The noise of the dance grew dim behind them.

"Darling . . . d-darling . . ." Lorcan suddenly squeezed her shoulder and bent at the waist. "I need to stop. Just for a moment."

Wynter pushed him back into an open doorway and propped him against a wall. They were in the antechamber of a small room, their only source of light the dim torchlight of the corridor outside.

"Are you all right, Dad?" His eyes were glittering in the gloom, his breath a laboured wheeze. He laid his head back against the wall and patted her arm, nodding.

All right then, just a moment to catch his breath and then they'd move on. She glanced around her warily. God, how vulnerable they were. She could still hear, faintly, the music of the dance; they'd hardly made any progress at all.

That's when the shouting started. Wynter turned her head to listen, and Lorcan grew tense and wary as the music stopped. The shouting was followed by screaming, like a brawl in a pot-house. There was the noise of footsteps running. And then, that most chilling of sounds, the "Gathering of The Guard" being played on the royal trumpets – the alarm that signalled an attack on the life of the King!

Assassin

Wynter and her father stood frozen in the dark as quiet footsteps sped up the corridor towards them. A young man raced past the door, just a blur of coat and pumping arms and legs, and then he was gone. Wynter started immediately for the hall, her intention to call for the guards, but she drew back as yet more footsteps approached.

Christopher Garron shot past, his long hair flying out behind him. He was there, then gone in an instant. Wynter leapt forward and out the door, not quite sure she'd actually seen him.

The fleeing man was almost at the end of the hall by the time Wynter skidded into the corridor. She saw him glance desperately over his shoulder, saw his panicked expression as Christopher gained on him. Saw Christopher take a sudden leaping bound into the air and kick his two feet forward to hit the man square between his shoulder blades, bringing the two of them down in a tangled, sliding heap.

Someone else ran past her, brushing her shoulder, but Wynter barely registered them as she took in the cold-blooded fury that was Christopher Garron.

He had got his feet under him even as he was sliding and, before the young man had registered the fact that they'd hit the floor, Christopher was on top of him.

It was his silence that most disconcerted her, that and the absolute precision with which he landed each blow. He hit the young man straight between the eyes with his first punch, knocking his head back into the floor, disabling him with that blow alone. But he didn't stop there. Christopher cocked his arm back, way back, and that was what Wynter would recall later: that pose and then the contact. Each separate punch divided into the moment when Christopher's arm was pulled back, his fist ready and then the instant when the punch landed on the young man's face. Blood sprayed out from the fellow's lips, his nose, his eye. Just blood, Christopher's fist and more blood. And Christopher completely silent, his face composed to hatred. His intention to beat every inch of life from this person who lay under him, limp and immobile since strike one, perhaps already dead.

The person who had rushed past her slid to a halt beside Christopher, and Wynter realised with a shock that it was Razi. She let out a little cry as she noticed his right sleeve, black and glistening with fresh blood, his hand red with it. As he fell to his knees beside the pumping fury of his friend, Razi's blood spattered onto the flagstones. One-armed, he grabbed Christopher around the chest and heaved backwards, pulling him off the target of his wrath.

"Enough! Enough! Christopher!" Razi shouted. "We need him alive! We need him *alive*, Chris! Stop!" He heaved back so violently that the two of them tumbled over, Christopher still as silent as the grave.

Then there were guards in the hall, pulling Razi and Christopher to their feet and snatching the beaten man up from the flags and snapping shackles on him. Razi growled at them and rebuffed their attempts to separate himself and Christopher, who stood looking at him with a dazed kind of confusion. And then, oh God! Christopher launched himself at the guards.

Screaming in Hadrish, his face contorted in red anger, he leapt into the air and loafed one of them right between his eyes, felling him like a pole-axed bull. "Where were you?" he screamed. "Where were you, you poxy whoreson cur!" And then, even as the first guard was hitting the floor, Christopher spun on his heel and with another brittle scream of rage, brought his knee slamming up into the groin of the big fellow next to him.

More guards closed in with a roar and Razi swept his arm up, yelling at them, "LEAVE! Leave, goddamn you all! Take your trash and leave!" And, amazingly, they did. Christopher and Wynter and Razi were left standing in the hall, panting and looking around them wonderingly, as if it had all been an illusion.

"Razi," said Wynter, reaching for her friend's arm, "you're bleeding."

But Razi wasn't listening. He was looking at Christopher, who was, in turn, gazing at the bright splashes and curlicues of blood that decorated the floor where he had beaten the young man.

"Christopher," Razi gently put his hand on the smaller man's shoulder.

Christopher turned to him immediately. He looked at Razi's arm, hanging limp by his side now, blood still dripping from his cuff. He scanned Razi's chest, his other arm. Finally he looked up into his friend's face, blinked, and took a deep breath as if surfacing from cold water.

"I'm all right, Christopher," said Razi, very softly.

"I saw you go down. That whoreson threw his knife . . . I saw you hit the floor. Good Frith, Razi! The spray of blood!"

Razi showed all his teeth in a wide grin. "You imagined that, friend. There was no spray of blood."

Christopher reached up suddenly and grabbed Razi by the back of the neck. He pulled the taller man's head down until Razi's forehead rested on his shoulder, then he wrapped his arm around Razi's back in a brief, fierce hug.

"Don't do that again, you fool." He banged Razi twice on the back. Wynter suspected it was intended as a gentle pat but fear and the aftershock of violence made into a solid thump. And then the two men parted.

"You'll need stitches," Wynter said. Razi nodded. Wynter put her arm around his waist and he leaned into her for a moment. "Let's get you and my father back to our rooms, Razi."

But there were more guards now, advancing down the corridor, and with them the King, his face a black mixture of anger and concern. Razi shot his two friends a look and began backing away from them, moving to intercept the King before he got a chance to sink his teeth into the ones who had refused to eat at his feast.

"Get Lorcan to your rooms, little sis," Razi whispered before limping away. "I'll see you when I can." And then he was gone, the guards, the councilmen and his father closing around him like a shroud and whisking him off up the corridor.

Lorcan was sitting in a chair in a dark corner of the ante-room when they went to fetch him. Wynter could see the knuckles on his hands gleaming white in the reflected light. She thought, with a flash of pride, *he's arranged himself to look stronger, in case they discovered him.*

He'd done a good job. Sitting straight, with his hands clutching the arms of his chair, his long red hair fell loose around his shoulders and his green eyes blazed from the gloom. He looked like a tiger in its lair or a dragon smouldering in its cave. Unassailable. Wynter came in with one hand up. Keeping her voice low, she used the affectionate tone that they reserved for when they were alone.

"It's all right, Dad. Christopher took the assailant down. The guards have dragged him to the keep."

"Alive?" Lorcan's voice was a hoarse gravel in the base of his throat. Wynter knelt by his chair and laid her hand on his, startled by how cold his flesh was.

"Alive," answered Christopher from the shadows. Lorcan's eyes leapt to him and Wynter felt the big man's body jerk in shock.

"Was it the King or the boy he was after?" Lorcan directed this question to Wynter, and she smiled knowingly at him. It would take much more than Razi's faith in Christopher to get Lorcan to trust a Hadrish stranger! She looked back at the young man hovering behind them and transferred the question to him with a raised eyebrow.

"He was aiming for Razi," Christopher replied. "He threw a knife across the room, nearly took Razi's arm off."

Now that the fight was over, Wynter could hear the aftershock trembling through Christopher's voice. In the gloom, she could just make out that he was cradling his mangled hands to his chest as though they hurt. *Small wonder they hurt*, she thought, *you beat that man to a pulp.*

"Christopher," she asked, "will you help me get my father to our room?"

Lorcan growled, but he was no fool either. He allowed the young man to come forward and, between the two of them, Wynter and Christopher got Lorcan back to his suite.

They helped him to his bedroom door, fully intending to put him to bed, but he shrugged free of them at the threshold and staggered inside, shutting the door behind him.

"Can I do anything more for you? Get water? Some food, maybe? Call a guard for your door?" Christopher asked, with one foot already out the door, his concern for Razi willing him away. Wynter shook her head, wanting him to go and protect her friend, wishing she could accompany him, but knowing she couldn't.

"Listen to me," she said, putting a hand on his arm. He went to draw away. "*Listen!*" He stilled, impatience humming off him like the resonance of a bell. "Do *not* sneak about. The lords will kill you if you're caught. And, Christopher, they *want* to kill you. You are Razi's ally, you don't fit in, you're . . . you're a danger. If you go sneaking about on your own they'll murder you under the pretence of thinking you an assassin, and that will be the end of you. Stay public, go about in the light . . . be *blatant*, Christopher. Do you understand?"

He maintained that hooded gaze for a moment, and then he said, "Will they let me see him?"

She shrugged. "You might as well try; it all depends on how strong Razi feels. If he's able to hold his ground against them, then yes, I think even the King would allow you in, if Razi demanded it. But be loud, Christopher, be obvious, make sure he knows you're there."

He nodded, turned to go, and Wynter caught his arm once more.

"Christopher."

He paused, patient now, waiting for more instructions.

"Thank you," she said, "I'm glad you're here."

She felt the muscles in his forearm jump and then he was gone, padding away from her with no noise at all.

He returned at the flux of the shadows, midnight by the northern clock. Wynter had been sitting in a chair by the window for hours, the scent from the orange garden balmy on her face, cool in her shift and her mother's dressing-robe. Her father had fallen into a sleep so sound that she'd been frightened by it. She checked on him regularly, laying her hand on his chest as he slept, feeling the rise and fall of each laboured breath, feeling the unnatural rhythm of his heart.

When Christopher returned, she was out of her chair and sliding the bolt open before she'd fully registered the sound of his knock. He was standing in the hall, a tray in his hand, no expression on his face. Wynter smelled toasted bread and butter, hot milk and cinnamon.

"My Lord Razi sends you his love and a tray of supper, my Lady." Wynter glanced past him and noted with shock that the corridor was now lined with guards, ten or twelve in all, positioned at attention from one end of the hall to the next. Dear God. There would be no privacy at all now.

"Come in, Freeman Garron, and lay the tray over there, please."

She went to shut the door, but Christopher shook his head slightly and made a show of crossing to the table and laying out the supper in full view of the nearest guard. Wynter drifted over to supervise. Christopher spoke without looking at her, his voice a whisper.

"There is a large, dark panel of wood in the far wall of the retiring room. If you turn the cherub sconce on its head, it will unlock a hidden door and Razi and I can access your room through a small corridor that leads from ours. Would this be all right?"

She nodded. He glanced up quickly as he organised pots of honey and butter and jam. "Razi has very little time and he wants to spend it with you . . . but we have to undo the work that that bloody quacksalver has done on his arm. He hopes you won't find it distressing if we do it here?"

She glared at him impatiently and Christopher's dimples flashed in amusement, his eyes sparkling. "Razi seems to think you a delicate wee flower. I shall detail your scorn for him."

Then he stepped back, bowed and left without another word. She shut the door and drew the bolt loudly, the guard across the hall staring all the while.

She hurried across to unlock the hidden panel. Moments later there was a knock, and the panel was pushed open. Razi came through first, stooped slightly and grey, his soft white shirt hanging loose at the right arm, a heavy wool cloak over his shoulders. He pulled her to him in a tight hug and she thought, as ever, how clean he smelt, how unlike most other people he was. "Sis," he murmured, "I'm sorry."

Christopher followed, a copper bowl of steaming water held out carefully ahead of him, his hands protected by thick wads of cloth. "Out of my way, out of my way! 'Tis hot!"

Razi broke away from her and limped over to put a rush mat on the table by the supper things. Christopher laid the bowl on top of it and disappeared back down the dark passageway. Wynter leaned in at the secret door and saw him turn right a few paces up, where light spilled out in a dim rectangle from Razi's rooms. From what she could tell in the gloom, the passage continued on past that patch of light, winding away in dark mystery behind the walls to God knows where.

"I can't believe the King doesn't know about this!" she marvelled.

"He does know," said Razi from behind her. He had dragged the armchair closer to the table and as she turned, he sat down gingerly and began to pull his uninjured arm from his shirt sleeve. "He just doesn't think anyone else does. Aaah!"

Wynter went to help him and together they got the shirt over his head. He was left in just his britches, the bandaging across his shoulder and chest vivid against his dark skin.

Wynter blushed to see the curling hair on his chest and stomach, and the dark circles of his nipples. They had swum naked together all their lives, and until Razi was eleven, had often slept in the same bed – Wynter and Albi against the wall, Razi curled around them like a guard dog. But they weren't children anymore and it felt strange suddenly to be in his presence like this. Razi seemed perfectly at ease, though, and she bit down on her embarrassment. It fled of its own accord anyway when he began to unwind the bindings, and the horrible mouth of his wound was revealed, its row of stitches like a collection of ragged insect legs poking up from the clotted gore.

"Oh Razi," she gasped, helping him with the last of the bandages. "Why? Why did the King do it? Could he not tell that this would happen . . .?"

Razi looked at her, bitterness etched in every line of his face. "He waited, Wyn, strung me along with this damned lie about Albi being on the coast . . . waited until Lorcan and I were in the reception rooms, ready to step out the damned door. Then he told us what . . . what he wanted me to do. Poor Lorcan, his face . . . But what could we do? We were surrounded by guards. Half the councilmen sided with the King, the others cowed into submission. If only . . . God, if only we had had time to think, to prepare, but the wily bastard sprung his trap and there we were . . . caught."

Christopher was beside them then, in that sudden way of his, putting a bottle of something down beside the copper bowl, laying cloths on the floor and across Razi's lap and over the chair. He looked patiently up at Wynter, and she realised he wanted her to move. She shuffled over to Razi's left arm and Christopher knelt on the floor in front of him, examining the long crescent of the wound that curved like a bloody moon between Razi's right breast and the square definition of his shoulder.

"Good job you're lefthanded, Raz. This is bloody deep."

Razi was sweating now, in anticipation of what was to come. He growled at Christopher, dread roughening his voice. "Just get that old fool's filthy stitching out of me, before it poisons my blood."

Christopher rubbed his hands with liquid from the bottle and the smell of alcohol and lemons filled the room. He lifted a little pair of copper scissors from the boiling water and snipped all along the row of stitches, cutting the threads just at the knot. His hands looked awkward, but moved deftly, sure in their work. He paid no heed to Razi's quickened breath or his high yelp of pain as he set a tweezers to the first ragged stitch and tugged it sharply from the flesh.

"Sit down, Wynter," hissed Razi, glaring up at her from under his curls. He had a death grip on the edge of the table, and his face had gone from grey to scarlet in the flaring candlelight.

Wynter sank onto the fire-stool. "Who was he?" she asked.

"No one knows." Razi grimaced and then leapt as Christopher removed the second stitch. "*Damn it!*" And again as Christopher rapidly tugged the third stitch and then the fourth in quick succession. "*Shit! Christopher! Shit!*"

Christopher sat back on his heels and looked up at his friend without a trace of emotion. "There are four more to go," he said, "Do you want a moment?"

Razi locked his lips together and panted in and out through his nose. He looked menacingly at Christopher. "Just. Bloody. Do it!"

"You need to shut up," said his friend, raising the tweezers again and focusing on the remaining stitches. "The guards will hear you."

Wynter tried to divert him. "But how did the attacker get in? You can't just waltz into one of those feasts!"

Razi shook his head and then inhaled another high squeal of pain as Christopher quickly tugged the remaining four stitches from his shoulder. Wynter reached forward and gripped Razi's corded forearm, her other hand rubbing his neck and shoulder with round soothing motions. "It's finished now. He's done," she said, and Razi laughed through the tears that were suddenly pouring down his face.

Christopher dropped the tweezers and the scissors onto the cloth by the copper bowl. Razi's blood spread out in delicately veined blossoms on the soft weave cotton. "I still have to stitch him back up," he said dryly and Wynter's stomach clenched at the thought of it.

"Let it bleed a while . . ." muttered Razi, his eyes shut.

Christopher nodded and pushed gently until Razi was leaning back in his chair. "Hold this," he said to Wynter, and she put her hand against the thick wad of cotton that he had placed under the wound. It caught the fresh blood before it trickled down Razi's belly and stained his britches. "Don't block the wound," Christopher instructed as he set about cleaning up. "Let it clean itself out.

"All right." She couldn't take her eyes from Razi's face, newly drained of colour and textured like dough. He had begun to shiver, but before Wynter could comment on it, Christopher pulled the cloak up from the back of the chair and draped it around his friend's shoulders.

Razi took a moment to gather himself, grunting inadvertently with each exhale, his mouth turned down, and his face old with pain. Then he opened his eyes to Wynter again.

"So," she said, her voice as steady as possible, her free hand still rubbing circles in the knotted wood of his shoulder and neck. "A stranger magically appears in the sanctity of the King's banquet hall without *anyone* noticing him, and manages to take a shot at the newly announced pretender to the throne?"

Razi winced at the title, but nodded.

"That's impossible, brother."

Razi nodded again.

"I smell conspiracy," said Christopher, shuffling things about on the table. "And the sooner we get that fellow up on his feet and singing a story, the sooner we'll get some answers."

Razi's eyes actually crinkled up into a smile at that, and he slid a mocking look at Christopher. "If someone hadn't beaten him out of all his senses, we might already *have* those answers."

Christopher replied by pulling a wickedly curved needle from the bowl of water, and threading it with boiled silk.

Razi looked away and moaned.

Wynter tapped his arm. "Where *is* Alberon, Razi? Is he dead?" There. She'd said it, and in saying it her heart overflowed with dread and grief. "He *must* be dead, Razi. Why else would Jonathon do this? And why won't he say what's happened him? Jonathon adores Albi, he *adores* him."

Razi looked at her, his face tilted so as not to see the needle, and took her hand in his. His eyes were black in this light, pits of liquid darkness. "Father is talking about *mortuus in vita*. He's already put things into motion."

Wynter's eyes widened in shock. Could this not end? Right now, could this not just end, with her waking up to a warm summer's day, down by the trout-brook, a basket full of fish, her line in the stream and Razi and Albi strolling towards her down the meadow? Could that not just happen?

She repeated the terrible phrase, her voice cracking. "*mortuus in vita*" – the King was declaring Alberon "dead in life"? It would be as though he had never existed. Even if her dear friend *was* alive, he may as well have been a ghost, because, once *mortuus* had been declared, Alberon was no longer a prince; he was no longer even a person. He simply was no longer *there*.

"Razi. He can't . . . what reason could . . .? He can't!"

"He can, and he intends to," said Christopher abruptly, holding up the needle. "And Razi intends to stop him. Now, let go of her hand, Razi, or you'll break it when I start to sew."

By the time Christopher was finished, Razi was trembling and sweating, and Wynter was crying silently as she held his shoulders down from behind. "He's just done now. He's just finished . . ." She kept whispering that in his ear, his damp curls brushing her cheek as she leant in.

Christopher looked into his friend's eyes, the bottle poised over the horribly aggravated wound. He was waiting for Razi to compose himself. Finally Razi glanced at him, gripped the arm of the chair even tighter, braced his legs and nodded curtly. Wynter pressed down hard on Razi's shoulders and Christopher poured the remaining liquid over the wound, disinfecting it and sluicing the clots away in an fragrant, hissing wash.

Razi muffled his scream in Wynter's arm, drumming his heels on the floor and grinding his fingernails into the wood. Christopher calmly pressed a fresh wad of gauze onto the wound and began to wrap his friend's shoulder in fresh bandages.

Once everything was done, Wynter wrapped the cloak around Razi and knelt behind his chair, hugging him, her head buried in his neck, his chin on her arm. He was drenched in sweat and shaking. Neither of them spoke.

Christopher got to his feet, all his tools and the numerous bloody cloths piled neatly in his arms. "I'll be back in a moment," he said softly and padded back through the secret door.

After a while Razi stirred, pushed back a little and patted Wynter on her shoulder. "I must go, Wyn. We have so much to do . . ."

"Where must you go? Razi . . .?"

But he was rising to his feet, pushing himself up with shaking arms. "I need to interrogate that fellow, the one who stabbed me . . . need to hear for myself what he has to say."

Wynter understood this. Understood the power that firsthand knowledge gave, and applauded Razi for his wisdom. But, dear God, he was swaying on his legs, blinking at her from swollen, bloodshot eyes, his naked torso slick with cold sweat. She put her hand on his chest and appealed to the physician in him.

"Listen, Razi, you need to dry off, let your body calm itself, put some warm clothes on. If you go down to the keep in that state you'll have pneumonia by dawn. And then where will Alberon be?"

He dithered for a moment and then sat back down, nodding. She shoved a beaker of still warm milk at him, and the pile of toasted bread. "I'll go get Christopher to bring you some dry clothes," she said and slipped through to the dusty blackness of the hidden passage.

"Christopher?" She crept cautiously into the dim interior of their suite of rooms. It had that scent of male about it, a scruffy, piled-up kind of feeling. Books and heaps of things were scattered about. She smiled, this was Razi. This was how she remembered his rooms all those years ago. She passed his door, it could only be his door, the room within was so cluttered.

"Christopher?" she whispered again, afraid to call too loudly in case the guards in the hall heard her. She moved on to the next door, this must be Christopher's room, silent and, except for a dressing trunk, bare of possessions, nothing out of place.

She heard a quiet scrape in the receiving room and went to the door, pausing to squint about in the gloom. Despite the heat, there was a fire in the grate. They had obviously lit it to boil the equipment and, in fact, there was a small cauldron suspended over it at that moment, the bowls, scissors, and other implements of Razi's trade bubbling away in its depths. The pile of bloody cloths was set neatly to one side and Razi's shirt lay crumpled on the floor beside them.

Christopher was standing by the window, blue lit by the moon, his back to her. He didn't turn around, and when he answered her, his voice was thick. He had to clear his throat to get any words out. "Does he need me?"

"No. I've persuaded him to rest a while. Told him I would get him some fresh clothes; his own are soaked through."

He nodded. "I'll bring them in a moment."

She turned to go, and then stopped. He seemed so lonely there. "Christopher . . ." she began, but couldn't think of anything else to say. He didn't turn, just kept standing, looking out the window and she didn't know how to comfort him so she left, returning to Razi whom she found asleep at the table, an uneaten slice of toast in his hand.

Torture

Wynter was standing in the kitchen of her old cottage. The sun slanted through the partially closed shutters and illuminated a vase of white poppies on the scrubbed table. She was so afraid. Her heart was hammering in her chest and there were black edges to her vision.

Outside they were murdering her cats. She could hear them yowling and calling out to each other in their pain and fear. She didn't want to see, but she couldn't help herself and she flung out a hand and knocked the shutter back.

They had slung washing lines across the yard, passing from the gables of the workshop across to the roof of the stable. The cats hung by their necks, silhouetted black against the white hot sky, the washing lines bobbing and swaying under their weight. There were dozens of them, dying slowly, their legs and tails thrashing and scrabbling at the air, their mouths open, pink tongues and needle teeth flashing in their swollen faces.

Their awful cat-wails, their high, baby-strangled yowls,

filled the sun-laden air, and Wynter felt she was going to be sick. But she was too frightened to run outside to help them. She knew that all she had to do was cut the lines and they might survive, but she was too frightened, and she just stood there as the terrible, unearthly noise clawed at her stomach and her heart.

"You can never be friend to a king, sis."

She leapt at the voice and turned to find Alberon sitting at the table, his crossed arms resting on the wood.

He had grown into a beautiful young man, the very image of his father, as like the King as Razi was different. The sun made fire of his red-blond curls and copper wires of his eyelashes. His big-featured face, his broad mouth, his sleepy blue eyes were all as she recalled them. He was looking at her with a sad kind of affection, and for some reason the sight of him made her want to weep; there was no joy in it at all, just a bitter, bitter sorrow.

He turned away from her and looked out the window, his face creasing in distaste at the sight of the cats. He got to his feet, stooping slightly to keep sight of the yard. He already had Razi's height, but there was a broad-shouldered, bullish physicality to him that was all Jonathon, more power than grace.

"The things we do," he said in sad wonder. "The things we find we must do." He gestured to the yard, and looked at Wynter with his vivid eyes. "Here comes the last of them now."

The horrible screeching started up again. They were bringing more cats down from the castle, great wicker baskets full of them, all tumbled together, clawing and screaming and terrified.

Wynter ran to the corner, her hand over her mouth, because she knew she was going to be sick.

She woke in the chair, alone. But the screaming continued. Razi and Christopher had left as soon as Razi was dressed, and she had sat herself down, vowing to listen for their return. She must have dozed off – the candles were burnt out. Two hours maybe? And now the air was full of screaming. Hollow and thready, but real nonetheless. She leapt to the window, and even before she looked down into the orange garden she knew what she would see.

Heather Quinn was racing through the trees, her mouth wide, her loose hair flying. The moonlight shone through her and almost made her solid as she flitted through the tree trunks and passed through the stone benches. She ran on transparent feet, her hands raised to the windows that overlooked the courtyard, begging for someone to listen.

Wynter had never seen Heather Quinn, but everyone knew what to listen for in the night, should Heather come calling. She had been a King's Mistress, Jonathon's grandfather's mistress to be exact, and had flung herself to her death from the Sandhurst tower. She was the castle harbinger, a foreteller of death, and people took it very seriously when she made her crazy, screaming circuit of the complex in the dead of night.

Down by the stables the hunting dogs began to howl in their kennels, their rising, ethereal wail a musical overtone to Heather's screams.

Wynter leant far out of her window, expecting shutters to open and lights to blaze, expecting people to begin shouting and calling and checking each others' rooms. But nothing happened around the courtyard except some discreet movements at windows, and some quietly closed shutters.

Heather's desperation grew as no one paid her any heed, and she ran a frenzied circle around the garden, her face turned up to the blank windows, pleading for attention. She spotted Wynter and her mouth stretched wider, a horrible gaping chasm in her distorted face. She turned at an unnaturally sharp angle and raced through four orange trees in her desperation to get to Wynter. Her eyes widened to saucer-sized voids and her hands seemed to stretch up, the fingers growing as she sped like lightning across the grass.

"Don't let her talk to you, child! They'll hang you from a tree."

Wynter leapt back from the window, partly from fear of Heather Quinn, but mostly at the shock of a cat-voice so close to her ear. Heather Quinn broke away as soon as Wynter was out of sight, cutting sharply left and flying past under the window. She shot out of the garden and passed under the fountain arch, her screams fading into the distance, headed for the river.

A small, marmalade cat nestled on the windowsill, hidden in the shadows behind the shutter. It regarded Wynter with phosphorescent eyes and she backed away from it, unsure of its intent. It blinked at her. It seemed to be waiting. Wynter looked about her, took a breath and curtsied as in the old days.

"All respects to you, mouse-bane," she said very softly, "well met, this night."

The cat sighed, uncrossed its paws and rose to its feet. It

dropped from the windowsill like an unfurling silk scarf, and landed with a barely audible *patta-pat* on the wooden table beneath. "Close the shutters, fool. You will be watched."

It had been so long since Wynter had heard cat-voice. That curious, whining growl, all long drawn-out and with too many *rrrrrrs*. Wynter couldn't help but smile at its familiar, impatient tone.

The cat watched her with all the inherent scorn of its species, and switched the tip of its tail, *pit-pat, pit-pat*, as Wynter quietly snapped the shutters closed.

As Wynter found and lit another candle the cat tutted, sighed and tapped its claws on the table, impatient to be given her full attention.

"So you're ready then, are you?" it said. "Quite sure, miss? Want to go bathe perhaps? Or take a stroll?"

"I'm sorry, good-hunter. I cannot see so well in the dark as you."

The cat *pffted* and turned its head as if to say, *oh please, don't bother. Flattery will get you nowhere with me.*

Wynter spread another curtsey and, knowing every cat's love for titles, introduced herself formally, "Protector Lady Wynter Moorehawke at your service, good-hunter."

The cat rose to its feet, suddenly furious, and Wynter was taken aback at its hissing anger.

"I *know* who you are, girl-once-cat-servant, why else would I be *here*? Do you think, after all that's befallen, we'd deign to speak with any but you?" It flowed around itself in a prowling figure of eight, grizzling under its breath until it managed to regain some self-control. Then it sat back down and directed its green-eyed glare at Wynter once more.

"GreyMother sent me to warn you."

"GreyMother? GreyMother lives?" Wynter laughed out loud in joy, but the cat just stared at her disdainfully until Wynter took her seat and composed herself.

"GreyMother lives, though old, very old now. And Coriolanus too, though much weakened and always poorly from the poison."

"I'm so sorry," whispered Wynter, tears once again springing to her eyes at the thought of her precious friends.

The cat looked at her as if she'd let loose a fart, its nose wrinkling in disgust. "What care I for your sorrow, human? I am here for revenge on he-who-betrayed-our-trust. That is all, and to use you as an instrument of his downfall. Don't speak to me of your sorrows. I despise them. We all despise them, as the nothings they are."

Wynter felt the tears roll down her face at the cat's awful hatred. "But I did nothing . . ." she whispered.

The cat stood up and prowled again, releasing a low irritated yowl. "Arrwwww. Hush up, hush up, creature. I do not *care*. Listen to my message and act upon it! That is all you need to do."

"I will not bring about the downfall of the King!" Wynter said, her voice suddenly steely, "I will not aid you in your destruction of the crown."

The cat turned sly eyes to her and smiled its needle-toothed smile. "The ghosts are surging," it said. "They are this very minute about to rise." It slunk across the table and brought its smiling face up close to Wynter's, "They will thwart your friend, he who is son-but-not-heir to the King."

"Razi?" exclaimed Wynter, half-rising from her chair.

"Yes, Razi."

"Bring me to him!" said Wynter and the cat's smile widened.

At the cat's direction Wynter slipped through the hidden panel in the retiring room. They passed the door to Razi's room and made their way into the pitch-black labyrinth beyond. The passages behind the wall were dusty and very dark. The cat had not allowed her to bring a candle, saying that the light might give her away, so Wynter had to depend on its voice to guide her through the impenetrable blackness. It perched on her shoulder, breathing instructions into her ear, its breath meaty and hot on her cheek.

She ran her hand along the wall for assurance, but sometimes the wall would just disappear and she would be assailed by a blast of icy air as she crossed the junction of a passageway. At those moments she would be gripped by the terrible fear that she was teetering on the edge of a precipice. She imagined a void yawning beside her, her feet a toe's breadth from its maw, and she was convinced that she would simply topple over sideways and drop forever into the eternal black. At these times, she would be gnawed with doubt as to how far she could trust this cat, who was obviously filled with hatred and had not even offered her its name, but within a few steps the wall would be there again, running along beneath her fingertips, a tangible surface to anchor her in the dark.

They seemed to go on forever, past endless corridors of cobwebbed wood panelling. Occasionally they would hear voices, usually muffled, sometimes loud, sometimes there would be music. Now and again a thin line of light would show through a crack in the wood, and Wynter was glad that the cat had forbidden her a candle.

They went down steps. They took numerous turns. The air grew colder and colder and Wynter knew they must be in the cellars. Or in the dungeons underneath the keep.

"Here," hissed the cat, "turn left."

Wynter found herself in a very short, corbel-roofed passageway. There was dim torchlight coming through from the main corridor, which was only nine or ten paces ahead.

They were deep, deep underground, in the most secret of the palace dungeons. Wynter hesitated, terrified, her breath coming in misty puffs in the frigid air.

"Turn right at the top there, and go down the steps," ordered the cat. "Tell he-who-is-son-but-not-heir that the ghosts will thwart him. Tell him to hurry in his inquisition."

There were distant screams echoing from somewhere up ahead. Terrible screams, nothing like Heather Quinn's, nothing like the nightmare cats'. Screams of unendurable agony.

Wynter panicked suddenly. What was she was doing here? What might she have to witness? She tried to retreat into the secret passage, meaning to rush back to her rooms and forget all about this fool's errand. But the weight of the cat slipped suddenly from her shoulders and before she could turn, it had gone, flickering back into the dark like a snuffed candle. She was left with no way back, no guide through the pitch-black maze of passages. Her only choice now was to go forward and face what lay ahead.

The screams grew as she slowly moved along the corridor. High, bubbling, unending, they made her feel sick;

they made her legs turn to water. She was suddenly filled with an urgent need for the privy.

She rounded the corner and found herself at the top of a short flight of stairs. She pressed against the wall, hugging the stone. The screams were so clear here, so full of human suffering. She was panting in fear and horror. She knew she was whimpering, but couldn't seem to stop.

The stairs led down into a room. The bottom steps were flooded with sulphurous light, shadows moved about, flickering up the walls of the stairwell, making nauseating patterns on the stone. The prisoner, the poor, screaming, tortured *victim* that was the source of the sounds, was very close to the foot of those steps.

If she descended three, maybe five steps, she would see him. She would see what was being done to him, and who was doing it.

There was a smell of fire, of smoke, of burning flesh and hair.

She could make out the scattered, burbling words that punctuated the inarticulate shrieking. The pleading, the promises, the prayers.

How could anyone listen to that and still continue to inflict such pain? How could anyone, for any reason . . .?

"What in God's name are you doing here?"

A cracked, appalled whisper from across the corridor. She turned her head to meet Christopher's wide, haunted eyes. He leant in the shadows of the wall opposite her, looking as though he could barely stand. His face was drawn and horrified and he smelled of vomit. "You shouldn't be *here*!" he exclaimed, his voice high with anguish. "*My God!* You shouldn't be *here*!"

The screams fell away to moans and sobs for a moment, and the two of them turned towards the light. There was a short murmured conversation. A thin ribbon of garbled pleading. Sharp, impatient words. Then the pleading again, rising to begging shrieks, *mercy, mercy, oh God, mercy*. And then that great agonised howling again, those clogged, bubbling screams that stole the power from Wynter's legs and brought her to her knees.

A shadow cut the light suddenly, soft edged and swirling as if walking through smoke, and then a tall silhouette came rapidly up the steps towards them. It was Razi. Wynter barely recognised him. The corners of his mouth were pulled down so far as to be hideous. His eyes were like live coals at the bottoms of tar-pits. He was smudged all over in soot and blood, and was shining with sweat. He looked like a monster cast in bronze, a horrific, horrified gargoyle forced to look on hell.

The screams continued to rise behind him as he topped the stairs. He flung himself on Christopher, who sobbed as Razi grabbed him and dragged him away from the wall. "All right," Razi said, hoarsely, "All right, you win! Give it to me. *Give it to me.*"

Christopher was snarling through his tears, and Wynter didn't think he heard what Razi was saying. He kept looking back down the steps. The victim was in a frenzy of pain, a series of high rhythmic shrieks tearing the air. "I should have killed him!" Christopher moaned, "I should have killed him! He'll never talk! You should have let me . . ."

Razi shook Christopher hard. There was a patch of blood on his shoulder where it had soaked through the bandages and his shirt. "I'm SORRY!" he screamed, pulling Christopher up close to yell in his face, "I'm SORRY! You were RIGHT! Give me the bloody KNIFE!"

Christopher registered Razi's words suddenly and started to scrabble at his boot to get his dagger.

Wynter was kneeling on the floor at the feet of the two men, completely disregarded. As she peered down into the sulphurous light she noticed a change in the air, a *drawing out* of the light, a low mutinous buzz that was rising up behind the sounds of torture.

"Razi . . ." she said, leaning forward over the top steps, staring into the light. It was drawing her like a whirlpool, it was sucking her down. "Razi . . . the ghosts . . ." she put her hand on the step below her, as though she intended to crawl down the stairs.

Razi turned beside her, Christopher's dagger in his hand. He stuttered forward a few steps and then stopped. Christopher sank to his knees on the floor across from her. He fell forward onto his hands, his face tilted to the light, his eyes blank.

The screaming had ceased. The light had turned from orange to white. The air was humming all around them, like bees in a hive.

"The ghosts, Razi . . ." she said, "the ghosts are surging."

The light seemed to burst.

Wynter felt her hands slide along the stone floor as she was pushed back up the corridor. She came to a stop against the stone arch with a gentle *bump*, rolling over, limp as a rag doll but still awake.

Light washed over her like watered milk.

Something big slid past her on the flagstones, brushing

her legs. Later she would realise it had been Razi, toppled onto his back and shoved up the corridor like a sack of grain.

Great blossoms of white light flared and scattered on the ceiling and walls. All the sound had been crowded from the air, pushed aside, no room left for sound at all. Wynter knew that if she opened her mouth to scream, there would be nothing to hear.

The light went on and on, like a comet passing overhead, moving, flowing and blossoming. Wynter stared up at it, unable to lift a hand or her head, dumb and motionless as a stone.

And then it was over. Stone was stone, flesh was flesh, and she was seeing and hearing and breathing again as if nothing had happened.

She rolled slowly onto her side, her body tingling. Her hair was crackling like summer fire. Her clothes were sparking, sending out little fireflies of light at every crease and fold. Her teeth hurt. Her lips were buzzing.

Razi lay in the middle of the corridor, staring at the ceiling. As she watched, he slowly bent his right leg. Raised his left hand and dropped it again. Blinked.

Across the hall she heard Christopher release a shaky breath.

They got slowly to their feet, and went to look down the stairs. For a moment the three of them stood in a row, silent. Then Razi led the way down into the chamber.

The fires were out, their coals and soot scattered about the floor in a thick gritty carpet. Ash scraped beneath their feet as they walked, stone cold where only moments before it had been searing hot.

The prisoner and the inquisitors were indistinguishable, apart from their clothes and their positions in the room. Bloody, pulpy messes, barely recognisable as human; they looked as though they had been skinned and then carefully dressed again.

Wynter could look only very briefly at what was left of the prisoner before she had to turn away. The horrible chair, the straps, the twisted legs and broken arms, all these things she saw only fleetingly, but they never left her. The chair was ringed about with tables that were laden with terrible instruments, coated now with grit and ash. Great angry iron spikes, hammers, clamps, brands, screws, pliers, and some whose purpose she didn't dare guess at.

Christopher would not come into the room. He followed them down the steps and she heard him pick up his knife from the floor, where it had fallen from Razi's hand, but he loitered at the entrance and came no further. He stood staring at the bloody remains of an inquisitor. His corpse had been shoved up against the wall by the door, a scarlet trail leading from it to the torture chair. Christopher's face was unreadable, but Wynter didn't think he cared too much about this man's fate.

Razi prowled the room, his footsteps scraping and echoing. The torch that he'd brought from the hall flared as he held it high and moved from body to body. He was checking for signs of life in the three inquisitors and the prisoner. When he had pressed his sooty fingers to the last bloody neck and found no pulse, he straightened and stalked back up the stairs.

Christopher and Wynter found themselves in utter

darkness. Rousing themselves, they sealed the room, locking the door on the awful blackness within, and, without discussion, followed Razi's footsteps, which led them along another hidden passage to the kitchen.

Fishing for Flies

False dawn was glimmering over the trees when the three of them came into the kitchen. They still had at least another quarter of the shadows before anyone but the fire-keeper would be wandering about. The old woman was actually just banking up the grate when they came slowly down the back stairs, and Razi snapped at her to leave them, his voice uncharacteristically harsh. She startled, bowed and scuttled off, shutting the door behind her.

Except for the little spit-boy, asleep in his crate of straw by the hearth, they were alone in the dancing light of the newly-stoked fire.

Razi got them beakers of water, horse-bread and butter, smoked fish, and they sat at the small table, not touching their food. Christopher was staring at Razi, his face hard, and Razi was pretending not to notice. Wynter was trying to keep her mind from dwelling on that chair, those instruments, and the memory of Razi stalking out of the smoke and firelight, bubbling screams rising up behind him.

"I'm SORRY!" shrieked Razi suddenly, rounding on Christopher and making Wynter jump. But he didn't sound sorry. He sounded angry, he sounded furious, and his face was scarlet with rage. Christopher just looked at him, a stone wall, and Razi pounded the table with his fist. "I'm SORRY, Christopher! I'm SORRY, goddamn you, I'm bloody *sorry*!" And he *was* sorry then, his anger melting like ice on a skillet, leaving only regret. He put his face in his hands, and his voice was cracking when he said, "I can't believe I let it go on so long."

Christopher's face softened for a moment and he moved his hand as though to reach out to his friend.

"Did you get anything from him?" Wynter asked. Christopher grunted in disgust and pushed back from the table with a screech of wood on stone. He went over to the fireplace and sat on the nook-bench beside the sleeping child. He turned his back on Razi and Wynter, his elbows on his knees, the fire outlining his taut profile in flickering light.

"Did you, Razi?" she asked again, her voice hard, purposely disregarding Christopher's obvious abhorrence.

"Not much," said Razi, tearing his eyes from the fireplace. "Just that Oliver sent him and . . ." he faltered, not looking her in the face.

"And? What?"

He looked at her then, the fire burning in his eyes, and she knew he was going to lie even before he wet his lips and opened his mouth. "That's all," he said, "Oliver sent him. That's all we got."

Wynter gazed at him. Oliver, her father's old friend, the King's beloved cousin. The man who had fought valiantly by the King's side all through the insurrection, disgraced now, and fled the palace for reasons known only to the

King. He had sent this man? But why? Why would he want Razi dead? It made no sense.

Razi slid a sideways look at her and she knew he was not telling her everything. Chuffing impatiently and pushing back from the table, Wynter glared at her friend. "What are you hiding, Razi Kingsson?" she said, "I'm not ten years old and in need of protecting now. Tell me!"

Christopher snorted in admiration and Razi ran his fingers through his hair, cornered. "There's . . . he kept babbling about some kind of machine . . . what he called, 'The Bloody Machine'. That, and Oliver . . . that's all . . ."

There was more. She could tell. Something Razi couldn't bring himself to say, and her intuition made her ask, "Did he mention Alberon?"

Razi glanced at Christopher, who turned to look briefly at them before facing back to the fire. Razi slid a glance at Wynter and shook his head, his gaze dropping to the table. She didn't believe him. He might as well have had *LIAR* written in burning letters on his forehead. But that was all right, she'd get it out of him later. Perhaps it was something he didn't want to say in front of Christopher.

"Why did the ghosts interfere, Razi?" Christopher said, speaking quietly. "What difference does any of this make to ghosts? They don't care about anything. And why should the cats get involved?"

Wynter answered thoughtfully, working it out as she spoke. "I think the cats thought that the prisoner knew something . . . that he had information that would harm the King. And they wanted him to survive long enough to give you that information. Jonathon betrayed them, Razi, he *poisoned* them. They want their revenge. The ghosts must want to protect the King. They must . . ." Wynter hesitated, confused at the very thought of it. "The ghosts must have taken sides!"

Razi gave her a doubt-filled look. Even Christopher glanced at her sceptically. "Ghosts don't take sides," he said.

"A machine," Razi mused, "The Bloody Machine . . . that's what he called it. The Bloody Machine."

"For Godssake!" growled Christopher suddenly. "He was talking about the chair! That's all! That damned . . . *contraption* you had him in! That's all!"

Razi flung his hand up and twisted his head away. "All right! all right!" he cried. "Just stop talking about it!"

They subsided into a bruised silence, over which the fire roared and crackled, the smell of smoke reminding them of the smoke-filled room with its odour of burning flesh and hair. Razi's hands tightened to knots on the table, his eyes tormented.

Christopher suddenly gasped in surprise, and Wynter and Razi turned to see the cause. The spit-boy had lifted his hand and was sleepily running his fingers over Christopher's loosely hanging fist. They watched as the little fellow, still comfortably curled in his sleep-shape, ran his fingers along Christopher's mangled knuckles.

"How do, mouse," whispered Christopher. "Thought you were asleep?"

"My Lord Razi woke me," murmured the child, his cheek resting on his fist, his eyes silver slits under his eyelashes. He was barely awake. "What befell your fingers, mister?"

Christopher put the child's exploring hand back under the blanket and pushed the greasy hair back off his little face. He ran his thumb across the sooty forehead. "Go to sleep," he said quietly, "your day will start soon enough."

The child's eyes began to drift shut as Christopher continued to run his thumb across his brow.

"Tell me," the boy insisted sleepily, his eyes still closed. Christopher chuffed a little laugh. Wynter was glad to see that even Razi, so downcast moments before, brightened noticeably, amusement gradually replacing the horror in his eyes.

"Tell me," implored the child, with all the drowsy persistence of the very young.

"They were eaten by a bear," whispered Christopher, with such easy conviction that for a moment Wynter believed him, though the story was patently ridiculous.

The child's eyes showed silver under his lashes again and he peered at Christopher across a huge chasm of sleep, not sure if he believed him. Christopher breathed another soft laugh. "I was fishing for flies . . ." he said confidentially.

"For flies?"

"Aye." Christopher's thumb kept up its easy stroking of the little forehead. "Ain't you never fished for flies?" The child shook his head, his eyes closing despite his best efforts. "Huh," said Christopher, "how do you feed your frogs then?"

The child's eyes stayed shut and Christopher slowly took his hand away, listening to the gentle rise and fall of the boy's breath. Wynter found herself yearning for the rest of the story. After all that had happened tonight, she wanted to hear more about frogs, and fishing for flies.

Christopher straightened and then chuckled as the sleepy little voice said, "Don't got me no frogs."

Christopher bent forward again, murmuring low so that Razi and Wynter had to strain to hear. The fire shot blue and lilac highlights through his curtain of black hair and outlined his chin in gold as he said, "Oh, you must get some frogs, lad. They are excellent good companions."

Razi stretched his hand across the table, palm up, and Wynter took it lightly in hers, as if they were children again, listening to Salvador Minare spinning his tales at the fire in Jonathon's chambers.

"How you fish for flies?" the boy mumbled.

"Well . . ." Christopher's scarred hand lay on the side of the small head. "You just dip your fingers in honey and wait. "'Course, I fell asleep, didn't I? And when I woke up, that bloody bear was making off with my fingers. I chased him, of course, and he dropped all but the two that are missing. And your good Lord Razi, he sewed the others back on for me, because he is a great doctor, and a most excellent man."

Razi put his hand over his eyes at that.

"You know what the worst part was, mouse?"

"Mmmmhmmm?"

"Those two fingers had all my best rings on them. Now, whenever I see a bear I follow him home to see if he's shat out my jewels."

The child squeaked out a little laugh of delighted revulsion. "Ew! You roots in bear poop!"

"Silly boy," tutted Christopher, "I use a stick."

The child was asleep, dropping off the precipice of consciousness as only the very innocent can. Christopher, his face still hidden, continued to stroke his cheek with his thumb, until Razi came over and put a hand on his shoulder.

"Come on," he said roughly. "Bed."

"I'll stay a while," Christopher said, his voice distant, not looking up.

"It's not safe," Wynter cautioned, more harshly than she intended. It was as though she and Razi felt duty bound to balance Christopher's tenderness with iron and rough stone.

"Razi will be all right," murmured Christopher, his eyes still on the sleeping child.

"For you, Chris," said Razi, squeezing his friend's shoulder, "It's not safe for you."

"Good Frith!" Christopher leapt angrily to his feet and ducked past them, pushing his way out of the fire-nook.

The cocks were just starting to crow as the three of them headed back to the secret passages and the uneasy comfort of their beds.

Mortuus in Vita

Wynter rose from the deepest of sleeps to the sound of someone hammering on the receiving room door, and the sight of a raven on her windowsill. The raven cawed loudly and eyed her with malevolent disinterest. It had a long strip of bloody meat dangling from its beak, and there were bloody tracks on the pale wood of the sill.

Cages, she thought, still gripped by sleep, *gibbets, blood and pain*.

The bird spread its huge wings, blotting out the light. Cawing again, it launched itself from the window and disappeared up to the roof, its cries like a rusty saw on knotted wood.

Wynter pushed herself onto her elbows. The shadows were short, the sun high and hot in her window. God, it must be midday or later, which would mean that she had slept like the dead for over eight hours! The hammering on the receiving room door grew louder. She struggled out from under the sheets and the netting, cursing Razi for the bitter draught he'd forced on her before bed. She could still feel its hold on her arms and legs, feel the sleep that kept sucking at her mind like a black river.

"I'm . . ." She cleared her throat and longed for water. "I'm coming!" she managed hoarsely, unbolting her bed-room door.

She heard Lorcan's bolt fly back as she passed through the retiring room, and she was amazed to see him come stumbling to his door, frowsy and tousled, in bare feet and long johns, last night's shirt hanging open to his belly. He had slept in, too! The lord and master of early rising!

"Whu . . .?" he said. He looked like a puzzled bear.

She opened the hall door and an irate courtier spread his hands at the sight of her in her shift and night cap. "It is the sixth quartering of the shadows!" he said in extreme agitation. Behind him a little page stood, patiently holding a large tray. He peeped at Wynter from around the taller man's legs.

Lorcan cursed violently behind her and addressed the courtier in alarm. "Has he been waiting all this time?"

The courtier looked him up and down, his lip curling in barely suppressed disdain, just the right side of dangerous insolence. "The King has more urgent things at hand than to wait for you, Protector Lord Moorehawke. He bids you make haste, and he shall meet with you when he's next free."

They were treated to one more glacial look, and the man turned smartly on his heel and left.

Lorcan flung his hands up. He grabbed his tangled hair and squeezed his head, looked around him in flustered despair. "God*damn*. God*damn* . . . where are my poxy boots?"

The little page cleared his throat and offered his tray to Wynter. "Compliments of my Lord Razi, some breakfast. It's all cold now, though."

Wynter took it. "Thank you," she said. The laundry-staff had deposited a neatly folded pile of their clothes by the door, the bill carefully pinned to the top layer. "Will you bring those in for me, little man?"

The page did as he was bid. He seemed young enough and innocent enough, but when Wynter asked him how fared the Lord Razi, the boy just looked at her with solemn, court-wary eyes and didn't reply. She pursed a sad little smile and nodded to dismiss him. He left with last night's untouched supper things, and she put the new tray on the table, lifting the cover with the sudden realisation that she was starving.

Lorcan came storming from his room, a boot in one hand. "What are you doing?" he exclaimed. "Get dressed!"

"Sit down and eat, Dad. Razi said . . ."

"Wynter! Get your work clothes on, Jonathon is *waiting*, he's been waiting for *hours*!"

His colour was very high. Wynter felt like grabbing him and telling him to *calm down* before he collapsed again. Instead she sat down and began to butter a scone, as though they had all the time in the world. The scone was rich and fluffy, ripe with sultanas. Lorcan suddenly couldn't take his eyes from it.

"Dad," she said, "the King is *not* waiting. You know that. He's gone off somewhere. It doesn't matter what business you have with him, he's going to ignore you for hours now, just to show you who's boss. Have some breakfast. Razi says you have to eat."

Lorcan's eyes drifted to the tray. He swallowed at the sight of the coffee, which he hadn't so much as smelled in five long years. Wynter had added cream and sugar and was pouring two big bowls of it. She pointedly put one of the bowls on his side of the table and took a long swallow from the other. Lorcan looked at the bowl, then at the flaky crescent breads, the herby lamb sausages, the boiled eggs and salt, the slices of fresh fruit. He swallowed again and Wynter heard the spit in his mouth.

"Just a bite," he conceded, dropping his boot and sitting down.

They cleared the plates between them, eating silently, steadily and with enthusiasm. Eventually there was nothing left but crumbs, and a half-bowl of creamy coffee.

Lorcan pushed back with a satisfied sigh. "Jesu Christi," he murmured. "That was magnificent."

Wynter laughed. She hadn't seen him this rosy-cheeked and replete in an age. He laughed back at her, his old merry self. The sun made emeralds of his dancing eyes. "Ah, girl," he said fondly, "you're a bloody tonic." And they grinned at each other across the devastation of breakfast.

After a few more moments of contentment, Lorcan straightened up and his face became serious.

"Wynter, Jonathon has offered me my licence."

Her heart leapt. "Oh Dad! That's *great.*" she squinted at him, waiting for his smile. Why wasn't he walking on air? "What limitations?" she asked, thinking it must be *very* limited for this subdued response.

"No limitations at all, love. All grades open, all tenders legitimate, any province, any city, free to practise."

"My God, Dad! I . . . that's . . . Hah!" She laughed and

spread her hands. "That's *incredible*!" Jonathon had just handed her father carte blanche to set up business anywhere he liked, using whatever staff he liked, taking on whatever jobs he fancied. It was the most unlimited licence of work she'd ever heard of. Lorcan should have been elated. Instead he was looking at her with a kind of gentle sorrow.

"It's hereditary, Wynter." She dropped her hands at that, stunned. "It's hereditary, in perpetuity. You get to carry it on. No one can ever take it away from you."

"Oh, Dad."

His eyes were huge and glittering in the streaming sunlight. Wynter put her hands on the table, palms down, suddenly cold all over.

She understood now. "He wants you to support Albi's disinheritance. He wants you to declare for *mortuus in vita*?" Lorcan nodded. "You *can't*. Dad, you can't. Tell me that you . . ."

"He has the licence papers, Wyn. He held them *this close* . . ." Lorcan raised his hand in front of his face, clenched into a fist, looking at it as though it was something vile and disgusting. "This close," he repeated.

"Dad," she reached across the table to him and he looked at her as if she was about to break his heart. "It's *Albi*, Dad. It's *Alberon*."

"I know," he whispered. "But it's also *you*, darling. It's you and what happens to you when I'm gone." He didn't say the rest. *I'll be gone soon. You'll be all alone. This is all I can give you.*

The sunlight reflecting in his eyes flickered as a shadow crossed the room, drawing his attention to the window.

Then another shadow briefly darkened his face. He got up to have a look.

"God help us!" he said, looking out the window, surprise and amazement. When the implications of what he saw sunk in, he said it again, low, heartfelt, hopeless. "God help us."

Wynter knew already, had heard the rattle and slide of their claws on the red tiled roofs. She had hoped they'd escape her father's notice. Ravens. Ravens were gathering. She turned and watched her father as he stepped onto the sill and leaned far out the window, balancing himself with one big hand on the top of the frame. For a moment all she could see were his long legs. Then she heard him curse and he slithered back into the room, his face drained.

"The keep?" she asked, not really a question.

"The keep," he confirmed, not looking at her. He put a hand on her head as he passed her by. "Get ready for work," he said, and went into his room, closing the door softly behind him. It was some time before Wynter heard him begin to get dressed.

Ravens over the keep. It could mean only one thing.

Jonathon had impaled the prisoner's body on the trophy spikes. A broken, bloody, vengeful flag high over the complex; the first of its kind to have been displayed there since Jonathon had taken the throne.

Wynter put her face in her hands for a moment, pushing her fingers into her eyes, shoving unwanted images back into dark rooms and shutting doors in her mind. Then she got up and went to get dressed, leaving the breakfast things to gather flies in the sweltering heat.

She put on her rough work clothes and clubbed her hair.

When she came out from her room, shouldering her roll of tools, Lorcan was standing in the receiving room. His tools were on his back, the sunlight in his plaited hair. They didn't talk. Wynter still had no idea where it was they were going or what it was they were meant to do, and she chose not to ask her father for details. Sometimes words just made things worse.

He turned and looked her up and down, nodded approvingly and said, "Ready?"

"Ready."

Then he straightened, set his shoulders and raised his head. Face cold, eyes hooded, Wynter's father disappeared in the blink of an eye and became the Protector Lord Lorcan Moorehawke. He didn't look at her again, just swept from the room with her in tow, master and apprentice striding forward on their business for the King.

It should have been very quiet at midday at the height of summer, but there was a steady undercurrent of activity in the halls. Grim-faced, eyes down, men were moving through the corridors like worker ants. They carried big paintings and small paintings, the images obscured with cloths. They carried statues, and stacks of manuscripts. All were heading in the same direction – out to the gardens.

She trotted obediently along behind her father, pretending not to notice. But she saw the strained look on the men's faces. She saw the pages and serving girls snatching distraught conversations as they passed in the halls. She saw the tension growing in her father's back. Then two men stumbled at the head of a short flight of stairs, the huge painting that they carried escaping their grasp. As they struggled to hoist it back onto their shoulders, the cover slipped and the image was revealed.

Wynter stopped in her tracks.

It was her favourite painting, the one from Jonathon's chambers. The one that held pride of place above the main fireplace in his retiring room: Alberon, Razi and herself, grinning happily in the garden.

Memories of childhood came pouring over her.

She recalled how she used to lie under the round study table, listening to Oliver and Jonathon and her father talking. She remembered kicking her feet and looking up at that painting through the tassels of the tablecloth. She was always amazed at how like the three of them it was. How unusually accurate a depiction of their true selves.

Razi was shown sprawled against a tree root, a book in his hand, looking down to where Albi and Wynter were sitting on the grass. Albi was cradling Shubbit, his beloved spaniel, and Wynter was looking out from the painting, her eyes full of curiosity. They looked so happy, like a proper family. Proper brothers and sister. She and Albi were about six at the time; Razi must have been ten.

The men righted the painting and started down the stairs with it.

Wynter was brought back to the present by her father's hand on her shoulder. She looked up into his guarded face. He was watching the men carry the painting down the stairs, the happy faces of the three children disappearing into the gloom of the stairwell.

Turning suddenly on his heel, Lorcan led the way down the side stairs and out through the small rose garden, from where they crossed quickly to the other side of the main palace building. There was a smell of fire in the air, and thick smoke drifted through the gardens from somewhere behind the complex. As they skirted the pond, Wynter caught a glimpse of the line of men carrying their various packages and bundles around the back of the buildings, heading for the source of the smoke, heading for the fire. A group of empty-handed men trailed back in the opposite direction, smoke in their hair, tension on their faces.

Lorcan mounted the granite steps on the opposite side of the garden and proceeded down a black and white tiled corridor. Suddenly Wynter knew where they were going and her heart sank. The library. *Oh, Dad,* she thought, *not the library.* The roll of tools was suddenly an ominous weight on her shoulder.

Lorcan opened the door, and there it was, just as Wynter remembered it, with its everlasting smell of wood and polish and sun-baked dust.

Jonathon had made this his life's work. In a time when books were regularly burnt, condemned, outlawed or banned, Jonathon had avidly gathered tomes and volumes of every type imaginable, in every language, of every creed, representing every philosophy known to man. He had been responsible for saving innumerable works of science and medical research from the many crusades, pogroms and purges that tore their way through the kingdoms around him. And then he had made the library freely available to anyone willing to pay a good scribe to make copies for their own use.

Standing in the enormous room, surrounded by the King's magnificent collection, it was impossible not to be impressed by the immensity of the project, the scope of his vision. It was the wonder of the Europes, perhaps even of the world, a tremendous shining light in the increasingly black void of ignorance that was foisting itself on the populations of the other kingdoms.

Wynter paused at the door and watched her father as he came to a halt in the centre of the room. He put his roll of tools gently down onto the floor and stood looking all around him. Wynter heard his throat click, and his shoulders rose and fell with a deep sigh.

It wasn't the books that he was looking at, though they were breathtaking in their own right. It was the bookshelves, the wall panels, the ornately carved ceiling beams. Thirteen years of Lorcan's life had gone into this room. Thirteen years of steadily carving and sanding and polishing the hard redwood that now glowed in the early afternoon sun.

At the far end of the room was the wall panel that he'd been working on when Jonathon had sent him away. The entire frame was pricked out in detail, but less than a third of it had been carved. It showed Jonathon, Oliver and Lorcan standing on the wooded path, their hounds flowing around their legs, their bows slung across their backs. Razi was with them, and Wynter and Alberon were waving to them from the steps. At the two children's feet lay some of the many cats that had been under Wynter's care, all sublimely recognisable in their individual quirks and poses. Like all of Lorcan's work, it was warm and domestic, lacking the stiff formality of much palace art. It hurt Wynter's heart to see it. It spoke of days lost, never to be retrieved.

Lorcan had chronicled all their years here, using his incredible talent to draw them out in wood. Often at

Jonathon's specific request, many times at his own whim but with Jonathon's blessing, Lorcan had detailed the births, the babyhoods and the childhood years of the palace children. There were countless flights-of-fancy poems, written by Jonathon and carved into the walls by Lorcan, so that the children would always remember when Razi rode his first horse, when Alberon caught his first fish, when Wynter broke her arm falling from a tree. The whole of their young lives were here, a permanent and indisputable reminder of what had gone before.

He had also perfectly captured the intense feeling of brotherhood and the happy camaraderie enjoyed by himself, Jonathon and Oliver.

Over and over again, all around the room, were images of Alberon and images of Oliver; their names were carved into numerous plaques, their crests incorporated into imaginary coats of arms. And now Wynter understood, completely understood, why it was that her father was here, the magnitude of the sacrifice that Jonathon had demanded from him in return for her future.

Lorcan spoke gruffly, with his back still turned to her. "You know what we are to do?"

"Yes," she whispered, her voice small.

Lorcan cleared his throat and picked up his tools. "You start on the smaller bookshelves," he said, "I'll take the walls." He made his way through the stacks to the far wall. Wynter didn't shift from her position at the door. Unable to move, she watched as her father took a rough file from his roll of tools. He stood before the big wall panel for a moment, looking up at it. Then carefully and with great precision, he began to remove Alberon from the picture.

At the first grating rasp of Lorcan's file on the wood, Wynter made her way to the smaller bookshelves in the far corner of the room. Carefully she chose her starting point, then bent and unrolled her tools. She selected a file, looked for a moment at the piece of art before her and then turned to her work, her mind and her face as empty as blank paper.

Secrets

*O*ver the next two days, Wynter and her father rose early and retired late. They walked to the library before dawn, when the palace was a silent tomb, and returned to their rooms long after midnight when the halls were an echoing crypt. Wynter felt as though they were the only people left alive. They spent each day with their backs turned to each other, working solidly and without rest. Each night they fell into bed, exhausted, and slept like corpses until dawn. Even when they paused to eat, they did not talk. Lorcan would sit, his back to one of the big windows, his face blank, chewing stolidly at his food, draining his drink and then silently returning to work. It was as though he had retreated down a long corridor and only saw his daughter vaguely, from a distance, through a fog.

No one came near them all day, no one visited them at night. Even Jonathon had yet to make an appearance, and though Razi sent regular gifts of food and drink to their room, he was nowhere to be seen.

After two days and nights of utter silence, Wynter's mouth felt fused, her lips stiff, as if they couldn't recall how to speak. She thought that her head might actually burst with the pressure of her unspoken thoughts; they were trapped inside her, bumping against each other like beetles in a box.

Her work, which had always been her solace and her joy, failed her now. As soon as she'd become absorbed, as soon as her hands would achieve that steady, hypnotic rhythm so familiar to her, her mind would slip its leash and wander into territory it shouldn't. Before she knew it, terrible images would rise up before her. She would see Lorcan, gasping in the dark, a wounded animal. Razi, grey faced and shaking, blood running down his stomach and pooling on the white cloth in her hand. Christopher, silent as a grave, his fist smashing into that man's face, blood flying up in a fine spray. But most of all, she would see that awful chair, those instruments, and Razi rising up out of the smoke and flames, haloed in screams. Her chisel would slip, her hammer falter and she'd have to clench her teeth and her hands, and force herself to be still.

She was alone with these images, they were her own personal devils, and more and more, as her solitude went on, she felt they were going to drive her mad.

And all day there was the incessant scrape of chisel on wood, the unending scouring of the file. Sounds that usually meant creation, pride and satisfaction. But now it was Alberon's face under the blade and Oliver's face, Albi's name and Oliver's name, all day long, curling away in slivers and spirals of fragrant red sawdust and shavings. Disappearing, a layer at a time, under the sharp edge of her own tools.

She longed for Razi. She longed for fresh air. She longed

to focus on something further way than the end of her nose.

On the morning of the third day, Wynter stood for a moment, looking at the little poem that Jonathon had written when Alberon's beloved Shubbit died. This was to be her next task, to wipe this moment of tenderness from history, to pretend it had never been, and she just couldn't begin. Finally she put her tools down and left.

Lorcan was grimly planing Alberon's name from a plaque in the lower corner of a redwood wall panel and he didn't look up as she passed him by. He kept his head bent to his work, his hair and eyelashes speckled with red sawdust. Wynter closed the door quietly behind her, telling herself that she'd only be a while.

She stood on the steps in the early dawn, looking up into the trees. Her hands and arms were still vibrating with the rhythm of mallet on chisel. There was a taste of sawdust off her lips, the scent of shaved wood permeating her clothes. But the morning smelled of living wood – yew and pine and damp birch, and it felt incredibly good to be outside in the daylight, with the air on her face. It was almost intoxicating.

She let her burning eyes drift along the trees. She took in the horizon, lifted her head to the grey and rose coloured sky. Gradually her shoulders and back unknotted and her neck relaxed. Through the open library windows she heard the steady, shushing grind of Lorcan's plane, shaving, shaving, shaving. Undoing three or four days of his beautiful work in a single hour.

She turned suddenly and walked away from that sound. She went down the long back steps and around by the birch trees, putting space between herself and the library. She wanted no more of this steady, daily unravelling of her father's legacy to the world.

Maybe Razi would be at the stables? It was barely past dawn and the deserted complex had a sleepy unearthly feeling, as though she were walking through a dream. She cut through the narrow alley between the spare horse stalls and the feed store. The exercise ring was ahead of her, and she could hear the *trit-trot* of a horse circling the arena. Dust spiralled across the mouth of the alley in the slanting early light.

She was passing the dim mouth of an empty stall when a low moan of pain stopped her in her tracks.

From behind the wooden wall, Christopher's voice gasped, "Stop! Wait!" low and urgent.

Wynter crouched down, her hand on her dagger, the words *ambush* and *assassin* scurrying across her mind.

Then another voice, feminine and impatient, whispered, "What is it?"

"Just hold on a moment . . ." Christopher again. There was a moment of rustling, and the woman giggled.

"Here . . . we go . . ." panted Christopher.

"What in God's name is that?" whispered the woman, doubt and fascination overriding the husky expectancy in her voice.

"*That* . . ." Christopher paused with a grunt. The woman giggled and then gasped, releasing a slow luxuriant *uhhhhhhh*. "That . . ." growled Christopher breathlessly, ". . . is your protection . . . against the likes . . . of me."

He made another sound, another moan, which Wynter realised instantly, and with burning embarrassment, wasn't pain at all. She fled up the alley, her cheeks blazing.

A sudden rage against Christopher Garron slammed her hard under the heart, like a punch to her chest. He seemed to be having no problem finding comfort! *He* seemed to be perfectly fine! But where was Razi? While Christopher pleased himself, where had he abandoned Razi?

She found him at the exercise ring, sprawled listlessly on a milking stool, his long legs stretched out in the dirt, his back to the red-washed feed-store. He was supervising a horse being put through its paces and was dressed for work, dusty leggings, dusty riding boots, a pale green, loose-weave tunic. But he looked utterly exhausted and she doubted he would have the energy to sit a saddle.

Wynter stopped, shocked at how drawn he was, how much older than his nineteen years he looked. Even his usually glossy mass of curls seemed tired – a dull, untidy mat hanging over his half-closed eyes.

There were six or seven enormous, black-clad guards dotted around the ring – bodyguards. One made to stop Wynter, but Razi waved him away, smiling at her and moving his fingers in greeting as she crossed the yard.

"Hello, brother," she said, kneeling beside him in the dust, and turning to watch the big horse cantering at the end of its lunge rope. It was magnificent, one of those arch, high-headed princes of a horse, uncut and fiery. "Is he one of yours?"

"Aye." He put a hand on her head and smoothed her hair with a long affectionate stroke. Then he let his hand drop tiredly back into his lap.

"Your tomcat is on the prowl," she sneered, and he turned his head questioningly. "Christopher," she clarified, "he's sowing his oats in the stalls."

To Wynter's great surprise, Razi laughed, so suddenly and loudly that the guards all glanced their way. "He found her, then?" He grinned, his teeth showing white in his brown face, his eyes sparkling. "I should never doubt him!" And then he laughed again, Razi's luxuriant, chuckling laugh, and Wynter had to smile in return.

Impulsively he took Wynter's hand in his, kissed it and held it loosely in his own, smiling to himself and watching the horse with renewed interest. His face was transformed with delight, and he was nineteen years old again. Tired, yes, and wan from pain and his recent ordeal, but not wasted looking, not defeated. It was such a radical and profound difference to how he had looked just moments before that Wynter felt all her anger at Christopher drain away.

She put her head on Razi's shoulder and despite her former desire to talk, she didn't speak. This was enough. All the terrible subjects that they should have been discussing, all the awful truths and secrets, Wynter let them lie beneath the horse's trampling hooves, let them be pounded into submission. They drifted up with the dust that rose from the exercise ring, and she was free of them for a brief and fragile interlude.

They sat quietly together, as the heat of the day built around them and they watched while the master groom put Razi's magnificent horse through its paces. Just as if they were any other brother and sister, on any normal morning. Razi murmured comments now and again. Wynter replied and occasionally she threw in a comment of her own. The groom shouted questions, and Razi answered them with a nod or a few words. On the periphery of their vision the guards stood like black, impassive cockroaches. Save for their presence, it was peaceful, a perfect moment of comfort that was doomed to end too quickly.

Wynter felt Razi tense beside her, and he slowly got to his feet. Following the direction of his gaze, she saw a councilman standing in the shadows of the indoor arena. He was keeping out of sight of the soldiers and staring pointedly at Razi. Wynter recognised him as Simon De Rochelle, one of the few councilmen who hadn't forced Razi to the throne. Beside him lurked a ragged-looking fellow, lithe, tanned and furtive. He had the stiffly rosined hair and beard of a west country Comberman, and he was covered in dust. *Straight in off the road*, she thought, *a messenger of some sort.*

Razi nodded to De Rochelle, and the two men melted back into the shadows.

"Wynter," Razi murmured, still looking after Simon and his companion. "Go tell Christopher that I'll meet him in the kitchens in the next quartering of the shadows. Tell him not to wander about."

"What's going on?"

He turned his head and glared down at her with all the authority of his royal heritage, and she felt a small flare of anger that he would think to use that look on her. But he didn't soften, and she sourly dropped her eyes.

"How do you propose to lose your guard dogs?" she asked.

He glanced coldly at the looming soldiers. "Just give Christopher my message," he said, "and I'll worry about the rest."

He went to walk away, and Wynter caught his hand, not wanting to part on such an unpleasant note. She needed something more from him before he left, but she wasn't sure what that was. She found herself gazing up at him, tearfully.

He swung back, impatient to be on his way, but then he saw the distress in her face. "Sis," he said tenderly, putting his hands on her shoulders, and then he faltered. What could he possibly say to her? There was no comfort that could be given with words, nothing soothing he could say that wouldn't be a lie or a platitude. They looked at each other for a moment, struggling to express how they felt without actually dragging all the terrible facts of their situation into the light.

And then Razi hugged her. He wrapped his arms around her and enfolded her in the warmth of his long body, bending his head down to rest his cheek on the top of her head. She let herself lean into him, and closed her eyes, breathing in his scent, that warm mixture of horses, sandalwood and clean linen. And for a moment she felt small and hidden and protected.

"Go on," he whispered, too soon, and he kissed the top of her head. Then he was gone, dust swirling around his legs as he strode across the sun-blasted arena.

The guards moved to accompany him, and Razi flung up a hand without looking at them. "Give me a moment," he ordered. When several of them continued to follow, Razi turned on his heel and levelled them with an unbelievably cold glare. "Goddamn you," he hissed. "Unless you're planning on wiping my arse, I suggest you give me a God-cursed moment."

The guards faltered and dithered, and Razi stalked away without waiting for their response. Then they turned back to the ring and let him pass around the back of the indoor arena, and out of their sight.

Wynter stood for a moment, the guards eyeing her. Then she slowly made her way back to the alley. The stall where she'd last heard Christopher was quiet now, and Wynter stepped into the dim interior fully expecting him to be gone.

He was lying on his back, his ankles crossed, his left arm covering his eyes and his right arm flung loosely out from his side. He was completely naked, his chest rising and falling in peaceful sleep.

Wynter gasped. She wasn't a stranger to male nudity, but there was such an air of open sexuality about Christopher that she caught herself looking in a way she'd never really considered before. For the first time ever she found herself wondering what it would be like to have a man press his body against hers. What it would be like to have a man kiss her in that way she knew men kissed women when they were expressing more than simple affection.

These thoughts brought such a giant, frightening surge of emotion that she squeezed her eyes shut and turned away. She was left with an impression of slim, well-made limbs shimmering against the dusky hay, shockingly dark hair against the pale skin of his chest and stomach, and, surprisingly, the dull gleam of silver snake bracelets hugging the tops of both of Christopher's arms.

He's Merron! she thought, her eyes opening in surprise. *He doesn't look Merron!*

She dithered for a moment, then she resolved to leave the stall and announce herself with a knock, thus giving

Christopher the chance to get dressed in privacy. But she must have made some small sound, a scuff or a rustle, because, before she could take a step, Christopher had leapt from the hay, making her skitter backwards in shock. He rose to his feet in one smooth action and took up a defensive crouch, his black-handled dagger held out, his other hand raised.

"*Cé hé sin?*" he said hoarsely in Merron. Wynter realised that she was silhouetted against the glaring light of the alley, and all Christopher could see was a black shape lurking in the doorway.

"It's me. Wynter."

"Oh," he sighed, and relaxed, lowering his knife and pushing his hair behind his ears. "Razi's in the exercise ring with the stallion," he said, gesturing casually towards the arena, and then he looked away to find his clothes.

He was completely unfazed by his nudity, and began to dress unhurriedly and without any self-consciousness. But he seemed surprised when she didn't leave, and then disconcerted when he caught her staring while he did up the stays on his undershirt.

Christopher cleared his throat pointedly, and Wynter turned away as he bent to pick up his underthings and his trousers. She didn't look again, and he rustled about behind her, sitting on the hay to pull up his trousers and put on his socks and tunic.

"I'm done," he said, and when she turned, he was just slipping the dagger into his boot. He leant forward, his hands dangling between his knees, looking up at her in puzzlement. "Do you want me to walk you around to him?" he asked, genuinely solicitous, but obviously confused at what he took for her reluctance to go to Razi. The sunlight emphasised the sloping bones of his narrow face as he tilted his head.

"You're Merron," she said, and then, in response to his surprised look, "I saw your bracelets. You belong to the serpent Merron."

"You know the Merron?"

"A clan of panther Merron used to winter in Shirken's forests. I got to know some of their customs. You wear the symbol of the serpent Merron."

Christopher put his right hand over the bracelet on his left arm and said earnestly, "They're not the originals. I had to have them remade." It seemed important to him that she understand this, as though it would be a crime to pretend that these were the original artefacts. "The originals were stolen from me." He unconsciously ran his thumb over the gap where his finger should be.

"I have no desire to cause offence," said Wynter, unsure of how he would take it, "but . . . you don't *look* Merron."

To her relief, he laughed, "I'm a bit small all right, aren't I?"

Wynter grinned back. Merron men were notoriously huge, broad and hairy creatures, every one. Christopher, on the other hand, would never be considered a large man; the only trait he seemed to share with his tribesmen was his incredibly pale skin, a feature for which the Merron were also famous.

"I'm mostly Hadrish by birth, I think." He smiled, his grey eyes clear in the sun. "And when I was growing up, the troupe spent a lot of time living and travelling in Hadra, so I suppose you could say it was my home country. It was the

master of my troupe who was Merron, and he took me in
when I were but a mouse." Christopher's smile grew wistful and he paused, obviously remembering the man with
great affection. "He raised me," he said softly. "He was my
dad . . . he was who I *called* my dad." He raised his eyes to
Wynter, questioning. "You take my meaning?" Wynter
nodded. "He took me to the Merron *aonach* – their great
fair – every summer, to catch up on his people, and eventually, despite my obscure origins, they adopted me! They
called me *Coinín*, Rabbit, on account that I could outrun
them all. Big, lumbering apes." He chuckled softly at that.

"You're a foundling, Christopher?"

"Well, I had me a mother for a while, but she wasn't so
inclined to hang about. Mind you, I was a terribly wild
infant!" He widened his eyes to illustrate exactly *how*
wild an infant he had been. "And in her favour, she stuck
by me for nearly four years! You would agree that she
showed excellent perseverance, had you any idea what I
was like!" He smiled up at her again, as though what
he'd said was amusing and not, as Wynter found it, unut-
terably sad.

How open he is about himself, she thought, *how like clear
water when compared to the usual courtier. If he were a trout
pool the fish would have nowhere to hide, and you'd see every
pebble on the riverbed.*

She cleared her throat. "Razi asks that you wait for him
in the kitchens. He won't be long. He asks that you please
do not wander."

A touch of amused irritation clouded Christopher's face,
and he looked away, sucking his teeth. "I'm not a bloody
baby, Razi Kingsson," he muttered.

Wynter snorted. "Razi thinks we're *all* babies. He thinks he has to protect us."

"And what's *he* up to, while I'm keeping myself safe and sound? I take it he's not *wandering*? I take it he's right where I left him, surrounded by guards, completely unassailable." Christopher's voice was dripping with amused sarcasm, and Wynter found herself pleased to have found someone with whom she could share her irritation at Razi's bullheadedness.

"He's in secret rendezvous with a councilman."

Christopher clenched his jaw, his amusement transforming to anger. "That Rochelle fellow?" Wynter nodded. "He have a messenger with him?" She nodded again. Christopher eyed her, trying to see her face. "What do they want from him, lass?"

She shrugged, genuinely ignorant. "I don't know, Christopher, I . . . I am not privy to his secrets."

Christopher turned away, his jaw twitching. He glared into the depths of the stalls for a moment and then abruptly shook himself. He flung his hands up and dismissed the subject with a gesture. "Pah!" he said. "A pox on the lot of them. They're not worth his spit." He stood up suddenly, brushing himself off, and shot a teasing smile at Wynter. "Best do as he says though, eh? Lest he sulk? But would you do me the grace of walking me to the kitchens? I can't seem to find my way around."

Wynter saw this for a blatantly transparent lie, but that didn't stop her from ducking her head in agreement and matching Christopher's step as they strolled out into the sunlight.

"How did you meet Razi, Christopher?" It felt strange to

ask such a blunt question, a bit like diving off a high rock. In court life such things were weaselled around for weeks. A piece of information gleaned here, a piece of gossip uncovered there. It went against all her training to be so direct. She steeled herself for the expected lie, for the usual glib evasions. For some strange reason, she hoped that they wouldn't come.

"I was playing at his aunt's wedding," he said.

Wynter stopped walking. "You were . . . you mean music? You were performing?"

He looked back at her, puzzled, and then it dawned on him, and he lifted his mangled hands. "Oh!" he said. "You assumed . . . No! Razi and I knew each other . . ." he shrugged, looking for a way to put it. "Before." He smiled.

Wynter felt a strong wave of pity cross her face, it just overcame her, and Christopher's smile fell away. His face became hard and still, like it had the first time they'd spoken, after she had snidely referred to him as a *tumbler of some sort*. She swallowed.

"Which . . . which of Hadil's sisters was it that got married?" she tried lightly. He held his resentful glare for a moment, and then he relented and accepted her offering in good grace.

"The tall fat one," he said with an almost genuine grin. "*What* a crazy witch! I was mortal terrified for that poor groom!"

Wynter laughed, though she had no idea who Christopher was talking about. She had never met any of Razi's mother's sisters. She was just delighted that Christopher had thawed.

He started walking again and she fell into step. They

passed into sunlight, and it beat on them like a golden hammer.

"I was at Hadil's house for the whole wedding ceremony, a good three weeks. Most days I would wander down to the stables, and Razi and I fell to chatting about the horses." He glanced shyly at her. "I know an awful lot about them, you know."

"Well, you *are* Merron."

He grinned and nodded, "Aye."

They turned the corner that would take them to the kitchen steps and the path ahead of them was suddenly full of life. Provisions were being delivered and there were carts and drays and many scuttling men and women.

"And you just stayed on with them," she queried, "when the festivities were over?"

Christopher tensed, and the unusually easy give and take of their conversation ground to a sudden halt. "Um . . ." he said, "When my time with Hadil was over . . . Razi . . ."

Wynter felt a knot tighten in the pit of her stomach as she realised that he was about to lie. He would do it badly, and she was certain that it embarrassed him, but he was going to do it anyway. The realisation that Christopher was about to deceive her unexpectedly knocked the heat from her heart. Why? Why should it upset her so? Deception was an integral part of life, and only days ago she had been berating his lack of guile.

But as Christopher feverishly groped about for the right words, Wynter felt a terrible disappointment growing in her. It was only then that she realised how light she had felt talking to Christopher, how much laughter he had managed to weave into the short time that they'd walked together. She swallowed back her bitterness as he cleared his throat and stumbled his way back into the conversation.

"Razi persuaded me to stay. To work with his horses."

What was he hiding?

Perhaps he's a thief, after all. Perhaps that's what happened to his hands. He stole from Hadil. It would be just like Razi's mother to demand the full rigours of the law. And just like Razi to take him in as charity afterwards. But why not just tell her? Didn't he realise that she'd find out anyway?

He threw her then by holding up his hands. "This," he said, clearing his throat again, "this happened about two months later. Bandits. The Loups-Garous . . ."

The name made her startle. "In the Moroccos?" she gasped. "That far south?"

He looked at her knowingly. "Oh aye," he whispered and she suspected that his dealings with the Loups-Garous were far greater than this one savage attack.

"Why?" she asked, gesturing to his hands. Again he faltered, and once again she realised that he was going to lie.

"I suppose I fought just a little too hard," he said quietly, spreading the fingers of his left hand, not quite managing to straighten them. "They were very upset with me."

Perhaps, thought Wynter with a flash of inspiration, *this is not so much deceit, as it is a need for privacy.*

Christopher smiled at her, his cheeks a high pink now, his eyes very troubled. "They took my bracelets," he said, as if that were almost as bad as them having ripped the fingers from his talented hands.

A shrill whistle cut across the noise of the nearby traders. It was Razi, stalking towards them, his face taut with well contained excitement. He was ringed by guards, and they seemed to loom over him with renewed vigilance, as if they had to make up for their laxity at the arena. They pressed so close that Wynter wanted to scream at them, *Let him breathe! Let him move!*

Christopher muttered, "Goddamn. They'll get him with child if they don't back off!"

Then there was the unmistakable *thwack* of a longbow being fired, and the guard to Razi's right keeled over onto his companion, an arrow piercing his head from temple to temple.

Thwarting the King

There was pandemonium. Suddenly everyone was shouting and running, pointing in different directions. The guards crowded around Razi and one of them tried to shove him back against the wall of the palace. Razi struggled to push free and see to the fallen soldier, though it was obvious even to Wynter that the poor man was dead.

Christopher grabbed Wynter by the arm, restraining her from running forward. He had gone very still and quiet, his eyes roaming the trees beyond the path.

A woman screamed, "There! There!" and pointed as some hapless gardener came round the far corner, his scythe over his shoulder. The guards turned as one, and the poor man took one look at their faces and fled, dropping his scythe to the grass as he ran. With a roar, all but one of the guards took after him, leaving only a big lumbering fellow to stand in front of Razi and shield him from further threat.

Wynter started forward, her hand up in frustration. "NO!" she shouted at the retreating soldiers. Suddenly, Christopher whistled sharply to get Razi's attention, and pointed high up into the trees. Then he was off up the path, cutting quickly right and heading upwards at tremendous speed through the woods.

Razi ducked from under the guard's arm and dodged away as the huge man made a panicked swipe at him.

"My Lord!" he bellowed as Razi escaped his grasp.

"Get the others!" Razi ordered the man. "Stay there!" he yelled imperiously, pointing at the few civilians who had run forward to join the chase. They came to an uncertain halt.

Razi took off into the woods, angling left, then up to intersect with Christopher's trajectory. Wynter was on Razi's heels like a shot. He was obviously still suffering the effects of his recent wound, for she rapidly overtook him, and went crashing through the scant underbrush to try and catch up with their quarry.

She could see Christopher ahead of her, haring through the dappled shadows, obviously fixed on his target. It was a steep hill, though lightly wooded, and the ground was slippery with leaves. Wynter was quickly winded, and before long her heart was hammering in her chest. She could hear Razi panting and struggling behind her.

She looked past Christopher and saw the assailant. An enormous man, his bow cast aside, running for his life through the trees. Christopher was angling past him, gaining height on the slope, and Wynter saw that he was intent on getting above the bigger man and bringing him down.

He's too big to hold! she thought. *Christopher will never keep him down!*

Christopher launched himself through the air from the slope above the man. He brought his legs up and around in the same action he had used on the first assassin, and felled the man with a flying kick to the chest. The two of them rolled in a flurry of leaves and debris down the slope towards Wynter.

Christopher landed awkwardly, and came at the assailant from a bad angle, his first blow landing poorly, his balance off. In the end, he was just too light to overpower the huge man and the assailant easily kicked him off. He sent Christopher slamming into a tree where he slumped for a moment, blinking and winded, before staggering to his feet.

By then Wynter was on top of them. She ran at the man and kicked him hard in the side of the head before he could turn on her. He spun away into the leaves, blood flying from his mouth, and before he could get back up, or before she could think, Wynter jumped and landed her full weight, feet-first, onto his back.

She felt a horrible cracking *give* beneath her boots. The man let out an agonised shriek, and Wynter tumbled off him in shock and revulsion. Then Christopher was there, and the two of them dragged the man onto his back.

Christopher slid in behind the man and wrapped his arm around his neck. He heaved so hard that the man's head and shoulders were pulled up, his eyes bulging from lack of air. Wynter flung herself across the man's legs and did her best to hang on. Razi arrived in a swirl of leaves and straddled his would-be killer, pinning his arms to the ground.

"Quickly," said Christopher. "We don't have much time!"

For what? Wynter thought wildly, and then had to tighten her grip on the man's legs as Razi knelt on his wounded chest, causing him to screech and thrash about in pain. Razi grabbed the man's hair and yanked his head back, loosening Christopher's grip and exposing the man's pulsing throat. Then Razi, his eyes cold, pressed his knife hard into the man's taut neck. Bright beads of blood showed along the blade where it bit into his flesh.

"I know you!" said Razi softly. "You're Jusef Marcos, one of my father's huntsmen. You fought by his side during the insurrection, you were under Oliver's command."

The man just rolled his eyes to meet Razi's, panting with pain. Razi grunted and struck him hard with the handle of his dagger, making Wynter wince.

"Who sent you?" he hissed, pressing the blade back to Jusef's throat.

Christopher's gaze flicked past Razi, down the slope. They could hear shouts rising up by the palace. "Hurry, Razi!" he urged, "Make him talk!"

Razi leant in close to Jusef's pain-creased face. "If you tell me who sent you, I promise to kill you quickly. You won't feel a thing." The man's legs jumped under Wynter's weight, and she clutched them convulsively. She glanced in horror at Razi's ruthless profile. His voice was so sure, so blackly cold. Christopher was staring past them, down the hill, his face tense.

"I am loyal to the crown," Jusef growled, then he gritted his teeth against the pain as Christopher twisted a handful of his hair.

Christopher bent his head down, and murmured in Jusef's ear. "You just tried to kill a royal prince, you syphilitic cur. That don't sound too loyal to me."

"I am loyal to the *crown*!" shouted the man again, bucking against their combined weight and then yelling at the pain it caused his ribs.

Christopher glanced back down the slope and his eyes widened. Wynter turned her head and saw that there were shapes moving towards them through the trees. Suddenly Christopher was talking, urgently and persuasively.

"Now you listen," said Christopher, his lips moving against the man's ear, "they're coming for you. They're already at the base of the hill now. If they get you they'll take you to the keep."

Jusef continued to struggle, despite his pain, but Christopher just kept talking, and as he went on, the big man gradually stilled, his eyes widening, and he began to pant with more than just pain. "Shall I tell you what those vultures did to the last fellow Razi gave them? First thing they did? They drew his eyes from the sockets. They were amazing careful, didn't even puncture them. You ever seen an eye drawn from its socket? It's like a bloody grape, so it is. They left them hanging from strings, swinging on his cheeks."

Wynters stomach lurched. *No Christopher! No! I don't want to hear this!*

"I kept wondering," mused Christopher, his tone conversational. "Could he still see?" Jusef's eyes rolled to Christopher, but the young man was bent so close to his ear that he couldn't have seen anything but hair and a portion of Christopher's cheekbone. "Then they took hot pokers . . . have you ever smelled that? Hot metal on flesh?"

Christopher's voice had dropped a register and Wynter tried to bury her head in her arms, so that she wouldn't hear the rest. But it was impossible to do so and still keep hold of Jusef's legs, so she heard Christopher say, "Well, anyway, they took those pokers, and they made certain that the poor miserable bastard would never shit again. You get my meaning?"

Jusef let out a hoarse yell of terror, and Christopher's voice dropped blessedly low so that Wynter was spared any further additions to her awful library of horrors. All she heard after that was Christopher's indecipherable murmuring and Jusef's strangled moans of fear.

She turned her head away and pressed her wet cheek against the man's trembling legs. A movement downhill caught her eye, and she started in panic at how close the soldiers were. They were nearly upon them and, oh God! Jonathon was with them!

"They're coming!" she screeched, "They're coming! Don't let them get him! Don't!"

Jusef screamed in panic.

"Tell me!" shouted Razi, his blade still pressed to Jusef's straining neck. "It's your last chance!"

"His Highness, the Royal Prince Alberon! It was Prince Alberon! He sent the word, my Lord! He sent the word that I kill you."

Razi snatched the knife away from the man's neck and sat back, horrified.

"Razi," hissed Christopher, his eyes on the huge body of men approaching through the trees. "Razi!"

But Razi was staring at Jusef, the knife dangling uselessly, his eyes wide with shock.

"Razi! Razi!" Wynter begged, her mind full of that chair, those flames, and the terrible images that Christopher had painted. "Don't let them! Don't let them!"

"Please, my Lord," whispered Jusef, tears running down his face. But it was too late. The King was already striding towards them, his face hard, his squad of guards on his heels.

"Good Frith," moaned Christopher. He whipped the knife from Razi's hand and, in full sight of the King and all his men, ended Jusef's life.

Wynter wailed. "NO! Christopher! NO!"

Razi leapt up, his face appalled and took two horrified steps back. "Oh God! Drop the knife!" he cried. "Chris! Drop the knife! They'll kill you!"

Christopher, looking stricken and terrified, dropped the knife to the ground. He rose to his knees, his hands up, palms out.

"He's unarmed!" Wynter called out, turning to face the advancing men. "He was protecting my Lord Razi!"

The King stormed across the small space between them, and Razi spun to intercept him. Jonathon's face was wicked with anger, and when Razi stepped between him and the still kneeling Christopher, Jonathon backhanded his son without any warning. It was a massive bear-like swat to the head: Jonathon was a huge man, as tall as Razi and broader. The powerful blow sent Razi spinning to the ground. He rolled a short distance down the steep slope and smacked against a tree, curling around his wounded shoulder with an agonised cry, even as he was trying to gain his feet.

Wynter yelled and leapt towards him, but one of the guards latched onto her arm and dragged her back. She struggled and he shook her so hard that her eyes vibrated in her head. Her teeth clicked together onto her tongue, filling her mouth with the bright copper taste of blood.

Jonathon strode past her, intent on getting to

Christopher Garron. Wynter fought the guard, straining to keep the young man in her sight. He was gazing up at the King who now loomed over him. Then Wynter saw the awful truth dawning in Christopher's eyes, and she stopped struggling. Christopher looked into the King's face, dropped his hands and accepted that he was about to die.

"Your Majesty . . ." he whispered, but got no further. Jonathon grabbed him with a roar, lifted him from the ground and swung him, head first, into the nearest tree.

Razi howled as he scrambled his way towards them, and Wynter resumed her frantic struggle against the guard.

"Christopher!" she screamed, "Christopher, no!"

Christopher's head rebounded off the trunk with a resounding *crack*. Incredibly, he didn't go down. Instead, he staggered backwards a few steps, his mouth open, his eyes dazed and then stood there, swaying drunkenly but not falling. A thin line of blood dribbled down his forehead and ran into his eye.

One of the guards eyed him with sneering amusement. He jabbed him with his finger, and Christopher staggered sideways a step or two without seeming to notice.

"Leave him *be*!" bellowed Razi, pushing his way through the ring of soldiers. "And let her *go*!" he snarled, slapping the guard's hands away from Wynter. She stumbled from his grip, rubbing the top of her arms, her eyes glued to Christopher.

Razi shoved the men aside in an attempt to get to his friend. But before he could reach him, Jonathon took the young man by the hair and slammed his head against the tree once more. This time, Christopher did fall, sliding smoothly to the ground with a moan, his eyes still open. Blood welled slowly from his nose.

Razi launched himself in a two-fisted blow at the King, punching him soundly in the chest. Jonathon staggered sideways and looked at Razi in genuine surprise, as if he'd just dropped from the sky.

The chief guard stepped between father and son, his fist raised, but Jonathon stayed him with a gesture. He looked Razi up and down with puzzled disdain and said, "What are you *doing*, boy?"

"He's my *friend!*" screamed Razi. "He was protecting me!"

Jonathon's face crimsoned with rage, and he grabbed Razi by the collar suddenly, and shook him until Razi gagged. "Your *friend? Your friend?* You're not a commoner, boy! You have no friends! You have subjects! He's your *subject!*"

Wynter put her hand to her mouth, not knowing what to do. She was like a child among giants, and she couldn't take her eyes from Christopher who was just visible behind the shifting screen of the guard's legs. He was lifting and dropping his right hand in a slow ineffectual movement, his unfocused eyes roving the dappled canopy above him.

"He was *protecting* me!" Razi's voice cracked with desperation, and Jonathon released him with a small push, causing him to stumble backwards.

"He cheated us," the King said, his voice dangerously low. "He killed a man we wanted taken alive, and he robbed the throne of its informant. He'll be taken to the keep, Razi, and we'll see how many more fingers he will lose before I feel repaid."

Razi cried out in despair, and this time three of the

King's guards grabbed him before he could fly at Jonathon's throat. Wynter sobbed loudly, then immediately pressed her lips shut, wishing herself invisible, when Jonathon turned his baleful glare on her. She saw him assessing her, and like beads clicking on an abacus, she saw plans and options and schemes form and shift and take shape in his eyes as he puzzled out her place in all this.

"What are you doing here, Protector Lady? Do the Moorehawkes thwart me too?"

Razi groaned and closed his eyes in desperate frustration. "Oh leave them *be*, Father! I beg of you!"

The King roared at him, making Wynter jump. Jonathon raised his fist to his son, but caught himself at the last moment and just shook it in Razi's now furiously defiant face. "Stop talking like *a peasant*! You do *not* beg! You *never* beg! You are the *heir apparent*!"

"I think the sun is in the King's eyes," growled Razi, spit flecking his lips, his teeth bared as he surged against the restraining guards, putting his face up to his father's. "His Majesty mistakes me for my *brother*!"

Father and son faced up to each other for a moment, like territorial wolves. Then gradually Jonathon's expression changed into something darker than rage. He looked at Razi in a new manner: an up and down, speculative manner. Wynter didn't like this new expression. It was remote and calculating, all Jonathon's fury fading in exchange for a carefully scheming assessment of his still furious son.

On the ground, by the tree, Christopher murmured something in Merron and rolled onto his side. The King glanced at him and gestured to his guards.

"Take him," he said casually. "Feed him to The Chair. Let the remaining inquisitors winkle him out."

Wynter screamed in panic and tried to push her way to Razi, but he didn't react. He had gone very wary and still, and was watching his father, his chest rising and falling in rapid, shallow breaths.

Two soldiers dragged Christopher up by his arms, and he hung between them, limp as a rag. He mumbled again in Merron: "*Is mise . . . fear saor.*" He tried to raise his head but couldn't, and his face was hidden in a tangled, bloodied net of hair.

Jonathon turned his head slowly back to Razi, and met his eye. Wynter saw the sly triumph in the King's face, and her heart skipped a beat.

"Well, boy?" asked the King.

"I will not wear the purple," said Razi, very quietly.

"Yes, you will," said the King. "You will sit without protest. You will eat at each remove. And you *will* wear the purple."

Razi shook his head slowly, in sorrow and despair. "I will not wear the purple," he whispered, his eyes glittering.

Christopher was making a real effort to move now. He managed to hold his head up for a few moments at a time, and kept trying to bring his feet under him. He tugged vaguely against the guards' grip.

"Girly?" he slurred, and Wynter's eyes overflowed with tears when she realised that he was calling for her.

"I'm here, Christopher," she said. "I'm all right!"

He raised his head slightly and peered through his curtain of hair, seeing nothing. "Raz . . ." His head dropped forward again, and he moaned.

"Take him," Jonathon ordered, gesturing without taking his eyes from Razi's face.

The guards heaved Christopher upright. "You're off to the keep, my lad!" one of them sneered into his ear. Christopher's eyes rolled open, and Wynter knew that on some level he understood what that meant. The guard realised this too, and grinned in delight. He whispered savagely in his ear again. "They're going to put you in The Chair!"

Christopher released a hoarse, terrified scream and began to thrash weakly against the big men. They laughed and started to drag him backward down the hill.

"No!" moaned Wynter. "Razi! No!"

But Razi was staring at his father, who was showing his teeth in a merciless, triumphant grin.

"You will attend the banquet tonight, and every night," said Jonathon smoothly.

Razi dropped his head.

"You will eat at every remove."

Razi shut his eyes.

"You will don the purple robe of heir."

Razi whispered, "Yes."

Christopher's cries were fading into the distance and Wynter's sobbing was harsh in the silence. Jonathon rubbed his hands. "Good! The Hadrish will stay in the keep tonight. You stay true to your word, and he will be released unharmed tomorrow."

"At least tell him he won't go to The Chair," Razi pleaded, raising his eyes to glare hopelessly at the King. "At least do that."

But Jonathon just smiled, and Wynter knew he would

do no such thing. He patted Razi's shoulder suddenly, with a tenderness that was obscene under the circumstances. Razi's lips trembled and his eyelids fluttered in suppressed rage.

"You will learn, son, that friends are a luxury that no king can afford. Your only duty, your *only* concern must be the welfare of state. Everything, *everything*, comes second to that. Including yourself."

Razi shrugged off his father's hand and turned away. Jonathon shifted his attention to Wynter, who was staring after Christopher, her hands pressed to her mouth, tears tolling down her face.

"Protector Lady Moorehawke," he said, his voice harsh. "Get back to work, and do *not* interfere again." Wynter raised her eyes to him, frozen to the spot. He didn't wait for her to respond, just motioned to his guards as he turned to go. "Take his Highness Prince Razi to his chambers. He is tired and wishes to rest until dinner. He will not want to leave his rooms. Have Jusef Marcos's widow and father arrested and taken to the keep."

And he strode off down the hill, leaving Wynter and Razi together in a ring of black-clad, stone-faced men, a body at their feet, their friend's screams still hanging in the air.

Carpenter and King

Lorcan must have heard Wynter crying as she raced her way down the path and up the steps, because he was already coming out of the library door when she ran into the tiled corridor. He barrelled straight out into the hall, staring around him in alarm, and came to an abrupt halt at the sight of her. Wynter flung herself into his arms, jabbering incoherently, her face a mess of tears. She was so uncharacteristically distraught, so unusually out of control that he just clutched her to him, his heart beating wildly against her ear. He dragged her into the library and kicked the door shut behind them, and, much as she tried, she couldn't stop screaming and moaning, tears and snot spreading liberally across the front of his shirt.

She should stop now. She knew that. She kept waiting for her father to push her away, to shake her, to shout at her, *get yourself together!*

But Lorcan just kept holding her against his chest, rocking her and stroking the back of her hair. He was crooning as if she were a baby. "It's all right, darling. It's all right, baby-girl. Shhhhhh . . ."

Eventually, the wild storm drained out of her, and Wynter was left beached on its shore. She sagged, clutching her father's shirt in both hands. Her knees were weak, her eyes burning. There were sobs and hiccups still, but she was regaining control.

Lorcan continued to hug her close. "There we go," he said, "That's my girl." She closed her eyes for a moment and floated on the strength and comfort that he still managed to give her, that he would always manage to give her, until the day he died.

"Oh Dad!" she said suddenly and buried her face in his chest. She began to weep quietly, in a completely different way to only moments before. A heartbroken, hopeless way, that was all about loss.

"Oh, baby-girl," he said gently, frightened now. "Come on, darling. Tell me what's wrong? Tell me what happened?"

And she did. As she spoke, Lorcan drew away from her slightly, holding both her hands in his, looking down at her with growing despair. When she got to the part about Jonathon arresting Christopher and forcing Razi to don the purple, Lorcan released a little moan of grief and shook his head. Turning away, he shuffled over to the wall where he had been working. He leant against the defaced picture panel, his head down, his forehead pressed to the wood. Then he sank slowly to the floor and lay down, his head back, his right arm over his eyes.

"Dad?" she whispered, her own grief forgotten.

She slid to the floor and scooted over to sit beside him, taking his hand in hers.

"Dad. Please don't leave me."

A tear slid slowly from the corner of Lorcan's eye and he

hitched a little breath. "I'll do my best, baby-girl." And he squeezed her hand before going very still for a long time.

Wynter sat for about two-eighths of a quarter, twenty or thirty minutes, holding his hand and listening to his breathing. This had happened several times since Lorcan's illness began, where he had just sunk to the ground and faded into sleep, usually after a long period of intense concentration, or late nights working, or stress. It was very different from those other gasping, sweating attacks, which were so full of struggle and desperation. Wynter was never sure which of these two she hated more.

He had been so very strained these past few days, after such a long period of hard travel, and the last two attacks had been so bad, and so close together . . .

She wished that Razi were here, with his knowledge and his calm authority. Even Christopher, padding about in the background with his quiet competence, setting things straight, being supportive. Thinking of the two men only made her worry how they might be now, especially poor Christopher. She had seen a head injury like Christopher's before, when a groom was thrown against a fence at Jonathon's tilt-yard. The poor man had been plagued by fits for the rest of his days. The thought of Christopher, that graceful, self-assured tomcat, in the grip of one of those foaming attacks was appalling, and Wynter pressed it down with all her might.

After a while, she heard the tramping of a large body of guards coming up the granite steps and advancing along the tiled corridor, but she didn't move. Even when the sounds stopped right outside the library door, she remained seated. She didn't intend disturbing Lorcan for anyone.

The door opened a little and Jonathon slipped inside, leaving his guards in the hall. He shut the door quietly behind him and came to a stop at the sight of Lorcan lying on the floor, his daughter hunched and scowling beside him.

"Is this how the Moorehawkes fulfil their duty to me?" he asked, but his voice was soft. "By sleeping?"

"Your Majesty has but to glance around this room to see how hard my father has toiled in your name." Jonathon's eyes slid a little to the right, but he did not really look around him. Instead, he stepped closer and peered down at her father with what Wynter was amazed to see was tenderness. Infinitely more tenderness than he had shown his own son less than an hour previously. She stifled her surprise and took advantage of the King's momentary openness while she had the chance.

"The Protector Lord is ill, your Majesty. I beg you please, allow my Lord Razi to attend him?"

Jonathon's eyes flickered and he spoke dismissively as he moved to get a better view of his old friend's half-obscured face. "He is your Royal Highness, the Prince Razi, Protector Lady Moorehawke. Do not misspeak again. And he is not a doctor; he is the heir apparent to the throne. The palace already has a doctor."

"Razi says he is a quacksalver!" Wynter exclaimed, her temper rising. The King levelled an opaque look at her and she swallowed her insubordination like bile. "Please, your Majesty," she said, courtly and low. "Will you not allow his Highness to attend the Protector Lord? Or if not his Highness, can you not find the good doctor St James, who was here before?"

"St James is dead, child. He died bringing Razi to the Moroccos. I will get Doctor Mercury to . . ."

"What are you doing, Jonathon?"

Lorcan's dry whisper shocked them both.

Wynter leant over her father. "Dad?"

Lorcan squeezed her hand, took his arm from his face and let it fall across his chest. He turned his eyes to Jonathon. He looked exhausted, and he barely moved his lips when he asked again, "What are you doing?"

Jonathon remained silent, but Wynter was completely thrown by his reaction to Lorcan. This was a man who, only today, had backhanded his wounded son down a hill, who had tried to crack Christopher Garron's head open against a tree and who was methodically erasing his most beloved heir from history. She found herself staring at him in astonishment as he looked down on her ailing father. He was examining Lorcan with the most heartbroken tenderness and regret. And more, a kind of shuffling guilt had crept into his demeanour, as though, in the face of his friend's distress, he could no longer keep his courtly mask from slipping. Wynter had never thought of the King like that before, as having to don The Mask. But looking at him now she realised that, of course, of all people he would have most to hide.

"Lorcan," he said, crouching down beside his friend. "Allow me to appoint another in your place. There is no need . . ."

Wynter's father's voice remained a rasping whisper, but his green eyes spat fire and his hand clenched tightly on Wynter's when he said, "You think I would let anyone else do this, Jonathon? You think I could possibly stand by and allow someone else to undo my work? *This* work?"

"What do you mean?" cried Wynter, dropping her father's hand. "Did you *offer to* do this, Dad? Are you . . .?"

Lorcan smiled tiredly, but the King glared at Wynter with what looked like confusion and hurt. Wynter wanted to shout at him, *who do you think you are? To look like that after all you've done?*

"What did you think, child?" Jonathon asked, "Did you think that I would *make* your father desecrate his own art?" Then he was suddenly angry. His face darkened and he flung an arm about in an expansive, grandiose circle. It was a movement more fitting to an auditorium than to crouching on the floor with a prostrate carpenter and his apprentice, and Wynter thought the King was like a spoiled child denying that he'd broken a vase. "Do you see Salvador Minare here?" he continued, "Burning his own manuscripts? Do you see Gunther Van Noos hurling his paintings on the fire? What kind of a man do you think I am? That you would accuse me of *making* an artist destroy his own work?"

The kind of man who hurls his son downhill and tries to expose a good man's brains to the light, Wynter thought, narrowing her eyes. Her expression must have been transparent as glass because Jonathon faltered and dropped his eyes, all his anger gone.

"You always were wicked quick to lose your temper, Jonathon Kingsson," said Lorcan, his amused hiss breaking the tension.

The King groaned and passed his hand over his eyes. Then he amazed Wynter by dropping down into the sawdust to sit with his back to the wall by Lorcan's head. He looked down into Lorcan's face and put his hand on his old friend's chest. Lorcan glanced up at him briefly. Jonathon sighed and laid his head against the wall, looking up at the sky through the library window.

"And you were always very quick to give your opinions, Lorcan Moorehawke. I should have shot you years ago."

Lorcan chuckled. "There's time yet."

They sat in silence for a moment, then Lorcan asked tiredly, "Will you kill the Hadrish?"

Wynter's heart squeezed and her eyes widened in shock at the casual way he asked it. He could have been asking, *will you attend the game?* or, *will you buy that horse?* for all the emotion he had just put into the question.

"I won't have to," Jonathon said tonelessly. "Razi is bright enough to get rid of him first. Besides, he's rather more useful alive . . . for the moment."

"He is Razi's *friend*!" exclaimed Wynter, dismayed at her father's disinterest in Christopher's fate. "He's a *good* man! He is loyal!" She didn't add the dangerously sentimental, *he makes Razi laugh! He makes Razi happy!*

The two men turned their heads to look at her, blue eyes and green eyes equally appraising of her. She felt tiny and stupid under their combined scrutiny.

"He's too dangerous," said the King dismissively. "He's unsuitable."

"There was a time," rasped Lorcan, "that people said the same about me."

The King grinned. "Ah, Lorcan, you are different."

"I know my place," Lorcan murmured, without a trace of bitterness.

"Aye," whispered the King, patting his friend's chest. "We *both* know your place. Razi doesn't understand things like that yet."

The men subsided into silence again.

Who are these men? thought Wynter. *I don't know them at all.* This was not her circumspect, courtly father, and this certainly wasn't the remote and demanding King. These men, she realised with a start, truly were *friends*.

"What ails you, brother?" It took Jonathon a while to ask it, and he did so reluctantly, as if by asking he might push Lorcan irretrievably over the edge of some precipice.

"My heart is failing me," Lorcan answered simply.

Jonathon closed his fingers slowly on her father's chest, gathering a bunch of Lorcan's shirt in his loose fist. "I will get Razi to attend you," he said quietly.

Oh, thank you! Thank you! thought Wynter, tears springing to her eyes.

Lorcan didn't move, but Wynter saw his eyes gleaming under the shadow of his arm. He blinked a few times in the silence, and then he rasped, "You know I love that boy." Jonathon tilted his head and tightened his jaw as if to say, *Don't! Please!* But Lorcan went on. "He was always a most excellent child, and now a great man. But he is no king, Jonathon. You haven't bred him for it. He is, and always will be, a doctor."

Jonathon growled but Lorcan continued, his tone grating, "For Godssake, man," he said, "it's what you've wanted for him since the day he was born, it's what he's trained for since he was eight years old. He has a God-given talent for it. He is a blessing to the world, Jonathon. What are you doing, that you would destroy him like this?"

Jonathon was quiet for a long time, and Wynter held her breath, trying to remain invisible.

"They will never accept him, Jon." Lorcan covered the

King's hand with his. "It doesn't matter what you do. Despite all his worth, despite all his talents, regardless of all the magnificent things Razi brings to this world, the people will only ever see him as your brown bastard." Jonathon winced at that, and Wynter recoiled at her father's unflinching bluntness. "And they will kill him, Jonathon. They will kill him rather than let him take the throne." Lorcan let his hand drop back to the floor. "You know that." That last was a whisper so soft as to be a sigh.

Jonathon breathed in deeply. Cleared his throat. "I have no choice," he said. "He's all I have left." His jaw muscles tightened and he turned his head to look down at his friend as though preparing for an argument. Lorcan didn't respond.

"Dad?" Wynter whispered.

"Lorcan!" Jonathon gripped the front of his friend's shirt and shook hard.

Lorcan gasped, startled and took his arm down from his eyes, staring blearily, "What?"

Jonathon and Wynter both released terrified, relieved laughs.

Lorcan frowned up at them, confused. He sighed and closed his eyes. "I can't do any more today, Jon."

"It *must* be done," Jonathon said, his voice hard. "If you cannot finish in time, then I *must* retain some help. I can't afford to wait. A team of woodworkers could get this whole room done in a few days. I'm delaying just to please you, Moorehawke! It's ridiculous!"

Wynter's hands knotted, but her father just nodded. "I know. I know. Just give me today. That's all I need."

Jonathon seemed to collect himself at that. He looked

away, and said quietly. "I will get my men to carry you to your chambers."

Lorcan's eyes flew open. "No you will *not*," he snarled. "I will *not* be paraded through the corridors like some fool in a tumbrel." He reached his hand up to Wynter and attempted to rise.

Jonathon rolled his eyes to heaven and pressed his hand down on her father's chest, pinning him to the ground. "Oh, stay easy, you bloody fool." He got to his feet and went to the door.

The King murmured to his men for a moment, and Wynter steeled herself for the awful moment when they would come in and force her father to submit to this humiliation. Then Jonathon shut the door and stood listening to the corridor, his hand up to silence them.

What was going on? Lorcan tilted his head at Wynter, and she shoved her shoulder under his and pushed. He got his legs under him, and between the two of them they got him halfway to his feet before Jonathon turned and saw them. He released a pretty spectacular oath and crossed quickly to catch Lorcan under his other arm and lift him the rest of the way.

At a knock on the door Jonathon pulled Lorcan's arm over his shoulder and wrapped his own arm around his friend's back. He glanced down at Wynter and nodded at her.

"Now," said the King, "my men have cleared the hall outside, and they'll clear each corridor as we go along, all the way from here to your rooms. No one will see you. Does that suit you, you stubborn rock-head? Or are you too bloody good to have the King help you walk?"

"Shut. Up," hissed Lorcan and leant forward to get the three of them going. Wynter and the King jerked into motion and, between them, they made it through the empty corridors with no one to witness his Majesty the King acting as a crutch to a lowly carpenter.

Leverage

Lorcan sat down on the edge of his bed, trying to regulate his breathing. After a moment's uncertainty, the King mumbled something about getting Razi, and fled. Wynter shut the hall door behind him, blocking out the curious faces of the guards. She leant against the wood for a moment, her eyes shut, her head spinning. Then she went back to her father.

Lorcan was trying to undo the buttons on his shirt and failing. Wynter brushed his hands away and took over. He let her for a moment, sitting quietly as she undid four or five of the fiddly little bone buttons. Then he shook himself and abruptly knocked her hands away. He pushed her from him, his cheeks flaming.

"Dad!" she protested. "Don't be stupid!"

"I'm not a bloody cripple!" he said harshly. "And I won't make you my nursemaid!"

"Have some sense!" she cried. "Who will help you if I don't? Let me undo your shirt!"

"No!" He pushed her away and then dragged the shirt

over his head with a ping and scatter of many buttons. Wynter flung her hands out in frustration.

"Oh great! That's just great! You're a stubborn *wretch*, Dad! You need a toe up your backside!"

Lorcan didn't respond. He let the shirt slip from his fingers and sank down onto the bed.

Wynter realised, with a pang of sympathy, that Lorcan hadn't the strength to lift his legs onto the bed. She lifted them up and over for him, and he rolled onto his back.

She reached to take off his boots, but he pulled his legs out of her grasp and moved them away.

"Jonathon will do it," he sighed and then shifted slightly and gritted his teeth against another stab of pain. She stood uselessly watching him for a moment and then began to creep quietly to the door.

Lorcan's breathing became abruptly deep and unnatural, and Wynter bit her lips and fled out into the receiving room, intending on running into Razi's suite and dragging him in by his hair.

But he was already on his way down the corridor when she ran out her door, his bag in his hand, his father on his heels. Razi nodded curtly to her under the glare of the guards, but his eyes were soft and reassuring. He put his hand on her shoulder when he came level with her, turned her smartly on her heel and guided her back into her chambers. The King followed, and shut the hall door behind them.

"Come on, sis," Razi said, and he marched her into her father's room and shut the door in the King's anxious face.

Razi pulled off Lorcan's boots and handed them to her, then she turned her back and fidgeted in the corner as Razi stripped Lorcan of the rest of his clothes and examined him. Finally she heard him pull the sheet up and Razi murmured that she could turn around now if she wished.

She was amazed to see that Lorcan was awake, lying on his side and watching heavy-eyed as Razi mixed a tincture in a beaker of water. Razi glanced down at him as he was putting some vials back into his bag, and seemed surprised to find Lorcan's green eyes open and aware. He finished what he was doing and then knelt down by the bed, his face level with her father's.

"Well," he said gently. "You haven't been resting at all, have you?"

Lorcan just smiled. Razi shook his head and patted the big man's shoulder. "I have mixed you a draught. It's much stronger than the last; it will force your body to take the rest it needs and you—"

"No . . ." Lorcan's fierce response caused Razi's lips to tighten and the young man to sit back.

"Lorcan—" he began sternly.

"No, my Lord! I cannot take your draught. And Razi . . . I am so sorry . . ." There was such heartfelt sincerity in this simple apology that Razi stared at him, his eyes growing huge in anticipation of something terrible.

"For what, good friend?"

"Tonight. The banquet. I must attend . . ."

Razi looked as though he had been hit. Wynter stepped from the shadows, appalled. She was about to say, *you can't! You haven't the strength!* And then the full import of what her father was saying struck her. Her father meant that he must show his support, his public support, for the King and his terrible decision to put Razi on the throne.

"Please, my Lord," Lorcan's words came out in a dry,

urgent rasp and he moved his hand slightly as if trying to reach for Razi. "I beg of you, I *beg* of you. Forgive me?"

Razi shut his eyes. Wynter thought he was going to turn away from her father. She could tell that Lorcan thought so too.

"I know . . ." began Razi, his head down, "that you are my good friend, Lorcan. You have always been a most . . ." His voice failed him, and he put his hand on her father's suddenly and squeezed hard. When Razi opened his eyes, they were glittering. "He has us both, dear friend. Does he not?"

Lorcan glanced quickly at Wynter and then back to Razi. Razi turned to look at her. She shook her head. *No,* she thought. *No. Do not lay this at my feet! I can make my own way! I don't need you to betray Alberon for me! Don't blame me!*

"I too have been forced to make a similar bargain today," Razi said, looking Wynter up and down, but not really seeing her.

"Your friend," whispered Lorcan. "How fares he?"

Razi's eyes were huge and threatening to overflow. Then he tilted his head up and took a savage breath through his nose, gritting his teeth until he regained some composure.

"Christopher is in the keep." He patted Lorcan's hand, then pulled away. "I have not seen him since my father tried to murder him by pounding his head against a tree." He stood up and began to busy himself with his instruments.

"Jonathon will not kill him," said Lorcan. "Not if you do what—"

Razi flung a vial into his bag with sudden vicious force

and slammed his hands onto the table. "If he touches him again! If he so much as—"

"Shhhhh," hissed Lorcan.

Razi glared at him. "Shhhhh," said Lorcan again, softer this time and Razi relented, nodding.

"My father cannot bear up to another feast, Razi," Wynter said quietly.

Neither man looked at her. Instead they locked eyes – green to brown – both knowing what was at stake. Both knowing that she was right.

"Give me a moment," said Razi suddenly. He strode quickly past Wynter, opening the door as though he expected his father to be lurking at the keyhole. But the King was sitting on the other side of the retiring room. He stood up expectantly, and Razi shut the door behind him as he stepped into the other room, leaving Wynter burning to know what was going on.

She glanced at her father, ashamed to eavesdrop in his presence, but to her surprise, he shifted his hand in a shooing gesture, urging her forward. She hurried to press her ear against the door, straining to hear the conversation in the next room.

Jonathon was exclaiming in exasperation, "We are *all* tired, boy!"

"No, Father! Not *tired*! Not bloody *tired*! Why aren't you listening? The poor man is *exhausted*! He has nothing *left*! Can't you understand? He has barely the strength left to keep his heart beating. He . . ."

"I *cannot* cancel the banquet. The arrangements . . ."

"What are they saying?" murmured Lorcan from the bed, and Wynter relayed the conversation in whispers.

"I need Lorcan by my side, boy!" The King was pacing, and Wynter could hear his voice, louder then quieter, as he passed to and fro. "I need him in public. I need him to be seen. The people love him. If they are convinced he supports me . . ."

"If you make that poor man take to the hall tonight, looking like he does now, everyone will be convinced that you have beaten him into submission, or poisoned him. He is *not fit*. He will shame himself and turn the people against you."

Wynter reported all this faithfully, though she stumbled on the words *shame himself* and glanced over at her father. Lorcan just listened quietly, his arm back over his eyes. What she could see of his face was expressionless.

There was a long moment of silence and Wynter realised that Razi might finally have found an argument that made sense to the King.

"Father," asked Razi cautiously. "Why are you doing this?" He spoke very quietly, Wynter could imagine him skirting warily around the King, who she envisioned hunched and snarling like a great beast, smoke dribbling from his nostrils. She held her breath.

"What are they saying?" murmured her father again and she opened her mouth to tell him, but Razi had resumed speaking and she pressed her ear to the door once more.

"What is worth this? The gibbets. The repression. *Inquisitors*, for Godsake? You were never a brutal man, Father . . . now it seems you will sacrifice anything, anyone . . . and no one knows why . . ."

Wynter related all this in a rapid whisper, then paused as Razi waited for his answer.

Lorcan shifted his arm slightly, his eyes gleaming slits. "Has he replied?" he asked quietly.

Wynter shook her head. The other room was silent. Then Razi spoke again. "Where is my brother? Where is Alberon?" There was still no reply from the King and Razi pressed on, his voice hard. "What is The Bloody Machine?"

"He has asked the King, 'What is The Bloody Machine?'"

At her words, Lorcan let out a tremendous howl of shock and despair, startling Wynter and making her spin around to stare at him, her back pressed to the door. At the same time Jonathon released a similar roar of horror from the next room.

"NO!" cried Lorcan, clutching the sheets in big gouging fistfuls and goggling at Wynter with terrified eyes. "NO!" He hoisted himself onto his elbow, his face scarlet, utterly distraught. "Get him in here!" he shouted, "Get him here now!"

"Who?" Wynter asked, confused.

"The King! The bloody King!"

When Wynter flung open the door Razi and Jonathon were on opposite sides of the room, both of them shocked and staring at each other, the King wild-eyed and devastated. "Majesty . . ." she began but her father roared from behind her, his voice filled with rage.

"Jonathon! Get in here, goddamn you! Come *here*!" He was gripping the mattress in a furious effort to keep himself up, and the sight of him had Razi exclaiming in horror and striding towards him. But Lorcan waved him aside and glared past him to the King, who was stepping warily forward, his face pale, his eyes hollow.

"You! You . . ." Words failed Lorcan and he ground his teeth in anger. The King just kept staring at him, his face unreadable.

"Dad," whispered Wynter, but she and Razi had been washed aside, left stranded by this far darker, older storm. Razi reached for her, and she took his hand.

"You promised me!" Lorcan growled, spitting fire. Jonathon tilted his head away as if to avoid some of the sparks. Then Lorcan's sudden burst of energy deserted him, and he sank abruptly to his side, his lips white. "*You promised!*"

Jonathon stepped towards the bed and stared down at his friend. Lorcan was the very image now of an angry corpse. His eyes glittering with rage, he glared up at the King. Then Wynter saw realisation dawning slowly in his white face.

"Jesu, Jonathon! You *always* intended to, didn't you? *That's* why you sent me away! It wasn't to negotiate with the Northlanders! It wasn't to play hostage of faith to that cur Shirken! It was so I wouldn't be in your way . . . It was . . . aaggh!" He lifted his fists to his face and keened inarticulately with fury. "And you dragged Alberon into it! Your lovely shining boy! And Oliver! *Oliver!* Oh. You bastard! Oh, Jonathon, you bastard!"

"You *built* it," hissed Jonathon accusingly. His fists were balled up, his shoulders hunched and he loomed over the recumbent man like a cliff about to fall. "You built it, you poxy hypocrite. Don't . . ."

"I was *seventeen!*" howled Lorcan. "And you *promised!* After the first time, you took an oath . . .!"

"Things got desperate here, Lorcan, you've no idea."

Lorcan snarled up at the King, "*Nothing* could be *that* desperate!" Lorcan's cheeks were wet with tears. Wynter had never seen her father cry like this before. She squeezed Razi's hand so hard that she felt his bones move under the skin. She felt like they were witnessing some form of combat. Some quick, murderous battle in which the King and Lorcan tore strips from each other's armour, exposing an unexpected depth of darkness beneath.

Suddenly Lorcan shifted his gaze to where she and Razi were standing pressed side by side at the foot of his bed, their eyes enormous, their faces those of frightened children.

"Get them out!" he hissed, "get them out!"

Jonathon turned to them then, his face aghast, as though he too had just realised they were still there. "Out!" he cried. "Out! Into the hall!"

Wynter felt Razi steel himself to stay. He kept her hand in his, but moved forward slightly, putting her behind him. He said nothing, but the King must have seen the defiance in his face because his lip curled and he clenched his jaw.

If he hits Razi again, thought Wynter, *Razi will hit back. He will really let fly. And the King won't know his own name for a week.*

She didn't think the King had any idea of the amount of raw strength Razi had hidden in his sinewy body.

"Get out!" Lorcan was waving his arms at them, "OUT!"

"Please, Razi." Wynter tugged her friend's hand, her eyes on her father's terrible colour, his desperate clutching at the sheets.

Razi followed her eyes, "Lorcan . . ." he said hopelessly

"GET OUT!" screamed the two men, and their children backed rapidly from the room. Jonathon pushed and bullied them out into the hall and slammed the door in their faces. After the briefest of moments they heard more shouting from Lorcan's suite as the two men tore into each other again.

The guards watched them from carefully neutral faces, their spear heads gleaming in the slanting night. Razi was staring at the door, his posture combative, his breathing rapid. He was wound up, ready to burst.

Wynter looked at the guards. Their blood was already high from the incident on the hill and the shouting from Lorcan's room had them on edge. She feared for the consequences to Razi should he start an argument with the King now. As it was, he could barely contain his rage, she could feel it trembling through his body like a river, raging deep underground. If he went head to head against the King there would be violence. And the way he was now, whatever he started he would damn well finish and that would be treason. He'd be hung, drawn and quartered without mercy or reprieve.

"Razi," she said quietly and tugged his hand.

Razi grunted and pulled his arm away, reaching for the door.

Suddenly the shouting stopped. They froze, their attention focused solely on what might be happening inside the now silent room. Razi's eyes widened, and Wynter suppressed a little whimper of fear as they listened in vain for some form of conversation. Razi lifted his hand to the door handle, but the door flew inwards before he could touch it, and Jonathon stood there, his face appalled.

"Help him," he said.

Razi rushed past him and Wynter followed.

"I've killed him, haven't I? He's dead!" The fear and regret in Jonathon's voice would have had Wynter gaping at him, had her father not taken up all her attention.

"Oh Razi! Razi! He's dead!"

"Shhh!" Razi held up his hand and they forced themselves to be very still. He bent over Lorcan, his face grim. Then he turned quickly, rummaged in his bag and drew out his little wooden trumpet and a small mirror.

"Son . . ." began Jonathon, but Razi rounded on him and snarled at him to *shut up*. The King stepped back, pressed his lips together and watched with tear-filled eyes while Razi held the little mirror to Lorcan's partially open lips.

Razi watched the mirror carefully, frowning. Then he put the trumpet to Lorcan's chest and listened. Wynter gripped the footboard and held her breath, concentrating hard, as though by being still enough and quiet enough, she too might hear what Razi strained to detect.

Lorcan was as still as stone. His eyelashes, his eyebrows, the fine, sleek beginnings of a beard on his unshaven cheeks, gleamed in the sun that streamed through his window. They gave a bright and fiery illusion of life to his motionless face. But his powerful chest lay unmoving. His big hands, heavy as marble carvings, rested on the white sheets.

Dad. Oh, Dad. Wake up.

Razi cast aside the listening device and bent over her father again, pressing his ear directly to the man's chest. His jaw twitched rhythmically as he ground his teeth. His expression was growing desperate.

Suddenly Razi reared up, lifted his fist over his head and brought it down in a fierce hammer blow to the centre of Lorcan's chest. Jonathon leapt and yelled in shock, but Razi completely ignored him as he bent and pressed his ear to Lorcan's chest again. Wynter sobbed as Razi's face drew down in tight frustration and despair. But once again he swung back and slammed his fist down hard onto Wynter's father's chest, yelling with the impact as if raging at Lorcan.

He pressed his ear to the big chest again, his face taut. Wynter and Jonathon held their breaths. Razi grunted and shifted position suddenly, putting his eye to Lorcan's lips. He stayed motionless for a moment, his face intense, and then Wynter saw his eyelids flutter, and a tiny smile lifted the corners of his mouth.

"Good fellow . . ." he whispered, and lay his forehead against her father's. His hand lifted slightly as Lorcan's chest rose in a shallow breath. Wynter lost sight of them then, because her eyes were blinded with tears. But she heard Razi murmur "good fellow" again. Then he began to shuffle his vials and potions about in a calm, methodical manner, and Wynter felt herself sink to the floor.

"Pick her up," she heard Razi say from far away, "bring her to her room and lie her on the bed, raise her feet on a pillow."

Distantly, as if in her sleep, Wynter felt the King lift her, carry her and gently lay her on her bed.

There were no dreams.

"Wynter."

She felt the weight of someone sitting beside her on her bed and knew at once that it was Razi. He stroked her hair and she opened her eyes. The light was dim, he'd lit a candle. She looked down; someone had taken off her boots and her belt, and covered her with a blanket.

"What happened?"

"You collapsed from exhaustion."

"I mean about my father, Razi. What happened to my father?"

"Lorcan is doing well, sis. His heart beats constant. He roused to consciousness a while ago, and Father and himself had a long, calm discussion. Then he agreed to take that draught. He should sleep until late tomorrow morning, and then we shall see how things are."

"Will he die?"

"He might." She closed her eyes. Razi stroked her hair. "But, in reality, Wynter, he's more worn out than anything else at the moment. If he does as I tell him, he might live a good long while yet. It just depends on his staying calm and resting."

"I'd better dye my dresses black then, because that's not going to happen.

It wasn't intended as a joke, but she sounded so forlorn and miserable that the two of them chuckled.

"What earthly time is it?" she asked, raising herself on her elbow and looking around.

Razi just patted her shoulder. "I have to go, sis. Will you come sit with him? I've ordered food and hot water for you from the kitchens. They should be here soon."

She eyed him. He was dressed in his scarlet long-coat and black britches, his suede gloves in his right hand. *He's going to the banquet,* she thought with regret, *it wasn't cancelled after all. Poor Razi.*

"You're wearing the scarlet," she said significantly, hoping that the King had relented. Razi looked down at his clothes.

"Alberon's coats need to be adjusted for me," he said bitterly. Then he stood abruptly, dragging his gloves on with savage little jerks. "Apparently they have the purple robe waiting for me in the royal rooms. I need to go now. Take care."

"Razi!" She slid from the edge of the bed, appalled that he was actually striding from the room with such a curt farewell.

He looked around in surprise, then his face changed and he dashed back to her and pulled her into his arms. "Sorry," he whispered in her hair. "So sorry, sis. I'm all rage and fire at the moment. I'm not thinking clearly. I'm not angry at *you*, you know that?"

She rubbed his back as he hugged her, trying to ease the iron-tight tension in his shoulders. "Have you had news of Christopher?" she mumbled.

He pulled away, avoiding her eyes, adjusting his gloves again. "No news."

She hesitated, then laid her hand on his, stilling his agitated fretting. "Perhaps I could take to the passages tonight," she offered. "I could see if . . ."

"NO! No, Wynter. Promise me!" He grabbed her hand, his face and his voice stricken with panic and fear. "Promise!"

She grinned at him, a watery, weakling grin. "Mother hen!" she chided. She punched his arm and he tried desperately to smile at her.

"Promise," he said, shaking her gently.

"I promise."

"Good girl. Now, please don't leave your rooms." He gazed tenderly at her for a moment. "And don't worry about Lorcan. He'll be fine." He kissed her on the forehead. "I'll be back soon."

And then he was gone, slamming the hall door behind him. The sounds made by a large body of guards retreated after him down the corridor, silence following on their heels like a curse.

What Price to Pay

*R*azi did not return that night, though Wynter waited until well past the first quarter. Lorcan continued to sleep peacefully and deeply, oblivious to her faithful vigil. Eventually discomfort and bone-weariness sent Wynter shuffling to her bed, where she dozed on and off in restless unease.

She was just sinking into a true, deep sleep, her mind falling away, when her father frightened her by appearing at her door. He clung to the doorframe and peered in at her, his mouth moving wordlessly and she gaped at him, as if seeing him through gritty clouds of smoke.

Eventually she rose to the surface of her fatigue, and Lorcan and the room snapped into sharp focus. It was early morning, just before sunrise and Lorcan was saying, ". . . darling? Wynter? Can you hear me?"

His hands were gripping the doorframe so tightly that it looked as though his tendons were about to pop through his skin.

"Wynter. I have a job for you today, if you're up to it?"

She answered him dryly, without a trace of humour.

"Get back into bed, you idiot. And I *might* come in and listen to your request. Otherwise, fall down where you are, and I'll step over you on my way to the privy."

Lorcan scowled at her and began to grope his way back to his room. "You're just like your mother!" he rasped as he disappeared around the corner.

She waited tensely as he laboured into his bedroom, then relaxed at the sound of him getting into bed.

"She must have been a blessed saint!" she called out, and pushed back the covers and prepared to wash and dress.

Beyond the window, shadows flickered across the fresh rose of the sky. Ravens again, but so many more this time. Jusef Marcos's body must have been added to the bloody remnants on the trophy spikes. She groaned in disgust and averted her eyes. There had been a time when robin-song and blackbirds woke her from her sleep. Now it was ravens, circling and cawing, their sharp feet scrabbling on the roof above her head.

What had their lives come to? That death greeted them from sunrise to sundown, and they had no choice but to run alongside it, and hope not to be caught in its net?

There was nothing edible remaining of the previous night's food, so she perched at the foot of Lorcan's bed in her work uniform, chewing on a stale crust of manchet, a beaker of water in her hand. Her father had refused anything to drink, and was huddled under his blankets, shivering despite the heat. He eyed her as she doggedly gnawed the hard bread.

"Go to Marni," he urged. "Get yourself something proper to eat."

She stopped chewing, and her hand dropped to her lap.

Go to Marni. Get yourself something to eat. How many hundreds of times in her life had her father said that to her? She hadn't heard it for years now, of course, but up until their exile it had been a regular, daily order. It had been the beginning of so many journeys to the kitchen. Journeys which she had first tottered on fat little legs. Then skipped, scabby-kneed and blithe. And finally raced with all the bubbling exuberance of youth. Journeys she had almost always travelled alone, but that had always been bookended by those two eternal stalwarts, her father and Marni. Comfort and strength at both ends of the trip, the knowledge of their presence always enough to carry her through the intimidating, sometimes dangerous, corridors of state.

How much longer do I have? she thought, looking at her father, *with you as my fortress and my friend?*

"Stop writing requiems in your head," he murmured, his lips curving upwards. It was an old joke of his, whenever she drifted off. But it was a bit close to the bone today, and he knew it as soon as he said it.

"Are you hungry, Dad?" she asked, as evenly as she could.

"Yes! I'm bloody clemmed!"

She laughed in delight and patted his foot. "How does scrambled eggs, manchet bread, and coffee sound?"

He made a ravenous noise, and she hopped off the bed and headed for the door. But a thought struck her as she was leaving, and she paused at the threshold. Perhaps this wasn't the right time, but last night's terrible fight was gnawing at her, and she had to ask.

"Dad," she said, "about that . . . about the . . ."

"*Don't!*" he said fiercely, his eyes huge and frightened. "Wynter, you can never mention that machine again. Do you understand? Not even in private, not even just between the two of us. As long as last night remains unmentioned, you will be safe. But Wyn, you need to understand . . . if it ever came to light that you know more than this, or that you seek to know more than this, Jonathon will kill you. And he'll kill Razi too." Lorcan held her eyes with his own and his voice dropped almost to a whisper, as though the walls, the bed or the ravens on the roof might overhear and report their conversation.

"He has already destroyed Oliver, and he is wiping Alberon from history. He has ruined everything he ever wanted for poor Razi. And he *loved them*, darling. He *still* loves them. But you are nothing to him. You understand? He would erase you, like that!" Her father clicked his fingers, his teeth bared. "And he would think nothing of your loss. So, please, do not give him cause. Do not let a mistake I made in my youth cost me the only life I hold dear."

She blinked, but didn't reply. He raised his head from the pillow.

"*Wynter*," he hissed, "*Please!*"

"What if the King is wrong? What if . . ."

"I don't care. He can't hurt you, I won't allow it." His voice was flat and filled with steel. "I don't *care* if he destroys the kingdom, Wyn. I don't care if he destroys *himself*, as long as he leaves you alone."

Wynter knew that wasn't true – both those things would break Lorcan's heart, but she knew what he meant. Unlike

Jonathon, Lorcan was not willing to sacrifice that which he loved for the sake of a kingdom, no matter how unique, how bright and shining that kingdom might be. Lorcan would always put Wynter first. She was the price he would never be willing to pay.

"All right, Dad," she said softly. "We'll never speak of it again." He relaxed his clenched fists and let his head drop back to the pillow. They smiled at each other. Then she scowled and jabbed a finger at him. "Stay in bed!" she ordered and headed out into the hall.

There were three Maids of the Bucket coming from Razi's room and another three waiting to enter, their heavy buckets steaming gently into the early slanting sun. Wynter frowned. It was very early for Razi to be filling a bath. The boiler men couldn't be too happy with him. He must have had them up at all hours, heating the water.

"Are we almost done?" whispered one of the waiting maids to the others as they exited Razi's suite, their empty buckets clonking hollowly against the yoke.

"Aye, thank Jesu. You lot'll be the last. Bloody ridiculous, a bath at this hour! Couldn't he have used the bathhouse like the rest of the court?"

The two of them noticed Wynter passing by, and ducked their heads in silence as she went on her way. *Razi would want to be careful*, she thought, *people will say he's grown tyrannical.* It was so unlike her friend to make unreasonable demands on the staff that she paused at the corner of the hall uncertainly, wondering if she should go check on him, but then she thought better of it and proceeded down the gallery towards the main stairs.

The kitchens were buzzing and Marni growled at Wynter, muttering about "folk too good to dine in the hall". But she made up a generous tray of breakfast for herself and Lorcan, and mixed a real heft of cream into the coffee jug.

"Off with you," Marni snapped and turned her attention to the barely contained pandemonium behind her.

The tray was heavy and Wynter walked slowly, carefully balancing it as she went. The palace was waking up, the corridors beginning to hum gently with the early morning traffic of pages and maids and fire-tenders and slops-carriers. Wynter made her way smoothly through the lot of them.

She was coming up from the back stairs and had just turned right into the lesser hall, when two maids ahead of her, their arms piled high with clean linen, paled and stopped in their tracks. As she passed them by, Wynter saw that they were gaping past her to the junction at the end of the hall. Whatever they saw horrified them, and as she watched, they backed slowly away and tried to disappear into the shadows of a deep alcove. Both of them were obviously distressed and one of them in particular welled up into tears which rolled fatly down her cheeks and spattered the neatly folded linens in her arms.

A vile and horribly familiar smell assailed Wynter's nostrils, and with it, all of yesterday's terrible events washed over her in a cold tidal wave of memory. She recalled, in a sudden trembling rush, the one thing that had slipped her mind this morning and her eyes filled with guilty tears. How? *How* could she have forgotten? She bit her lip and fought hard to keep her composure.

Down the hall, two of Jonathon's personal guard were walking slowly towards her. They were matching their pace to that of their prisoner, and it was clearly much too slow for them. Christopher Garron was stumbling along between them, and despite her best efforts, Wynter couldn't help but gasp at his wretched condition.

His hands were bound before him and secured to his waist with a shackle belt. His feet were restrained with a leather hobble and he was shuffling along with all the care of an extremely ancient man, as if every movement might cause pain. Both of his eyelids were grossly swollen and bruised, and he kept his head tilted back, stiff necked, his eyes slits against the light. He was breathing carefully through his partially opened mouth, his nose being completely clogged with dried blood. The entire lower half of his face was coated in rusty smears and his long hair was a tangled, ratty mess of blood from his scalp wound, debris and sweat. His clothes were filthy and spattered in dark stains.

As Christopher got closer, the smell became almost unbearable. Stale piss and damp, mouldering straw: the unmistakable reek of a dungeon cell. All prisoners smelled the same no matter where you went, but by any standards the stench off Christopher was appalling. They must have thrown him into the filthiest pit they'd had available. The two maids lifted their bundles of linens and buried their noses in the fabric.

He didn't see her as he shuffled past. Wynter thought that maybe he couldn't see much through those partially closed eyes. Even this dim light was obviously bothering him.

They turned him roughly at the bottom of the stairs to the middle gallery and he stumbled against the hobble as he tried to take the first step. The guards paid no heed to Christopher's stifled moan of pain at the jarring misstep. They just grabbed an elbow each and one of them said gruffly, "Step up." They waited till his groping foot found the step and then pulled him onto it with a rough jerk. He gasped, found his balance and groped forward with his foot for the next rise. "Step up," the guard instructed again and they repeated the movement all the way up the stairs

By the time they disappeared round the bend at the top of the steps, Wynter was shaking so badly that she had to lower the tray to the floor and kneel there for a moment, her hands clenched together in an effort to get herself under control. The two little maids remained in the alcove, staring at nothing, saying not a word. They were still there a good four or five minutes later when Wynter picked up the tray and continued on up to her suite.

She took the winding back stairs. She couldn't stand the thought of having to pass Christopher on the main stairs, or in the halls. She didn't want to see the way people would look at him, the mixture of triumph and pity that she knew would paint the many faces he'd have to endure on his way to Razi's room.

Why had they left the shackles on him? And why hadn't they brought him around in private? She groaned. Why was she even bothering to ask herself these questions? When she knew the one and only answer to them all. They had done this on Jonathon's orders, to humiliate

Christopher, to send a message to others and to put Razi firmly in his place.

By the time she got to her suite there wasn't an iota of expression on her face or the slightest trembling in her hands. Razi's suite was silent, Christopher's clothes lying in a foetid pile in the corridor outside the firmly closed door. Jonathon's soldiers were gone and the hall guards watched her blandly as she let herself into her rooms.

She went straight to her father's bedroom. He was asleep again and she set the tray down on his bedside table and went to leave.

"Where are you going, darling?"

She knelt down by his bed, bringing her face level with his. "I thought you had gone back to sleep."

He frowned and his eyelids fluttered and she saw him struggle to open them again. "Damn Razi and his bloody potions."

She chuckled. "He'll be very peeved. That was meant to keep you under until at least noon!"

Lorcan cleared his throat and went to sit up. She laid her hand on his shoulder. "Dad, they brought Christopher back. I want to go to see him, then I'll come have breakfast with you, all right?"

His eyes were suddenly clear and alert. "Did you see him? The Hadrish?"

Wynter's reaction shocked even herself. Her eyes filled with tears and overflowed, her lips began a stupid, girlish trembling, and she had to clench her hands together to disguise another bout of hectic shaking. She bit down hard on the inside of her cheek and nodded.

"Darling," murmured Lorcan. "You should stay away from that boy."

"I just want . . ."

"I know, but he's a dangerous boy to hang your hat on, baby-girl."

She straightened, shocked. "Dad! I'm not . . .!" She swiped furiously at her eyes and wiped her nose on her sleeve. "I don't have any *feelings* for him! It's just . . . he's Razi's friend. And he's a good man! I only . . ."

"It's all right to have *feelings,* darling. But you might want to pick someone less . . . that lad has no future here, you know that."

And do we? thought Wynter suddenly. *Do we have a future here?* Instead she said, "I'm only going to see if they need anything. I'll be back in a moment."

Lorcan grabbed her hand as she stood to go, "Wyn," he said, hunting for words. "He . . . the Hadrish. He's been through a bit, by the sounds of it. Sometimes, when a man has been through something bad, he . . . when he gets somewhere private and safe, he might react in a way that he may not want a woman to see."

He looked up at her, frustrated at his inability to explain to this suddenly adult version of his little girl how unmanned Christopher would feel at a display of weakness in front of her. And she looked down at him, shocked at his uncertainty, and thrown by the fact that he had just called her a woman.

"All right, Dad," she patted his hand awkwardly. "I'll be back in a minute."

"Wynter . . ."

She turned at the door, wary. "Yes?"

"You shouldn't let the guards see you. You should take the secret passage."

Her shocked surprise made him chuckle and he curled around himself a little in delight.

"Who told you?" she asked.

He chuckled again, a rusty version of his usual rolling laugh, and waved her on with a breathless gesture. "Who told me?" he wheezed. "Who told me! Hah . . . what a tonic! Who do you think *built* them, girl . . . oh . . . who told me, indeed!"

He was still chuckling away to himself when she turned the cherub sconce in the retiring room and slipped into the darkness of the secret passage.

"Razi?" she knocked at their wall and gave the panel a little push. To her surprise, it slid open and she hesitated, wary of walking in on top of them. She could hear low murmuring from the far bedroom, Christopher's bedroom. The air was sharp with a high, medicinal odour, which did nothing to mask the residual stench of the dungeon. The shutters were obviously drawn, and dim candlelight softened the gloom.

"Razi!" she called, a little louder this time, and moved cautiously over the threshold.

He stepped from Christopher's room, still dressed in last night's clothes, though he'd cast the long-coat aside. He had a bloody cloth in his hand and he glanced back into the room before stalking towards her, his expression obscured as he passed from the candlelight into the shadows.

"You can't be here yet," he said firmly and took her by the elbow, manoeuvring her back into the passage. "He needs some time."

"Wait, Razi, *wait*." She pulled her arm from his grip and put her hand on his chest, resisting his attempt to back her from the room. "How is he? I just want to know."

Razi continued to try and walk her from the room, and she punched him hard in the chest. "Stop crowding me, Razi! STOP!"

He made a strange little *oh* sound, and stepped back immediately, his hands up. She took a chance and stepped back into the room.

"How is he?" she peered up at him.

"He needs a bath," managed Razi, "he . . . has a terrible headache. You can't see him, Wynter. He needs some time . . ."

Then Christopher called softly from his room, "Razi." It was barely audible but Razi turned on his heel and disappeared into the room as quick as Wynter had ever seen him move. She stood listening to their quiet conversation, feeling very uncomfortable and off balance.

"Let me see her." Christopher's voice was soft, but what he said was not a request.

"Chris. Give yourself a chance . . ."

"I need to see her."

"I already told you she's fine."

And now Christopher was pleading, still in the same soft whisper, and there was no way that Razi could withstand the desperation in his voice.

Razi came back to the door, angled in such a way that he was nothing but a long narrow shape against the light. "Come on," he said quietly.

Christopher was sitting at a little table, various vials and bottles and cloths and a bowl of steaming water at his elbow. He was wrapped in a loose Bedouin-type striped robe of many colours, and his filthy hair was tied back off his face. He was still stiff-necked and shaking, and he peered at her from barely opened eyes. "Wynter?" he said, hardly moving his lips.

"Yes."

"I can't see you."

She stepped closer, into the circle of light. He seemed to be looking her up and down, trying to make her out through the awful swelling of his face and the poor light.

"Did they hurt you?"

That surprised her so much that she didn't answer right away. He leaned forward, his breath quickening, scowling against his impaired vision, grunting with the pain that his frown brought him. She could hardly understand it when he said, "Answer me. You need to tell me. Did they hurt you?"

She stepped closer again, swallowing her revulsion at the terrible smell. "No, Christopher. Nobody hurt me."

The doubt in his face was obvious. She forced strength into her voice when she repeated, "Nobody hurt me, Christopher. I spent a peaceful night in my own bed."

He believed her then, his lips cracking as he grinned in relief. "Ahhhh," he said softly, the slivers of his eyes sparkling brokenly in the candle light. "That's grand so. That's fine . . ."

"I'll let you have your bath."

He nodded stiffly and closed his eyes against the light, taking delicate little breaths through his abused mouth, pain overtaking him for a moment.

"I'll come see you later?"

He made no acknowledgement, and she thought he might have drifted away.

She turned to go and he said suddenly, urgently, "You

promise? You'd tell us . . . if they hurt you?" Why did he keep asking? Wynter wondered if he was delirious. He continued, "It . . . if you don't talk about those things . . ." his hands began to shake rapidly under the cover of the robe's wide sleeves and he drew them to his chest. Suddenly his lips were trembling and his breath was coming fast and ragged as he tried to finish his sentence. "It gets to be like . . . m-maggots in your head. If you don't tell. It'll eat you up."

"I swear," she said. "I swear, Christopher. Nobody laid a hand on me."

Razi grabbed her shoulder and pulled her from the room. She let him manhandle her to the secret door, before she came to herself enough to lift her arm in protest and push him back.

"What was all that about?" she hissed.

"Nothing, nothing. I'll explain later."

"Jesu! Razi!" He was really starting to infuriate her. But she lost all her rage when he stifled a sob into his hand and leant down to rest his head against her shoulder, muffling a brief, violent storm of silent crying into her neck. "Oh, Razi," she whispered, reaching up to wrap her arms around him. It's all right. It's all right, Razi. It's all over. He's safe."

He coughed suddenly and pushed away from her, scrubbing his face with his sleeve. "He's still a touch confused," he ground out. "They kept him awake all night, threatening to take him to the chair. Once they even . . . strapped. Him. In." He took a sharp breath, released it, went on. "Left him . . . waiting for the inquisitors that never came.

The two of them looked away from each other, both

blinded momentarily by their own seething cloud of rage, then Razi continued quietly. "There was a woman, and a man. But the woman . . . he could hear her. They told him it was you. He thought, all night, that the poor creature was you."

Wynter felt the blood ebbing from her cheeks. What he must have been through! Then she thought of the woman. "Marcos's widow?"

She felt Razi nodding in the shadows beside her.

"They . . . Razi. They didn't hurt him anymore than . . ."

"Any more than what, Wynter?" Razi's rage bubbled over finally and he raised his voice to her, his shoulders hunching defensively. "Any more than my father trying to murder him? Any more than confining him in that hideous place? Any more than tormenting him all night until he's unmanned with worry and fear?"

"Razi Kingsson . . ." Christopher's soft voice admonished from the next room. "I'll thank you to kindly refrain from using the word 'unmanned' when discussing me with such a delightful woman."

That sounded so like the old Christopher that they both laughed despite themselves. Razi covered his mouth with his hand, his eyes brittle and hectic as he looked to the door of his friend's room. Wynter broke away suddenly and ran back in to Christopher.

She didn't even think about what she was doing, she just ran straight up to him and squeezed him fiercely around the shoulders, making him moan and gasp in discomfort. Then she kissed his bruised lips, soft and quick. She pulled away just as fast and backed to the door.

He put his hand to his mouth, his eyes unreadable under all the bruising, but a definite smile on his lips.

"You better get Razi to de-louse you, lass. I'm a mite pestilent at the moment."

"I'll see you later, Christopher," she said softly and slipped out to the secret passage, returning to her father's room.

Public Perception

"*I* don't think I can do this, Dad."

"Why not? You're used to dealing with other teams. You often negotiate for me."

"You've always been *there* before! I don't think I can face them alone."

Lorcan tilted his head on the pillow and looked at her with equal measures of sympathy and exasperation. "Wynter! You have to do it sometime! Or do you plan to quit the business when I'm gone?

Wynter scowled. "Stop that!"

"Seriously!" he spread his hands, half-joking, but she could tell by the tightness in his voice that he was starting to work himself up. "What do you plan to do when I'm dead – hang up your guild badge, and make yourself into some lad's kitchen slave and breed sow?"

Her cheeks blazed. "Dad!" she gasped, mortified.

"That lusty fellow next door, there. He'd fill your belly every year for you, no problem. Wouldn't that be lovely?"

"Dad!" she cried, stamping her foot in embarrassment and fury. "That's *enough*!"

"Well then, stop acting like a bloody *girl*!" shouted her father suddenly, his colour high, his anger genuine. "Do you want to bloody kill me with worry?" he cried. "What have we been doing all these years, if I haven't taught you to cope without me? Good Christ! Wynter!" There was fear in his eyes. "*Tell* me you can do this! Tell me you're fit! Or else . . ." he trailed off, lifting his hands in wordless panic. "What . . . what will become of you?"

"All right, Dad, all right." She stepped closer. "The master will be all right, I suppose. But how do I cope with the apprentices?"

"The master will be fine," said Lorcan, soothingly now, his tone gentle. "It's Pascal Huette, he's a good man. My father and I worked with him many times. He's talented, competent, progressive. He's courtly. I promise you that once you've proved yourself in command, he'll make the apprentices toe the line."

Wynter clenched her hands together and took a deep breath. "Goddamned apprentices!"

Lorcan's mouth twitched and his eyes sparkled at her when he said, "Aye, they're a bloody pain in the arse."

She gave him a dry eye. "Ah, stop it," she said.

"You can do it, baby-girl." He nodded at her, his eyes solemn. "You're fit. And it's just for one day. I'll be with you tomorrow."

Wynter looked at his white lips and tired face, and nodded uncertainly. "I know you will, Dad."

"Go on then."

She took a deep breath, flexed her hands, straightened her back and left.

There was activity at Razi's door as Wynter exited her

suite, and she pretended to check something in her belt purse, watching the proceedings from the corner of her eye.

It was the tailor, delivering a neatly folded stack of purple coats. Razi was accepting them as though they were a basket of adders. He nodded to dismiss the man and then stood watching him leave, his face tight, the pile of coats in his arms. The steam from Christopher's bath was billowing past him into the corridor, and it gave Razi the look of a rangy god, descending through clouds.

A page was waiting and he cleared his throat until Razi turned his hooded eyes to him. "His Majesty, the Good King Jonathon, wishes to remind your Highness that your presence is required in the council room at the second half of the eighth quarter."

"Tell his Majesty that I will be otherwise occupied."

The page seemed to be expecting this reply and handed over a note, sealed with Jonathon's crest. Razi's jaw twitched, and he shifted his burden of coats and took the note, breaking the wax seal and snapping the paper open with one hand. Rapidly scanning the missive, his breathing quickened and his face flushed as he read the message.

The page looked steadfastly at the wall while Razi ground his teeth and made a visible effort to suppress his rage. Eventually, he managed to grind out a terse, "I shall attend."

The page snapped off a relieved bow and hurried away.

Wynter stopped fiddling with her purse and moved casually up the hall. "Your Highness," she said, her tone formal but her expression soft. Razi snapped his eyes to her and she saw that he was barely in control of his emotions.

"How fare you?" she asked lightly, her eyes saying more.

He handed her the note. It was very brief. Written in Jonathon's elegant hand, it simply read, *The Inquisitor General requests that the Freeman Christopher Garron, Hadrish, remain available for further discussion.* It was signed "*Jonathon Kingsson III* ".

Wynter re-folded it carefully and looked up into her friend's face. Within Razi's rooms there was the sound of gentle splashing. Christopher's ruined clothes lay in a heap at their feet, the smell nauseating despite the medicinal steam that filled the air.

Wynter swallowed hard. Though he was staring at her, she didn't think Razi was seeing her at all, it was as though he were scanning some invisible interior landscape, peopled by predators and shadowed by horrors that only he could see. He clutched the coats against his chest, creasing the carefully pressed brocades and crushing the velvet collars.

Wynter put the note on top of the coats. "You're creasing them," she said, and she pulled his hand gently to loosen his crushing grip on the expensive cloth. Razi focused on her then and despite the guards, she kept holding his hand and looking up into his face, giving him a rare, unguarded public smile of affection.

Razi breathed out a sigh and smiled back, squeezing her fingers, his face pained. He went to say something, and then he frowned. He looked down sharply at her hand. He looked over her shoulder at the watching guard. He looked at her face. Then he glanced around suddenly at the very public hall, and he snatched his hand away from hers.

The note wobbled and dropped from the coats to the floor and Wynter bent to retrieve it and replaced it on the pile. When she looked back up at him, Razi's expression had completely changed.

His eyes were hooded, his face cold. He was standing very straight, his posture remote. "This must end," he said firmly.

Wynter wasn't sure what he meant. "I will see you tonight," she assured him.

"No," he said, and stepped back, putting his hand on the door handle. "I shall be otherwise occupied." And he shut the door in her face without looking at her again.

She stood for quite a long moment, looking at the dark panelled wood of the door, Razi's last words a little seed of ice in her chest. There was silence from within the suite, no sounds at all. No conversation. Wynter knew that Christopher's bath was just to the right of the door, in front of the fireplace. Had Razi spoken to him, even quietly, she would have heard the murmur of their voices, but there was nothing. Razi must have either been standing, motionless and silent on the other side of the door. Or he had passed by his friend and gone into the other room without a word.

Goddamn you, Razi Kingsson, she thought and the strength of bitterness in her heart caught her by surprise. *Goddamn you and your damned secrets and your pushing people away.* She kicked the door childishly, and then laid her hand against the wood. *Come back*, she thought. *Come back out and give me a hug.*

But he didn't, of course, and she eventually patted the door gently, as she would have liked to pat Razi's shoulder, and made her way down to the library.

Wynter stood outside the library with her heart hammering

in her chest and her cheeks ridiculously red and hot. Her tools felt unbearably heavy on her shoulder. She wasn't going to be able to do this! She just wasn't!

She thought about the cluster of gangling apprentices that were bound to be on the other side of the door and felt her stomach roll like a carp in a jug. She was quite certain that she was going to open the door, stumble, trip, fall, fart and then puke.

Wynter slapped herself in the face, hard enough to bring tears of pain to her eyes. She took a sharp breath and held it. Exhaling slowly, she opened the door and stepped into the room. She didn't look around her until she'd carefully shut the door. At the click of the latch she was suddenly in control. Her cheeks were cool, her tongue was loose and able, her belly was calm. She raised her eyes to the small knot of youths in front of her and took them in with one cool sweeping glance.

There were five of them. Two first years, two third years, and one fourth year apprentice like herself. None of them were chartered for the green, in fact all but the fourth year lad wore only basic black laces, and none of them had guild approval for wages. They were, for the most part, the usual rough-looking, sly-eyed bunch. They turned as one to stare at her, at first with surprise and then with sneering laughter. The older boys eyed her with undisguised lechery.

"What we got here then?" crowed a slim, shock-haired fellow, looking at her crotch and licking his lips. "This a bloody joke or what?"

"Who told yer you could wear them clothes?" asked one of the small first years, his peaky little face sharp with accusation.

Wynter swallowed. She knew that their master was here, lurking in the stacks somewhere, pretending not to notice that she'd arrived. He would be listening to how she handled his boys, using it as a measure of her worth. This was make or break for her in terms of how she would get on with his team, she had to get this right, because there'd be no second chances.

"Mebbe she'd be here to give us some relief," laughed the shock-haired boy and his eyes roamed over her breasts. His companions whooped and knocked each other about in crude delight, though the smallest one couldn't have been more than seven or eight.

She ignored this coarse opening volley and looked each boy up and down with slow, cold deliberation. She had already taken in everything she needed to know about them, but now she was using her father's old trick of marking each boy and dismissing him as unimportant. She passed over the first years as if they were thoroughly beneath her contempt and turned her attention to the third year apprentices.

Wynter purposely started with the one who had first spoken to her, the foul-mouthed, shock-haired boy. She looked pointedly into his face, down to the guild mark on his tunic and then to the black laces in his boots. When she got to his laces, she allowed her eyebrows to lift a little as if to say, *oh, is that all?*

Then she did the same to his companion, a raw-boned, freckle-faced lad with striking blue eyes and crooked front teeth. He frowned at her scrutiny and glanced at the fourth year boy for support. Wynter had already realised that the older boy was the one she'd need to deal with, but first she made a show of glancing at the third year's laces and dismissing him with a tut. Only then did she turn her attention to the important fourth year lad.

He was of medium height, a stooping fellow of about seventeen, with a round good-natured face and a head of silky brown hair, clubbed, as was befitting his status, at the nape of his neck. He had stayed watchfully in the background as his companions had jostled and pucked and leered, and now he was regarding her with careful interest. She took in his face, the guild mark, his boots. She allowed her eyebrows to rise approvingly at the yellow colour of his laces, and let herself nod. A good grade, only one level down from the green. She let her eyes meet his, and caught him flicking a glance down to her guild approval pendant. His lips twitched and he met her eyes, his face guarded.

"I've no doubt your master has left you excellent instructions, and that you are hard at work on his behalf," Wynter said, speaking directly to him and only him. "I'm sorry to have interrupted you. Please, I beg you, continue with whatever tasks he charged you to perform. My master is most eager that we make progress."

This put a large burden on the boys. If their master had not left any instructions, then it implied that he was lazy and incompetent and that his early absence from the workplace was a great dereliction of duty. Wynter knew that apprentices were unruly and insubordinate to a boy, but loyal beyond belief to their master. For these boys to continue their larking now would be a bad reflection on the man who supplied them with their bed and board, and on whom their futures depended. It would also shame him in front of another master's apprentice.

The fourth year sucked his teeth for a minute and examined her face, a small frown growing between his eyebrows. "Why ain't yer master here himseln?" he asked.

The shock-haired fellow leapt in, his tone suddenly earnest and inquiring. "I heard Lord Moorehawke don't support this *mortuus in vita* thing! I heard he ain't even been to no banquet or nothin' since that pagan Arab bastard been taken to the throne! That's why he ain't here, ain't it?"

Wynter opened her mouth to reply, but the other third year interrupted her. He had a surprisingly cultured voice and he looked her up and down when he said, "My mother said the Lord Razi has put a spell on the King. That he has bewitched his way to the throne . . ."

"Sure his ma did bewitch her way to Jonathon's bed when the King were but a lad!" squeaked one of the first years.

"He shook her off quick enough," sneered the shock-haired lad, "Black-eyed bitch! Didn't take long for the King to come to his right mind and get himseln a decent Christian woman 'afore 'twas too late."

"Not 'afore that brown bitch pushed out a bastard, though! And she murst have cast another spell on him now, for harn't he tossed out his golden boy for that black devil?"

"Bloody brown heathen."

Wynter felt her head spinning. Their voices were all blending into one great rush of hate, and she felt her control of the situation draining away. It was like listening to Northlanders talk! *Decent Christian woman? Pagan Arab bastard?* When had religion and race ever been an issue in this kingdom? When had they started talking about spells and bewitchings as though they were something to be reckoned with?

The fourth year was speaking to her, and she forced herself to concentrate on his wary, thoughtful voice as he said, "I suppose we have ter replace his Royal Highness, the Prince Alberon, with the Arab bastard, do we? Scrape out the true heir and carve in the pretender?"

Wynter blinked at him, her heart scurrying in her chest. Her eyes felt dry and hot. She moved her tongue around in her mouth to try and get it wet enough to speak. When she did finally get something out, she was shocked at how even her voice was, how reasonable her words.

"My master is detained with business of state," she said. "That is why he cannot attend us today." She drew a note from her jacket, making sure that the crowding boys could see Lorcan's crest on the wax seal. "I have a note from him for your master." The fourth year looked from it to her, his face neutral. "And if you examine the carvings on these walls," she continued, "You will see that there will be no need to replace the prince with his brother. Lord Razi is, in fact in all of these pictures already. He is in more of them than even the Royal Prince Alberon, as Lord Razi was born first and was here longer."

The boys frowned and glanced around them. Wynter realised suddenly that none of them knew what either Alberon or Razi looked like. To these boys, her two friends were just names, one representing a brown bastard, one representing a golden boy. That was all, just names, just icons. And with this revelation she understood the true depth of what Jonathon was going to achieve here.

By erasing Alberon from history, by destroying every

reference to him, every picture of him, every carving, Jonathon could make whatever he wished of Alberon's memory. Alberon could become anything – a gibbering imbecile, a lunatic, a murderous lout, a dangerous tyrant. Jonathon could make *anything* of Alberon, because most of his people had never even seen him, had never known his face or the truth of his character. Poor Albi. Soon he would be nothing, or worse, he would be remade into a monster.

Jusef Marcos's last words came back to her in a rush: *His Highness the Royal Prince Alberon! It was Prince Alberon! He sent the word, my Lord! He sent the word that I kill you.* She could not reconcile herself to that. Could not impose her image of the wild, grinning, impulsively affectionate Alberon, bounding and sunny, with that of an evil, scheming man, hidden in the shadows, dispatching assassins intent on the murder of his own beloved brother. She felt tears threatening and bit her tongue and looked again at the group of boys who were still staring about them, trying to figure out who was who in the numerous carvings that filled the room.

Wynter took a deep breath and said harshly, "So, what work did your master leave you?"

The shock-haired boy sneered at her, "What business be it of yourn, wench?"

The fourth year slapped him suddenly on the back of the head, "Tat it, Jerome. Get yer roll to the back stacks and start on that frieze, as what yer were told."

Jerome gaped at his companion for a second. The fourth year held his eye, and eventually the other boy blushed deep and moved off to the large stacks. The other third year drifted away, and the two small first years dithered, hopping from foot to foot as if they needed to piss.

"What are we meant to do, Gary?" whined one of them.

The fourth year rolled his eyes to heaven. "Why doesn't yer ever listen, yer little maggots? Get yer to them little shelves over there and lay out yer tools and I'll be with yer now." The two boys scampered off, and Wynter heard them pushing and giggling as they made their way to the smaller book cases.

The fourth year, Gary, looked at her, his face solemn. He spoke to her in a low voice, and Wynter thought she heard a heavy measure of sympathy in his voice. "It pains me ter do this work," he said honestly. "Yer master has done some right excellent beauty here. 'Tis a sin ter wipe it."

She looked into his gentle eyes and said nothing. He grinned at her with a mouth full of rotten teeth. "You done well with them lads," he said and she let a little smile touch her eyes. "I'll take yer ter my master, eh?"

Wynter nodded and Gary led her through the stacks to where Pascal Huette had been biding his time. He was a small man, wiry and grey, his face angular, his pale eyes gleaming from a complex nest of wrinkles. During the course of the day, Wynter would come to realise that his apprentices adored him and that Gary was, in fact, his son.

They spend most of the next few hours walking through the friezes and picture panels, as Wynter described what it was her father wanted done. Pascal had at first assumed that they were replacing Alberon and Oliver with some object – a tree, a horse, something to fill in the gaps. When Wynter explained that Lorcan just wanted the figures planed down to the blank wood and left as a gaping hole in the picture, an obvious and glaring absence, Pascal looked at her thoughtfully.

"He wants no additions?"

"No, Master Huette."

"Naught to disguise the gaps?"

"No."

She produced the letter and handed it to him, waiting patiently while he read it, which he did slowly and with difficulty.

When he'd finished, Pascal folded the paper and looked around the room. "God help us," he sighed. "'Tis a bloody crime I'm partaking in. But it will be done, lass, and done well. Your master can trust us."

"He fully expects to join you tomorrow, Master Huette, and we will work by your side."

Pascal looked at the floor, sucked his teeth in a gesture he shared with his son, then glanced at her again. "Lorcan don't really support this here travesty, do he, lass? He can't possibly believe it right that the Arab take the throne?"

Wynter looked at his kind eyes and pondered his oblique manner. *Who can you trust?* she thought, *who but yourself?* Pascal Huette may well have been kind, but he could also be foolish. He may seem versed in the subtleties of court, but what if he was incapable of keeping a secret? It was obvious that Lorcan respected this man, but still, she noted, he had not trusted him enough to tell him of his illness. Her reply was quiet and bland, "My father will do his duty to the King, Master Huette."

Pascal nodded, looked her up and down, and flicked his gaze to where Gary was bent over a shallow frieze. It was a long, flowing, exuberant panel, Alberon running his hounds after a fox, the carving as full of life and joy as the boy himself had been. Gary was carefully shaving Alberon's figure from the wood, his sweeps slow and meticulous so as to preserve the beautiful work her father had done on the hounds and the surrounding foliage. Pascal Huette watched his son for a moment, his face sad.

"Aye," he murmured, "I can well unnerstarnd your father's mind."

"My Lord Razi does not want this either, Master Huette. He is loyal to the Prince."

Pascal's face creased into a knowing grimace and he glanced at Wynter indulgently, as if educating her in her innocence. "Oh aye," he snorted, "I'm sure they had to beat him to the throne. I'm sure they had to drag him kicking and screaming to that level of power."

The unwitting accuracy of the man's words brought Razi vividly to Wynter's mind. The way he'd resisted the guards at that terrible first banquet, his father's plan only freshly revealed to him. The look on his face as they had pressed him down into his brother's throne. She ground her teeth and had to press her nails into her palms to stop from yelling the truth into Pascal's knowing face. She recalled staring helplessly as Christopher, bloody and screaming, was dragged away to the keep, the very real threat of his death by torture hanging over Razi's head ever since.

"I assure you," she whispered, "My Lord Razi wants no part of his brother's inheritance. He *is* loyal."

Huette tilted his head kindly and patted her shoulder. She pulled away, cursing the tears that she couldn't seem to banish from her eyes. "Sure didn't he sit all last night long in his brother's chair, lass? Making merry and eating his brother's portions? Next yer know he'll be wearing the purple and tending at the council as if he had every right to rule." He seemed to misinterpret her shining eyes as fear, and his face became even kinder and he rubbed her arm comfortingly. "Yer carn't blame him, really. It's in their blood, yer see. A pagan like him, they don't have the same fealty, do they? They just don't unnerstarnd."

He shook his head sadly and looked around at his boys, "I can't stand to think what this place'll be like oncet he takes power. Mebbe they have the right idear up North," he said thoughtfully, watching his son as he concentrated on his work. "Mebbe we ort ter just send the lot of 'em packing. After all, iffin they can't be bothered ter e'en worship proper . . ." he trailed off, deep in thought, while Wynter stood rigid with horror and speechless fear.

Any further conversation was interrupted by Jerome's high voice at the door. "There ain't no bloody ladies here, you fool. Piss off!"

"WAIT!" Wynter shouted, "Wait!" She sprinted to the front of the library, swiping at her eyes and biting hard down on her lips to get some control. Her wild arrival surprised Jerome into stillness and shocked the little page that he was trying to bully out the door.

"Who do you seek, child?" she asked unsteadily.

"Why you, Protector Lady."

At the use of her title, Jerome's eyes popped open like heated chestnuts and all the apprentices shot up like rabbits to look at her anew.

"Good Christ!" murmured Gary, looking her up and down. "A lady, no less!"

The little page held a letter out for her, the King's crest

evident on the seal. He was mortally terrified of the five apprentices, and the paper trembled in his fingers.

"His Majesty, the good King Jonathon, expects a reply, my Lady."

"Good Christ!" repeated Gary, and Jerome paled at the sudden revelation of her powerful standing in court life.

Wynter snapped open the note, sniffing deeply to clear her nose and blinking the script into focus. Her heart dropped at the curt message.

You are required to attend tonight's banquet in place of your father. Be ready by the tenth quarter.

Wynter groaned and looked to the heavens.

"His Majesty requires a reply," squeaked the little boy. Wynter gritted her teeth, knowing what she'd *like* to say to his Majesty. But she swallowed her anger and took a deep breath instead. The page must have seen the black fury in her face, because his eyes slid to the wall and he stood waiting, his face carefully blank.

"Tell his Majesty I shall attend," she hissed and the little boy bowed and scampered quickly off.

Wynter stood for a moment, holding the note and looking at nothing. When she finally focused on her surroundings, the apprentices were standing about, their hands hanging loose at their sides, their faces solemn and almost afraid.

Do I look that upset? she thought.

Though he could have no idea what was going on, Gary seemed as though he wanted to say something comforting. But every time he opened his mouth, he appeared to think the better of it and stayed silent.

She turned and walked back to where Pascal was waiting

for her. Slowly she secured her tools back in their roll and shouldered them. She looked around the room, her eyes roaming the pictures, the happy faces, the merry little poems.

Pascal was watching her with kind, intelligent eyes, and Wynter forced herself into politeness.

"I cannot do this today, Master Huette. Do you think I have given you enough information that you may continue until my return tomorrow?"

"Oh aye, lass, no bother."

She looked at him and he smiled.

"Thank you," she said flatly, and left.

Distance

Razi was just leaving his suite when Wynter turned into the hall. It was well into the second half of the eighth quarter and he was going to be late for his council meeting. Jonathon's guards were moving about the hall like restless horses, but her friend took his own sweet time locking his door and adjusting his gloves.

The tailor had done an incredible job on Alberon's clothes, and Razi looked magnificent in the elaborate purple coat. But Wynter thought he was thoroughly unlike himself. His usual loose grace seemed trussed-up and confined in the heavy brocades. He was like a tightly bound, carefully contained version of the wiry, striding man she knew him to be.

"Your Highness," she said, hurrying towards him, longing to discuss what she'd discovered in the library. She knew that he wouldn't have time to talk here, but she wanted to grab him and make arrangements to meet later, before the business of the day swept him from her. But when Razi turned to her, his expression stopped her dead in her tracks.

Even with all her years' experience of seeing her father donning his courtly mask, Wynter had never been so shocked at a transformation. Razi's face held no warmth for her, there was nothing in his eyes but impatience, and he twisted his mouth in irritation as he tugged his glove and turned to go.

"I am busy, Protector Lady, you will have to wait."

She called after him as he strode away, "I will see you at the banquet then, your Highness!"

He came to an abrupt halt, his shoulders hunched, his hands frozen in their relentless fretting with his gloves. He took a breath and turned to look at her, his face stony.

"What do you mean?" he asked quietly and it was obvious that, as she had suspected, he didn't know about Jonathon's demand.

"His Majesty has done me the honour of offering me my father's place at tonight's meal." They locked eyes for a moment, Razi's face unreadable.

"You are a fortunate girl, are you not?" he bowed coldly. "I shall see you there." And he strode off down the hall without a backward glance.

Wary of the hall guards, Wynter allowed herself only a moment to watch him leave, but her mind was churning. Would he not offer to be her escort? Was he not going to walk her to the hall? She had been counting on Razi's support as she entered the unknown territory of the royal rooms, and the protocol-laden nightmare of dining at the royal platform. But he was retreating from her and she realised that she hadn't the energy left to be upset with him. She just turned, tired, disappointed and empty, and let herself into her suite.

Her intention was to go straight into her father's room, but there was a note on the receiving room table. Wynter's hopes soared when she saw that it was sealed with Razi's crest. She dropped her tools and snatched it up, snapping the seal in excitement. But when she read the page, all her hopeful joy deserted her, and her heart dropped.

The note was in Razi's official hand, squared off, eminently readable, completely impersonal. It was a neatly written list of instructions for her father's care, meticulous notes of times and volumes of medicines, suggestions for diet and strict guidelines for rest. She read it and knew that it meant Razi would not be attending Lorcan as frequently as he would like. That he was doing his best to ensure that her father received a continuous level of care, even in his absence.

It filled her with panic, this neat list. It spoke volumes of Razi's intent to distance himself from them. It heralded a sudden, determined pulling away. Wynter held the note and felt the maelstrom howl around her. She battled the image of herself and Lorcan, spinning and vulnerable. Alone again, and for the first time maybe lacking the strength to make it through. Tears filled her eyes again, and she bunched the paper in her hand, the temptation to fling it away almost too great.

A thin sheet came away from the back of the main note and fluttered to the floor. She looked at it, and even before she read it, the sight of Razi's sloping, rushed, personal handwriting made her close her eyes in overwhelming joy and gratitude. The damn tears rolled down her cheeks and dripped from her chin and she scrubbed them away with an impatient snort.

Dear Sis, Forgive me, forgive. The world has not enough sorrys to enable me express how terrible I feel. Understand this: I will not weaken. You can no longer approach me as a friend. I will never again show you any tenderness. Do not attempt to reproach me or rekindle our affection, it will never be possible. But I swear to you, and I pray you never forget, I love you, my little sister, my darling girl. Be safe.

Your adoring brother eternal, Razi.

She read the note, and re-read it, and read it again. *Goodbye*, it said, *goodbye, goodbye.*

He would not have planned to write this note. She guessed that he originally intended a cold and brutal break. But this was Razi, and he wouldn't, in the end, have been capable of such cruelty. His writing was almost illegible, badly blotted and smeared, his left-handed penmanship smudging the ink in his haste. He must have dashed it off at the last minute, unable to set her adrift without some recognition of how deeply he felt for her, of how much her love meant to him. She didn't care about the tears now. She just let them fall.

Oh Razi. This is wrong. All wrong. This is all so wrong.

A curious, detached sorrow came over her then, and she'd never felt anything like it. She made no effort to hide her tears as she unthinkingly shambled into the retiring room and stood at her father's door.

Lorcan was still in bed, though it was obvious that he'd been up and washed himself and combed his hair. The chamber pot had been emptied and cleaned, so the maids must have been around. She wondered if he had lain abed while they were here, but it would be hard to imagine him doing that. It was more likely that he had roused himself to leave everything outside his bedroom door, and had locked himself in until they were done.

He didn't notice her standing there, which was in itself alarming. He was lying half on his side, his right hand curled by his face, looking out the window with an expression that seemed relaxed and unguarded. His eyes were roaming the tops of the orange trees, following the flitting movements of the many multi-coloured birds that made their home in the branches. His room smelt of warm, clean skin, tincture of opium and orange blossom. It was heavy and peaceful, and she could not intrude on it with her loneliness and her selfish tears.

Wynter backed slowly away and retreated to her room, quietly washing her face and hands and brushing out her hair before going in to see him again. Her father noticed her this time, and he grinned drowsily and dragged himself up a little straighter in the bed.

"Baby-girl!" he drawled, his raspy voice a balm. "How went it?" He patted the edge of his bed, and settled back heavily into his pillows.

She swallowed her desire to bury her head in his shoulder and weep out her loneliness and despair. Instead she went and perched next to him and tried to smile. "Hello, Dad. How fared you today?"

"Oh, Razi was in and out, fussing and fiddling . . . bloody boy . . . and I'm bored out of my mind . . . I need news and gossip." His words were thick as slow-flowing honey, and Wynter glanced at the telltale brown glass bottle and half-empty beaker of water on the bedside table.

She adjusted the covers and patted his hand. "Did Razi give you some tincture of opium?"

He sighed and his smile grew dreamy and blissful. "Oh aye. He claimed I wasn't *relaxed* enough." He breathed happily, "I must say, it's wonderful. No more pain."

Her father's unwitting acknowledgement of his constant pain squeezed her heart. She looked away, for fear he'd notice the pity in her eyes.

"I'm to take your place at the banquet tonight," she said, for want of something better to break the silence.

"Oh bloody hell," Lorcan moaned, wiping his hand over his face. "What a pain in the arse for you." And he left it at that, his eyes heavy.

Great! thought Wynter, *Great sympathy there.* She eyed the brown glass bottle wryly. *Maybe I'll have a little swig of that beforehand. Float my way through the proceedings on a nice fluffy cloud.*

"Tell me . . ." he asked with a lazily amused smile, turning his head on the pillow to see her better, "what think you of Pascal? And how were the apprentices? Rotten to the core? Lecherous thugs? Did you have to beat them into submission?"

She did her best to chuckle, but he took one proper look at her raw eyes, her unsteady mouth and his face fell into pantomime concern and dismay. "Oh God in heaven," he drawled. "What *have* they done? Have they set fire to the library? Pissed on the books?"

That actually made her grin and she pucked his arm. He nodded fondly at her and took her hand in his.

"Darling," he said, "We'll get through this. It's all just wind and farce. We just have to duck the debris and hang on until the bitter end."

"Dad . . .?"

Something in her tone sharpened him, and he waited while she plucked up the courage to speak.

Oh, she thought, *I shouldn't do this. Not now. It's not fair of me! He's not strong enough.* But was there ever going to be a time again when Lorcan would be strong enough?

"The King is wrong, Dad," she said suddenly.

He tutted impatiently and tried to pull his hand from hers, but she tugged back and forced him to look at her. "He's wrong, Dad. He's *wrong*. When you said that the people would never accept Razi, you were right." She shook her head in disbelief at the memory of the apprentices. "The things those boys were saying." She looked him in the eye. "The things Master Huette was saying! It was . . . it was like listening to Shirken. It was just like being up North again. It was awful."

He knew exactly what she was talking about; she could see the sorrowful recognition in his face. "They're looking for someone to blame, baby-girl. A reason for their trouble. They think that if they can find that one reason, and deal with it, then their troubles will end."

"But they're blaming *Razi*. And not just that. They called him a pagan! They were talking about *decent Christian women.* I . . . I couldn't believe it. When have Southlanders ever talked like that?"

Lorcan chuffed a little laugh out his nose, and squeezed her hand. "Wynter, it's not too long ago that Southlanders were burning each other at the bloody stake!" He fought the inertia of the drug, cleared his throat and went on, his mind sharper than his tongue. "You've no idea . . . what people were like . . . even . . . even in my grandfather's day. They're just reverting. When people are scared, they turn into the most awful beasts. It's just the way they are. There's naught to be done."

"But it's Jonathon's fault!" He frowned at her raised voice and gave her a warning, slant-eyed look. "Dad, don't look at me like that! It *is* his fault. He's tearing the kingdom apart, and he's blaming everyone but himself . . ."

"You don't understand . . ."

"Do *you*? Tell me how *you* understand, and then explain it to me. Explain why it is that our good King has thrown everything out? Everything! All the tolerances, all the progress, all this kingdom's magic! His most beloved, most *wonderful* son, Alberon . . . and Oliver? Dad, Oliver? His great friend, that brother of his heart?"

At the mention of Oliver, Lorcan shut his eyes. "Stop it," he moaned.

Wynter shook his hand, forcing his eyes open. "The King is *wrong*. You know it! Whatever this machine . . ." He looked at her sharply, his lips thinning. *Do not mention it*, his face said, *do not say those words*. "This thing, whatever this thing was, that you made when you were young. How could it cause this?"

He shook his head. He would never discuss that with her. Never. She pressed on regardless.

"What could it have wrought, that would cause Jonathon to bring about the usurpation of his own heir? At the great risk of toppling the crown? The man is crazed!"

Lorcan shook his head again "You mustn't . . ." he whispered.

"If this continues – the gibbets, the repression, the *mortuus in vita* – everything will be ruined. We will become like all the others." Wynter spun her hand in a circle, indicating all the kingdoms that surrounded them, rancid with hate and self-imposed ignorance and fear. "It will be like a candle snuffed in the depths of night."

Lorcan pressed his head back into the pillow and looked up at the ceiling, his face hopeless. "I thought we could just do this," he whispered "Just go blind and deaf and dumb, and walk through this and out to the other side."

"And what would there be on the other side, worth walking out to?" she asked gently. "Do you think whatever it is will turn out to be worth the shutting of our eyes? Would *you* want to live there?"

The unspoken question hung between them. *Would you want me to live there without you? A woman alone, in a world like the one we just left up North?*

"What do you want me to do, girl?" he asked hopelessly. "You can see I'm bloody powerless."

She leaned forward and smiled uncertainly. "Dad. I want you to let me look for Albi."

He stared at her, and then he laughed, a hard, horrified bark of laughter. "This isn't the Easter hunt, girl! Alberon isn't crouched behind the wainscoting in the banquet hall, or hidden beneath a bush in the bloody garden like a painted egg! He's off up the forest somewhere, on the run with Oliver. With the King hunting him down like a dog"

She sat back triumphantly, and gave her father a knowing, tight-lipped look. "Oh, is he? And how long have you known that?"

He sighed. "That's *all* I know. I swear it to you. Oliver fled after Jonathon got it into his head that he was trying to usurp him. He had him declared traitor. Alberon followed very soon after, taking sides with Oliver against the King."

"My God. Did they really try to overthrow the crown? Alberon? And Oliver? Those most loyal of subjects?"

Lorcan frowned up at the ceiling, obviously just as incapable of reconciling himself to the thought as Wynter was. "It *is* hard to believe," he mused.

"Well, there's only one way to find out! Who better to tell us than Alberon himself?"

"Oh, enough!" Lorcan pulled his fingers from hers. He forced himself to sit up straighter against his pillows, shaking his fiery head to clear it. "Enough!" he cried, holding a hand up to silence her. "Let's say you did manage to sneak a horse and supplies out from the palace without being caught. Let's say you set off up the mountains at a gallop and travelled for a while without getting raped or robbed or murdered. And suddenly, *lo*, you find Alberon, camped in the road, cooking himself a fish supper! What in *hell* are you going to do then?" He looked at her so earnestly that she burst out laughing.

"After all that! I'd ask him for a bite to eat!" she said.

"Jesu Christi!" he flung his hands up, and sank back in defeat. "You're so like your bloody mother."

"Actually," Wynter took his hand again. "I think I'm quite like my dad."

He snorted, "Oh shush," he said, but he drew her hand to him and held it clasped to his chest. "You'd never find him anyway," he said quietly, "there's nowhere for you even to start. I'm not going to worry about it."

"And if I did find a place to start . . ."

"If you did, you'd want to be bloody quiet about it, Wynter. Because you'll be actively taking sides against the King."

Wynter swallowed. *Treason*, he was telling her, she would be committing treason.

There was a long moment of silence between them. Lorcan watching the sky, Wynter pondering her next move.

"How's your Hadrish boy?" asked Lorcan suddenly, surprising Wynter from her thoughts.

She laughed. "He's not *my* Hadrish boy, Dad! Stop it!"

His lips curved and his eyes sparkled. "Still and all, though. I bet you're dying to go check on him."

"Oh, that's *enough!*" She snatched her hand from his. "You're a menace! You were swearing me off men this morning!"

"Does he play cards?" Lorcan asked, and the question so threw her that she coughed in surprise, losing her breath for a minute.

"Does he . . . what?"

"Your Hadrish, does he play cards?" he repeated slowly, emphasising each word for her.

"Dad . . ." she said uncertainly. "Christopher's in pretty bad shape . . . I doubt . . ."

"Go ask him," he urged.

"*Now?*"

"Now. I'm bored beyond endurance here all day. I need some company while you're supping my beer at the banquet."

"But . . ."

He waved his hand at her. "Go, go! . . . I promise not to gamble . . . it's just for fun."

Wynter eyed him as she got up. "Yes," she said, dryly. "I think that would be wise."

"Ohhhh," he crowed, raising his eyebrows accusingly, his

gaze not quite steady. "You think he'd best me, eh? You think he'd be my match?"

"Even with his brains dribbling out his ears, I think Christopher Garron would walk home with your eyes in his pocket tonight."

Lorcan grinned blearily, and waved her out. "We shall see! We shall see!"

Wynter shook her head and headed into the secret passage to see if Christopher felt up to beating her father at a game of cards.

A Game of Cards

The shutters in Razi's suite were still closed against the evening light, and the candles had been extinguished so that the retiring room was very dark. Wynter could barely see. She had to feel her way around the dim shapes of furniture and the many piles of books and scattered objects on the floor.

Shuffling, banging and quietly cursing, she eventually groped her way across the small space and peered in at Christopher's door. The shutters let in a diffused light, which, though still very dim, allowed Wynter to make out the interior of the room.

"Christopher?" she called softly, and stepped over the threshold.

He was on the bed, curled on his side, lying atop the covers. He was dressed in his long Bedouin robe, his bare feet tucked up, his fists pressed to his forehead. Wynter thought at first that he was sleeping, but as she neared him she saw the slits of his eyes gleaming in the soft light, watching her as she approached the bed. She could hear his soft breathing.

"Christopher," she said again, her voice laden with sympathy, "How fare you?"

He didn't reply, but his eyes followed her as she knelt by the side of his bed.

There was a strand of sweat-damp hair caught in his eyelashes and Wynter gently pulled it free and tucked it behind his ear. He closed his eyes at her touch, but opened them again quickly and focused on his hands as though to keep his eyes shut made him feel ill. He swallowed delicately.

"Is the pain very bad?" she asked needlessly.

His lips twitched, his dimples lost in the terrible bruising that had spread down his cheek. "I'm mortal feared my head will fall off," he whispered.

"Have you taken nothing?"

"Willow bark tea."

Wynter snorted, he might as well be taking milk for all the good that would do for this kind of pain. "No hashish? No tincture of opium?"

"Oh, how I wish . . ." he moaned longingly, "but Razi is afeared to dose me too soon. He says I must wait."

"For what?" she exclaimed. It seemed so cruel!

Christopher chuffed a little laugh at her indignance and gasped and swallowed again. "To ensure my brains haven't run to jelly, I suppose. 'Tis just 'til sunset."

Wynter glanced at the shutters. The light was getting old; he wouldn't have long to wait now. She leant down to examine his damaged face, almost laying her head on the bed beside his bared arms. His warm skin had a spicy scent all of its own.

Her red hair, where it spread on his covers, glowed in the

gentle light from the shuttered window. "Just like a polished chestnut," he sighed. His breath was spicy warm like his skin, and she closed her eyes and inhaled without thinking.

"Uh . . ." she faltered, snapping her eyes open. What had she been about to say? "R-Razi has left my father some tincture of opium, Christopher. Would you like some?"

He shut his eyes in pained gratitude. "Oh, yes please."

She hesitated, then she said, "My father was wondering if you'd like to play a game of cards, to pass the time?"

"All right," he whispered amenably, his eyes still shut, and Wynter wondered if he was truly aware of what she was asking. Or perhaps, did he think he had to entertain Lorcan in exchange for the opium?

"You don't have to, Christopher, I can bring you the dose here if you prefer."

"Would *you* prefer I stay here?" It was a genuine question, no trace of bitterness or guile. It deserved a genuine answer.

"I would prefer if you come in to my father," she said, and he smiled, a definite smile, that finally revealed a trace of dimple in the dark bruising on his cheek.

It took a long time to help Christopher from the bed and into the secret passage, but she got him there in the end. He carried two fat pillows from his bed, and Wynter steadied him with an arm about his waist as he hobbled along, valiantly trying not to move his head or neck.

"Stay here," she whispered, and left him leaning at the secret door to her suite. She went in to close all the shutters and light some candles in her father's room.

At the sight of her, Lorcan pulled himself up in the bed.

"Oh!" he exclaimed "Has he agreed?" He leaned clumsily towards the drawer in his bedside table.

"Jesu!" snapped Wynter as he began tilting forward. She pushed him back before the whole long length of him could slide out onto his head.

Lorcan fell back against his pillows, grinning, and Wynter got his games box from the drawer and tossed it to him on her way out for Christopher. Her father immediately began a bleary hunt for his pack of cards.

Christopher was waiting at the secret door like a patient shadow. Wynter slipped her arm around his waist and got him moving forward. She saw Lorcan glance up as she helped Christopher into the room, and the smile slid from her father's face as he got his first look at the results of Jonathon's brutal attack.

Wynter knew that Lorcan was a practical, often calculating, and sometimes quite ruthless man, but she saw an almost tangible rage rise up in his eyes at the distorted mess Jonathon had made of Christopher's face.

"Good Christ, boy. Are you sure you . . .?"

Christopher waved his concern away and sat gingerly on the edge of Lorcan's bed. His body twisted awkwardly as he tried to look at Lorcan without moving his neck. "Shift your legs," he whispered, and Lorcan slid over to make room for him.

Wynter propped Christopher's pillows against the footboard, and the young man took a deep breath and carefully hoisted himself up and over. He slowly inched his legs around so that he sat facing Lorcan and finally he sank back against the pillows with a shaky sigh. He sat for the longest moment, tense and immobile, his eyes lightly shut.

Wynter regarded the whole process with held breath and clenched hands. She met her father's eyes over Christopher's dark head, and Lorcan glanced significantly at the opium. "I'll mix you that draught," she said, patting Christopher's shoulder and busying herself with the vials and pitchers on Lorcan's table.

"That would be lovely," Christopher whispered. Then he straightened cautiously and peered at Lorcan. "Wh-what're we playing?" Lorcan hesitated and Christopher waved a hand at him, "Come on. What you got? F . . . French deck?"

"Aye," said Lorcan holding up the big picture cards. "How about a hand or two of piquet?" he suggested.

Christopher made a noncommittal gesture. "We'd have to strip the deck," he said and the two men looked at each other. They continued to sit like weary stones, neither lively enough to begin.

Wynter handed Christopher the beaker of diluted tincture. "I'll strip the deck if you like, but you'll have to say aye or nay now because I've to dress for dinner."

Christopher carefully drained the draught, tilting his whole body backwards to avoid kinking his neck. Wynter put her finger to the end of the beaker and helped keep it steady as he drank it down. She took the empty cup and he straightened with a gasp and slowly wiped his mouth. "Noddy," he breathed finally and Lorcan gave a satisfied little grunt.

"Noddy it is. You're the elder," slurred the older man and laboriously doled out two cards each, turning up the top of the deck.

Wynter shook her head at the two of them. They were

peering at their first hands, barely able to make out the suits, let alone calculate their points. "God preserve us," she muttered and went into her room to wash and dress.

As she went about preparing for dinner the noise of their conversation increased, and by the time she was dressed, there was a sustained, though predominantly monosyllabic exchange going on between the two men.

Night was falling. Pretty soon she'd have to go down to the hall. She closed her eyes. Damn it. She sighed and sat down on the edge of her bed. Damn it. She lay back slant-wise on her covers and let her head hang from the other side. Damn it.

She could see out the window from here, upside down, and gazed into the sky. The stars were out in their multi-tude of brilliance, though the sky was still a dark blue. The crickets were agitating the air in the orange garden.

Wynter had slipped Razi's note into her bodice, and it was a small crackling presence against her heart. *Forgive me, forgive.* That was all well and good, but what was she meant to do next time they met? Even when they were in private was she to call him, "Your Royal Highness Prince Razi" and bob and curtsey like any courtly moppet? Make crippling small talk? Swallow down her hurt when he swept on by?

She knew what she'd *like* to do when next she saw him, and it wasn't an act of sisterly devotion either. She imagined with grim satisfaction the sound her riding boots would make connecting with his stubborn rear and showed her teeth in a grimace-like smile.

But she wasn't able to sustain this self-protecting anger, and the longer she lay there, the more likely she would be to turn to maudlin self-pity. She bounced up suddenly, popping off the bed like a jack-in-the-box. Pushing her hair back off her face with a violent little sniff, she shook herself and stalked out to spend what was left of the evening with the two equally infuriating, but still happily available lunatics in the next room.

Lorcan glanced at her as she totted up the scoreboard. He looked down at his cards and then turned his eyes back to her again, his eyebrows raised. "You look handsome in that dress, baby-girl."

Wynter tried to keep track of what she was doing. "I've been sitting here for twenty minutes, Dad. Are you only noticing me now?"

At the end of the bed, Christopher tilted his head back and tried to open his eyes a little wider. "What's she done to herself?" he asked Lorcan.

"She put a dress on."

"Oh," he said, "I saw her in a dress once. *Fierce* handsome!"

Lorcan smirked at Wynter. *See?* that smirk said. *What did I tell you? Your Hadrish boy!*

Wynter gave him a warning glare.

"I prefer the sight of her arse in a pair of trousers though," mumbled Christopher as he looked down at his cards again, apparently unaware he'd spoken out loud.

Wynter gaped at him and glanced at her father whose eyes had grown to saucers and whose hands suddenly looked very large and capable of snapping a Hadrish neck.

Lorcan leant forward. He was opening his mouth to let launch a tirade at the unsuspecting young man, when he was distracted by the sound of a body of guards arriving in the hall outside.

As one they all froze, suddenly alert as rabbits. They heard a key turn in the lock of Razi's door and a quiet snap and thud as it was opened and shut again. Razi was back.

It hit them all more or less at the same time: Razi was back to an empty room!

"Wynter?" Lorcan asked, "Did you leave him a note?"

Wynter gasped and leapt to her feet. Christopher made a dismayed little sound as they heard a door suddenly bang back against a wall next door. Razi bellowed Christopher's name and they heard him knocking something over in his panic.

"*Quickly!*" Christopher gestured wildly to Wynter. "Before he runs out into the hall!" but she was already flying out the door and into the secret passage.

Razi was actually at his hall door, his hand on the handle, when she pushed her way into his rooms.

"Razi!" she hissed, "Stop!"

He spun to her in a frenzy of terror and panic. "They've taken him! They took Christopher!" he cried. "Oh God, Wynter!" He clutched his head, gripping his curls with eye-watering force. "Oh God! What have I *done?*"

Wynter flew across the room and grabbed his arms, pulling him down so that his face was level with hers.

"He's all right!" she whispered. "Christopher is with us, Razi! He's inside! He's playing cards with Lorcan!"

As her words slowly percolated through his terror, Razi's hands loosened their grip on his hair and the panic gradually seeped from his face.

"Honestly, brother, it's all right," she said, patting his arm. "I'm sorry we didn't leave you a note. We never thought . . ."

His eyes filled with tears. He closed them briefly, and then he gently shrugged her hands from his arms and stood to his full height, looking around his rooms as if at a loss as to where or who he was, or what to do next.

"Come on," she said, and took him by the hand and led him unresisting through the passage to Lorcan's room.

When Wynter came back into the bedroom Christopher had turned awkwardly toward the door, his face anxious. Razi didn't enter, he just leaned his long body against the doorframe and looked at the two men with weary relief.

"Sorry, Razi," Christopher whispered contritely.

Razi rested his head against the wall. "Did you get your draught?" he asked, every word suffused with tiredness.

"Aye."

Razi nodded. "I must go," he murmured and turned to leave.

His three friends exchanged concerned looks.

"My Lord!" said Lorcan, "Go you to the banquet?"

Razi only turned his head slightly, his back still to the room. Wynter saw his weary profile as he spoke. His eyes were shut. "I am your Highness the Royal Prince Razi, Protector Lord Moorehawke. You must address me by my proper title."

He waited through the shocked silence and nodded when Lorcan whispered, "Aye . . . your Highness. My apologies."

"I *am* on my way to the banquet. Why do you ask?"

"I hoped you might accompany my daughter, your Highness. She is inexperienced in the manners of the royal platform, and I thought . . ."

Razi held up his hand, cutting Lorcan off and already heading into the gloom of the retiring room as he spoke. "Be ready in ten minutes, Protector Lady, I shall not wait."

They sat in stunned silence for a moment. Then Christopher sighed "Well," he said quietly, "that's you told, Lorcan."

Lorcan quirked a sad little smile. "Aye," he said. "That's me told."

Wynter hesitated for a moment, and then drew Razi's note from her bodice. She handed it to Lorcan and he read it without comment, his jaw tightening.

"What is it?" asked Christopher, straining to make out what they were up to.

Lorcan looked to Wynter for permission and she nodded.

"Can you read?" asked Lorcan kindly.

"Aye."

"Here," Lorcan leant forward and handed the note to Christopher.

The young man took it, moved it too and fro, angled it, shifted his head with a pained little grimace, and finally found a position from which he could see the writing. He read it slowly, his lips moving. "Oh," he said. "Poor Razi."

"We're a danger to him," said Wynter.

"Oh, Wyn," sighed her father, taking her hand. "That's not it, darling."

"He thinks *he's* a danger to us . . ." breathed Christopher.

"Yes," Lorcan agreed, nodding slowly.

"But the closer we are to him, the more vulnerable he is," insisted Wynter.

"Aye. Jonathon just has to *glance* at Christopher there.

Or have one of his guards smirk at you, darling. And Razi has no choice but to roll over and show his belly."

"Poor bastard," said Christopher absently, and Lorcan didn't even grimace at his choice of word.

A sudden realisation struck Wynter. "Jonathon will never let you go," she said to Christopher.

"She's right, boy." Lorcan said, "You're his best leverage to get Razi to do whatever he wishes. Jonathon's going to want you around for a long, long time."

"Good Frith!" breathed Christopher. He stared at Wynter and Lorcan and they both gave him identical, pitying looks. *Now who's the poor bastard*, is what he knew they were thinking.

Freedom to Leave

The next morning Wynter woke to a blessedly cool dawn. Outside was grey with mist and it drifted in her window. It was a glorious relief from the unrelenting heat, and she spread her arms on the pillows and revelled in it. It wouldn't last. The hazy sky was already washed with rosy sunrise and Wynter knew that within the next quarter, this sweet coolness would have given way to another blistering, sun-blasted day.

All her recent worries suddenly fell on her as if from a great height and pressed down on her chest, squeezing her heart. She rolled to her side with a groan and turned her face into the crook of her arm. Why couldn't she have stayed asleep? It had been blissful and dreamless, and she wanted it back. She closed her eyes and tried to force herself to sink under the surface of her thoughts, tried to drift back down into that delicious well of innocent oblivion.

Instead, her wayward mind travelled back to last night's excruciating banquet. What a nightmare it had been, with its endless protocol and the constant, whispering scrutiny of the falsely merry crowd. The King's guard had been a looming wall of intimidation at every turn, and Razi! Good Christ, Razi! Cold, aloof and unapproachable. On their walk to and from their rooms, he had spared her no words other than those that procedure demanded. Once in the hall itself, he had cast not a glance in her direction, unless to indicate where to turn or whose hand to shake first.

Even during the interminable after-dinner dancing, Razi had paid her no heed. He had spent the night sprawled on his brother's throne, a dour, brooding presence. Had Wynter not known the true heart of the man, she would have judged him a sullen, black-hearted knave. He did himself no favours with the attending crowd.

This memory speared her heart, and she grunted in frustration and rolled onto her back. She could get up now, get dressed, go arrange food, and look in on her father. She could get an early start on the library. Instead, she closed her eyes and let the damp air settle on her face and arms. Birds were making little waking up noises in the orange trees. A cock crowed in the stable yards. Wynter began to float dreamily, and tried to go with it. Maybe if she relaxed she would fall back asleep.

She heard her father say, "I am cold," and she opened her eyes when someone answered. It was Razi. Their voices were quiet, but clear as bells on the still air.

"Is it your feet, Lorcan?"

"Aye."

"I shall fetch another pair of socks from your chest, if you like?"

Lorcan replied tiredly that he would appreciate it. There was quiet scuffling about for a few moments. Then Razi said, "Is that better?"

It must have been an improvement, because Razi murmured an almost inaudible, "Good."

Wynter lay still and looked at the ceiling. She listened with sorrow to the private decency of the same man who only last night had glowered his way through the feast and scowled and grunted at everyone who approached him.

Her father mumbled something and Razi replied, "It is just for one more day, Lorcan! That's *all* I'm asking of you."

Lorcan's voice was tight with frustration. "I have much to do, your Highness. I need to oversee the library! And I need to get an idea of which way the tides are flowing out there! It will be fatal to fall out of touch."

"Lorcan," Razi admonished gently, "you will *die* if you do not rest as I have asked. I cannot be clearer with you. You will die, and you will leave our lovely girl all alone in this awful mess. I cannot believe that that is what you would want."

"For want of one bloody day abed?" Wynter could hear the sneer in her father's voice.

There was no reply. Wynter knew what expression Razi would have on his face. She could clearly imagine his brown eyes, steady and immutable, not backing down. And she knew her father would be valiantly trying to stare him into submission, and failing. She sat up and quietly swung her legs out of bed.

There was silence. Then her father grunted in defeat.

"So," Razi said, no triumph in his voice. She heard small sounds as he laid things out on Lorcan's table. "I can trust you to do as I have asked?" A pause in which her father must have gestured or murmured. "You are sincere, Lorcan? There will be no scurrying about behind my back? Because

I cannot be seen to return today, and I must be able to trust you."

"Aye! *Aye!*" Impatient and sharp.

"Thank you. Now, I will not give you the opium today, for fear you begin to crave it. I am, instead, leaving you this hashish. Eat one of these portions with your breakfast, dinner and supper. I have arranged good, wholesome meals to be delivered . . ."

"Sounds delicious. . ." murmured Lorcan snidely.

"Do not be sour."

"Well, I'm not hungry."

"That is just the opium talking . . . you will be clemmed soon, particularly if you take the hashish, it's powerful good for restoring a lost appetite. Here, drink this."

Wynter put on her robe and padded into the retiring room to peer in at her father's door. Razi was stooped over the big man, his face calm and attentive, his hand poised for the return of the cup. He was dressed in a loose white shirt, leggings and riding boots. His crop lay on the bed at Lorcan's feet. He must be heading down to the horses. She leaned against the doorframe and watched them. Lorcan handed Razi the cup he'd just drained, and made a face.

"Gah! Tastes like bloody horse shit!"

As Razi turned to put things into his bag. Lorcan lay back and watched him carefully, his eyes assessing.

"Would the Hadrish be up to spending time with me today?"

Razi paused a moment and then went on with his tidying. "Christopher will be in a lot of pain today, perhaps even more so than yesterday. But I have given him a draught, and I will leave it up to him."

"I like him," said Lorcan suddenly, as if surprised.

Razi said nothing.

"I suspect that there are feelings between him and my daughter."

Startled, Wynter slipped out of sight and stood listening from around the corner. There was a long pause, and Razi sighed quietly.

"There was a time, Lorcan, that to hear it would have made my heart soar. At one time I had hoped . . ." Razi's wistful voice trailed off.

"But now?"

There was a decisive sound of Razi snapping his bag shut. "Freeman Garron will not be here long enough for any of my hopes to be realised."

Wynter's heart contracted with unexpected grief at this news.

Then her father said, "The King will never let him go. You know that." And this filled Wynter with such fear that she didn't know what she wanted or how she even felt. There was silence from the next room and she stepped back to the door and looked in. To hell with skulking around corners while her menfolk discussed things that affected them all. They didn't notice or see her, and she did nothing to draw attention to herself.

Razi was standing, side-on to her father, and the two men were regarding each other with knowing, tension filled faces. Razi dropped his eyes and placed his bag carefully back on the bedside table. He went to speak, hesitated and then, with the air of someone about to make a reluctant confession said, "I intend to make myself a very unpleasant addition to the royal platform, Protector Lord."

Lorcan winced. "Razi," he moaned, "You will get yourself killed."

"And where would his Majesty be then?" Razi sneered. "Hunting one heir like a rat in a cellar, and burying the other in a Musulman graveyard in town? My father is mad, Lorcan, but he is not stupid!"

"Then he will hurt that Hadrish boy in ways you cannot possibly imagine. I *know* your father, and I am telling you, you have no chance against him."

Razi stood looking down on Lorcan, his face stony. Then his body sagged slightly, curving in on itself in weariness. "I will figure something out," he said quietly.

"But until then you must be careful, for your sake – and the Hadrish's. You must bide your time."

"Yes," breathed Razi, watching the brightening sky, "I have enough on my conscience with Christopher already."

"Wynter tells me that he is Merron?" asked Lorcan carefully.

"By adoption, yes."

Lorcan flushed, fidgeted with his covers for a moment and then murmured awkwardly. "They are an uncommonly lusty people, Razi."

Wynter heard the now rare laugh in Razi's voice when he said, "Aye! That they are! But you can trust Christopher, Lorcan. He will do naught to harm our girl."

Wynter's cheeks blazed, but she wasn't sure how to take that. What did Razi mean by *harm* exactly? Would Christopher not be *interested* in her?

"If he has feelings for her . . ."

She lifted her eyes, searching Razi's gently amused face.

"You can trust him, Lorcan. I promise you."

"Will you tell me something? Honestly . . .?"

Razi turned his face away slightly, regarding her father through warily narrowed eyes.

Lorcan held up a hand. "I am not asking you to betray a confidence. But . . ." he bit his lip. He met Razi's eyes. "I want her safe."

Razi stared questioningly, and Lorcan sighed.

"Is he a thief?" Lorcan finally asked and held up his hands, waggling the fingers. "Is he a criminal?"

Razi looked at Lorcan's fingers and swallowed. "He told me that he'd already explained . . ."

"Well, he didn't."

"Christopher is no thief, Lorcan. And if he lied it was only to protect me." Wynter was stunned by the bitterness in Razi's voice. His voice was trembling as he answered her father's question. "He is a good, honest man. I made an enormous mistake bringing him here. My friendship has caused him nothing but trouble since day one, and now he is ensnared as a pawn to my father. I wish I had sent him home when first I—" He cut himself short and looked down at his feet.

Lorcan dropped his hands to his lap and regarded him compassionately. "So what happened to . . .?"

But Razi's expression changed even as Lorcan was speaking, and the big man's voice trailed away as he watched his young friend come to some great and sudden realisation. There was something dawning in Razi's face, a huge, surprising rush of inspiration. He had an idea.

Lorcan's gaze drifted and he jumped a little when he saw Wynter standing in the early morning shadows. She met his eye and tightened her lips. *You were talking about me, you old meddler!* Lorcan raised an eyebrow and ducked his head. He gave her a little shamefaced, *you caught me* smile. She narrowed her eyes in mock aggravation.

Razi remained oblivious to everything, completely pre-occupied by his racing thoughts. It didn't look like he intended answering Lorcan's question anytime soon. "Of course . . ." He stood very still a moment, his mouth half open, his eyes distant. "Of *course* . . ." he said. "But how . . . without getting him killed?" He began to walk slowly from the room. Wynter opened her mouth to say something to him as he approached, but he didn't notice her.

Instead, he turned abruptly back to Lorcan and retrieved his crop from the bed. "I'll need this," he said, holding the crop up and nodding absently. He tapped Lorcan's foot with the tip of it. "You stay abed and do as you have been told." With that, Razi wandered thoughtfully from the room, blind to everything but his inner calculations, sliding the secret door shut behind him.

Wynter met Lorcan's eye. "Jesu!" said her father, "what was that all that about?"

Wynter didn't know, but for some reason it made her heart race in her chest and filled her with fear for her two friends.

It was still extremely early when Wynter reached the library. She knew that Pascal and the apprentices had an hour's journey from town to reach the palace every day, and she did not expect them to be there until the beginning of the next quarter. So it was quite a shock when she opened the library door and found them all standing, raw-eyed and anxious, in the centre of the room.

It was obvious that she had interrupted something. Gary was hugging Jerome, while the others stood about in a loose, shuffling, helpless circle. At her entrance, Jerome immediately broke free of Gary's arms and turned his back, quickly swiping tears from his eyes. Pascal stood a little to the rear of his boys, his face stricken.

Wynter closed the door carefully behind her, and put her roll of tools on the floor. "What is it?" she said warily.

To her surprise, Gary rounded on her, his face red with anger and fear, and Pascal did nothing but watch. "Where is yer *master*?" Gary snarled. "You said he'd be here! Where is he?"

Wynter blinked at the ferocity of the questioning.

"Where is yer *master*?" repeated Gary, his gentle face changed utterly in his distress.

"Yer *know* where he is!" howled Jerome suddenly, flinging his arms up and turning to show his tear ravaged face. "*Everyone* knows where the good Protector Lord is! Poisoned! Taken from the King's side in his time of need! The only working man on the whole royal platform! The only decent soak in der whole bloody crew! Poisoned! And you," he pointed a shaking finger at Wynter, "dancing with the evil bastard what done it! Dancing and making merry while decent men are dragged ter der . . . d . . . doom!"

Pascal raised his hand to quiet the boy's wild torrent. "Hush, Jerome."

Gary grabbed his friend's shoulder. "Tat it, Jerome," he said gently, his wary eyes on Wynter. "Tat it!"

Wynter raised her hands in placation and she addressed Pascal, her voice calm and low, despite her rapidly escalating panic. "What has happened?"

It must be something terrible, she though frantically. *Something huge!* These wild accusations, this barely contained aggression . . . none of that had been evident yesterday. Something must have happened! Someone must have said or done something, because these accusations hadn't sprung from nowhere.

"How can yer *do* it?" cried Jerome. "Take yer father's place at the feast? And he locked away! Dying mebbe. No one ter see him all day but you and that Arab? How can yer – shaking yer arse all night in the black bastard's face! Suppin' from his cup like a harem wh—"

"Hush, Jerome . . . come *on*!" Gary pulled his friend back, trying to steer him away from Wynter, his face alarmed. Wynter stood with her mouth open. Her stomach and heart frozen in icy shock.

Jerome began crying almost hysterically, pulling aimlessly against his friend's grip. Gary's face crumpled with sorrow and sympathy, and he tried to gather his friend into his arms, pulling him away from the others who stood, distraught and useless around the thrashing boy.

Pascal, with tears in his eyes, gestured to the back of the room, and Gary and the other third year manhandled the weeping Jerome through the stacks and behind the bookshelves at the other end of the library. His distress was still audible and now and again, he would let out a wordless howl, as if he couldn't contain the grief within him.

Wynter wanted to say something, to ask something, but she wasn't sure what. Her mouth opened but nothing came out. Pascal came and stood beside her, his jaw working, obviously fighting an overwhelming emotion. Finally he managed a tremulous hiss.

"Protector Lady," he said as if trying to give her a chance. "Where *is* your father? We came here this morning hoping he'd be here. Hoping we'd be able ter talk to him . . .." he looked Wynter up and down. "Where is he, lass?"

What could she say? Without betraying Lorcan's vulnerability, what could she possibly do? Wynter looked Pascal in his eyes, and tried to look convincing, but she was terrified that all she was managing was to look shifty and scared. "My father is detained on business of state, Master Heutte," she said, keeping her voice soft. "I cannot find a way to convince you otherwise; you shall just have to take my word for it. Please, you cannot possibly think that I would aid in my own father's downfall? That I would *poison* my own father?"

Pascal continued to eye her warily. His little first years had retreated behind his back, their peaky faces glaring out at her from the safety of his shadow.

"Everywan sawd yer dancing with the Arab," whispered one of them, and Pascal pushed him gently out of sight.

Wynter wanted to shout, *I was not dancing with Razi!* She wanted to say, *I'll dance with whom I damn well please!* She wanted to ask, *who told you such bloody lies?* but none of those things would matter a penny. It would only lead to her having to defend herself against this atrociously inaccurate gossip. She lifted her gaze from the little boys and looked Pascal straight in the eye.

"What has happened?" she asked.

"They've arrested Jerome's cousin, and his wife and the two childern. They took them in t'middle ard' night. Left the wee baby crying in its cradle till Jer's mam found it at dawn."

"Jesu Christi!" Wynter covered her mouth with her hands and gaped at Pascal. "What . . .? On what charge?"

"Sedition."

"Good God! And . . . the children?"

Pascal was looking her up and down, his face wary, attentive. She realised, with a shiver of despair, that he was watching her for deceit. "They allus take the childern, lass. You knows it."

She nodded, yes, in the past they had always taken the children. Always. Whole families thrown into jail. But not since Jonathon, never under his reign. She shook her head. She looked around her for a moment. Jerome was sobbing steadily at the back of the library; she could hear Gary mumbling to him.

"Why?" she repeated.

"Donny's wife . . . Jerome's cousin's wife. Her sister's husband was murdered by the Arab, who said he had tried ter kill him."

Wynter snapped her eyes to him in disbelief. "Do you . . . do you mean Jusef Marcos?" she said.

Pascal nodded. "Jusef were a loyal man. He were loyal ter the crown, lass. He were murdered fer it, and his good wife gone missing, and his old dad."

"He shot a guard through the *head*, Master Huette! He tried to *kill* the Lord Razi!" She almost said, *I saw it myself! I saw him fling the bow from him as he raced away*, but something made her stop.

Pascal was looking at her very hard. "They beat a poor gardener ter death fer it too," he said. "Did he also shoot a guard through t'head? Or were he jurst another outspoken man who irked the Arab's eye?"

Wynter remembered the gardener, trotting unsuspecting into the middle of things, flinging his scythe from him and fleeing at the sight of the enraged guards. Oh, that poor man! She put her hands to her head, and closed her eyes for a moment. "And people think that Razi *killed* those men, for . . .? Because . . .?"

"The people don't think narthin. They *know*. They know it's acause them men spoke out fer the Royal Prince Alberon."

"God help us!" Wynter whispered. The utter conviction in Pascal's voice had her digging her nails into her scalp. "And now they're arresting Jusef's associates? His family?" *Oh God.* It had become a purge. Jonathon was just making things worse and worse. What were they going to do? She looked up at Pascal again. He was hard eyed and watchful. "You are in danger, Master Huette."

"You don't harve ter tell *me* that," he whispered coldly. He put his hand on the knotted head of the little first year who was trying to peep at her, and pushed him back out of sight again. They were all in danger. If the arrests spread to Jerome's immediate family, then his friends and their families and all *their* friends were in imminent danger of arrest, and of questioning and of execution.

At the back of the library Jerome and Gary were arguing now.

Gary was saying, "Yer need ter just calm down! Just hold yer horses 'til me dad tells us what ter do!"

She could hear poor Jerome's wavering voice, his words too garbled to make out from here. But Gary interrupted him with a yell, "Tat it! Tat! Yer wanner get yerseln kilt? Just tat it, Jer!"

Jerome began crying again, loudly and without restraint. Then the sounds were muffled, as if Gary had suddenly drawn his friend into a hug. Wynter saw a little hand reach around from behind Pascal's leg and discreetly take hold of the old man's fingers. Without looking down, Pascal enclosed the first year's hand in his and held on tight.

"Let me talk to my father," whispered Wynter, dragging her eyes up to Pascal's face. "Please stay here," she said, "Please, *please* do not let Jerome leave the library."

Pascal did not even nod. He was still standing in the exact same position when she shut the library door behind her.

Hopeless Causes

Wynter closed the door softly and stood for a moment, leaning against the wood. She didn't know what to do. It was a measure of her confusion that she had committed the unthinkable crime of leaving her tools in the library with another master's crew. That was the equivalent of leaving the family jewels on a tree stump in a gypsy camp, but she couldn't bring herself to return for them now, and anyway, those boys were hardly in the mood to pilfer.

Dear God, she thought. *What an evil mess.*

And what was to be done about it? In reality, when the wheel of state had begun its roll against you, there was very little that you could do, except tuck your head in your arms and hope it passed over you. Jerome's family would live or die regardless of anything Lorcan could do or say. Even if Wynter were able to persuade Razi himself to intercede, it was unlikely that the King would halt a purge. Eventually these things took on a life of their own, living and dying as a beast might live and die, for as long as it had the strength and energy to continue on, eating everything its path.

Wynter groaned. Why had she allowed herself to get to know these men? It would be so much easier had they remained faceless, nameless, voiceless shadows. It wouldn't have made their inevitable destruction any less wrong, but it would have been easier on her, not knowing.

God, they hadn't a chance, and she had just committed her father to the hopeless task of aiding them. What's more, these were guildsmen. Guildsmen! The King was taking on a lot by targeting them. The carpenters' guild was a huge and powerful organisation, shamelessly outspoken and independent.

Wynter opened her eyes. Now there was an idea. Perhaps, by some stroke of madness or delusion, Jonathon might be unaware of how unhappy his people were. If the King could be made to understand just how virulent public feeling was, he might reconsider this new, overwhelmingly dangerous policy of antagonising his subjects!

But Wynter could not approach the King herself. And if she told Lorcan, he would leap from his bed without a thought for his health and go wading into the stormy waters of state, long before he was ready to cope. If she approached Razi, as things stood now, he might well turn silently away. She had two options: getting her feelings hurt or risking her father's health. Wynter knew there was no competition. She turned left down the hall and out the door, taking the path down to the stable yards.

She could hear Razi's shouted instructions as she approached the exercise yard. He was calling out to the grooms. "Where did she hit, there?" "Was that her right fore?" and "Raise that another rung now, Michael!" Razi was practising at the jumps.

As Wynter neared the ring, the thundering noise of the horse became a physical vibration in the air. She could feel it hammering through the earth beneath her feet. She had always loved that particular sound: the steady trot of the horse on the straight, quickening in the approach to the hurdle, the anticipatory *thu-thud* as the horse bunched its great hindquarters before the leap, and then the sudden and absolute suspension of noise, like a silent *whoop!* as the horse left the ground and sailed through the air.

It was a sound heard nowhere but here. In all her travels she had never once seen, or even heard reference to this type of riding. It seemed absolutely unique to Jonathon's kingdom, and she had missed its elegance. Its sense of beauty for beauty's sake.

She turned into the yard, and saw that Razi was astride a powerful chestnut mare, one of his long-legged, arch-necked Arabs. Wynter had never seen a horse as light on its feet. Razi was running her through a circuit of seven jumps, kicking up the yellow dust as they went. He guided the horse into the hurdles without a trace of fear or hesitation. Rising and falling smoothly in the stirrup on the straights, sitting down into the saddle and leaning forward into each jump. His hands were easy on the reins, his sinewy body shifting effortlessly in harmony with the animal. Razi was utterly concentrated on the task at hand, completely in control.

He would call out after each landing, and the grooms would scurry about in response, raising or dropping the bars on the jumps. They shouted out replies to his questions, telling him if the horse was hitting the bar, what leg was dragging or knocking, and Razi would adjust the approach accordingly and try for a perfect round the next circuit.

Gone was his previous tension, the almost frightening air of iron-willed containment that Razi now habitually wore. His face was flushed with the exercise and fresh air. His eyes were clear and bright, alert with the joy of his work. He was utterly focused, and Wynter realised that he had left the world behind him. At this moment, nothing existed for Razi but this; his own body and this huge animal and the way the two of them were working together to perfect their partnership. It was as disciplined as a dance, and as beautiful to watch, and Wynter could not bring herself to intrude on it.

She settled herself against the corner of the alley wall and glanced around, taking note of where the guards were situated. Her eye fell on a bright patch of colour on the far side of the ring, and she straightened and stared. It was the orange cat. The same fellow who had approached her the night of the first attempt on Razi's life.

It was perched on a fence-post, regarding Razi with calculating eyes. Wynter saw one of the grooms notice. Frowning, he picked up a stone and flung it, missing the cat by only an inch. The stone hit the post just under the cat's neatly folded paws, but the animal did not jump or startle. Instead it turned its disdainful gaze at the groom, stood up, shook itself and dropped from the fence-post as of its own accord. The groom glared at it until it had slunk from sight.

Wynter turned her attention back to the ring, just in time to see the big mare toss her head and rip the rein from Razi's weakened right hand? At the sudden, lopsided break in communications, the horse shied and side-stepped and hopped, causing the grooms to spread their arms and scuttle about like crabs.

Razi was too good a rider to be unseated. He gathered the reins in his left hand, sat firmly into the saddle and clamped down hard with his thighs. He drew the horse in a tight left-handed circle, and crooned at her until she came to a roll-eyed halt under him.

He sat erect and masterful in the saddle until the horse was calm. But then he alarmed Wynter by leaning forward, his face creased with pain, and she noticed his right arm remained hanging by his side, the hand limp and white against the dusty fabric of his leggings.

She went to step forward but a voice behind her said, "Don't you have work to be doing, Protector Lady? Wood to shave? Carpenters to berate?"

She turned and looked up into the smooth good looks of Simon De Rochelle. He curled an unfriendly smile at her, and held her eyes for a moment before stepping past her into the ring.

In the short time it took for the groom to cross the ring and take the mare's rein, Razi had straightened, his momentary display of weakness gone. Wynter was sad to see that his remote, courtly mask was back in place. He slipped free of the stirrups and swung his leg across the mare's neck. Sliding unaided to the ground, he landed sure-footed and light, nodding as De Rochelle advanced towards him. Wynter saw him flexing and bunching the too-white fingers of his right hand.

All of Razi's attention was fixed on the councilman and he didn't see her waiting uncertainly by the corner. She bit her lip and hung back, not wanting to discuss anything in front of De Rochelle.

"What news?" Wynter heard Razi say.

"He's arrested all of them. Men, women and children."

Razi tightened his jaw and looked away.

"My Lord . . ." De Rochelle went on, but Razi warningly glanced at the guards.

"Simon!" he snapped.

De Rochelle's back straightened, and Wynter heard him take a sharp irritated breath. "Your Highness," he corrected himself.

Razi nodded. He turned, and began leading the councilman away from Wynter, whom he still hadn't noticed lurking by the alley.

"Good man, Simon," he said. "You must remember. I would not like to lose you over a slip of your oily tongue."

De Rochelle chuckled and ducked his head as they headed towards the indoor arena.

Wynter opened her mouth to call Razi, but his next words to De Rochelle stilled her. "If the King begins a purge," he said, tapping his crop against his thigh. "It will go badly for him with the people."

So, Razi knew then. Would he act?

"Badly for the King means disastrous for you, your Highness."

Razi's voice trailed out of earshot as they headed into the big barn, but not before Wynter heard him say. "But disastrous for me is wonderful for my brother, Simon."

God help us, Razi, she thought with a start. *What games are you playing? Have you no concern for your own life?*

She hesitated for a moment, then turned to leave, but

spun back as Razi suddenly dashed from the barn. Gone was all his courtly composure, and his face was creased with worry. He looked around the arena until he found her, then he gave her a most searching look. De Rochelle must have said something about her presence. Razi met her eye, his expression alarmed.

"Protector Lady?" he called across the sun-baked exercise yard. "Is all well?"

She flicked a glance at the guards. *Don't forget yourself Razi!* she thought, and bowed formally. She realised that Razi thought her father or Christopher were in need of him, and in his concern, all his carefully constructed aloofness had fallen away. She kept her voice cool as she said, "All is most well, your Highness. I was merely taking the air."

Razi gave her an uncertain look, nodded and turned back to the barn. Simon De Rochelle watched her from the shadows until she left.

As Wynter retreated up the alley, a flash of movement at the end caught her eye and she broke into a run. She cleared the corner of the feed-store just in time to see Gary Huette racing back to the library as fast as his legs could carry him.

Damn! Oh goddamn it! Damn it to hell!

He was going to report back to the others that the Protector Lady had not, as she had promised, gone to speak to her father. But had run instead to her lord and master, the murderer, the poisoner, the usurping pagan bastard, Razi the Pretender.

Damn it! She kicked the wall in frustration and yelped and hopped and cursed under her breath. *Oh, good Frith!* as Christopher would say.

She walked back to the palace completely at a loss. Should she go to the library and try to explain? Would they listen? What if they tried to leave, believing that she was plotting behind their backs? Jesu. If that happened they'd have to explain why to the guards. They'd bring a whole lot of trouble down on themselves.

There was nothing for it. She'd have to go talk to her father.

She let herself into the suite and came up short at the sight of Christopher He had dragged one of the round chairs into the retiring room, no mean task in his current condition, and positioned it outside her father's open bed-room door.

Christopher was sitting upright and wary, staring at something within Lorcan's room. One hand had a death's grip on the arm of his chair. In his other hand Wynter was alarmed to see his black dagger, steadied against his knee, the blade forward and at the ready. The tip of the knife shook slightly. Christopher was afraid.

Wynter locked the door and waited for Christopher to acknowledge her presence.

"Girly?" he hissed, without looking around.

"Yes," she whispered, reaching for her own dagger.

"There's a ghost in your father's room."

Jesu. There were no resident ghosts in these apartments! That meant it was a visitation. A spirit wilfully breaking its sphere of influence, acting on impulse and of its own accord. Never a good thing.

Wynter swallowed and slid her dagger back into place. "Christopher," she said softly, advancing on the tense young man. "You don't need your knife."

She could hear Christopher's ragged breathing as she got closer and realised that he was terrified beyond belief.

"It's been here for an age," he whispered, his bruised eyes glued to the apparition, which remained out of Wynter's sight in her father's room. "I came in to visit with your father, but he were asleep, so I came out to fetch a pillow, and when I got back . . . it were here. Standing over him. Just looking."

Is it . . . is it a woman?" she asked uncertainly, thinking of Heather Quinn and of all that a visit from her would mean.

She sighed with relief when Christopher said, "No, lass. It's a man. A soldier. I'm mortal feared it's going to do to your father like those others, and I have no idea how to stop it . . ." Christopher gestured with his knife and said uncertainly, "should it . . . commence to glowing . . ."

Wynter understood that Christopher feared that there would be another surge, like the one that had killed the inquisitors and their prey.

"It's all right, Christopher," she said, moving to his side and putting her hand on his arm. "Ghosts don't tend to harm." Despite her words, she was still reluctant to look into Lorcan's room.

"Oh aye?" said Christopher dryly. "Tell that to the raw meat we left in the dungeon a few nights ago." He pulled his knife hand free, and continued his anxious surveillance of the ghost. Wynter took a deep breath and leaned across him, resting her cheek on the top of his head as she peered around the doorframe into Lorcan's room. She cried out softly at the sight of the apparition, and Christopher jumped. He exclaimed in alarm as she tried to push past him.

"No!" he hissed, and grabbed her wrist, pulling her away from the door. His gap-fingered grip felt odd on her arm, but he was quite amazingly strong for such a slim person.

"It's all right, Christopher," she said again.

She crouched down level with him so that he didn't have to bend his neck. She put her hand on his and tried to gently pull his crushing fingers from her wrist. "I know him! He won't harm me."

Christopher's eyes slid back to Lorcan's room.

Lorcan was asleep, lying atop the covers in his robe and nightshirt, his long hair fanned on the pillow like blood. Rory Shearing was standing over him. He was gazing down at the sleeping man with an expression that could have been resentment or could have been distress, it was hard to tell.

Don't let him be a harbinger, thought Wynter, turning to look. *Don't let him have come for my dad.*

As if reading her thoughts, Christopher whispered. "What does it want?"

Wynter rose slowly to her feet, Christopher held onto her wrist a moment longer, then let her go. She crossed quietly into her father's room and stood at the foot of Lorcan's bed.

"Hello, Rory," she said.

Old Songs, Best Left Unsung

*G*hosts rarely focus on that which doesn't interest them. So Rory Shearing ignored Wynter completely. In life, he had been a good fifteen years older than her father, but Rory had died so many years ago that Lorcan's age had caught up with his, and now they could have been peers.

Rory tilted his head, and some trick of the light against his transparent face made it clear that he was, in truth, regarding her father with enormous love and sympathy. The conviction that Rory was a harbinger rose up again like vomit in Wynter's throat.

Behind her, Christopher was trying to stand, and she whispered to him to stay where he was. He must have decided to obey her, because his frustrated gasps and mutterings abruptly ceased. Wynter glanced around at him and had to smile at the way he was glaring at Rory, his useless dagger held at the ready, should the ghost decide to attack her.

"Who is he?" Christopher whispered, his eyes on Rory.

"It's Rory Shearing," she replied softly. "He was my father's commander in The Haun Invasion, during

Jonathon's father's reign. A great warrior and a good man. My father was very fond of him. He led the defence of Profit's Pass?"

She phrased it as a question, thinking it impossible that Christopher wouldn't know of the Battle of Profit's Pass. But there wasn't an iota of recognition in his face. *Why should there have been?* she realised. Christopher couldn't have been more than three years old at the time of the invasion, and living way up north in Hadra. He would have been blissfully ignorant of the terrible, brief war that had threatened this distant Southland kingdom.

"Rory, Jonathon and my father took a small group of men, and against all odds, defeated the last of the Haunardii at Profit's Pass," she explained. "Rory's men were out-manned, outmanoeuvred and under-supplied. They were cut off by the weather and practically starved, but they defeated the enemy, broke up their supply route and turned a certain defeat into a victory within weeks."

Christopher grunted in admiration, and Wynter turned back to watch Rory as he stood over her father. "Poor Rory died very soon afterwards," she said. "He was only thirty-three, same age as my father is now."

"Your father must have been fierce young."

"Seventeen."

Rory continued to ignore them completely; they may as well not have been there. He seemed to be waiting for something.

Wynter had to admit that she was very surprised to see him here. Apart from the fact that this wasn't Rory's usual sphere of influence, Lorcan and Rory Shearing's ghost had never communed in the past. In fact, her father had often tried to discourage Wynter's regular visits to the avenue that Rory haunted.

The dead should remain dead, darling. You're only halting his ascent to heaven, encouraging him to hang about.

But she had been a wilful little minx, and despite her father's gentle disapproval, she'd always returned to her wistful playmate. Wynter knew that she must be honest with herself now, there could only be one reason for the spirit's wordless vigil over her father's sickbed.

"Rory," she whispered, tears in her eyes. "Are you here to . . .?"

Lorcan moaned in his sleep, and Wynter heard him gasp as if in pain or fear. "Dad . . .?" she said, her fingers tightening on the footboard. Both she and Rory leant forward slightly as the big man's breathing quickened and he shifted uncomfortably on the bed.

"Stop him!" cried Lorcan suddenly, making Wynter jump. "Stop!" And his eyes flew open and snapped immediately to where Rory's ghost was leaning over him. Rory smiled, and Lorcan gave him a quizzical look. "Rory," he whispered. "I was dreaming of you.

"That you were," said Rory, his voice as subtle as snow falling on snow, so subtle that you could almost convince yourself you hadn't heard it.

Lorcan glanced down to where Wynter stood, silent and staring, at the foot of his bed. "Baby-girl," he whispered, obviously alarmed to see her there. He glanced across at Christopher. Then he looked up into the ghost's kind face once more. "Oh, Rory," he said softly. "I'm not ready!"

Rory Shearing shook his head. "Not my job," he smiled, and Lorcan relaxed with a shaky sigh.

"Thank Jesu!" Lorcan said, and Wynter closed her eyes and leaned her forehead on the footboard in relief.

"What do you want?" Christopher asked, his voice hard and suspicious. Lorcan glanced at him, frowning, but Rory ignored him altogether. To Rory, Christopher didn't exist. Wynter probably didn't exist at this moment. Only Lorcan existed, because Rory was trying to tell him something.

"The boy," Rory said to Lorcan, gesturing with his hands, and trying to concentrate. "Jonathon's . . ." his voice trailed off, and he gazed wordlessly at Lorcan for a moment, his hands poised.

Wynter groaned. She had forgotten about this frustrating ghost talk. Trying to speak to them was like trying to hold water in your fingers. It seemed they were too distant to keep track of many things. After a while, most of them focused on only one subject. Like Heather Quinn and her obsession with death. Or the Hungry Ghost and its obsession with food. But Rory was trying very hard to concentrate, she could see that, and she willed him to get a train of thought going that he could communicate to them.

"Jonathon's boy?" asked Lorcan, keeping very still, trying not to disturb the ghost's efforts. "Which of his boys? Alberon, is it? The young boy? The white boy?"

Rory closed his eyes and swayed like water-weed for a moment, drifting in and out of focus. "Jonathon's boy," he whispered, as if recalling him in a dream. "He does not understand . . . just paper. Just . . . ideas."

Christopher growled impatiently, and Wynter and Lorcan shushed him as one.

Rory opened his eyes again, staring down at Lorcan.

"The men," he said, very clearly, his voice almost a real sound. Lorcan's lips parted in dismay. He gazed up into Rory's urgent face and Wynter could tell that the words *the men* had significance for her father.

"*Our* men, Rory? The twenty-four? Our twenty-four?"

Rory blinked at him, his face puzzled, he had forgotten already.

Lorcan pulled himself up in the bed and reached his hand out, as though to grab the front of Rory's ragged uniform. His fingers passed through sun-filtered air.

"Rory! Do you mean the twenty-four?"

"The twenty-four," repeated Rory, his face clearing. "Aye. The men."

Lorcan abruptly put his hand to his eyes, and Rory watched as the big man struggled with some inner turmoil. The ghost's face was unusually alert now, really *seeing* the man before him. Wynter began to feel uncomfortable at the way Rory was staring at her father. Ghosts weren't meant to focus on you like that. It wasn't done. Rory's tissue paper words drew Lorcan's gaze back up, and Wynter saw her father swallow down his emotions and grind his teeth in an effort to listen without tears.

"They have forgotten," Rory told him, "everything but victory."

Lorcan's distress turned to confusion. "What do you mean?

"The men. The boy. Ideas. Old songs best left unsung. It was all for naught . . . all for naught, Lorcan . . . He used it again."

Lorcan nodded, his eyes hollow. "I know."

"Now . . . he wants to take it back . . ."

"He's right to, Rory. He should. We all agreed."

Rory leant down, and without warning, brought his ghostly face up dose to Lorcan's. The big man recoiled from the sensation of ghost breath on his skin and Rory leaned closer. For a moment, Lorcan was staring directly into the dead man's eyes. And the dead man was staring back. Lorcan's hands began to shake, and he made a desperate noise in his throat. He seemed unable to look away.

"The men *don't* agree," hissed Rory. "*They're* with the boy!"

Wynter jerked in panic as her father began to choke.

"Hey!" Christopher shouted from the door, and Wynter heard the chair scrape as he pushed himself from it. "HEY!"

Lorcan released a horrible rasping breath, as though he were being strangled, and Wynter leapt forward as Christopher stumbled his way to her side.

"Dad!" she shouted.

But then Rory stood up, breaking eye contact, and Lorcan slumped forward, his hand to his throat, his face scarlet. He immediately held a hand up, and Wynter and Christopher came to an obedient halt.

Wynter fidgeted at the edge of the bed, glancing anxiously between Rory and her father as Lorcan got himself under control. Behind her, Christopher staggered like a drunkard and grabbed at the footboard, his knife still held out in shaking defiance of the ghost.

Rory Shearing was standing dreamily looking down at the now glaring Lorcan.

So," rasped the big man, his hand still to his throat. "Where is he? The boy?"

Rory tilted his head, looking quizzical.

"Rory!" Lorcan slapped the bed loudly, demanding that the ghost concentrate. "RORY! Sharpen up!"

Rory frowned, and seemed to focus on Lorcan again, "Yes . . ." he said. "The boy . . ."

"That's why you're here, isn't it? To tell me where the boy is? You can't possibly think it's right. That he bring it into use? That he drag it all out into the light? After all . . ." Lorcan paused, and his voice dropped to a whisper. "After all you sacrificed to bury it."

Rory frowned suddenly and looked behind him, as though he'd heard a sound. Instinctively they all followed his gaze. He was staring intently at the far wall, but there was nothing there that they could see.

"Rory?" asked Lorcan uncertainly. "Where is Alberon?"

Rory tore his eyes from the wall. "That is what you need to know?" he asked.

"Yes!" said Wynter suddenly. "Yes! Dad! Tell him *yes*!"

"Yes!" said Lorcan.

Rory looked behind him again. "I must go." He glanced at Lorcan. "I will do my best." He ducked his head and raised his hands, as though someone had shouted in his ear, and looked behind him again. "I have to go!" he cried, glancing about him in panic as if uncertain where to turn. He bolted suddenly, and Lorcan yelled and pulled his legs back as Rory passed through the bed. Without a sound, the ghost disappeared into the far wall.

They looked about tensely for a moment, waiting to see if anything would arrive in pursuit of him, but there was nothing. Just the faintest scent of gunpowder in the air.

"Good Frith," murmured Christopher as Wynter guided

him around to sit on the edge of the bed. "You palace folk lead interesting lives."

Lorcan looked at his daughter. "Seems like fate is pushing us to find that boy," he said.

But what for? thought Wynter. *When we find him, do we help him? Or do we deliver him to his father and his doom?*

To Wynter's surprise and dismay Christopher slowly lowered himself onto his side and curled up like a cat on the bed at Lorcan's feet, his head in his arms.

Lorcan and Wynter exchanged a look of alarm. "Are you all right, boy?" asked Lorcan.

"Oh aye," whispered Christopher, his voice muffled by his arms. "I just need a moment to hold onto my breakfast."

Wynter patted his foot, and Lorcan grimaced in amused sympathy. "You stay there as long as you like, boy, you make a grand bed-warmer." And he tucked his toes in under Christopher's belly.

"Agh," exclaimed Christopher softly. "Your feet are like blocks of ice."

Lorcan lay back on his pillows. He folded his hands on his chest, gazing thoughtfully at the ceiling. "Rory Shearing . . ." he mused, his face grave. "I need to think."

"Lorcan," Christopher asked, head still cocooned in the protection of his arms. "Has this to do with The Bloody Machine?"

Lorcan started and gave the young man a frightened look. "Hush, boy!" he said. "What you don't know won't kill you."

Christopher snorted. "Oh, I'm not so certain about that. I know less than nothing, and I'm still getting my head kicked in."

Lorcan's expression vied between amusement and despair as he looked down at the young man at his feet. Without thinking, Wynter reached and covered Christopher's feet with the hem of his robe.

"Thanks," he said.

"Bloody theatre folk," grated Lorcan, poking Christopher gently with his foot. "Always with the dramatics." Then he leant back and resumed his pensive observation of the ceiling.

Wynter looked at her father's pale face, the ever present trembling in his fingers, and she made a snap decision. She turned to leave.

Lorcan glanced at her in alarm. "Wynter!" he said sharply, as though it had just struck him, "What were you doing here anyway? Is there trouble in the library?"

"No, Dad," she said, turning to smile at him. "I just wanted to look in on you, that's all. I'd better go."

At the hall door she paused, her hand on the key. An image came very clearly to her mind of Pascal Huette, reaching down to enclose that child's hand in his own. She knocked her forehead gently against the wood of the door. *They left the baby, crying in its cradle.* Jesu Christi. Her father would never forgive her – she'd never forgive *herself* – if they didn't at least *try* to save these men.

She went back into Lorcan's room and stood resignedly in the door. Lorcan glanced across at her. Before she even spoke, he was dragging himself up and heaving his legs over the side of the bed.

The Protector Lord's Men

"God help me . . . I hate this." Lorcan's voice was tight with uncharacteristic bitterness, and Wynter assumed that he was referring to his physical weakness. She said nothing, just patted his arm and continued to keep watch up and down the torch-lit passageway, ready to warn him should anyone appear.

They had taken much the same route that Jonathon had shown them the day he'd half-carried Lorcan back to his rooms, and, so far they had been almost completely free of public scrutiny. But this was the last section where it would be possible to remain secluded from the public eye, and Lorcan had stopped to catch his breath, and to try to gather his wits before donning the mask of Protector Lord. He was sweating and shaking, and Wynter was more and more convinced that she'd made the wrong decision telling him of the apprentices.

They had left Christopher sitting up on Lorcan's bed, his head tilted back against Lorcan's pillows, squinting disapprovingly as the big man made himself presentable. "You're a bloody fool," Christopher kept saying. "Razi will kill you dead." Now she was wondering if Razi would even get the chance. She resisted the urge to ask, once again, that they return to their rooms. Lorcan had become quite irritable with her the last time.

"I hate this constant panic. I wish I could just have a moment to sit down and think," Lorcan continued, and Wynter realised that he hadn't been speaking about his illness at all.

He was reading the ceiling in that pensive way of his, his eyes roaming the carefully layered cobbles as if deciphering Sanskrit. "I hate this constant reacting," he said. "It's all I seem to have done for the last five years. React, react, react. No time to plan, no time to organise any kind of defence, before the earth shifts and the tides turn, and we're on the move again. Oh Wyn!" He groaned suddenly, putting his hand to his face, and for the first time in her life, Wynter heard defeat in her father's voice. "I'm too tired for this. I'm just . . ." He took a deep breath.

Wynter bit her lip in sympathy. But even as she was putting a comforting hand on his chest and opening her mouth to say, *it's all right, Dad. Let's go back*, Lorcan was pushing himself from the wall and looking purposefully at the short flight of steps at the end of the passage. "Up those steps, across the rose garden, another flight of steps, and then the library," he said, as if making a deal with himself, "all right." He breathed out and launched himself forward, looping his arm across Wynter's shoulder.

"Once we're at the top of the steps you'll be in full view," she grunted. "You'll have to walk alone, Dad.

"Just get me there, girl!" his angry growl silenced her. They took the steps with careful deliberation, and paused at the top for him to gather his defences. Then Lorcan pushed back his shoulders, took a breath and stepped out into the sun.

The rose garden was empty as they closed the door behind them, but Lorcan didn't bend from his rigidly self-imposed pretence. He walked slowly, with squared shoulders and ramrod straight back, his only concession to his terrible condition the bruising grip he had on his daughter's shoulder. Wynter kept just a touch too close to his side. She glanced up at him. *Who do we think we're fooling?* she thought, *look at him!*

The granite steps into the other wing were almost his undoing. There were only six, but Lorcan stood at the foot of them, staring, his body shaking. Then he dug his fingers into her shoulder, leant forward and took each step like a man assaulting a mountain crevasse.

At the top, he sagged, and she moved to put her arm around his waist. "Stop that!" he hissed savagely and straightened.

Then they heard the shouting.

"Shit," said Lorcan tonelessly and started forward again.

Once inside the cool shadows of the tiled corridor, the sounds were very clear. At the end of the hall, the library door was open, and inside was the source of all the noise. Small children were bawling. There was an old man shouting, and other men too, yelling. Over it all, the mingled voices of three young men were screeching in fear and anger.

"Oh, good Christ," moaned Lorcan, moving as fast as he could.

We're too late, thought Wynter mournfully.

But three things gave her hope as they rounded the corner and entered the library. There was no blood. There were only three soldiers. And they were only ordinary hall guards and one gate watchmen. There was no sign of Jonathon's personal guard. If any of that group of huge, relentless men had been present, it would have been the end for these boys. As it was, the situation might be salvageable, but only if they acted quickly.

The guards were in the process of grappling with Pascal's crew, attempting to drag Jerome and Gary from the protection of the group. The two hall guards held Jerome suspended between them. He struggled wildly and kicked and spat. The third guard was prying Gary from the clutching arms of the other boys. Everyone was shouting and screaming, the small boys crying piteously through their anger. Pascal was striding up from the back of the library, a wooden mallet ready to strike down on the head of the man who threatened his son.

Things were just on the point of no return.

Lorcan paused, unnoticed, in the doorway. He drew himself up to his full height, let go of Wynter's shoulder and roared. "What are you *doing* with my *men*?"

Lorcan had a deafening bellow when he wanted, and the room fell still under the ringing aftershock of his voice. The men turned to look at him, wide-eyed. They recovered quickly and for one moment, Wynter saw rage storm up in the eyes of the soldiers: *who the hell did this carpenter think he was?* One of them actually stepped forward, a snarling retort on his lips. Then the gate watchman recognised her father and snapped to attention.

"Protector Lord Moorehawke! We caught two of these

boys sneaking off the grounds without papers. When we tried to question them, my Lord, they ran and we pursued."

Oh thank God! Not part of a purge then, not a court sanctioned arrest. Just a panicked attempt to flee that had gone wrong.

Wynter saw the boys regarding her father with round-eyed wonder. So here he was! Every working boy's hero. The carpenter, the lowly working man, granted title and power by King Jonathon himself. The magnificent Protector Lord Lorcan Moorehawke, he who had saved the King's life when they were boys. Hero worship shone out of the boys' tearstained faces, and Wynter prayed that her father could live up to the challenge of saving their lives.

Only Pascal seemed to notice the terrible pallor of her father's face, the slightly hunched shoulders, the unsteady hands. She saw sorrow dawning in his face. He came to a stop behind the group, lowered his weapon and gazed sadly across their heads at Lorcan. Wynter didn't know if his grief was on account of Lorcan's suffering, or because the fate of his boys rested on the shoulders of such a mortally-ill man.

Lorcan surveyed the boys coldly, and took a chance on them not having concocted some story. "I told you to wait for your papers, you little maggots. What do you think you're up to?"

The boys swallowed and looked uncertainly at the guards.

"Beg . . . beg pardon, my Lord . . ." answered the quick-witted Gary in a parched voice. "We forgot."

Jerome just stood, owl-eyed and shocked, his lips trembling.

Hold it together, thought Wynter. *Hold it together, good lad.*

"You forgot? You *forgot*!" Lorcan's roar made everyone jump. One of the first years began crying again, but Wynter swore she saw a smile tug the corners of Pascal Huette's lips. "Well, see if you *forget* when I dock you a day's wage, you moronic chard!" Lorcan took two long steps into the room and gestured at the guards who were smirking sideways at the scarlet boys. "Do you think these good men have naught better to do than hunt mice? Make your apologies!"

Gary turned immediately, stiff-limbed and numb. His face looked as though it might crack from tension when he said, "Beg pardon, good sirs. We didn't mean ter waste yer time."

The guards turned their hard faces to Jerome, who they still held tightly by the arms. His throat worked as he tried to force some sound past the fear blocking his throat, but all he could manage was a squeaking terrified hiss. The guards just laughed, and one of them shook him.

"Say you're sorry, squeaker!"

"You are dismissed." Lorcan's order was cold and it sliced across their amusement like a butcher's blade. The guards realised that they had overstepped the mark. These were the Protector Lord's men, his and his alone to abuse and admonish. They released Jerome, who staggered away from them, and they snapped to attention, their faces carefully neutral. "Next time you see my boys," said Lorcan, "they will have their papers, and you will have no need to abandon your post in pursuit of honest guildsmen." He gestured sharply to the guards, and they left with a salute and the careful closing of the library door behind them.

Silence settled in the room. Lorcan stood watching the door for a moment, his face blank. Wynter stepped closer to him. His eyes were very heavy, and he seemed to have drifted away for a moment.

Pascal Huette's voice came softly through her concern. "Get the Protector Lord a chair, Gary. *Gary* . . . get the Protector Lord a chair."

There was a sound of scraping and soft footsteps, and Gary and a third year brought one of the reading chairs around from the sitting area and set it quietly down behind Lorcan. They retreated to their master's side and watched as Wynter laid her hand on her father's chest, and spoke softly up into his face.

"My Lord," she said. "The apprentices would like you to do them the honour of taking a seat."

Lorcan focused on her, then looked over at the ring of uncertain faces regarding him from the other side of the room. "You idiots," he said, without a trace of humour or affection. "Why didn't you wait like my apprentice told you?"

A row of curious eyes turned to Wynter. She saw confusion there, mixed with a small measure of shame and an even bigger measure of suspicion. Gary and the third year dropped their eyes, the small boys continued to gape. Jerome hadn't even lifted his gaze from the floor; he looked as though he might fall down. Pascal kept his eyes on Lorcan.

"Won't yer do us the honour of taking a seat, my Lord?" The old man's voice was gentle, but without any dangerous pity.

Lorcan looked behind him at the chair he'd carved with

his own hands. He hesitated, as if deliberating refusing their offer, but Wynter knew he was calculating his chances of getting into the chair without losing his balance. He glared back at the ring of men, lifted his shoulders briefly in a shrug that said, *oh, why the hell not, if you're offering.* He sat down stiffly, arranging himself in an imposing and easily-maintainable position. Wynter placed herself at his back, and the two of them glowered across at the men. The carpenters quailed at the full weight of a double-barrelled, green-eyed Moorehawke glare.

"Well?" snarled Lorcan, "My apprentice, speaking in my name, left you specific instructions to sit on your arses and await me. What in blazes were you doing, rabbiting about against the guards?"

Pascal remained silent, seemingly content to allow Lorcan to reprimand his boys, or perhaps considering himself included in Lorcan's scathing ire. Gary shuffled uncomfortably, lifted his eyes to Wynter and dropped them again. "She went ter the Arab," he mumbled, "She didn't go ter you at all."

"Rest assured, young man," hissed Lorcan, leaning forward like a snake spotting a mouse. "Next time you go spying on a woman of the Protector Lady's status, you'd better hope she's as discreet as my daughter. Had the Protector Lady opened her mouth about your presence, the King's guards would have seized you, and cut you into little cubes and fed you to their hounds."

Gary's eyes flickered to Wynter again, and she regarded him coolly from behind her father's chair. Lorcan continued, his tone merciless, "They would have done this, because it is how the King would have willed it. Even that good man, his Highness, the Royal Prince Razi, wouldn't have been able to save you. Do you know why?"

Gary blinked very rapidly and shook his head.

"The reason his Highness, the Royal Prince Razi, would be unable to aid you is because the Royal Prince is as powerless in the face of the King's will as you or I. Do you understand what I am saying to you?" Lorcan let his eyes travel from face to thoughtful face, resting finally on Pascal. "Do you understand?" he repeated, speaking directly to the older man now. "The Royal Prince is a subject under the law to the King. He is a *subject*. He is following the *King's will*."

Jerome seemed to wake suddenly from a bad dream, and looked at Lorcan with red-rimmed eyes, as if seeing and hearing him for the first time. He released a long shaky breath. "Yer trying ter tell us that that pagan Arab bastard ain't oercome with joy ter be setting his arse on the heir's throne? That what yer trying ter say, Protector Lord?"

Pascal and the others swallowed hard at Jerome's audacity, but none of them moved to silence him, or to distance themselves from his words.

Dear God, thought Wynter, *these sentiments run deep. This boy is in mortal fear of his life. They are all of them in mortal fear of their lives . . . and still they go on.*

She looked at the row of pale and staring faces and could not help but admire their tenacious loyalty to Alberon. And by the same token, she could not help but marvel at how much they obviously trusted her father, to speak so dangerously in his presence, knowing as they did his proximity to the throne.

Lorcan bared his teeth and he speared Jerome with a

glare. "Let that be the very last time you malign a man on the grounds of his race, his creed or the circumstances of his birth, boy." He held Jerome's eyes until the young man dropped his gaze. Lorcan let his eyes fall on each face again and his voice softened a fraction, rising above icy to just shy of cold. "His Highness, the Royal Prince Razi . . . and mark me well, guildsmen, *that* how you will refer to him, on pain of imprisonment, by order of *the King* . . . The Royal Prince regards his present position on his brother's throne as a *stewardship*. He is as loyal and as faithful to the heir as you or I. Do you mark me?"

The apprentices frowned uncertainly.

"Do you *mark* me?"

"What of the purge, Lorcan?" Pascal said, at last, speaking for them all. They gazed at their hero in fear and the barely sustained hope that he could save them from a hideous end.

Lorcan hesitated, and Wynter knew that his hesitation was premeditated. Not a word her father said now, nor any little tic of expression, or gesture he made, would be unconscious, or done for anything less than effect. He hesitated, and so the men knew that a purge was not something he felt he could control. Yet when he spoke, there was a measure of hope in his words. "It is not yet certain, Master Huette, that there is a purge. From what limited information I have been given, it would appear that it is only the immediate family of the assassin, Jusef Marcos, that has fallen foul of the King. Am I correct?" Jerome's eyes filled with tears. Pascal nodded. "Then it is possible it may end there."

Jerome looked around him for a moment, lost. "What of

my cousin, Lord?" he said, turning his swimming eyes to Lorcan. "What of their childern?"

Lorcan's voice was gentle when he said, "Mourn them. With my sympathies."

Jerome's bottom lip shook and his eyes overflowed, and Gary pulled him to him with an arm around his shoulder.

"In the meantime," said Lorcan, his voice hard again. "Take a lesson from that excellent man, the Royal Prince Razi, and *cease your continuous harping against the King.* Guildsmen, if you do not want a purge, for Christ's sake, stop encouraging one."

"You want us ter stay silent?" This was from Gary, unexpectedly bitter, and unwilling to concede, his arm around his friend's shoulder, his father uncertain and distressed at his back.

"I want you to bide," said Lorcan, his voice surprisingly gentle again. "Like good men, like loyal and patient subjects. Bide and do his Majesty's will. And believe me when I tell you, *trust* the Royal Prince Razi, who toils in active patience for the return of his brother."

This seemed to sink in. Even Jerome stood silent then, in blinking thought, processing all the Protector Lord had said.

"Pascal," murmured Lorcan, "Put your boys to work."

And this the man did, directing them to their various occupations until gradually the library filled with the sounds of planing and filing, and the steady gentle tap of small gauge mallets hitting delicate chisels.

Finally, Pascal came over and crouched at Lorcan's knee. He managed not to keep glancing at Lorcan's hands or to search his face too closely.

"Are we safe, my Lord?" he asked, his voice low.

Lorcan moved to put his hand on the other man's shoulder and immediately thought the better of it, gripping the chair again with brutal force. "I am to dine with the King tomorrow, Pascal." The importance of this showed in Pascal's face and he glanced apologetically at Wynter. Lorcan would be showing his support of the King on the Royal platform, in the exact way that had so enraged the apprentices when Wynter had taken his place. "I will do my best to mention how loyal, how steadfast, and how honest a group of men you are."

The old man's eyes brimmed and he nodded. "Thank you, my Lord. My boys . . ."

Lorcan interrupted sharply. "But understand," he said. "I cannot protect fools. You must rein them in, Pascal. You must marshal your boys and their acquaintances. Or we shall see innocent blood, the like of which hasn't been known since our grandfathers' time. And if that happens, I will wipe my hands of you and walk away with nary a backward glance." He held the man's trembling gaze. "Are we clear?"

"Aye, my Lord," mumbled Pascal. "We are clear."

"Go about your work now."

The old man made his way to the end of the library, and recommenced with the picture panel that Lorcan had left unfinished.

Lorcan sat still for a long moment, his head bowed, his hands gripping the arms of the chair. Wynter waited patiently. Eventually, without raising his head or moving at all, he murmured softly, so only Wynter could hear, "Are they occupied, my darling?"

"Aye," she breathed, glancing around at the industriously turned backs and the averted eyes. He pushed himself forward, and she slipped her hands in under his elbows as he painfully got to his feet.

Wynter's eyes darted from boy to boy, but none of them raised their eyes or turned their head from their work. Even when Lorcan staggered, and she had to catch him around the waist and give him a moment before starting forward, all eyes were kept discreetly turned. It was unnatural for such a group of boys, this tact. Wynter wondered if it was out of respect, or out of self-preservation? Perhaps they felt that what they couldn't see wouldn't harm them, and so kept their eyes down. Keeping themselves safe from the knowledge that all their hopes of salvation were pinned on Lorcan's slowly bowing shoulders.

New Quarters

$\mathcal{T}$he journey back was awful. Lorcan managed the brief public sections with trembling stoicism, his fingers gouging welts in her shoulder, more and more of his weight leaning on her. But once they reached the secret passages and the quiet stretches of cellar, he finally let himself acknowledge his growing helplessness, and the awful unceasing pain of his condition seemed to overtake him. He groaned quietly. Occasionally he gasped, "Oh God. God help me. I can't do this. I can't."

Wynter staggered along in the constant fear that he would sink to the ground and leave her unable to assist him. She determined that he would not die here, frightened and comfortless with no candle to succour him against the shadowy approach of death.

"Keep going!" she encouraged, "Keep going!" Somehow he kept on, until they reached the end of the final stretch of private corridor and came to a stop at the small door. They had to pass into public view just once more now, in order to access the hall that led to their rooms.

Lorcan leant his head against the door. "Wynter," he groaned, "Wynter . . ." and shook his head.

"We're almost there! Please! You can make it!"

He turned his head and looked at her in the dimness. *I cannot,* his face said. *I have come as far as I can. I cannot go any further.*

"When we get to our rooms," she promised, "you can take some hashish! You can lie on your bed! Dad! You can sleep for the rest of the day and the night. How wonderful does that sound?"

He took a deep breath and pushed her off him suddenly, propping himself against the wall, his legs shaking. He let her go, cautiously testing his balance. He tilted his head. "Get Christopher. Quick. Can't stay up much longer . . ."

The hall to their rooms was thronged with servants coming and going. They were removing things – Razi's things. *Oh God! Oh God!* her mind screamed in panic. *What now?* But she pushed ruthlessly past the scurrying pages and maids, their arms piled high with books and scientific equipment and clothes, and dodged her way to Razi's door where she knew Christopher must be.

He was leaning against the far wall of the receiving room, his arms crossed, watching bleakly as the suite was cleared of Razi's belongings. As Wynter slid to a halt on the threshold, Christopher jerked from his reverie, winced and pushed himself unsteadily from the wall.

Jesu, she thought, *he looks no better than Dad. I'll end up carrying them both back.*

"What is it?" he said. She didn't answer, but at her desperate pleading look, he started forward and fell into weaving step with her as she stalked back through the stream of domestic staff.

"Good Frith! You stubborn bollix!"

Lorcan managed a laugh at the young man's exclamation, and Christopher and Wynter were just in time to shove themselves in under his arms and catch him as he slid down the wall.

This we can do for you, Dad. Wynter thought, her arm brushing Christopher's as they both clutched her father around the waist and helped him along. *This much we can do.*

They finally got to Lorcan's room, and Christopher helped him into bed. He slipped discreetly out while Wynter eased off her father's boots, his tunic and britches. Then Lorcan pushed her away and crawled under the covers in his long johns and shirt. He curled on his side, as he often did when the pain was bad. She fetched him one of the fragrant little hashish biscuits, and watched as he wearily propped himself on his elbow long enough to eat it, and drink some water. Then he lay down without a word and covered his face with his hand, waiting for her to leave.

"Rest well," she murmured, but Lorcan didn't reply.

When she went into the receiving room she found Christopher leaning against the frame of the opened hall door, his arms folded. He was openly gazing at the bustling activity in the corridor and, for once, Wynter didn't feel like berating him for his lack of tact. Instead she crossed and stood beside him, watching as Razi's things were taken away.

They were silent for a while, then Christopher murmured softly, "This cannot be good for him."

They all understood the reasons for Razi's sudden and distressing remoteness, but this was a step too far. It served no purpose that Wynter could fathom. Whatever Razi's behaviour must be in public, and no matter how aloof he remained in private, wouldn't he want to sleep at night protected, and surrounded by the people who loved him?

It seemed to her that Razi was needlessly casting himself adrift in the cold, black waters of state. Leaving Christopher, Lorcan and herself warm and cosy in the little nest that he had engineered for them, while he spun further and further away into the dark. Surely that kind of isolation would be agony for a man of Razi's innate warmth?

"I'm sure he must have his reasons," she said doubtfully.

"He's a stubborn bollix," Christopher said. "Just like your dad."

Wynter laughed. Impulsively, she slipped her hand into the crook of Christopher's arm and briefly pressed her forehead to his shoulder in a gesture of amused solidarity. "What will we do with them?" she asked, and smiled into his face. Then she too, turned to resume her undisguised monitoring of activity in the hall and, without thinking, leant comfortably against him.

To her surprise, Christopher tensed and straightened, almost pulling away. He put his hand on hers as if to lift it from his arm. Wynter kept her eyes fixed on the hall. It was a gesture that she hadn't even thought about, this taking of his arm, this leaning in. Now she regretted it, and not because it was so dangerously open and unguarded, but because it had been so obviously unwelcome. She found herself embarrassed and also horribly disappointed.

"Wynter," Christopher said unhappily. "You know. I won't be . . ." he hesitated, scrabbling for words, and tried again. "Razi, he . . . he wants . . ." He looked awkwardly down at her and paused. She flicked a glance at him, began to pull away, then saw the warring emotions in his marred face and felt the tension in his body as he tried to work something out in his head. Christopher seemed to come to a decision then, and squeezed Wynter's hand tighter into the crook of his elbow. "To hell with that," he said bitterly, and turned his eyes back to the hall, gripping her hand tightly where it lay on his arm.

Christopher began to unconsciously stroke his thumb across her knuckles as his eyes roamed the crowded hall. "Curse me," he muttered. "But that man has a powerful mountain of possessions."

The man in question chose that moment to round the corner, his face like thunder. He saw the two of them at once, and Wynter felt Christopher tense as Razi's hooded brown eyes dropped to their linked arms. But Razi swept into his suite with barely a pause, and they heard him immediately start shouting at the staff.

"Hurry the hell up, you laggards! This was meant to have been completed an *hour* ago!" There was muttering and apologies, then Razi's angry voice again, railing in an utterly uncharacteristic way against his underlings. "At least get my God-cursed dressing-trunk and washstand to the new rooms so that I can change for court! *NO!* Don't maul my medical bag, you drooling idiot! I left *specific* instructions that it wasn't to be touched!"

Wynter winced at Razi's tone, and Christopher straightened and gently took her hand from his arm. "That ain't our lad," he murmured. "That ain't our lad at all."

Razi stormed from his room, a small portfolio in one hand, his medical bag in the other. Without a glance in their direction, he turned and began dodging away through the now frantically hastened staff.

"Your Highness!" called Wynter, but Razi either didn't hear, or chose to ignore her.

"The Protector Lord has need of you, your Highness!" Christopher's raised voice stilled Razi at the corner.

Razi glanced back at him, his face still black with anger. For a moment, Wynter thought he would leave, but he took one look at her face and turned back immediately, striding through the crowd and passing her without a word, to enter the suite. Christopher shrugged wearily at her, and followed their friend inside. Wynter followed suit and shut the door behind her.

Razi hesitated at the threshold to Lorcan's bedroom, frowning at the manner in which the big man was curled in his bed. He looked at Lorcan's boots and the heap of his clothes discarded untidily on the floor, and Wynter cursed herself for having forgotten them. Razi looked darkly at herself and Christopher, and they came to a shuffling halt beside him, their eyes averted.

He went to shut the door on them, but Christopher reached his hand out, and held it open. Razi met his eyes, and Christopher held his ground, frowning in confusion at his friend's animosity. Razi dropped his gaze and turned away, leaving the door open so that Wynter and Christopher could follow on his heels.

Razi's face grew even darker as he got a good look at the Lorcan. "What have you been up to?" he growled, glowering down at the shivering man.

Lorcan rolled an eye to him and looked away, shifty as a thieving hound. "Oh," he rasped, "You know. This . . . and that."

"Good God," said Razi quietly, looking him up and down. And then he yelled and threw his bag onto the bedside table, upsetting the cups and vials already there, sending things crashing to the ground. "Can't . . . can't you people just . . . Can't you just *DO WHAT YOU'RE BLOODY TOLD?*" He kicked the table, hard, and the remaining things bounced and jiggled and fell over.

Everyone froze for a moment, stunned by his sudden outburst of violence.

"All right!" Razi said, turning on Lorcan, his face suffused with sarcastic bitterness, "all right, Lorcan!" He grabbed his bag and snapped the catch. "You want to act like a bloody child? Fine! Fine! I'll just knock you the hell out! I'll . . ." he rooted viciously in his bag for a moment, and drew out the bottle of tincture of opium. "I'll knock you bloody *out* and you'll have to . . . you'll . . ."

"That is *enough*, Razi," said Wynter, coming to stand on the other side of the bed, staring at Razi, her hand protectively on Lorcan's shoulder.

Razi glowered at her, breathing hard.

"What has happened, Razi?" Christopher's quiet voice drifted from where he leaned wearily at the bedroom door.

Razi paused, his eyes closing briefly. And then he unstoppered the tincture of opium and poured a few drops into the bottom of a beaker.

"What has happened?" repeated Christopher, a little impatiently. "Why have you removed yourself from our rooms?"

"It is unnecessary," added Wynter, "and not healthy to sever yourself so utterly from those who love you."

Razi paused at her words, then added water to the tincture. "I will not stay," he said finally. "I cannot."

"Razi . . ." groaned Christopher impatiently.

"It matters *not*, Christopher!" Razi slapped the cup down on the table, and reached to help Lorcan sit up against his pillows. "I simply *cannot*. Let that be an *end* to it!"

Wynter leant across and tried to assist her father from the other side. Lorcan shrugged the two of them off and struggled to sit unaided. Razi let the big man flounder for a moment, before reaching under his armpits and heaving him forcefully into position. He went to hand him the beaker of draught, but Lorcan caught Razi by the wrist and pulled down until the younger man had to either spill the drink or stoop to his eye level.

"What the hell has happened?" said Lorcan, not unkindly. "That you need to withdraw so thoroughly?"

Razi's anger wavered and his mouth became unsteady. "There have been . . . insinuations. Rumours that I cannot bear to tolerate."

Lorcan stared into his eyes. "What?" he said, trying to read Razi's face, still gripping his wrist. "What have they said?"

"Certain of the councilmen, those who . . ." Razi laughed, a dry bitter sound. "Those who support my brother . . . have . . . in an effort to discredit me . . ." he glanced desperately at Christopher, shook his head and ground his teeth.

Lorcan slowly released Razi's arm, his face taut. He took the beaker. "Then you are right to draw away," he said softly.

Wynter did not understand. She looked from her father to Razi, hoping for a clue. "What?" she asked finally. "What have they said?"

"Oh!" Razi threw his hands up in frustration, his cheeks burning. "It doesn't matter! Suffice it to say I cannot tolerate it!"

"What have they *said*?" insisted Christopher.

"That you are my catamite, Chris!" shouted Razi at last, spinning and holding his hands out, his eyes wide. "My catamite! I will not tolerate it!"

Lorcan winced and Wynter gasped, and the two of them turned involuntarily to look at Christopher. They expected rage, but the young man just squinted at them, obviously not understanding. "What does that mean?" he asked uncertainly. "What is a catamite?" To Wynter's amazement he turned to her, "Wyn," he asked, "what does it mean?"

She felt her face grow hot. "It means, Christopher . . . um . . . that Razi. That he has . . . that you are . . . his toy. That he has fashioned you as . . . his plaything . . ." she ducked her head, too mortified to expound, and almost immediately Lorcan surprised them all by murmuring something in Hadrish.

Christopher knew *that* word, all right. They watched as his jaw dropped and Wynter waited for the outrage, the hurt. To their immense surprise the young man just threw up his hands in relief and laughed.

"Oh Razi!" he said, "Is that *all*! Oh, friend! You don't know a bit of me, if you think that matters! And as for yourself, what does it say about you? Except that, were you so inclined, you'd have excellent taste in men!" He grinned at his friends, expecting them to share the joke.

Lorcan dragged his hand over his mouth, shocked, and looked sideways at Razi. The tall young man glared at Christopher, his body bowing forward with the strength of his emotion. "It may not matter to *you*, Christopher, but it matters to *me*." The light drained from Christopher's face at his friend's cold rage. "You are *not* in one of your bloody Merron camps *now*! The rest of the world doesn't share your people's dubious tolerances for such men, and I for one, will not be associated with their practices."

Christopher blinked, and Wynter saw him stiffen with anger and hurt, his scarred hands knotting at his sides, his bruised mouth compressed to a thin line. They all stood in awkward silence for a moment, then Christopher turned and walked stiffly from the room.

Razi looked at the empty door, then turned and began to put things back into his bag. "That draught . . ." he began, but his voice failed him on the first try. "That draught," he said again, much stronger, "is very powerful, Lorcan. You won't be fit for anything but sleep for the next good long while. So you will have no opportunity to gad about and orphan your daughter." Lorcan just silently watched Razi's face as he finished tidying. "If you need me," Razi continued, snapping his bag shut and not meeting Lorcan's eye or looking at Wynter. "Send a page to fetch me, any time of the day or night." He turned to leave.

"You are right to move out," repeated Lorcan slowly.

"But you are a fool if you let this come between you and a true, loyal friend."

Razi listened to this with his back turned, his head tilted, and left without replying.

Christopher must have been standing or sitting in the receiving room, because they heard Razi say before he left, "I have business to discuss with you, Christopher. First I must wash and dress for court, but I shall return within this quarter, and I will speak to you here."

"Oh aye," said Christopher. "We should be sure and have Wynter attend as chaperone, in case this dubious Merron compromises your Highness's virtue."

There was a moment of stillness, and Wynter's heart dropped when Razi coolly replied, "You will be fit to travel within a week, Freeman Garron. I want you to be ready to leave as soon as I tell you."

All the sarcasm had gone from Christopher's voice when he said, "Oh, Razi. So soon? What of Wynter?"

Wynter strained to hear a reply, but there was none. Only the abrupt click of the hall door shutting, and then silence.

Papers

Christopher was still in the receiving room when Wynter finished with her father. He had taken her favourite seat by the window and was gazing down into the orange garden, his arm on the sill, his face grim. Wynter dragged a chair from the other side of the room, pulled it close enough that Christopher's knees brushed the arm of it, and sat down.

"My father is asleep," she said.

He didn't turn to look at her, uncharacteristically morose. She nodded in understanding, closed her eyes in companionable silence and leaned her head against the wall.

"How can you bear this place?" he said quietly. "It's poison. It's like breathing poison, day after day 'til your spirit sickens and dies."

Wynter opened her eyes. The sun was reflecting off something in the garden, the glossy leaves of the trees perhaps, and the ceiling shimmered with dancing light. The room smelled of fragrant orange blossom and the uniquely stirring spice that she'd come to associate with Christopher.

"Why don't you leave here?" he said. "Put Lorcan in a cart, pile all your belongings around him and just go." She smiled at that. He made things sound so easy!

"Why do you grin?" he asked. "You said it yourself: you're not dependent on the throne for your bread. Use your talents, Wynter, set up a shop somewhere safe and free. Move away from all these vipers and parasites."

She sighed and closed her eyes. "It's not that simple, Christopher. People can't just set up shop where they like. You need papers, licences, and we don't have them . . . Not until the King releases them." She tilted her head to look at him. He was gazing at her, still as a statue, his hands on the arms of his chair.

"There must be somewhere you can *go*!" He insisted quietly, and she was surprised to hear desperation in his voice. "Your father is a lord! Surely he has lands . . .?"

"You don't understand," she said. "My father is a *Protector* Lord. It's just a title, that's all. It means *he who will protect the King*. It's very powerful and it has many privileges, but there is no land attached to it, Christopher, and only a small annuity. Once outside of these palace walls, we must truly fend for ourselves, and we cannot do *that* until Jonathon releases our papers. So, you see why we can't just go? You understand?"

"I don't want to just abandon you here, girly. How will you manage?" Christopher shook his head, and though she found his concern for her touching, she had to laugh at his solemn protectiveness.

He looked so hurt that Wynter reached forward, smiling, and laid her hand affectionately on his face. "Christopher, I don't need you to . . ." she said, then paused, looking into his eyes. He turned his cheek into her palm and held her gaze sadly.

The atmosphere between them thickened, and Wynter's smile faded. Just for that moment, she let herself acknowledge the fact that Christopher was leaving. Razi truly was sending him away. She ran her calloused thumb over his bruised and lacerated eyebrow. She might never see him again. "Christopher," she whispered, no humour at all in her voice as she took in the damage the King had wrought on him. "*Look* at you. This place will kill you if you stay."

"And what of you?" he asked softly, his eyes searching hers, his cheek still resting in her palm. "We'll be leaving you all alone."

She knew he was right. Razi was becoming more and more a distant moon, and Lorcan . . . poor Lorcan, how long did he have left? Truth be told, thoughts of the future filled Wynter with dread. But as she looked at Christopher's worried, battered face, she thought, *there's nothing you can do about it, Christopher Garron, except get yourself killed.* She gave him a confident smile. "I'm *fine* here," she said. "It's what I'm bred for. There is nothing you can do for me here, Christopher, that I cannot do for myself."

The dimples showed slyly at that and he gave her a wicked smile. "Oh, I wouldn't be so sure of that!" he smirked, and she bared her teeth at him and swatted his cheek lightly so that he play-acted agony and they broke apart without awkwardness.

They sat for a few moments, leaning back in their chairs, a pensive silence settling between them. Christopher's eyes drifted shut. "Lord. I am just about worn to a thread."

Wynter patted his knee in sympathy. "Go lie down."

But he just sighed instead. "Our Razi is in a bad way, ain't he?" he murmured. "That remark . . . about my people." He snorted in disgust. "I swear . . . I ain't ever been so close to punching him."

"Those things they've said, though, Christopher . . . they'd upset any man.

He opened his eyes to look at her again.

"Up North," she said, "They'd hang a man for those sort of . . . activities."

"I know all about the North," he said with quiet disdain.

Wynter regarded him closely and realised there was so much she didn't know about him, so much she didn't know about Razi. Her eyes narrowed in thought and she sat up straight, her head tilted.

"No," he said with an amused smile, "I'm not."

"Not what?" she said, startled.

"I'm not what they say I am. It just ain't the way I'm made."

She blushed, then hesitated and bit her lip. *And Razi?* she wondered. It was hard to think of Razi in that way at all. She had never seen him as anything other than just . . . just Razi. She met Christopher's eyes and he grinned stiffly against his bruises, amused at the question in her face.

"Would it make a difference to you?" he said. "If he were? Would you think any less of him?" His grin faltered when she didn't answer, and fell away entirely when she had to acknowledge to herself that it *would* make a difference. She wasn't sure *how* she would feel about it, but it would make a difference. Christopher shook his head in disappointment. "You people," he said. "You . . ." He left the sentence unfinished, just spread his hands and dropped them again in despair. He glowered out the window, mulling things over in his head. "Razi, Razi," he murmured, "What are we to do with you?"

Wynter was still staring pointedly at him, and he grimaced and flung his hands up again in exasperation, "Good Frith!" he said, glaring at her. "It's just lies, all right? When Razi finally unbends enough to enjoy a bit of sport, it's a woman he takes to his bed! Now! You have it! I wish you joy of the knowledge! You can continue to look on him with unblemished pride and love! He is excellent and perfect and not at all *dubious*!"

Wynter laughed, too relieved to take his anger seriously, but he turned stiffly away to look out the window again, his face grim, and she realised that he was genuinely upset with her.

She shook his knee, trying to lighten his mood. "We were brought up to call it the *loving* act, you know. My father told me it's an expression of love, not sport!"

"Oh, I have no doubt!" snorted Christopher. "Half of Razi's problem is that he's forever confusing the sport with love. He can't seem to relax himself enough to just have some bloody fun. He's too busy running off getting his heart broke by every set of brown eyes as looks his way."

"But surely . . ." she checked herself and sat back, amazed to find herself discussing this subject without the slightest blush, and with *Christopher* of all people. She frowned and thought about that for a moment. This was a subject that usually reduced her to a paroxysm of stuttering and scarlet mortification. And yet . . . she looked up at him. He was regarding her with puzzlement, still not quite over his anger but wondering what the pause was all about.

"Surely," she continued, settling back in her chair and watching him. "It's all the better when you are in love?" This was what her father had told her, that the act was an extension of your love, that it should be saved for a man she loved completely and who she trusted to love her the same. She realised that she wanted very much to hear what Christopher had to say on the subject.

"I'd say it's very *much* the better when you are in love," said Christopher, staring back at her. "That's what my dad told me anyway."

"But . . . you don't know?"

He paused, his eyes slipping from hers. "I ain't never combined the two," he said softly.

"You've never been in love, Christopher?"

His lips parted, he began to say something, hesitated, and snapped his mouth shut with a grimace. Wynter swallowed. Christopher kept his eyes down for a moment and then met her eye again. "I ain't never combined the two," he repeated with one of those sudden and unexpected flashes of shyness.

Wynter smiled, "Me neither," she said, "having never experienced either." She shocked herself with that little bit of daring, but Christopher just smiled affectionately at her and they let the subject lie.

The silence carried on comfortably, and then Christopher sighed and ran his hand lightly over his face. Wynter could see that he was utterly spent.

"Razi says that you should put warm cloths on your face," she told him. "The better to speed your body's expulsion of the bruises."

"Aye," he sighed and began to push slowly to his feet. "I have water keeping warm by the fire in our rooms."

"I'll fetch it," she said, leaping to her feet, but he waved her down and continued to rise.

"No. No. It's all right." He shuffled into the retiring room, heading for the secret door. "I'll do it myself, and if you don't mind, I'd quite like to lie down for a bit. Anyway, I know you've much to do . . ." His voice trailed off as he wandered to the back of the other room. Wynter got up and watched as he pushed the panel to one side.

"You know, Razi asked that you wait here," she reminded him.

"Razi can kiss my Merron arse," he said wearily, and disappeared into the shadows, the panel clicking shut behind him.

The day passed in many small activities, and Razi certainly didn't return within the quarter. Wynter came and went. She paid the overdue laundry bill and checked the horses. She prepared, and signed in proxy, the carpenters' egress papers and delivered them herself, checking on their work and assuring herself of their continued safety. She accepted the delivery of a good meal, and returned Lorcan's portions uneaten.

Lorcan could not seem to get warm, so Wynter arranged for a fire-tender to set and light a fire and shore up a supply of fuel. Soon Lorcan's room was an almost unbearable furnace, the grate blazing, the summer sun sweltering through the windows. But the big man still shivered under his covers.

Razi arrived late in the evening, knocking loudly and

sweeping past her as soon as she opened the door. He seemed rushed and distracted, and barely acknowledged her presence. He came to a halt in the middle of the room, and looked all around him.

"Where is he?" he asked, as if he'd only left Christopher sitting for ten minutes and was shocked to find him gone.

"Razi!" she exclaimed. "It's been hours! You surely didn't expect him to still be waiting?"

Razi blinked at her in confusion, and it was obvious that he did indeed expect Christopher to be waiting. "I . . . I needed to speak to him *here!*" he said, as if that was all that mattered.

She put her hands on her hips and compressed her lips in frustration. "Well," she snapped, "Christopher says you can kiss his Merron arse."

Razi gaped. "Wynter!" he admonished, shocked. Then he looked away, ran his hands through his hair, thought for a moment, "He's probably asleep, I'll have to bloody knock. Damn it . . ." he threw his eyes to heaven. "There's nothing for it. I'll have to go in through the hall!" He strode past her, heading for the door. "Sorry, sis," he said absently, "must rush." She smiled at his unconscious endearment.

He paused at the door, and spoke over his shoulder without looking at her. "You understand, he'll be gone within the week," he said firmly.

"So you've said," she replied.

"I mean it. Once I've set things in motion, he'll have to leave as quickly as possible. There'll be no turning back."

"What do you intend to do, Razi?" Wynter asked, her stomach instantly knotting around itself.

He finally looked directly at her. "I want you to stay

away from him now, Wynter. It will be easier for you both. I know . . . I know that everything always seems so simple when Christopher is around. He's so straightforward He has a way of making a person forget themselves, and that's fatal for people like us."

It hurt to acknowledge this, it cored her heart, but she nodded. "I know," she whispered.

Razi hesitated, as if he wanted to tell her something else. Then he squeezed his eyes shut and shook his head grimly. "All right," he said and left.

Moments later, she heard him hammering on Christopher's door. It took a long time for their friend to answer. She heard Razi's deep voice speaking gruffly, but she couldn't tell if Christopher replied or not. Then the soft thud of their hall door cut off all sounds.

Wynter drifted into the retiring room and stood very still, trying to hear the voices from next door. The fire in Lorcan's room blazed and crackled, and even the retiring room was almost too warm to bear.

"Wynter?"

She turned at the sound of her father's voice.

"Yes, Dad?"

"What are you doing, standing there?"

She blushed and opened her mouth to explain, when the secret door slid open without warning, causing her to jump and reach for her dagger. Christopher hobbled out of the darkness, his face furious, his long black hair tossed and tangled as though he'd leapt from his bed in a panic.

To her surprise he dodged past her, his eyes down, and limped straight into Lorcan's room. He didn't say a word to her father, just padded barefoot to the chair that was wedged into the furthest corner of the room and lowered himself into it. He sat silent and stony, eyes cast down, his hands clenched into fists on his lap.

Lorcan regarded him uncertainly. It was obvious that the poor man was still mostly asleep and thoroughly confused at his young friend's behaviour.

Razi came in then, stalking through the secret door and into Lorcan's room, his face like poison. "Don't be so bloody childish!" he cried, coming to a halt in the centre of the room, glaring down at the top of Christopher's dark head.

Christopher said nothing.

"Goddamn you, Chris! You think I won't discuss this in front of them? You think my God-cursed pride will keep me silent? Is that why you're here?"

Christopher looked up at that, his eyes gleaming dangerously under their swollen lids. Razi held his hand out, "Give me the keys."

Christopher drew his clenched fists to his chest and glared defiantly at his raging friend.

"Give me the God-cursed keys!" bellowed Razi, and Wynter leapt across the room and, without thinking, whacked him on the back.

"This is my *father's room*, Razi Kingsson! What do you think you're doing?" She was angry with Christopher for bringing this in here, but she was *raging* with Razi. At least Christopher was being quiet.

Razi glanced at Lorcan. The big man was peering at him as if through a dark glass from a long distance, mildly puzzled but nothing more. Razi glanced at Wynter and then turned back to Christopher, his hand out once more, his face grim. "The keys," he said quietly.

Christopher shook his head stiffly, his fists knotted at his chest, his sleep-tangled hair falling every which way around his shoulders.

Razi dropped his hands, his face tight, his jaw working. "All right," he said, his voice dangerously low. "All right, then. To hell with your keys." He looked around and quickly spotted what he was looking for in the corner. He crossed the room in two long strides and had pulled the ties on Lorcan's roll of tools and unfurled it before Wynter could do anything more than yell in protest. She leapt at him and tried to grab his hands as he snatched a chisel and a small hammer from the neatly organised pockets.

"Hey!" she shouted, appalled. "Those are my *father's*!"

Christopher rose from his chair, his face distraught as he stared at the chisel. "No!" he cried.

Wynter tried to snatch the tools from Razi and he shrugged her off, surging to his feet.

"No! No, Razi!" Christopher was actually begging, and the despair in his voice made Wynter turn to him in shock. He stumbled after Razi as the tall man strode purposefully to the door. "Don't!" he implored, "Razi, don't! *Please* don't break my father's trunk!"

The frantic pleading in Christopher's voice was alien and heartbreaking, and it froze them all in their places.

Lorcan said, "Good Christ . . . Razi . . ." his disapproval palpable in the silence.

Christopher held his hand out then, a set of little silver keys dangling from his scarred fingers. "Take them," he said, utterly defeated. "Take them. Go on. Just . . . don't break the trunk."

Razi looked at his friend's despairing face. He looked at the keys. He handed Wynter back the hammer and the chisel. She took them with numb hands and watched as Razi slid the keyring from Christopher's finger.

"It's the only way," he said softly, but Christopher flung his hand up and shook his head, his face creased in pain and disappointment. Slowly, he made his way back to the chair in the corner and sat and put his head into his hands.

"What," said Lorcan slowly, "What is the . . . only way?"

Razi glanced at him and clutched the keys, looking uncertain.

"He's going to get my papers," said Christopher. "He's going to show them to the King." He lifted his head, his face bitter and distraught. "He will *kill* you, Razi. You told me . . . you *said* . . ." He shook his head and turned to Lorcan in despair. "He'll bloody kill him. Lorcan! Talk him out of it!"

"No," said Razi and held a hand up to silence Lorcan, his eyes on Christopher. "He won't kill me, Chris, and he won't kill you either. He's going to do *exactly* what I ask of him. He's going to give you safe conduct to the Moroccos. He's going to let me go to Padua. He is going to bow to me, or I swear to heaven, I *will* release those papers to the council, and they will have me tried and jailed and disinherited by sundown the same day. And there would be nothing Jonathon could do because he *wrote the bloody law.*"

"What law?" hissed Wynter. Razi ignored her and she grabbed his arm and shook it, heartily sick of him. "What *law*?" she yelled.

Razi looked down at her, his eyes hard and glittering

with bitter triumph "Father's anti-slavery law, sis. His infamous, wonderful, unique anti-slavery law.

Wynter backed off, releasing Razi's arm as if burned. Razi grimaced at her, a sour, crooked expression that was nothing like a smile.

"No, Razi," she whispered. "No!" She shook her head and looked over at Christopher, praying that he would refute what Razi was saying. He just raised his head from his hands and gazed bleakly at her. "Christopher," she said. "No!"

Razi continued mercilessly, that horrible travesty of a smile still on his lips. "Christopher is my slave, Wynter. I bought him. I paid good money for him, my fellow human being. I sat in an auction room and placed my bids and he was sold to me, just like a horse, or a dog, or a piece of meat." He leant his head down to stare into her eyes, and he nodded grimly at the horror and disgust he saw there. "Good," he said, and stalked from the room, Christopher's keys in his hand.

The Tidy Plan

"Stop it," said Christopher wearily.

"Stop what!" snapped Wynter.

"Stop looking at me as if I've done something wrong."

A sharp retort rose in Wynter throat, but she bit it back when she realised that she had, in fact, been glaring at him with undisguised rage. The realisation caught her by surprise and shamed her. She glanced at her father, who was just dropping his gaze to the floor, and she understood that he, too, must have been silently berating Christopher with his eyes.

Why? Why were they so angry with *Christopher*? Why had she suddenly found herself wishing that he'd never been here, that he'd just go away? She sighed. *Oh, it's not your fault, Christopher. It's none of it your fault.*

How could Christopher have helped the fact that he'd been bought and sold? Or that it had been Razi who had bought him? *Razi*, of all people. Razi, who must have understood the consequences of such a foolish action. Wynter raised her head and stared at Christopher again. What on earth had possessed the man? It was such a dangerous, such a *stupid* thing for a Southlander to do.

"I've done nothing wrong," Christopher insisted, mis-interpreting her stare. His voice was quietly defensive. "And neither has Razi. Though he's uncommonly devoted to his bloody guilt and self-recrimination, so don't be directing those looks at *him* either."

Lorcan groaned in frustration and despair, and rolled onto his back, his fingers pressed to his eyes. Wynter, at a loss for what to do or say, wandered to the foot of her father's bed, and sat looking at the floor.

"I assume he emancipated you," rasped Lorcan.

"Of course," sighed Christopher. "He gave me my papers the day he bought me. Hired me as his horse doctor that same evening."

"I assume that's the reason he bought you?" asked Lorcan, still not looking at him, "In order to set you free?"

Insofar as an ex-slave is ever free, thought Wynter, for they only ever had their own word and some flimsy papers as proof that they'd been released, and they were for ever prey to re-capture and re-sale.

There was a long silence, and Lorcan and Wynter looked over at Christopher. He was gazing at his hands. "Suffice it to say," he murmured, "I was in an unbearable situation, and Razi saved me from it." He spread his hands, making his usual futile effort to straighten the finger on the left. "'T'ain't his fault things went so wrong. Lorcan?" he asked, his voice breaking, "Will Jonathon kill him?"

"I don't think so. I think that Razi is right, Jonathon will let you go. I suspect that Razi will arrange for you to send him a message from the Moroccos, letting him know that you are safe. Then he will send you the papers . . . It's an awful risky deal for you though, Christopher. You'll have to travel unpapered down the goddamn port road, you'll have pass through three separate jurisdictions, and you'll need to voyage to the Moroccos unsupported and evade the check-men there until you get your papers back."

Christopher sighed into his hands. "It doesn't matter," he said, every syllable weary.

"Where are you branded?"

Wynter gasped, and Christopher looked pleadingly up at her father. *Don't, Lorcan. Please!*

"Come on, boy!" he demanded. "Where are you *branded*? If you're challenged, would they have to search to find it?"

Christopher continued to balk, but Lorcan pressed and eventually the young man sighed. "My arse," he murmured reluctantly. "They branded my arse. It's only the broker-mark, they don't ever want those to show."

"Oh Chris!" murmured Wynter in sympathy.

But Lorcan grunted and stared at him, thinking hard. "That's not too bad," he said pragmatically. "You're lucky, had you been sold on, your house-master would have branded your arm or your chest, maybe . . ."

"My face," interrupted Chris softly. "The house I was destined for, they would have branded my face."

Wynter and Lorcan regarded him in frozen silence for a moment. Then Lorcan swallowed and went on, his voice even. It's a lot more work for a check-man to rip off your trousers than it is to pull up your shirt. If you're lucky no one will bother to search you that carefully. You might be all right!" he said and made a strained attempt at a grin, "that is, if you keep your arse covered for once in your life!"

Christopher gazed bleakly at Wynter. "It doesn't matter," he said again.

"Yes it does!" she snapped. "Razi is putting everything on the line for you! You'd *better* care enough to survive!"

He frowned miserably at her tone and looked away.

But she was just too frightened to speak gently, and her harsh words hid a deep anxiety for her two friends.

A runaway slave. Without his papers, that's what Christopher was, a runaway slave. Depending on which jurisdiction he was caught in, he could be subject to mutilation, resale, perhaps even death. And Razi, as long as he was here and had those papers in his possession, he could be tried as a slaver, a purveyor of human flesh. He would be subject to imprisonment and loss of his lands, he would lose his licence to practice and suffer automatic disinheritance. It was one of the most severely punishable crimes in Jonathon's kingdom.

They were both in so much danger. It hardly seemed worth the risk. But try as she would, Wynter couldn't manage to contrive a neater plan.

She sighed and put her head in her hands.

When Razi returned, that is how he found them. Wynter and Christopher on opposite sides of the room, their heads down. Lorcan on his back, his arm over his face.

Wynter looked up when she noticed him in the door. She had expected Razi to have the papers in his hand, but, of course, they were secreted on his person somewhere. Hidden, like the note she now always carried against her heart.

He looked at her, trying to read her expression. She

smiled sympathetically. It seemed to melt something within him, that smile, and he blinked, relieved and vulnerable for a moment.

Christopher raised his head, letting his hands dangle between his knees. They locked eyes. Razi gestured with the keys. "I tried not to disturb your things," he said softly.

"Thanks," said Christopher and held out his hand.

Razi brought the keys to him and dropped them into his palm. "I'm sorry," he whispered.

"Would you have broken my father's trunk, Razi?" Razi hesitated and Christopher held up his hand. "Doesn't matter!" he said, quickly averting his eyes. "I don't need to know."

"When will you tell the King?" asked Lorcan.

Razi glanced at him. "Tomorrow; I have an appointment in the seventh quarter." He paused, looked Lorcan up and down, tilting his head in concern. "How fare you?" he said. Lorcan grimaced, and waved a hand, but Razi kept staring intently. "The heat in here is barely tolerable, Lorcan. Yet you are cold, are you not?"

Lorcan frowned and he flicked a glance at Wynter. Her hair was plastered to her head, her face flushed. He looked at Christopher who had loosened the stays on his robe, exposing his chest, and rolled his sleeves to the shoulder. A nervous kind of panic came over Lorcan's face and his eyes darted sideways.

Razi reached down suddenly and grabbed Lorcan's hand. He palpated the fingers, frowning. He jerked his chin at her, and Wynter slid off the bed. Razi reached under the covers and felt Lorcan's feet. "Wynter," he said, in an aside. "Get a warming-pan for your father's feet."

She scurried to obey.

Razi crouched down by the bed. "Well, friend, it seems there aren't enough drugs in the world to keep you asleep. You must have the constitution of a bloody water-horse." They both chuckled, and Razi continued with a fading smile and no small measure of emotion. "Lorcan, I am *begging* you to stay abed." Lorcan looked at him and Razi took his hand. "I'm *begging* you, please, to promise me that you will stay abed. Will you do that for me? Will you allow me to rest easy about this one thing? Just this one single thing? Please?"

"I swear it," said Lorcan softly.

Razi closed his eyes in thanks, squeezed Lorcan's hand and rose to his feet. He turned to Christopher.

"Chris. From now on you are to keep all your doors locked. Do not answer a knock, except that you hear my voice or Wynter's. And do not take any food, other than what I give you, or Wynter does. Do *not*, I beg you, leave your rooms." They regarded each other solemnly, Christopher almost resentful. "*Christopher*!" insisted Razi and his friend sighed and turned away, nodding in mute agreement.

"All right." Razi turned to go, and saw Wynter watching him from the fireplace.

"And what of you, Razi?" she asked quietly.

He huffed a breath, and that twisted non-smile returned to his face. "What of me?" he retorted.

"Who will take care of you?"

He could make no answer to that.

"Do you really think Jonathon will agree to your travelling to Padua?" asked Lorcan.

Razi frowned blankly at him, as though uncertain of his meaning. Christopher watched his confusion for a moment, then sighed dramatically, drawing everyone's eye, and rose stiffly to his feet. He crossed the room slowly, and as he passed Razi, he patted him on the chest.

"When *I'm* on my way to the *Moroccos*," he said softly, meeting Razi's eye. "*You* will be on your way to *Padua*. Remember?"

Razi's face cleared, and he turned his head after Christopher, watching as he hobbled from the room. They heard the panel slide back, and they all listened as Christopher made his slow way down the secret passage and into his own rooms.

"What will you do in Padua?" asked Wynter, after the strangeness of the moment had passed, "now that everything has changed?"

Razi shook himself, and breathed deep. "Oh, you know!" he said, with a sarcastic little wave of his hand. "Study. Practise medicine. Dodge assassins. Watch from afar as my father destroys his kingdom. That manner of thing."

"You are surrendering," said Lorcan evenly.

Razi glared at him. "What else would you have me do?" he asked bitterly. Lorcan dropped his eyes.

"What of Alberon?" whispered Wynter.

Razi turned cold brown eyes on her, his face hard. "What of him?" he said with a challenging look, and then strode to the door and left, passing through the secret passage so that he could be seen exiting from Christopher's suite.

Wynter stood in the blistering heat, listening to

Christopher's hall door open and close. She heard the bolt draw. She waited to see if Christopher would make his way back to them, but Lorcan and herself exchanged a rueful look when they heard the secret panel to Christopher's room slide shut and the locking mechanism click. There would be no card games, or amusing conversations tonight.

"Wynter."

She jumped at Lorcan's voice and realised that she'd drifted away. She looked back up into her father's grave face. "We must begin to plan your escape."

Step One

The forest was blazing, a blinding inferno surging up into the night sky. Sparks and stars mingled against the darkness. The great logs roared and hissed, the wood splitting explosively in the heat, each loud report making Wynter leap with shock. She was deafened by it. The heat was tremendous. The deep throb of unseen drums reverberated in her chest.

Big men and tall women moved calmly against the luminous flames.

Christopher stood beside her. He was naked and filthy, fading yellow bruises like leopard spots all down his body. His bracelets were gone. He was gazing at the sparks as they shot upwards to die amongst the stars. He swayed to the rhythm of the drums, his eyes distant.

"Christopher!" she shouted, the roar of the fire swallowing her voice.

He turned to her at once, grinning vacantly.

"Where's Razi?"

Christopher raised a hand to the dark trees behind them and she saw Razi stumbling drunkenly towards them. He was staring into the fire, his mouth open, his face streaming with tears.

"Stop them!" he shouted, stumbling from tree to tree, his voice a desperate thread against the roaring fire. "Stop them!"

The drums sped up, their stately pulse becoming a wild beating frenzy. Wynter turned instinctively to the flames, filled with dread. There was a deafening, violent rush of air and an enormous dark shape plummeted downwards, crashing into the ground with a huge concussion that bounced her from her feet and flung her into the darkness beyond the firelight.

She woke with a start and her first thought was, *today is the day that Razi tells the King.* It was still dark grey pre-dawn, the air cool and damp again with mist. She shook the anxious dream from her, the noise and smoke, the tremendous heat, all sliding away rapidly in the cool morning air. Only Razi's face stayed with her, tear-stained and shocked, begging for them to stop. *The dreams don't always come true*, she told herself.

Frowning, she slipped from bed, wrapped herself in her mother's robe and padded quietly in to check on her father.

Lorcan was sleeping. Wynter could hear his steady breathing in the dark. His shutters were closed, the gloom impenetrable except for the faintest glow from the nearly dead fire in the grate. Moving as quietly as possible, she lit a candle from the embers and began to shovel ash into the waste-bucket.

Today is the day I tell Marni, she thought.

She gathered a little pile of still glowing embers in the centre of the hearth, piled tinder on top, and blew gently until it blazed. Slowly she fed in fuel and soon a merry little fire danced and blazed in the grate, filling Lorcan's room with light, and the heat he couldn't seem to get enough of.

This is day one of our goodbyes.

Still kneeling by the grate, she turned to look at her father. He looked peaceful and beyond pain; she wished that he could remain like that.

From this moment, we are beginning to separate, she thought. *Christopher, Razi and I. Soon Dad will be all alone. How can I do it? How can I leave him alone?*

How wonderful it would be if Lorcan could wake whole and well again. If he could stretch his powerful arms over his head, grin and leap from bed as he used to when she was a small girl.

When Wynter was tiny, he used swing her up onto his shoulders and they would walk the meadow before breakfast. She would knot her chubby fists under his chin and the sun would come up and glitter in the dewy grass. It would set fire to Lorcan's hair, and she would rest her chin on his head, surrounded by its luminance. They would breathe the free air together, and watch for foxes and shy deer.

I love you so much, Dad, she thought, her heart twisting.

Lorcan sighed and his hands knotted, then relaxed on the covers.

He deserved so much more than this. He deserved peace and companionship. He deserved a loving circle of friends. He deserved a comfortable well-tended convalescence in his own home. He did *not* deserve *this*. This annexed state, isolated and besieged and alone. Constantly vexed and fretted at, so that his body could not heal. Where were his friends? Where was the King, that man who had called him brother, who had loved him so well their entire lives?

He is not so important to them. He is second always to bigger things. She bowed her head, the light from the fire playing across her hands. "I know my place," Lorcan had always said, and this was it. Second, always second to matters of state. And now . . . *And now I, too, will leave him,* she thought. *Even I . . . because there are things that are more important, more important than this lovely man who has given me all he has, who has never failed me.*

She could not bear these thoughts. She couldn't. They would kill her. So she pushed to her feet and crept to her room. She would wash herself and she would dress, she would arrange for breakfast, she would talk to Marni and she would wait for news of Razi. This is what she would do. One thing. Then another thing. Then another. And in that way she would get through this day, hands clenched, teeth gritted, head down. Today and every day to come, she would get through them all, one step at a time.

She was emptying her washing water out the window when Lorcan called her, his voice strained and panicky, from the next room. She flung the tin basin back onto the washstand and rushed to his door, her heart hammering.

"What is it, Dad? What . . .?"

He was propped half on his elbow, a fist knotted against his belly. He looked at her from under his hair as she crossed the threshold of his door and ground out, "Get Christopher."

"It's very early, Dad. He'll be asleep. I was going to wait and invite him to breakfast . . ."

"Get him!" he was desperate now, "Just get him, girl! Please!"

She fled into the secret passage and ran the short distance to Christopher's room. She fought the urge to just hammer on the secret panel and scratched gently instead.

He'll be asleep, she thought, remembering Razi's insistent and repetitive pounding of the day before. *I'll never wake him.* To her surprise, she heard a small sound behind the panel and she risked calling softly through the wood.

"Christopher? It's Wynter. My father has need of you!"

The door slid to one side, soft candlelight filled the gloom. Christopher was fully dressed, smelling of soap and toothpowder. He was backlit by the candles, a distinctive, lean shadow in the door. "What is it?" he asked in concern, "Is he unwell?"

"I don't know!" she cried softly, "he wants you!"

He herded her ahead of him through the passage, his hand on the small of her back. When they got to the bedroom, Lorcan held a hand up to keep Wynter at the door. Christopher crossed quickly and leant over him.

Lorcan whispered to him, his eyes flicking to Wynter as he spoke. Christopher's face was obscured by the fall of his hair, and he nodded and answered in a low soothing manner. The young man went to straighten, and Lorcan grabbed his wrist and looked up at him. He mumbled something, pained apology on his face.

Christopher leant down once more, placed his free hand on Lorcan's and squeezed. "Friend," he murmured, "I would have been livid had you not. Think no more on it."

Then Christopher crossed to Wynter and guided her from the room by her elbow.

"Does he need Razi?" she asked, panicky and tearful.

"No, lass," he said gently. "Your father just needs a bit of a hand, a strong arm to lean on." He looked her in the eye as he began to shut the door on her. "Go organise breakfast," he said.

And then she was outside in the dark, while Christopher gave her father the help that Lorcan would never allow her to provide.

To her shock, Marni hit her. A fierce angry blow to the face that threw Wynter back into a table full of wooden beakers, tripping her and bringing the whole lot crashing to floor. She lay there, her arms over her head, her ear ringing. Cups bounced and clattered and rolled off in all directions. Marni stood motionless in the corner of the storage room, her little blue eyes round, her big mouth hanging open in horror.

Wynter was stunned. Though Jonathon had often inflicted his temper on the boys, and though Marni was never averse to a cuff behind the ear and a sharp swat to the rear, Wynter had never been beaten as a child. The big woman's assault thoroughly overwhelmed her. She found herself confused and paralysed, waiting for the next punch.

When Marni finally emerged from the corner and loomed over her, Wynter flinched and rolled into a tight little ball. Marni reached a huge paw and grabbed Wynter's arm, pulling her to her feet and she yelped in fear. But the big woman just clutched Wynter to her, crushing her against her enormous breasts, the smell of butter and fresh dough and apples washing over her. Wynter gasped for air as the giant arms squeezed, and Marni rocked her to and fro like a baby.

"Oh girl! Oh girl!" she moaned, "Are you crazy? Are you

bloody gone in the head? Ohhhh . . ." she trailed off into keens and moans. "My little babies," she sobbed. "My poor little babies . . . what times, what terrible times!"

Wynter wriggled and squirmed until she had a little breathing space between one bit of flesh and another. "Will you do it, Marni?" she gasped. Will you help?"

Marni continued to squeeze and to rock, and instead of replying, she laid her cheek down on top of Wynter's head and cried until Wynter's hair was wet.

An hour later, Wynter made her way from the kitchen with a rush basket full of freshly boiled eggs dangling from her arm. She carried a tray laden with fragrant manchet bread, a huge jug of creamy oatmeal porridge, and a pot of coffee. She had a stinging red hand print on the side of her face and a ringing in her left ear. Most importantly, she had Marni's sworn promise to aid her in her escape, and to help nurse her father after her departure.

Wynter had taken step two, and if her heart couldn't exactly be called light, it was at least calmer than it had been this morning.

The sun was fully up by the time she got back to the suite, and the receiving room was flooded with clear light. She locked the door behind her, and began emptying the tray onto the table. At the sound of her entrance, Christopher slipped from Lorcan's room and came to look over her shoulder with an appreciative sigh.

"Oh *my*," he said, inhaling deeply. "I'm fair clemmed." He leaned across her and stole a chunk of manchet, scurrying backwards and shoving it into his mouth before she could swat him. He grinned stiffly at her.

"How's my father?" she whispered.

"He's grand, lass. Just proud," he gave her an affectionate look. He s a big strong man and you're still his wee
baby-girl. There are some things . . ." He shrugged, not
knowing quite how to put it.

She tutted and threw her eyes to heaven, it was easier to
cling to irritation than it was to wonder what Lorcan would
do when Christopher was gone.

"You inviting me to breakfast?" he asked, diplomatically
changing the subject. Otherwise, you know . . ." he cocked
a hangdog look in her direction, "I'll starve, all alone and
neglected in that big empty suite!"

Christopher's narrow face was beginning to regain some
of its definition, the swelling retreating a little from the
fine sloping cheekbones and jaw. His clear grey eyes were
getting easier to see under the heavily bruised lids. Wynter
was filled with a sudden, almost uncontrollable rush of
affection for him and the two of them paused for a
moment, smiling in the sunshine.

"Will we take the lot in to your father's room?"
Christopher suggested. "It might encourage him to eat."

Between the two of them they carried the table into
Lorcan, and laid everything out again. Christopher had
opened the shutters, and the room was bright and airy,
despite the outrageous heat. Lorcan watched them, heavy-
eyed, from his pillows and shook his head when they
offered him food. Christopher just laughed at him and,
while Wynter was eating a boiled egg, he somehow got half
a bowl of porridge and a little bit of coffee into her father
without Lorcan even really noticing that he was being fed.
The big man fell asleep like a baby, suddenly and deeply
and without warning.

"Christopher," whispered Wynter.

He turned from where he'd been standing, looking down at her father, his expression miles away. She held up a bowl of porridge and a spoon. "You've eaten nothing. I thought you were clemmed?"

He made a growling sound and leapt at the food, emptying the bowl in a few monstrous scoops, and looking at the jug to see if there was more. She filled his bowl again and he wolfed it down just as quickly, sighing with pleasure as he scraped the bowl clean.

"Christopher," she said with a frown, "Did you not eat yesterday?"

He had opened his mouth to reply when a loud knock on the hall door made them start.

"OPEN IN THE NAME OF THE KING," a voice bellowed. They looked at each other in startled horror.

"You need to go!" hissed Wynter, already throwing a couple of eggs and a lump of manchet into the little rush basket. She flung them into his hands and pushed him to the secret door as another loud knock shattered the air.

"OPEN IN THE NAME OF THE GOOD KING JONATHON!"

Lorcan jerked awake with a start and looked around him in confusion. "What?" he said.

"I'm coming! One moment!" she called out loudly as she ran back into Lorcan's room and quickly poured a bowl of coffee. She thrust it into Christopher's free hand and then shut the door in his face, turning the angel-sconce to lock the mechanism and rushing to answer the door to the King.

A Concerned Friend

Jonathon stalked in without a word and gestured for Wynter to shut the door behind him. She did so with a wildly beating heart, glancing anxiously at the squad of enormous guards crowded into the hall. She then turned to the King, and bowed formally, waiting for permission to speak.

Jonathon stood with his hands on his hips, the sun burning in his hair and beard. In this confined space, and dressed as he was in his court garb, the King was beyond intimidating. He seemed to fill the entire suite. He looked all about him, his face grim, and finally, he turned reluctant blue eyes to Wynter, as though she were the last person on earth he would want to talk to.

"Well, girl?" he said grudgingly, looking her up and down. "Where the hell is your father?"

"Your Majesty . . .? My . . .?" She gaped at him, was he serious? She couldn't believe it. Where did he *think* her father was? Had Razi not told him of Lorcan's condition? Jonathon must have seen her confusion blaze to anger, because his eyes grew wary despite the unchanging superiority of his expression.

Wynter drew herself to the limit of her height and spoke formally, through gritted teeth. "The Protector Lord is gravely ill, your Majesty. In fact, he was peacefully sleeping until your guard's *bellowing* woke him."

Jonathon blinked.

"Has your Majesty not spoken to his Highness, the Royal Prince Razi, about the Protector Lord's health?"

Jonathon flung out his hand. "Enough with the God-cursed titles, child! No, I have not spoken to Razi about your father! I have not passed two words to that bloody boy in three days," his face darkened at the thought of Razi. "Goddamn him." Shaking himself, he turned to look into the receiving room. "He is abed then? Lorcan?"

"Aye, he is abed. Razi has forbidden him leave it."

Jonathon turned an icy glare at her. "He was well enough to defend those damned boys against my guards yesterday. Doesn't sound like he's having too much trouble getting about to me."

Wynter's heart dropped and she paused, paralysed for a moment with shock. Then, as smoothly as possible, given the rage that numbed her lips, she said, "My father was in the library on your Majesty's *business*. Huette's boys had got into a misunderstanding with their papers and my father sorted it out, as is his duty."

"Yet he cannot attend my council or be seen in court, is that it, Protector Lady? He has energy for his guildsmen, but not for his King?"

There was no hesitation this time and Wynter's voice was cold and low when she replied, "The journey to the library nearly killed my father, your Majesty. It brought him to his knees. If it were not . . ." she paused, she had almost said, *if it were not for Christopher* but thankfully, she bit it back in time, switching smoothly instead to say, "if it were not for his great spirit, he would not have made it back at all. His Highness Prince Razi was most irate."

Jonathon gazed at her a moment, his face unreadable, then he turned without warning and swept towards her father's room. Wynter hurried after him with a cry of outrage, "At least let me prepare him, your Majesty!" But Jonathon had passed though the retiring room before she could stop him.

He halted in the entrance, and she had to slip past him to get into the room. Wynter had become so used to Lorcan's rapid decline that she was no longer thrown by the devastation it had wrought on him. Jonathon however, was seeing him anew and he remained at the door, motionless and staring. Wynter crossed to the bed and stood quietly by her father's side. She wondered how much of their conversation Lorcan had heard. She flicked a glance at him and decided not too much. He was watching Jonathon with hooded eyes, his face expressionless, his head heavy on the pillows. She looked back to Jonathon, and the two of them silently regarded the King.

Jonathon frowned. His eyes skittered over Lorcan's face, the white lips, the darkly shadowed eyes, the beginnings of hollows in the pale cheeks. The King's jaw tightened, and he stepped uncertainly to his friend's side. Lorcan followed his movements with his eyes.

"Your daughter says I woke you," Jonathon said, glancing down on Lorcan from his great height.

"No matter," Lorcan's voice was surprisingly strong, his usual confident rasp. He sounded alert, his mind sharp.

This seemed to surprise and comfort Jonathon, and he finally looked properly at his old friend. He nodded and sat carefully on the edge of the bed. "She tells me that Razi has confined you to your bed."

"He is most insistent."

There was a small, heavy-laden silence.

"Have you not been speaking to Razi?" asked Lorcan carefully.

Jonathon grimaced, "We orbit each other . . . at a distance." He shook his head. "He has been a bloody trial to my patience." He looked sideways at his old friend and murmured darkly, under his breath. "Things have been said . . ."

"Lies," said Lorcan immediately. "Court gossip and slander."

"Still . . ." Jonathon shook his golden head again and snarled, "Still."

"He has distanced himself with commendable speed."

Jonathon looked thoughtfully into the fire. "Still," he said again, "It would be much simpler to just throw the Hadrish back in the keep. No chance for accusations of unnatural behaviour if he's chained in a cell . . ."

Wynter felt herself grow rigid with fury, but Lorcan just sighed and waved his hand. "Just let the damned pain in the arse go, Jon. Send him back to the Moroccos, get him out of the way."

Jonathon flicked a suspicious eye at Lorcan. Lorcan didn't flinch. "I need him here, you know that." He looked briefly at Wynter, then turned back to the fire. "He's my only lever."

Lorcan sighed and let it go. He lay placidly in the bed while the King watched the fire. Wynter fought to push her hatred and disgust back down in her chest before she said something she would for ever regret.

"How fare you, Lorcan?" asked Jonathon softly, not taking his eyes from the fire.

Wynter ground her teeth, and Lorcan didn't bother to reply. They knew that Jonathon wasn't asking out of concern for his old friend's health. At Lorcan's continuing silence, the King turned to look at him. He startled at the cold green stare that Lorcan was levelling his way.

Jonathon's eyes flicked guiltily away, then back again. Then he scowled, seemed to recollect he was the King and straightened so that he was frowning down at the man in the bed.

"When will you be fit to do your duty, Moorehawke?"

"Only God knows, your Majesty."

Both men's voices were equally cold, equally intractable.

Jonathon tipped his head in warning, "I *need* your public support, Protector Lord."

"Then perhaps you should have your guards parade me about on a litter with a sign around my neck, your Majesty, for I can do no more than I have."

They glared at each other for an instant. Then Lorcan's face softened slightly, "Look, Jon," he said quietly. "I am *spent*. Can you not see it? I am spent." He spread his big hands in warm regret. "Just give me some time."

Jonathon looked at Lorcan from under lowered brows, then raised his gaze to Wynter. She took an involuntary step back at the calculation in his eyes, her spine cold. Lorcan reached convulsively for the King's arm. "*Jonathon*," he breathed, his face alarmed, the word a warning and an entreaty.

Jonathon shook Lorcan's hand from his arm and stood, his eyes still on Wynter. "I will see you at the banquet tonight, Protector Lady; you may have the honour of taking your father's place." He bowed to her, and then to Lorcan who was regarding him with cold hatred. "I wish you a speedy return to health, Protector Lord. I look forward to your return to my side."

They listened to him leave, the steady tramp of his guards fading quickly from earshot. Lorcan's lips were compressed and trembling in rage, his hands wringing the covers. Wynter put her hand on his shoulder. "Don't be upset, Dad. It's just another banquet! At best, I'll be bored to death, at worst, I'll have to dance with Warrick Shardon and have my toes broken."

He reached up and grabbed her hand, clutching it to his chest. He absently stroked the calluses on her palm, the worthy scars on her knuckles. All the years they'd spent working at their independence . . . as if they'd ever really had a chance, what fools!

"At worst you could be poisoned by his opposition," he said bitterly, "at worst you could be stabbed, or shot. At worst Jonathon could decide to betroth you into his circle, just to keep us near him. He could send you to a convent, just to control my words. He . . ."

"Dad!"

He squeezed her hand hard and brought it to his lips, his eyes clenched shut. "Oh Wynter!" he moaned, rocking slightly in distress "Oh baby-girl! At least tell me Marni has agreed! At least tell me that!"

"She has agreed," she whispered, beaming at him with every ounce of false cheer she could muster. "Did you ever doubt her?"

Lorcan nodded. " Good," he said, regaining some of his composure. "Good." He took a deep breath and then he released her hand, pushing himself higher in the bed, "Go get that boy now," he said with a wave of his hand, "none of us should be alone today." But as she moved away, he seemed to have a thought and reached for her arm and looked into her eyes. "We should tell Christopher of our plan," he said softly, "it alarms him that you might have to stay here alone. It will do his heart good, on his journey, to know that you will be safe."

"No, Dad!" she blurted.

Her vehemence shocked him, and he pulled back to look at her closely. "You fear he would tell Razi? Give you away?"

No, Dad, that's not what I fear at all. I fear that, should I try and deceive him as I am deceiving you, Christopher would see right through me. And if Christopher guesses what I really have planned, he would chain me in the keep, rather than let me leave. And you, Dad, would probably hand him the keys.

She nodded gravely at her father. "Yes, I think he would tell Razi. Razi wants me to stay here, and I think that Christopher would feel obliged to take his side over mine."

Lorcan smiled at her, his eyes kind. "I think you underestimate that boy's esteem for you, darling."

She squeezed his hand and leant in close, her voice teasing. "Dad! Do not tell *that boy* what we're planning! Regardless of his so-called *esteem*."

He held his hands up in surrender. "Whatever you wish!"

Wynter went to the secret door and slid the panel open, her thoughts miles away. A white shape moved quickly in the dark, and she leapt and stifled a scream as Christopher's pale face was revealed only inches from her own. She staggered back, her hand to her dagger. Lorcan shouted at her, "What is it?"

"Christopher!" she cried, "What in God's name . . ."

The breakfast things were at Christopher's feet, and Wynter realised that he'd never moved from behind the door. He had, in fact, been waiting in the dark all along.

Had he been spying? But no, she saw it in his eyes, that fierceness she had seen before, when he'd been protecting Razi. And she knew, all at once, that he had been waiting in case they needed him. She wondered how he had planned to get to them, had things taken a turn, but the look on his face told her that nothing would have stopped him, had she cried out.

She straightened, breathless, and shoved her dagger back in its sheath. Running a shaky hand over her face, she breathed deeply and tried to get her body to calm itself. In his own contained way, Christopher was trying to do the same. He slowly dropped his hands, sheathing his own dagger and straightened from his crouch. His face gradually lost its tense, dangerous mask. He looked away, a little dazed, his breathing shaky.

"I thought . . ." he said, "I thought I'd wait . . . just in case."

She nodded wordlessly and gestured for him to come on in. The two of them made their uncertain way to Lorcan, who smiled indulgently at them from his pillows, as if they were small children or a couple of amusing puppies.

Another Bloody Feast

"Stop pacing, boy! I'm exhausted just watching you!"

Lorcan's irritated growl drifted to Wynter as she locked the hall door behind her. Sighing, she lowered her roll of tools to the floor and leant her head against the frame, listening to the men fretting in the next room.

"What time is it now?" Christopher asked, his lilting voice tight.

"Good Christ! You just heard the bloody bell! It's half past the sixth quarter!"

"In *proper* bloody time, Lorcan! What's the time on the *Northern* clock?"

Lorcan's voice softened slightly and he said, "It's one o'clock, boy . . . Just one. There's still an hour to go."

"Good Frith. I . . . God curse him . . . I swear . . ."

Wynter listened to Christopher's inarticulate anxiety, and closed her eyes against the panic that threatened to unleash itself in her heart. She had left the library early, distractedly thrusting the egress papers into Pascal's hand, muttering something about state business. She had seen the horror in Pascal's eyes when she hadn't bothered to organise her tools before tying the roll shut, but she ignored him and flung the roll carelessly onto her shoulders. She couldn't remember doing one single tap of work all day anyway, she might as well be here.

She wandered into the retiring room and went to lean in Lorcan's doorway, her arms crossed against the tension in her chest. Lorcan was slumped against the headboard, his cards laid out in an untidy game of patience. Christopher was prowling a tight figure of eight in front of the fireplace. They both noticed her at the same time, and paused, looking at her expectantly, as if she might have news. She spread her hands at them in exasperation. *For Godssake! What the hell would I know?* And they turned away from her with identical grunts of disappointment.

Lorcan snapped a card down onto the bed.

Christopher did another circuit in front of the fire and broke off to look out the window.

"Get away from there," snapped Lorcan, as if for the hundredth time that day.

Christopher angled away from the window and returned to the fireplace. He came to rest for a moment, then started pacing again. Wynter felt his nervous energy starting to grate on her. She didn't know how her father hadn't yet killed him, she'd only just arrived and already she felt the urge to stamp on Christopher's head.

Razi must be preparing to meet the King now. He had probably been ready for hours. He was probably standing, right now, in his rooms. Alone. Waiting.

Jesu.

She broke away from the door and paced to the other side of the retiring room She got to the wall and paced back to the door again. She came to a halt. She clenched her arms tighter around her chest.

Jesu Christi.

Christopher's soft boots went *pat pat pat* on the wooden floor.

Lorcan snapped another card down.

"Dad." Lorcan looked up at her expectantly. "Jonathon would meet him in the private appointment rooms, would he not?"

Lorcan nodded. It was hardly likely that the King would choose to meet his son in the thronging chaos of the public rooms. No matter how discontented Jonathon was with Razi, he would never make him wait in that long hall, packed in with all the other patiently waiting petitioners.

Wynter looked significantly at her father. The private appointment rooms were only two floors down, almost directly below their suite. "I just want him to see me, Dad. I want him to know . . ."

Christopher had come to a complete halt and was staring at her, his eyes wide and hopeful.

"You can't let the guards see you, darling," Lorcan warned softly. "The hall to the rooms will be filled with Jonathon's soldiers." Wynter felt her chin beginning to jut in stubborn defiance, but Lorcan went on thoughtfully. "Razi will probably approach from the middle gallery staircase, coming up the blue corridor. If you take the twelve-step backstairs and come out the dwarf door, you could stand in the alcove by the music library. That way, when Razi comes up the steps to turn into the hall . . ." Lorcan raised his eyes to her, "he'll see you."

"I'm coming too," said Christopher firmly. One look at his face told them that there was no point arguing.

Half an hour later they stood, silent and staring, pressed side by side at the end of the short corridor. They could hear Jonathon's men in the hall around the corner. If they took just ten or eleven paces forward and turned left they would be right amongst them. Wynter did not want to think about that, about being surrounded by those big men again. These were the same men who had laughed when Jonathon had beat Christopher's head against the tree. The same men who had taunted him and dragged him, screaming and bleeding, down the hill to the keep.

Wynter tried to keep her breathing calm and quiet. She concentrated on the stairs ahead of her. What if Razi took a different route? What if he arrived, as was his custom now, surrounded by men? What if he swept by and never raised his eyes to look at all?

Beside her, Christopher stood motionless and patient as stone. His eyes had never left the top of the staircase, and if he was as nervous of the guards as Wynter, he certainly didn't show it.

They had been there for what seemed like a long time, and Wynter was beginning to wonder if Razi had already gone in, when Christopher straightened suddenly, and stepped away from the wall. She stepped forward too, her shoulder brushing his arm, and strained to hear what had caught his attention.

There! Boots on the stairs. One man, striding upwards. Razi!

He came quickly up the steps, his head down, and for an

awful moment Wynter thought he would continue on and turn the corner into the hall without seeing them. But at the very top, just before stepping into the sight of the guards, Razi came to a sudden frowning halt, his head down, his eyes unfocused. He stood there for a moment, one hand on the wall, the other clenched in a fist by his side.

Then he suddenly focused on the floor at his feet, took a deep breath and squared his shoulders. Wynter saw Razi's mask slip into place. His uncertainty, his fear, all those things, slid underneath somewhere, and his cool, insouciant court-face rose to the surface like ice. She saw his eyes, almost lost under his loose fringe of curls, harden and his brows rise up in haughty contempt. Then he snapped his back straight and flung his head up, and looked right into her eyes.

Razi's mask shattered into a million pieces at the sight of her, and he stumbled two steps backwards before collecting himself. His eyes slipped from her to Christopher and back again. He blinked rapidly as if trying to clear them from his vision.

Wynter felt her face crumble, *Oh God*, she thought, *we've done the wrong thing, we've done the wrong thing!* But they were here now and the damage was done, so she put everything she could into her eyes. *I love you*, she tried to show him, to tell him. *I'm with you. You're not alone.*

Razi's eyebrows knotted and his eyes grew huge and liquid. He took another step back.

Then Christopher stepped forward. He raised a finger to his lips and frowned sternly at his friend. Razi locked eyes with him, desperate. Christopher took his finger from his lips and straightened smoothly, his feet together, his face composed. He lifted his hand to his brow, put his foot forward and then swept down in the most perfect, most *courtly* bow Wynter had ever seen.

Razi released a silent, laughing sob. He looked down at his friend's bowed head, nodded and took a deep breath. He squared his shoulders again. Christopher held his bow for a long moment and when he rose, Razi's mask was back in place. The two men looked at each other down the length of the corridor, their poses formal, their faces set.

Razi ducked his head in a little nod and Christopher smiled and nodded back.

Razi met Wynter's eyes. There was the briefest moment of softness, the smallest lifting of the corners of his mouth and then he bowed. And though she was still in her work clothes, she immediately spread him a curtsy worthy of the finest dress, holding the dip for a very long time, so that when she rose he had moved on, as was befitting a royal prince in the company of his subjects.

"You look beautiful, baby-girl."

"Thank you, Dad." Wynter continued to hover in the bedroom door, running her hands nervously over the emerald satin of her skirts. It was almost time for the banquet, she had left it until the last minute to get dressed and now she must go.

Lorcan regarded her from his bed. He was huddled miserably under a mound of covers, shivering again despite the roaring fire. Christopher stood beside him, stripped to his undershirt and britches, barefoot, his sleeves rolled to the shoulder. He was sweating in the tremendous heat, his eyes and his bracelets gleaming in the firelight.

Both men were looking at Wynter as though she were about to be thrown on a sacrificial pyre. They had waited all day for Razi and were exhausted from it. The anxiety and fear they all felt for him had left them numb, and they both had a staring, sleepless look around their eyes. Wynter longed to go back in and sit with them, but she would be drenched in sweat within moments and it would ruin her damned dress.

Anyhow, she thought, *I've no time left*.

She had hoped she would have Razi to walk her to the hall, had hoped he would guide her again through the royal rooms. But Razi hadn't arrived, she knew now that he would not arrive, and she had to resign herself to going alone. *Please let him be all right. Please. Please.*

"I must go," she said.

The men nodded and she turned and made her way out. Before she opened the hall door, she looked back. Christopher had come to Lorcan's door and was watching after her.

"Christopher," she said. "Do *not* wander."

He just looked at her, his face lost in the shadows, and then he melted back into her father's room.

". . . I remind you that the *King* is a scholar."

"That may well be, but he's also a dab hand at cracking skulls . . . that boy, however, wouldn't know one side of a quintain from another, not like Alberon . . ."

"Excuse *me*, but have you seen the King's face? For an effete, the Arab . . ."

The courtiers paused as Wynter strolled through their well dressed ranks. Someone ahead of her was speaking authoritatively, his back turned.

". . . a beating won't be enough. In my grandfather's day they burned sodomites at the . . ."

One of his companions hissed, "The Hawk's ears." The Conversation turned smoothly to hounds, and Wynter moved on without a pause.

She dodged gracefully through the densely packed crowd of men and women, nodding and bowing her head, and exchanging passing pleasantries. Suddenly she found herself in an open space with no one around her, and she looked around in confusion. She was about ten feet from the Royal Door and it was as though someone had drawn an invisible circle on the ground and told everyone to stay outside it. Conversations carried on behind her as if nothing was different.

At the centre of this wide circle of casually turned backs stood Razi. He was facing away from her, and Wynter per-mitted herself a brief pause and a secret sigh of relief at the sight of him. He was tugging at the shoulder of his purple long-coat, preparing himself to enter the Royal rooms, and she frowned at the sight of his right sleeve hanging loose and empty.

Knowing that she was being watched from the corner of every eye, Wynter advanced on the unsuspecting young man. She cleared her throat politely as she came up behind him and said in a clear court-voice, "If you please, your Highness is blocking the door."

When he turned to her, Wynter couldn't help it, she made a sound, a high squeak of distress, and her mouth dropped open.

Razi! Oh Razi, what did he do to you?

Razi looked coolly at her and she had to force her mouth to shut. It took a second or two for her to remember to drop into her formal curtsy. She held the dip longer than necessary, struggling to regain control of her expression. Then she straightened and looked up at him with well-contained fury.

Next time I see the King, she thought, *he'd better pray that I am unarmed.*

Razi's face was a battered mess, his lip split, his eye bruised. His right arm was held tightly in against his chest and he moved stiffly, as though in pain.

Wynter met his eye, anger distorting her vision. *I will kill Jonathon,* she thought, *I will take his own sword and . . .*

Then to Wynter's utter amazement, Razi winked at her. He leant forward in a stiff bow and while his curly head was level with hers, he whispered, "You should see the King, sis. He can't even walk straight."

He straightened with a triumphant smile, and beamed a crack-lipped grin down on her. "Protector Lady," he said loudly, "I have not seen you this long while. Would you care to accompany me into the rooms?" He offered Wynter his arm and she took it in a daze. The two of them turned to the door, and as the page ushered them in, Razi, his voice carrying all down the hall, said, "Have I told you I'm going to Padua . . .?"

The Defiant Spirit

"*R*ory?" Wynter kept her voice soft, and she glanced up and down the avenue for fear of prying eyes. It had been four days since Razi had secured permission to leave and there was still no sign of Rory Shearing's ghost, or the information he had promised. Time was growing short.

Tomorrow morning, Christopher would leave. Two days after that Razi would be gone, and on that day, she, too, would have to make her farewells to her father. Her emotions began to rise up at the thought of it, but she pushed them carefully back down into the pit of her stomach. She could still feel them in there, roiling and nauseating, but she did not allow them to intrude on her, or interfere with her plans. Wynter had herself as contained and tightly locked down as the keep.

She waited for the shimmering of the atmosphere that would signal Rory Shearing's arrival, but the air stayed placid. Rory had not heard her call. She sighed and bit her lips in frustration.

Everything was in place. Razi had spent the last couple of days provisioning Christopher for his long trip to the

Moroccos. Besides Christopher's own horse, Razi had supplied him with two spare horses and a fully laden pack mule. It had galled Christopher not to be involved in the provisioning of his own journey, but Razi still considered it too dangerous for the young man to leave his room. Christopher accepted this rule with less and less grace as the days wore on.

At the same time, Wynter and Marni had been surreptitiously provisioning her own secret journey. Things were going smoothly and fast. All she needed now was her information.

Wynter looked up and down the avenue again. It was late. Dusty evening light was slanting between the chestnut trees, and the crows and ravens from the keep were cawing sleepily and rustling their wings in the branches. The high prayers of the Musulmen had just ended, and from the tilt yard Wynter could hear the soldiers practising at the quintain and the heavy *thwock* of archery practice in the long meadow.

She took another chance and called out softly to the shimmering air, "Rory! I *need* you!"

Lorcan was not improving. She knew it, he knew it. They all knew it. He was too weak to venture any further than a chair by the window, and he depended on Christopher for help with all but the simplest of personal tasks. But he had at least shaken that terrible chill from his bones, and they no longer had to stoke his fire to a furnace heat.

Christopher was anxious for him, and fretted over what would become of Lorcan after he was gone. The two men had spent most of each day together, talking and playing cards and, despite Christopher's growing frustration at his interminable confinement, he couldn't bear the thought of leaving the big man alone.

Two days ago, Razi had introduced them to a dapper little man, Marcello Tutti – Razi had tentatively suggested the man as an aide for what he diplomatically called Lorcan's "convalescence". The little man, neat and dark and charming, had sat with Lorcan for a few hours on two mornings, chatting amiably in Italian, doing this and that when necessary, and Lorcan had declared himself very happy with him. But Lorcan had forbidden him to start as his aide until after Christopher left, and so the young man remained a permanent fixture in the suite, his heart a little easier at the thought of Lorcan and Wynter having someone other than himself to depend upon.

The clock bell rang half past the ninth quarter and Wynter huffed impatiently and ran her hands over her hair. There had been no more God-cursed banquets, thank Christ, Jonathon having chosen to dine in private until the bruises faded and his limp improved. But, right now, dinner would be waiting in her rooms and the others would begin to question her absence. Christopher would be looking for any excuse to come fetch her, just so that he could stretch his legs outside of the suite.

"Damn it!" she muttered. She would have to go; she couldn't take the chance on loitering any longer.

"Your defiant ghost does not fare well, girl-once-cat-servant; his fellows harry and berate him so that he is worn to a mist from running."

Wynter turned warily to find the orange cat blinking at her from under a bush. It rose nonchalantly to its feet. "Do not fret your flame-coloured head, miss, there's none about to see you commune with us." It stalked out into the dusty sunshine and looked up at Wynter, no trace of warmth in its green eyes.

"What has become of Rory?" asked Wynter reluctantly.

The cat shrugged, "He struggles."

"With what?"

"With he that is twisted and not know his name."

Wynter bit her lip in exasperation. She sometimes believed that cats spoke like this on purpose, just to toy with humans and laugh behind their tails.

"I do not understand you," she said tightly.

The cat huffed as if her comprehension was none of its concern. It switched its gaze across the dusty path, and narrowed its eyes at some small vermin only it could see. The tip of its tail twitched, and it licked its lips. "Fret not," it said as it stalked carefully away, its eyes locked on its prey, its body taut and flowing low to the ground like a murderous orange shade. "I shall come fetch you should the defiant spirit manage to evade and materialise. Go . . . the others seek you . . ." It came to rest by the foot of a bush, perfectly still apart from the incessantly twitching tip of its tail.

Wynter walked quickly away, her spine prickling. Just before she turned off the avenue she heard a rustle and a thump and some small animal squealed in horror and pain. She shut her eyes and shivered; the cat had seized its prey.

Wynter let herself into the suite to the sound of Lorcan's breathless laughter. Christopher was insisting loud and vehemently, ". . . no! I *swear* it! Why can you not believe it?"

They stifled their chuckles at the sound of her entrance, and Christopher came cautiously to Lorcan's door, peering around the frame. He dropped his head in relief and called back over his shoulder, "It's that daughter of yours!"

"Fat lot of good *she'll* do us with her hands empty of food!" said Lorcan, and he raised his voice to shout to her, "Where's our dinner, woman?"

She laughed at the two of them and lowered her tools to the floor. "Where's *mine*, you lazy old goat?"

The two men were sitting by the fire. Lorcan, fully dressed for the occasion in britches and boots and a loose white shirt, sat in a round chair filled with cushions, his feet on the fire stool. Christopher was just lowering himself back onto the pile of cushions that it had become his habit to lounge against when the evening came in. They grinned at her expectantly and she spread her hands.

"Don't look to me for entertainment," she warned. "It's not in my nature to amuse." This entertained them mightily for some reason, and she flopped down on the cushions by Christopher and leant her head back against the wall. Much to her frustration, they showed no sign of producing any food and, instead, returned their attention to their chess game. "Seriously, gentlemen, where's my dinner?"

The men smiled secretly at each other and her heart leapt. Razi must be going to join them! He had turned up at all hours of the day and night in the last few days. Whenever he could escape from his guards, or from the pressing activities of his daily grind, he would make his way through the secret passages and spend whatever time he could in their company. They would hear a small scratching on the panel, as of a mouse, and there would be Razi, stooping in at the door and grinning. He rarely could stay, but sometimes his arms would be filled with maps and rolls of papers, and he would lift his chin to Christopher and they would disappear into their suite for hours, planning Christopher's route to the Moroccos. Oh, she hoped Razi could escape, for this night of all nights, not to have him here would be a crime.

Lorcan went to say something, but they all paused and grinned at the faint scratching on the secret door. Christopher and Wynter leapt to their feet at once and stumbled, laughing, around each other in their rush to get there first.

Razi ducked in the door, smiling, a covered pot in his hands. It smelled wonderfully of spices and gave off a delicious steam that made Wynter's mouth flood. Razi carried it stiff-armed to the table that the men had set up earlier with bowls and tea glasses, and Christopher ducked back into the passage and trotted to his own rooms for a moment. He returned with a flagon of white wine and a basket of fancies.

"Where did you get them?" asked Razi suspiciously, eyeing the basket as he uncovered the pot of food.

Christopher raised his eyebrows. "I have my sympathisers," he said.

Lorcan snorted. "Little plump-arsed, blondie maid brought them this morning. All pouting and boo-hoo-hoo."

Christopher winked at him. "She appreciated my services," he said piously.

Razi looked uncertainly at the food, and Christopher

rolled his eyes and stuffed a cake in his mouth, his eyes challenging. Razi looked appalled.

Wynter inhaled the steam from the pot with an almost carnal greed. "Good Christ, Razi! If he's poisoned he's poisoned, more dinner for us! Serve it up, man!"

They ate from the bowls with their fingers, like the Musulmen did, their tea glasses on the floor at their feet. Lorcan stayed in his chair, picking at his food, and, like a harem full of concubines, the others flopped down on the cushions at his feet, eating earnestly and silently for a moment, as the full force of their hunger hit them.

"Good Frith, man. This is excellent good! I had a longing for this since we left home. How did you manage to get the use of the kitchen?" Christopher refilled his bowl as he spoke and reached to refresh Wynter's tea.

Wynter and Lorcan choked a little and looked at Razi in surprise. "Did you cook this?" asked Wynter.

Razi looked at her over the rim of his bowl, carefully scooping the last scraps into his mouth with his fingers. He smiled with his eyes and nodded.

Lorcan shifted in his chair in order to get a better look at the young man who was leaning against his footstool. "Well," he said, "*I'm* bloody impressed." Razi tilted his curly head back against the arm of Lorcan's chair and smiled at him.

"Oh aye," breathed Christopher, finally kicking back and wiping his fingers on his napkin. "My cooking will keep you going, but Razi's will make you glad to be alive." He belched politely and patted his stomach with a contented sigh.

They worked their way through the cakes, and all had a

little wine, and the evening went pleasantly forward with easy conversation and much laughter. No one spoke of Christopher's departure, no one mentioned Razi's family and no one pondered the uncertainty of the Moorehawkes' future. As far as this evening went, there was no future. There was just this, four friends, their bellies full, talking lightly of amusing things. And the evening went well for it and they were happy for that small time.

They talked well into the depths of the night.

". . . do you recall . . .?" laughed Christopher, leaning forward to shake Razi's knee, "How he got it into his mind that you'd trade the stallion for one of his daughters?"

Razi grinned, his cheeks hot. "Aye! Parsimonious old rascal! Would rather part with one of his own, than hand over a purse . . ."

Christopher turned to Wynter and Lorcan, tears of mirth in his eyes at the memory. "Raz . . . Raz couldn't figure it! All these women kept coming to the tent . . ." He sat up straight, tossed his hair back in a womanish manner and fluttered his eyes, he waggled his backside on the cushions like a woman walking suggestively and murmured in a soft, feminine voice, "Would'st like some more sweets, Lord Razi?" He tilted his head and looked under his eyelashes at Wynter and Lorcan. "Would'st like me to fetch thee some water, Lord Razi?" He leant forward and breathed very suggestively, his features heavy, his voice husky, "Would'st like me fluff thy pillows, Lord Razi?"

Lorcan roared himself into a coughing fit, and Wynter hid her grin behind her tea-glass. Razi blazed red and, grinning, he swatted Christopher on the back of the head. "Oh shush, you bloody menace."

"Did . . . did the old man get the horse?" choked Lorcan, bending forward with breathless mirth.

Christopher raised an eyebrow. "What do you think?" he asked.

Lorcan roared again and Razi shouted in protest, holding his hands up to try and still the laughter. "He paid a fair purse! He paid a purse!"

"I have no doubt . . ." murmured Wynter slyly, leaning forward to fill her tea glass. "That he paid the purse . . . but not before his daughters got their due . . ."

The men roared again, and she smiled into her glass as Christopher grinned at her from across the cushions.

It was growing late and they subsided suddenly into comfortable silence.

"Sing us a song, Razi," murmured Lorcan sleepily, his head leaning back.

Razi smiled and shook his head. "Not tonight, I don't have the heart for it."

"Christopher?" asked Lorcan carefully, mindful of the implications for the young man.

But Christopher just smiled warmly, "Not unless you're fond of rusty metal hinges, I'm afraid. I sing like a crow!"

They chuckled and Christopher turned his eyes questioningly to Wynter. Lorcan waved his hand, "Oh, you may as well ask the moon! She'll never sing in company, though she thrills like a lark when alone."

Wynter kept her eyes on Christopher's and to Lorcan's obvious shock said softly, "I don't mind, Dad. What would you like to hear?"

Lorcan regarded her quietly for a moment, his face still.

"Sing 'The Lilies of the Field are all under His Care'," he said softly and Wynter's heart melted.

"All right, Dad."

Let me get through it without tears, she prayed, and opened her mouth and sang. She knew that it had been her mother's favourite hymn. It told of God's love for all living things and of his understanding of their plight. It spoke of comfort in the blackest hour, and the calm and joy that came after even the longest storm. It was a song that spoke to Lorcan's heart, and Wynter put everything she could into it, closing her eyes to block out all but the music, opening her throat to let out all of the song.

She finished and opened her eyes to find the men watching her, their eyes soft.

"You should sing more often," murmured Christopher.

They retreated into comfortable silence for a time, and looked into the fire. Wynter had feared heaviness and sorrow, but it was just a return to the gentle quiet of before, each of them comfortable in their own space, happy and safe with the people they loved.

Lorcan shifted in his chair and Wynter glanced at him.

"Dad?" she asked in concern, sitting straighter.

Her father had a hand over his face. She could see his fingers were trembling and his lips, just visible in the shadow of his hand, were a thin compressed line. Christopher got smoothly to his feet.

"Would you like to lie down, Lorcan?"

"Aye," whispered the big man, and Christopher looked pointedly at the others.

Wynter felt a little pang of jealousy, but Razi and herself rose obediently to their feet. They kicked the cushions against the wall and put the tea things on the table before moving to the retiring room to wait.

They sat at the round table in soft candlelight and listened as Christopher got Lorcan slowly into bed.

"What will he do without him?" said Wynter. *What will I do without him?*

"Tutti is a good man, sis. He was with me in the Moroccos. Without him St James's death would have been much . . . much more difficult for the poor man."

Wynter looked at Razi, his bruised face was thoughtful and sad in the gentle light. He looked into the candle flame, the gold flecks in his eyes vivid. St James had been a particular friend and protector to him, Razi having been apprenticed to him at the age of eight and having spent most of his life learning from him.

"What became of him, Razi?"

"He died of the cancer, I think. It was very slow. It was very . . . bad."

"I am sorry, Razi."

He looked at her, smiling. "Aye. Thank you." He continued to smile at her, his big eyes warm and tender. "Marcello will make sure that your father is well tended. You will need do nothing but love him and be there for him when . . ." He faltered and looked away, all his professional detachment deserting him at the thought of Lorcan's inevitable decline. "You will be able to remain his daughter to the very end, and he will not have to endure the thought of you becoming his nurse. I am glad to have been able to do that for you . . . It breaks my heart that I must leave him, Wynter. I . . . my only consolation is that he will have you by his side."

Wynter felt her hold on her emotions begin to slip. She shut her eyes. They would all be leaving him. Her father would be alone, all alone at the end. She put her head into her hand. Oh, how could she do this? How? She didn't think she was physically capable of going through with it.

There was a small movement in front of her, and Razi was there, kneeling at her feet. She looked up at him, and he brushed her hair off her face. "No tears," he begged. "Not tonight, eh?"

She nodded. "No tears," she agreed and took a deep breath.

They looked around as Lorcan's door opened, and Christopher peered out at them. They got to their feet and went to speak quietly by Lorcan's door.

"He sleeps like a stone," whispered Christopher.

"Chris," said Razi. "You must be ready to leave very early tomorrow. I still do not trust that my father won't try and prevent your departure." Christopher nodded, his eyes slipping to Wynter.

Razi sighed, "We should all to bed," he said. Christopher nodded again and moved to go back into Lorcan's room.

"Christopher!" said Razi, his voice sharp. "You should get to bed *now!*"

"I'm sleeping here," said Christopher, indicating the cushions.

Razi huffed impatiently. "You need a *good* sleep! You must be sharp tomorrow!" he demanded, "Go to your own bed!"

Christopher stepped over the threshold suddenly and put his hand on Razi's chest. He frowned up into Razi's insistent face and spoke firmly and low. "Look, for the hundredth time, Razi Kingsson, I'm no bloody baby. I'm sleeping in *here*, on those cushions." He took a fistful of Razi's shirt and tugged it gently to and fro, holding Razi's eyes with his own. "There's an end to it."

Razi's face softened, and he nodded. Christopher smiled up at him. "You know . . ." said Razi softly, "I may not . . . I may not make it out tomorrow . . . my father . . ."

Christopher's eyes tightened in suppressed emotion, but he patted his friend's chest in understanding. Before he could pull away, Razi gripped Christopher's hand and held it over his heart, his face solemn, his eyes full.

"By God, Christopher. Be careful . . . please."

"Once I'm outside those walls, friend, I will run like a bloody rabbit. They will never find me."

Razi leaned forward suddenly and wrapped his arms around Christopher, hugging him close. Christopher unhesitatingly looped his arms around Razi's back and squeezed. They stood like that for what seemed a long time, Razi's cheek on Christopher's head, Christopher's face pressed into Razi's shoulder.

Then they parted.

"Try and come tomorrow," said Christopher unexpectedly, his voice unsteady.

Razi nodded, not at all hopeful. He backed to the secret door. Wynter raised a hand to him as he loitered in the dark, his eyes bright in the shadows. He twisted a shaky smile at her and then he slid the panel shut. Christopher leaned into the wall, his eyes lost in shadow, his face turned to the secret door.

"We should to bed, Christopher."

"Aye." He looked across at her. "Will *you* rise with me tomorrow?"

She nodded fervently.

"Thank you," he whispered and he went in to lie on the cushions, his back to the fire, his eyes on Lorcan.

After Wynter put on her shift, she stood for a long moment looking at her bed, cold and neat in the blue light of the moon. Then she pulled the extra covers off the end and went in to Lorcan's room.

Christopher looked up in shock when she came back in. His face was bright with tears and he scrubbed at them self-consciously. Wynter paid him no heed and shuffled around to the cushions that lay between Christopher and the fire.

"Thanks," he whispered as she spread the blankets down on him. Then she settled behind him, getting under the covers and lying down on the cushions.

They stayed like that for a while, Christopher with his back to her, she lying on her side facing him, her cheek resting in her hand on the pillow. The two of them watched Lorcan as he slept.

After a while Wynter moved over and looped her arm around Christopher's waist. She laid her cheek against his back and closed her eyes. Her arm was relaxed against his stomach and she was just drifting to sleep when he took her hand in his own and pulled it up to press it against his chest. She fell asleep like that, the length of his slim body warming her, the strange gap-fingered pressure of his hand, a gentle reassurance as he held her palm against his heart.

First Goodbye

The moon had set and the sun not yet risen when Wynter woke. She was warm and comfortable, nestled into cushions, and it took a while for her to recall where she was. Then she remembered Lorcan's room, laughter, good food and friendship. She had slept all night by Christopher's side.

Christopher was up and about. At some stage, Wynter must have rolled in her sleep to face the fire, and she lay still now and watched his slim, dark shape crouched against the flames. It took a moment before she realised that he was dressed and already prepared for his departure.

Oh, Christopher. So soon?

His face was intent as he poured water from the kettle into Razi's silver teapot and eased the lid shut. He did not notice her watching him. As she looked on, he put honey and lemon slices into the waiting tea glasses. Her heart twisted when she noticed that he had prepared four servings. It appeared that Christopher would not give up hope of Razi being able to join them.

He was dressed for travel, wearing a dark, long-sleeved

tunic that covered his hands to the knuckles, dark riding breeches, and knee-length, hard-soled riding boots. He had a travel-belt around his hips, loaded with purse, ammunition and powder pouches, a buckler and a strange looking knife that Wynter had never seen the like of before. She could just see the handle of his black dagger at the top of his right boot.

Christopher carefully placed a spoon in each glass, ready for the tea to be poured, and Wynter frowned as she took in his precise, methodical movements.

There was something very odd about him. What was it?

Christopher's fluid curtain of hair was pulled severely back and coiled against his head. He had bound it tightly in place with a fine black scarf. His narrow face looked older. His easy, smiling mouth, his glancing eyes, seemed dangerous and set. He looked shockingly different to the lounging smiler she was used to. If Wynter met this man in the street, or saw him in a tavern, she would check her purse and make sure not to turn her back on him.

Wynter watched as Christopher stirred the tea. He turned his hard, expressionless face full into the light, and the answer came to her in a sudden rush of pride and sorrow. This, she realised, was Christopher's mask.

Kneeling by the fire in front of her, preparing the glasses of tea that were to be his farewell breakfast, Christopher was, in his mind, already on the road. Already anticipating the time when he would be alone and unprotected, travelling the perilous roads to the south, he had slipped into the persona that would make others think twice before they took him on. One glance at that face and it was easy to overlook the fact that this was but a slim, pale man with vulnerably damaged hands and no friends in sight.

Wynter pressed her cheek into the cushions at that thought and bit her lip against a prickle of unwanted fear for him.

Christopher, still blissfully unaware of her scrutiny, took a napkin from his pocket and unfolded it on the hearth to reveal one of last night's cakes He knelt motionless for a moment, regarding it. The firelight played across his silently moving lips. Then he carefully broke it into four, and, quickly, as if aware of the rapidly passing time, ate a portion, threw a portion in the fire, put a portion in his pocket, and with the final portion in his hand, stood and crossed to the bed where Lorcan slept soundly on.

Witchcraft, thought Wynter with a pang of fear, and immediately berated herself. *You've spent far too long up North, Wynter Moorehawke. Their intolerance has poisoned you.*

As Wynter watched, Christopher kissed the remaining piece of cake and carefully placed it against Lorcan's lips. He did this so gently that Lorcan didn't even flinch. Then Christopher slipped the offering under Lorcan's pillow and stood, his face lost in shadows, looking down on the big man.

Wynter found this unbearably moving and she rolled over purposely so that Christopher would know she was awake. He turned his head to look at her and his face was instantly transformed. There was his tomcat smile, there were those sly dimples. His eyes came alive.

"How do, girly," he whispered. "Did I wake you?"

She shook her head with a smile. "Were you praying, Christopher?"

He looked shocked for a moment, then smiled again, looking down at Lorcan with sad fondness. "I suppose so . . ." He chuffed a little laugh, "It's been a long time since I did ritual . . . but it felt like the right thing to do."

"Christopher is an odd name for a pagan," she observed softly

He looked over sharply at the word pagan, but softened almost immediately and grinned. "It were my mother that named me. I doubt the word meant anything to her but a sound." He looked down at Lorcan again, and murmured absently. "Though I suppose she might have been a Christian, who can know?"

He brushed a strand of hair from Lorcan's face and turned back to the fire. It was so strange to hear his normally soft footsteps, now loud and rapping in his hard-soled boots. He hunkered down by the fire and poured two cups of tea, strong and pitch black, the way the Turks drank it. "Here," he whispered and handed her a glass.

They drank in silent companionship, the fire a soft crackling undercurrent to their silence. Wynter found it hard to be sad; it did not seem real that Christopher was leaving. It just felt normal to be sitting here, in this easy quiet, her feet tucked under her, the blankets pooled in her lap. Christopher sat on the hearthstone, his legs stretched out in front of him, his ankles crossed. She examined his profile as he watched her father sleep. He held his tea glass under his chin between sips, inhaling the lemon scented steam, his expression unreadable.

"Wynter . . ." he whispered suddenly.

"Yes?"

He looked at her, his face dark against the fire, his eyes gleaming. "I am glad that you will be with your father when it is his time to die."

This was such a bald statement, so utterly without polish or evasion that Wynter's throat closed over for a moment. She did not know what to say to him and found herself staring, her eyes huge, as he continued.

"Not so much . . . well, of course, yes, it is so much the better for Lorcan that you will be there. And for that I am also grateful, because I have come to love him very much. But . . ." he seemed to consider something a moment, then he put his glass down on the hearth beside him and turned to look at her again, leaning forward, his elbows on his knees. "Wynter. My father and I were taken by the slavers in a little village on the Hollish border. Our troupe had been invited there to play a wedding. We were meant to stay a week, but it was all a ruse. When we got there, the village had been invaded by the Loups-Garous; they had come for their sevenths . . ." he paused, looked at her uncertainly, "You . . . you understand about the sevenths?"

Wynter nodded, her mouth dry. She knew all about the custom of the sevenths. Dear God. The Loups-Garous. That vicious, uncontrollable tribe of nomadic creatures. The bane of the Northlands wilderness. They would converge on a village, take it over for five days, help themselves to the food, the shelter . . . the women. Seven years later they would return for their choice of the strongest and hardiest of the children produced by their unions. Woe betide a people who didn't hand over their sevenths. It was a system that had been in effect for generations. Some villages had even come to regard it as an honour and

welcomed the Wolves with banquets and the free choice of
their daughters. Wynter shivered. "But Christopher," she
whispered. "I did not know that the Wolves dealt in slaves."

The shining reflection of Christopher's eyes met hers,
and his voice was dark with meaning when he said, "There
are so many things people don't know about them . . . For
one thing, folk think that all the sevenths grow up to be
Loups-Garous, but that ain't the way; most of the sevenths
actually end up sold as slaves. He glanced at Lorcan, then
back to Wynter, keeping his voice low. "The village had no
sevenths to give them, there had been an outbreak of the
smallpox and all the wee uns had succumbed." Christopher
tilted his head and spread his hands. "So the village offered
us instead. There was no wedding, there never had been, we
were their *gift* to the Wolves. The magnificent Garron
Troupe, famed in all of Hadra for our skill in music and
song."

"Oh Christopher . . . I'm . . . that's just so . . ."

He shrugged and waved his hand, as if to say *no matter*.
He glanced at Lorcan again. "There were six of us in the
troupe. All very talented. Most of us . . ." he paused. "Most
of us . . . pretty. They knew as soon as they looked at us, as
soon as they looked at the girls . . . they knew they'd get a
good reward. So they took the deal."

The cold that had been planted in Wynter's chest at the
mention of the Loups-Garous spread to her belly. She tried
not to imagine the depths of meaning behind Christopher's
spare words. "Wh . . . what age were you, Christopher?"

"I was thirteen, or was I fourteen already . . .? I'm not certain. You know . . ." he looked up at her, frowning as if it
was still a puzzlement to him, ". . . before all that happened,

I had such a great life. I was the luckiest lad in the world, everything was such *fun* . . ."

He sat staring a moment, then shook himself and continued quietly.

"It's a long journey from Hollis to the Morrocos. It got on to winter. They had picked up a fair string of us along the way by then . . . *goods* they called us. Goods. Somewhere . . . I guess it was the Midlands somewhere . . . We were all roped together, crossing this moor. A long empty road across this moor. Naught for miles. Naught for *miles* . . . Just snow. Something happened to my father." He made a motion over his stomach, pushing his hand into the pit of his belly and grimacing as if to indicate what had happened. Wynter winced and leant forward to take his hand, but he just squeezed her fingers, then gently separated from her, as if unable to continue while being comforted. His voice was strangely flat and emotionless, "He got a pain in his belly and couldn't walk. After a while we couldn't carry him anymore, because he was in too much agony." He stopped completely for a moment, then jerked to a start again. "They unshackled him and left him by the side of the road in the snow. He was curled in a ball. He . . . was crying. I couldn't help."

"Oh, Christopher . . ." she reached for his hand again and he pulled back, inhaling deeply and holding his hand up, as if to silence her. He shook his head, looking away.

"Look . . ." he whispered, "Look, all I'm saying is. You're lucky." He looked her in the face then, pointedly catching her eye. She sat back on her heels, her stomach cold. He suspected. Christopher suspected that she was going to leave, and he was trying to tell her not to.

"You will *never* forgive yourself, lass," he said, his gaze intense. "If you aren't here. It's not something you can get back. There's no second chance. That's all I'm saying. There's no second chance." He held her eyes for a moment, then nodded and patted her hand. "I must go," he said softly.

Wynter sat, staring at nothing, her hands folded in her lap, too stunned and too numb to say or do anything.

Christopher rose to gather up his things. When he was ready, his jacket on, his saddle and his tack on one shoulder, his dressing case on a little trundle by the door, he stood and looked uncertainly down at her. He asked softly, "Are you angry with me, girly?"

She looked up at him in shock. He was standing in Lorcan's doorway, ready to leave, his face miserable. All this time he'd been getting ready, she'd sat like a stone and now he thought she was . . .

She leapt to her feet and slipped past him into the retiring room. "I need to get my robe, Christopher. Wait for me."

"Oh no," he hissed in alarm. "You can't, I'm going through the secret passages; you'll never get back."

She paused in the doorway. "I'll scale the orange trees and climb through my window if I have to, Christopher Garron. You're not going to the stables alone with no one to wave you farewell."

She pulled on her robe and her soft indoor-boots and belted her dagger around her waist. When she hurried back into the retiring room, Christopher was standing just outside Lorcan's door, gazing in at her father who still slept, oblivious as a baby, his face turned to the fire. Christopher had placed a glass of tea on his bedside table, and it steamed gently in the firelight.

"It's the hope of things lasting that does us in, ain't it?" Christopher said quietly, his eyes on Lorcan. "If only we could shake that stupid illusion, the belief that *this* time we'll be able to stay. This time, things will last. Then we'd all be much happier."

Wynter stayed very still for a moment, trying not let those words burrow into her heart and break her down completely. "Aren't you going to say goodbye to him?" she asked.

"I don't want to wake him."

Wynter hesitated uncertainly. She wasn't sure that it was the right thing to do, to just leave like that, but Christopher bent and shouldered his saddle, looping his tack across his arm. He took the trundle by its handle, ready to go. He glanced at her, waiting patiently for her to slide open the secret door.

She did and then stepped into the passageway, moving aside to let him get past her, since he would have to lead the way. He didn't move, and she glanced up expectantly. He was still standing in Lorcan's doorway, the light from the fire dancing in distorted shadows across his face. He was staring through her, as she stood in the darkness of the passageway and his eyes were miles away.

"Christopher . . .?" she whispered.

Suddenly Christopher dropped the saddle and tack to the floor and fled back into Lorcan's room without a sound. Wynter rushed after him and came to halt in the doorway, tears springing to her eyes.

Christopher had fallen to his knees by Lorcan's bed and

was shaking the big man urgently by the shoulder, his face distraught. "Lorcan," he whispered, "Lorcan. I'm going. Lorcan. I'm going now. Wake up."

Lorcan gasped, and his green eyes snapped open, startled. "Whu . . .?" he said, staring without comprehension into Christopher's face.

Christopher tried to say something. He grimaced, baring his teeth and curled in on himself slightly as if he had a pain in his chest. He grabbed at Lorcan's hand and pulled it to him squeezing it to his lips. Big tears stood out in his eyes, shivering, but not falling "I'm going . . ." he managed finally, staring into Lorcan's face. "I'm going away . . ."

Lorcan blinked at him, still obviously confused and disorientated. He searched the young man's face, as if seeking a clue to who he was. "Christopher . . ." he breathed.

"Aye. Aye . . ." Christopher had run out of words and he just kept holding on to Lorcan's hand and looking into his face.

Lorcan seemed to have no idea what was happening, his green eyes never really cleared, and almost immediately they began to flutter closed again. Christopher watched him, his mouth quivering, as sleep took the big man under again. Gradually Lorcan's breathing returned to the steady, innocent cadence of sleep.

Christopher made a desperate little sound, his eyes liquid, his body trembling. His hands were shaking as he clutched Lorcan's hand to his chest. His eyes opened wide and the shivering tears overflowed abruptly in two shining trails down his face. He took a huge breath and held it. Wynter could see that he was in a fierce internal battle for self-control. She thought for a moment that he would fall on her father and shake him again, try to wake him properly so that they could say goodbye.

But Christopher just relaxed suddenly, and released his breath in a long shaky sigh, swallowing hard. His hands were trembling when he put Lorcan's hand back down on the covers, but his face was set, and he was back in control of himself.

Christopher leant over and gently kissed Lorcan's cheek. "I'm leaving," he whispered. "I wanted you to know. God protect you, Lorcan Moorehawke, and watch over you, on your journey to the better place."

Escape

Christopher seemed to know exactly where he was going. He moved confidently through the blackness, turning unerringly left and right. He led her up and down stair-cases, ducked through tiny archways, passed by echoing, chilly voids. Wynter could hear his hand trailing the walls, and he counted under his breath as each panel passed by under his fingers. At first, the trundle had made a terrifying amount of noise in the confined space, but Wynter had quickly picked her end off the ground and they carried it between them through the winding darkness.

Finally they came to the top of a flight of stone stairs, and Christopher pushed his way up and out of a trapdoor, which seemed to be set in open ground. Wynter followed him up the steps and found herself in the echoing space of the indoor horse arena.

Good God! She thought, looking around her in the vague twilight, *We must have been underground for the best portion of that journey.*

It was still very dim, but the air was beginning to shimmer with pre-dawn light. They were rapidly running out of time.

Christopher was calm now and he showed no trace of his earlier distress. He glanced at Wynter, shifting the saddle higher on his shoulder, and waited patiently as she shut the trapdoor and hid it again under loose straw. She took the handle of the trundle from him and followed behind as he led the way to the big double doors. They peeked out. It was very hard to see in this shifting non-light and they carefully scanned the exercise yard, before slipping into and moving along the deeper shadows of the walls until they got to the stables. Wynter wished that she had worn darker clothes; she stood out like a moonbeam in her white robe and shift.

She kept watch at the alley while Christopher tacked up his horse. The sturdy little animal had whickered and snorted happily when they entered the stalls, and Christopher quietly smacked his lips and made breathy noises to her in reply. Wynter glanced back at him; he worked quickly and with the ease of familiarity. The horse nipped his tunic and lipped his hair, snuffing fondly down the back of his neck as he tacked up. He scrubbed between her eyes, murmured gently to her in Hadrish and led her out into the alley between the stalls. He brought the horse to where Wynter was peering out the door and the two of them stood, nervously waiting.

It was very quiet, the sky starting to pale. Christopher's horse moved behind them, stamping gently, blowing hot breath down their backs. The air was chilly and Wynter began to shiver in her shift and robe. She hugged her arms tightly around herself and hopped from foot to foot.

Oh God, she thought, *where are the pack animals? Where are the extra horses?*

Razi had promised that they would be ready, he had told Christopher to wait here, that everything would be set to go. Christopher should be leaving *now*. Wynter looked up at the roofs of the barns: they were starting to show against the sky; it was beginning to get light. Christopher *had* to leave before dawn, had to catch the gate sentries by surprise. He had to hand over his egress papers and be gone before anyone knew he was out of his rooms.

Jonathon would want to control every inch of this journey, would want Christopher in his power for as long as he could manage to keep hold of him. Soon the hall guards would be hammering on the suite door, seeking to escort him to the stables. It wouldn't take long for them to discover that his rooms were empty. Christopher had to be well gone by then, out of the complex, well on his way to losing himself on the little winding roads leading south. Wynter started to shiver in earnest, the misty air and her growing fear combining to chill her to her bones.

Without saying anything, Christopher moved behind her and gently put his jacket over her shoulders. Wynter found herself unexpectedly engulfed in Christopher's spicy scent and the delicious warmth of his body. She was about to say *thank you*, when he drew her to him, wrapping his arms and the jacket tightly around her and holding her close. He casually rested his chin on the top of her head, and resumed his surveillance of the alley.

Wynter found herself completely overwhelmed by the tenderness of this gesture, and to her horror, and without any warning, she sobbed loudly. Christopher's arms tightened around her in surprise and he said, "Oh girly". The quiet protectiveness in his voice cracked something inside

Wynter's chest and the tears that had been threatening all morning finally forced their way to the surface. Mortified, she lifted her hands to her face and tried to pull away. But Christopher tightened his arms a little more, and, as Wynter's tears streamed down her face and soaked the dark sleeves of his tunic, he began gently to rock her to and fro.

Christopher would not release her. He held her against his chest with gentle, insistent strength and, quite suddenly, Wynter realised that she had nothing left to fight with, she had no energy left with which to pretend. She stopped struggling and slumped against him in defeat.

"All right," he murmured. "It's all right . . ."

Wynter leaned her head back against his shoulder and gave in to her tears.

Christopher bent his head forward and rested his cheek against hers. His skin was smooth and cool against her face. "Shhhhh," he crooned, cradling her against his chest, "Shhhhh. It's all right, sweetheart. I promise. Everything will be all right. Don't worry . . ."

She twisted in his arms and burrowed against him, pushing her face in against the warm skin of his neck, snaking her arms around his waist, pulling him closer. He continued to whisper in her ear, telling her it was all right, everything was all right, and then his lips were moving in her hair as he spoke, and against her neck, murmuring reassurances. She inhaled his scent, her tears drying against the fabric of his tunic, and his words lost meaning and the sound of his voice was all that mattered.

She turned her face against Christopher's neck and moved her cheek against the cool smoothness of his cheek. His hand was in her hair then, cradling the back of her head, and his lips were on her lips. Soft, unbelievably soft, his mouth moved against her mouth. She pressed up into his kiss, her lips parting, and for a moment, that was all there was. His warm mouth moving against hers, the scent of him, the encompassing safety of his arms.

A soft cough in the alley shocked them apart, and then Christopher was pushing her behind him, reaching for his knife, a growl in his throat. But it was only Marcello Tutti, his eyes soft, his cheeks pink, as he led the pack mule and spare horses up the alley, trying hard to pretend he hadn't noticed their kiss.

Wynter hid herself behind Christopher for a moment, wiping her eyes and trying to get her knees to support her weight. Christopher's jacket began to slip from her shoulders, and she absently shrugged her arms into the sleeves. She heard Marcello whispering as he came up the ally.

"*Buongiorno, Christi. Mi dispiace ma . . .*"

Christopher replied softly, "*Ciao, Marcello. Non importa . . .*" As he spoke, Christopher reached behind him and took Wynter's hand in his. She stepped to his side and they stood pressed together, hand in hand as Marcello brought the horses to a halt before them.

The little Italian bowed to her, his eyes gentle. "*Buongiorno, Signora Della Protezione.*"

She smiled faintly and bobbed her head.

"*Marcello,*" said Christopher, "*Dov'è il Signore Razi?*"

Marcello spread his hands and shrugged sympathetically. "I am sorry, Christopher. Il Signore, he can't get away . . . his father, you know. He keep . . . ah . . . the eye?"

Wynter felt her heart twist, and Christopher's face

creased in sorrow and disappointment. He hesitated and looked away a moment before nodding, his lips tight. "Can't be helped," he murmured.

"I, too, must leave you," said Marcello regretfully, "The guards, they keep the eye on all Razi's allies, in hope that they will be catching you in your escape. I must make myself to be scarce." He handed the lead rope to Christopher and bowed, "Take good care, Christopher. Be safe." He backed quietly up the alley and then turned and hurried quickly from sight.

They stood for a moment, hand in hand, looking blankly at the empty air where Tutti had been, the animals shifting gently in the narrow space. Then Wynter shook herself to life and turned to press her hand urgently to Christopher's chest. "You must go now!" she insisted, looking up into his face. "The cockerels will begin to crow soon!"

He moved slowly, turning his head in a daze and then suddenly he, too, snapped awake and turned quickly to secure the lead rein to his horse. Wynter nervously rubbed her arms and kept anxious watch up and down the alley. She huffed in exasperation as, instead of mounting his horse, Christopher hurriedly crossed to the barn door and began scooping out a hollow in the earth with his fingers.

" Christopher . . ." she hissed, but stopped as he took the remaining piece of cake from his pocket and dropped it into the shallow hole. She blinked as he carefully covered it and patted the earth back down. He bowed his head, his lips moving, and then straightened.

"Here," he said, crossing swiftly to her and withdrew a package from under his shirt. He pressed it into her hands and she looked down at it in surprise. It was a sheet of paper, folded many times, stiff and bulky. "I meant to give it to you in your rooms. It's a map of the secret passages She looked up at him in amazement. "You might need it," he said, "but *don't* try to use it as you go along. Memorise your route *first*, it's too dark in there to try and use a map."

They looked at each other, his eyes gravely holding hers as she held the map to her breast. Then Wynter pushed him gently to his horse. "Go," she said. "Go."

Christopher broke away from her with a cry of desperation and whirled, putting his foot in the stirrup and hopping to gain momentum for the rise into the saddle. He began to mount, but he never swung his leg across the horse's rump. Instead, Wynter saw his eyes lift to the end of the alley and he froze, standing straight in the stirrup, staring at something out of her sight. His face hardened, his brows lowered, and he curled his lip into a dangerous snarl.

Slowly Christopher lowered himself to the ground and lifted his strange knife from his belt. Wynter immediately unsheathed her dagger and crouched, ready to fight or flee. Christopher pushed his horse aside and Wynter saw what had set him on alert.

A huge man loomed at the end of the alley, a sword in his hand. He was nothing but a giant dark shape against the open air, but it was obvious by his size that he was one of Jonathon's personal guard. He moved to the centre of the alley, blocking their exit, and lifted his sword.

"You go now, girly," said Christopher, and unhooked the buckler from his belt. He stepped forward and crouched, holding the unusual knife at the ready. The ornate handle was shaped like a squared-off cup, and Wynter saw that

Christopher's entire hand fit into it. He was gripping it somewhere inside, and it covered his hand and wrist with a solid metal brace so that the blade stuck straight out from his metal-clad fist, like a wicked extension of his arm. "Go on," he repeated softly.

The man at the end of the alley hesitated slightly at the sight of Christopher's weapon. Wynter sidled out from Christopher's side and crouched down, her own knife hand held out, her free hand up in a defensive gesture. Christopher hissed in aggravation at her, but said no more about her leaving.

For a moment, the three of them remained motionless, waiting for someone to make the first move. Then the big man began to advance down the alley towards them, menacingly swinging his weapon from side to side. Wynter and Christopher tensed for battle. Then they jerked and flinched as a tall figure reared out of the shadows behind the man and dealt him a ferocious blow to the back of his head. He went down on his knees without a sound and swayed there, his sword hand falling loosely to his side. The tall figure stepped forward and they saw that it was Razi, his distinctive silhouette unmistakable against the rapidly paling sky. He lifted his left arm once more, a wooden cosh clearly visible in his upraised fist, and he dealt the guard another resounding crack to the head, watching coldly as he collapsed at his feet like a sack of grain.

He looked up at them then, his face invisible, his posture contained. He pointed to his chest, made what Wynter took to be a gesture to his eyes and then made a circling movement with his hand. He was going to keep an eye on their surroundings. He pointed at Christopher, and then pointed in the direction of the gate. Very faintly they heard him whisper, "Hurry!"

Christopher took a step forward and gazed up the alley at his friend. Razi paused. Christopher hesitantly raised his hand, holding it up in farewell. Then he touched his forehead, his mouth and his chest, bowing slightly as he did so, his eyes still locked on Razi's silhouette. For a long moment Razi didn't move, then he repeated the action, bowing slightly to his friend and holding it for a long time. Then he grabbed the fallen guard by the jacket, dragged him into a stall and was gone, swallowed by the deep shadows of the barn.

Christopher could wait no longer. In one quick movement he sheathed his knife and hooked the buckler to his belt. Gathering the reins in his right hand, he put his foot in the stirrup and hoisted himself into the saddle. His horse snorted and shook her head and side-stepped under him with a whickering neigh. Christopher clucked to her and pulled back the reins and sat down hard to make her stay easy. Wynter moved in and put her hand on the sturdy neck, looking up at him.

There were no words. What could they say? *I love you? I will see you soon? Wait for me?* What did any of that mean in this situation? He was going. He would never be back. There was nothing they could do about it.

The horse moved under him again and stepped sideways and tried to turn. A muffled shout from behind the barns made the two of them startle and look up. In the dim stalls, they heard a brief dash of metal, another muffled exclamation and a thud. They stared, straining to hear.

Then Razi's tall figure, stooped and running, shot along the back wall of the stalls and disappeared around the corner.

Wynter turned urgently to Christopher. "Go!" she hissed, and slapped the horse's shoulder, causing it to jump forward on him. He took it as she meant it and urged the anxious creature into a trot, leading the line of animals up the alley. Wynter stepped back as the laden pack mule jogged by and watched as the line of horses got to the corner, and turned out of her sight.

She watched the dust of their passage hanging pale in the air, then she took off after them, sprinting to try and catch up.

At the edge of the exercise yard, instead of trying to follow along the horse path, Wynter cut down between the barns, raced across the paddocks and pushed through a hole in the yew hedge. She ran through the gardens, her feet flying in the dark, blind and moving on instinct, until she broke through the shadows into the wide expanse of the main thoroughfare and the gravel drive that led to the gates.

Christopher was advancing on the gate, his spare horses and the pack mule making far too much noise for comfort. As he reached the big arch, she saw a sentry step forward and faintly heard his voice challenging Christopher to produce his papers. Christopher bent forward, and she saw the guard reach up to him. There was a long pause, during which she saw Christopher turn in the saddle and look back. She resisted the urge to lift her hand. The sentry said something and Christopher turned back to him again.

She startled and whirled as someone dashed across the gravel to her. It was Razi. He came to a sliding, breathless halt beside her and clung to her shoulders. They turned to watch anxiously as the sentry walked away from Christopher's horse and into the gatehouse. There was a momentary, agonising silence, and the sound of the gate chains came drifting across the morning The shadows under the arch were split with a thin line of grey as the great double horse-gates were opened. Then Christopher was silhouetted against the morning light as he urged his horse through the gates and out into the free air. He took off at a high trot, they could see him already on the upward slope and heading for the trees as the gates began to slip closed. He had made it out.

Let him stay safe, prayed Wynter desperately. *Let him stay free.*

Razi tore his eyes from Christopher's retreating back and looked down at the hand he had resting on Wynter's shoulder. He frowned and tilted his head in confusion, staring at her clothes. The gate swung shut with a thud. Above the trees, the sky was just shimmering to palest lemon. The cockerels in the barnyard began to crow. "Wynter," said Razi quietly, "is that not Christopher's jacket?"

The Twisted Man

Wynter pulled distractedly at the dark fabric of Christopher's jacket, running her fingers down the wooden buttons, pulling the collar up around her face. She had no doubt that it was his only jacket and squeezed her eyes shut in a mixture of regret for him and selfish bitter joy that she had this piece of him, scented by him and warmed by his body, to keep for her own.

Razi looked anxiously all about them as the light rapidly grew in the sky, and the trunks of the trees began to take definition in the morning air. He tightened his grip on Wynter's shoulders and drew her into the deep shadows that lingered beneath the trees. "Sis," he whispered, "let me return you to your rooms now. It is not safe."

Wynter nodded absently, her mind still filled with Christopher, but as Razi turned her on her heel and began to guide her back towards the palace, two things happened that made her abruptly dig in her heels. Firstly she saw a discreet flash of movement under the trees that made her startle. She looked quickly away before Razi noticed the direction of her gaze, her heart hammering in anticipation.

And secondly, as Razi put his strong hand on the small of her back and murmured that they should hurry, Christopher sprang vividly to her mind. Wynter recalled how he had been unwillingly confined to his room these last four days or more. It occurred to her that the poor man had been dependent on Razi for every meal, forbidden to participate even in the provisioning of his own journey home. In an effort to keep Christopher safe, Razi had, to all intents and purposes, made him a prisoner. Razi gently pushed her, trying to get her moving again, and she realised that this was what he intended for *her*. If Razi had his way, he would lock Wynter up in Lorcan's suite, safe and protected and completely helpless until he himself was gone and – as Razi saw it – no longer a danger to her. But she couldn't afford that! She had things she needed to do! Things that she could not allow Razi be party to.

To Razi's obvious shock, Wynter stopped dead in her tracks and twisted from his grip.

"Wyn . . ." he said, and she held her hand up to stop him.

Wynter raised her chin.

"I'll make my own way from here, Razi."

"But . . ." he was completely thrown at her sudden coldness. He looked around in confusion for a moment, then she saw his face clear with understanding. He leant down to look pleadingly into her face. "Oh, Wyn," he said. "Don't be angry with me, please. He couldn't stay. Can't you see? He couldn't . . . They would have . . ."

The hopelessly misplaced guilt in his voice almost shattered Wynter's resolve and she moved to comfort him, then stopped. She let her face harden. She could use this, Razi's inaccurate interpretation of her motives, she could use it. She stepped back into the shadows and drew Christopher's jacket tighter around her.

"Just let me be a while, Razi. I can find my own way back."

His face fell, his eyes wounded. Then his expression darkened and he stepped closer to her, leaning over her from his great height. "Now, you *look*," he said, his voice low, his eyes intent. "I just knocked five of my father's personal guard cold off their feet. Worse, even, than what my father might do about it, is the fact that the men themselves might seek revenge upon me. And I shall not have them get to me through you. I will *not* have *you* pay that price for my actions! You are *safe* in your rooms, Wynter, and I intend to get you there. So stop acting the stubborn *baby* and *do* as you are *told*!"

Wynter jut her chin at the familiar tone. All Razi's advantages of height, of strength and of birth were suddenly heavy in his voice, and Wynter lowered her head and glared at him in warning that he could not do that with *her*. She would never, ever, allow him to become his father, *never*, not in her presence at least, not in relation to their friendship. He locked eyes with her, his face set, and then his eyes cleared suddenly as he became aware of how he was snarling into her face, how he was looming over her, this small woman in her shift and robe, vulnerable to him and alone in the dark. He stepped back so fast that he almost stumbled, and stood a couple of paces back from her, his hands hanging by his side, lost.

She held her hand out, her voice soft. "Razi," she said gently, and he glanced at her, fearful of her ire. "I promise you that I shall take care. I just need to be alone for a small while. I will walk in the yews, I may stroll down the chestnut avenue and then I shall go back to the suite. All right?" His lips parted in helpless distress and he blinked. Wynter's heart wrung for him. She kept her hand up to prevent him following, and began to turn slowly away, her eyes still on his face. "Go get some rest, Razi. Please. You're all worn out. Go get some rest . . . and I shall see you later."

She walked quickly away, sticking to the shadows, staying deep in the trees. At the corner of the gardens, where she would pass behind a hedge and out of sight of the drive, she turned and looked back. Razi was still standing amongst the trees, his arms hanging loose by his sides. He was facing away from her, staring over the bailey walls to the outside hills and that small bit of wild forest visible to him against the dawn sky. He looked like a lost soul, abandoned and completely alone. Wynter clenched her jaw and forced herself to turn away.

Mist began to rise up from the damp morning grass as Wynter put distance between herself and Razi. The world coalesced into grey on grey. The sky became vivid with sunrise. She stayed close to the hedges and walls, keeping herself small and inconspicuous. Despite what she had said to Razi, Wynter had a deep fear of Jonathon's men, and the idea of falling victim to their wrath terrified her. It was still very cold, and she buttoned Christopher's jacket around her as she slipped along.

Eventually she came to a good place, quiet and secluded but open enough that no one could sneak up on her. She tucked her hands under her armpits and loitered at the base of the yellow dovecote. She didn't have to wait for

long. The orange cat slunk casually from the blackness of
the yews and came to a sighing halt in the grey haze of the
morning light. It yawned idly and sniffed, grizzling and
tutting as if Wynter had interrupted a particularly good
nap and it were impatient for her to get down to business.

You came for me! thought Wynter irritably, but she held
her tongue and her patience, and finally the cat rolled its
eyes and tipped its head to the avenue of chestnut trees.

"The spirit waits," it said. "He has not much time for
loitering; I suggest you hasten."

Wynter cursed in exasperation, and resisted the urge to
kick the cat across the courtyard. She ran as fast as she
could to Rory Shearing's avenue.

"Rory!" she hissed, coming to a skidding halt on the
leafy path. "Rory! I'm here!" *They'll kill me if I'm caught! I'll
be gibbeted! I'll be hung!* She called out again, regardless.
"*RORY!*"

There was nothing for a moment, and then she felt it,
that particular prickling of the skin, the strange expansion
of the light that signalled an apparition. Rory materialised
right in front of her and she staggered back a few paces with
shock. He was in an awful condition. "Rory!" she gasped in
dismay.

He swayed in front of her, apparently finding it hard to
see or to focus on her. There were patches of him missing,
faded away entirely, just gone, and what was left of him
kept flickering quickly on and off and fading in and out of
focus. He slumped and swayed, and staggered from side to
side for a moment until he got his ghostly feet under him.
He looked past her, blinked, turned his eyes back to her,
tried to focus. Finally he seemed to see her. "Child," he

said, his voice a moth wing against a window pane. "I seek your father . . ."

"No, Rory!" cried Wynter urgently. "My father is too ill! You are to deal with me! Understand! Bring your news to me!"

Rory squinted at her uncertainly. He lost his grip on the conversation and his eyes drifted to the left, his lids slipping closed, his head drooping. He began to lose definition.

"RORY!" Wynter clapped her hands loudly

Rory slammed back into focus again, snapping his eyes to hers. "He will not travel!" he shouted as if waking from a violent dream. He focused on Wynter, staring into her eyes, and she gasped and felt her spine snap painfully straight. Rory, in his desperation, was concentrating too hard. It felt like cold water rushing through her, freezing inside her. Her body forgot to breathe and her heart stuttered in her chest. She choked on the word *stop!* and tried to lift her hand.

"He will not travel . . ." said Rory again, hopelessly, and then disappeared completely as his strength deserted him. Wynter, released from his terrible scrutiny, slumped to her hands and knees, gouging in the leaves as she tried to force a breath into her frozen lungs. A few yards away, Rory floated back into being again, but weak now, and sagging. He did not look at her, just drifted in the shadows, his arms wrapped around his stomach, his head down.

The cat hissed behind Wynter suddenly, its voice sharp with fear. "Soldiers! They are almost upon you!"

The urgent warning sent Wynter scrabbling mindlessly off the edge of the path. Rory faded from sight. She flung herself onto her stomach and wriggled through the leaf mould until she was hidden beneath the gnarled branches and thick foliage of a laurel. Thank God for Christopher's jacket. Without it, she would have been a vivid white shape in the gloom of the undergrowth. She tried to push her lower half deeper into the bush, hiding the pale skirts of her shift and robe. She pressed her face into the dirt and froze as three soldiers staggered through the trees and came to an unsteady halt right in front of her. Their boots scuffed and dug at the leaves as they tried to keep their feet, and she saw with terrified relief that they had erased all traces of her presence on the path.

It was three of Jonathon's men. One of them was barely conscious, leaning against his companion with buckling legs and a heavy head. The third man was obviously in command, and he paced ahead of the others, scanned the trees and then stalked back, grabbing the injured man's arm and shouldering half his weight.

"Graham is coming," he growled and the men moved forward a little and then stood waiting. Their companion hung supported between them, moaning slightly now and again. "No sign of Norman. God curse it."

"I don't see no Hadrish trailing along behind him, neither."

The commander swore as the fourth man limped up through the trees, calling as he did, "Did you get him? Did you get the little sod?"

The others growled a negative, and Wynter sank deeper into the cold mulch as their compatriot carne to a halt right by her, his boots inches from her face. "Shit," he groaned, "someone hit me . . ."

"It was the Arab."

There was a round of snarling retorts to that information.

"I'll kill the bastard!" The new man exclaimed with violent intent.

His commander let fly a kick, connecting sharply with the soldier's shin. "That's a Crown Prince you're talking about, Graham, watch your fool mouth!"

Graham yelled and clutched his leg. "He ain't no bloody prince!" he grunted, his voice tight with pain. "*Alberon* is heir! It don't matter how many times the King denies it, it won't make it any less true."

Wynter thought that Razi must have properly scrambled this man's brains, if he felt he could talk to his superior like that.

Sure enough, the commander flung the wounded guard into his companion's arms and dealt Graham a massive blow to the face. The man staggered back, crashing into the laurel and almost treading on Wynter's hand before getting his balance. Wynter managed to stop herself from flinching or crying out, and she pressed her cheek into the ground. Blood flooded her mouth and she realised that she had bitten her lip. She sucked hard at the wound and stayed as still as humanly possible.

"The Arab is a *Crown Prince*," snarled the commander crowding against the man. "You will take your damned lumps from him as if he were the King himself. You understand?" The commander's boots were toe to toe with the soldiers. He must have been snarling into the man's face. "If that Arab tells you to bloody jump, all I want to hear from your bloody mouth is 'Aye, sir! How high, sir!' Are we clear, Graham?"

"Aye, sir," replied the soldier softly.

The commander maintained his close intimidation of the man for a moment, then stepped away. "Never fret, lad," he said in consolation. "The King will exact revenge on your behalf. He'll never let us down."

Wynter slowly closed her fingers into the cold leaves, her fear for Razi a solid lump in her throat.

"Do you think the Hadrish got out, sir?"

"Aye," said the commander thoughtfully, "I do." He turned and Wynter assumed he was looking in the direction of the hills. "No matter," he murmured. "The lads in the forest will get him . . ."

"We should head out after him too, sir."

"No. First you get Lionel to the doctor, then you find Norman. I must report to the King." He began to walk back to the palace. The others remained where they were, and he called to them as he left, "Should you meet the Arab, restrain yourselves from murder . . . you hear?"

The two men muttered a low, insincere chorus of "aye sir." The commander jogged away.

"'T'aint murder if he falls down the stairs," murmured Graham.

"Oh aye, or drowns in a horse trough . . . man like that, anything could happen him."

Muttering darkly and growling to each other in mutinous tones, the men gathered themselves together and began to move off in the direction of Doctor Mercury's quarters. The wounded man's feet dragged in the leaves, two rutted tracks from the toes of his boots marking the path they took away through the trees.

The soldiers passed quickly from sight and earshot, but

Wynter found it difficult to crawl back out from hiding. It took a tremendous effort of will to get her arms and legs co-ordinated enough to move, and when she finally sat up out of the filthy leaves, she had difficulty standing because her legs were shaking so badly.

Rory was watching her from the path. She stood and faced him, leaves in her hair, her face and hands filthy, her shift smeared with moss and clay. "Where is Alberon, Rory?"

"He that knows . . . will not travel. He is twisted, and does not yet know he is dead . . ."

"Does not know he is dead? Is he a *spirit*, Rory?" She considered this. Some spirits had very limited spheres of influence. "Can *I* go to *him*?"

Rory looked uncertain. He began to drift without walking, like thistledown being shifted by the wind. He was as flimsy as mist, vague and unfocused. "The others . . ." he murmured distantly. "They object . . ."

"Where must I go, Rory? To meet this man?"

Rory raised his eyes, looking over the trees to some-where Wynter couldn't see. "The others . . ."

"Aye, Rory. The others object . . ." Wynter tried hard to keep the impatience from her voice. God knows, Rory looked to have paid the price for his defiance of "the others", whoever they might be. "But I *must* talk to this man. I *must* find Alberon, Rory! Help me!"

He directed his gaze to her, and she tried not to flinch as he drifted towards her, his eyes roaming her face. He came very close. He was shifting, like reflected water, his features rippling in a way that could not bode well for him.

Can ghosts die? If they can, then this must be how it looks.

Rory brought his face close to hers. It was still his face, his gentle, intelligent, wistful face, the face of her childhood playmate. But standing this close and with Rory staring so intently, Wynter, for the first time in her life, felt the grave off him. She could hear it moving under his skin, invisible but tangible to the soul, the squirm and struggle of all that happened to the body after death. She felt that, if she just looked hard enough, she would *see* the corruption vibrating beneath the surface.

"Rory . . ." she whispered, horrified. "What has befallen you?"

"I will hold them off . . ." he sighed. "While you speak to the man . . . but I cannot distract them long, and when I yell for you to run, you must *run*! Fast and far. You understand, little Moorehawke?"

Wynter nodded mutely.

Rory's attention drifted away from her, and he bobbed gently, like a leaf on a pond. "Tonight," he murmured. "When the world is still . . . I will meet you there." He began to fade away and she reached for him in panic.

"Rory! Where? Where will I meet you? Where?"

He focused again, looking at her in surprise. "Why, the keep, dear . . . he will not leave the Chair . . . he does not understand that he has been released."

Wynter felt the cold wave of understanding wash over her. She took two unwitting steps back and turned her head away slightly, narrowing her eyes against the thought. "Rory," she whispered. "Do you mean . . .? Rory, is it the boy? The assassin?"

"The Twisted Man, girl. Aye. The Tortured Man." Rory was exhausted, his voice barely audible. "Tonight," he sighed, "when the world is still, I will meet you there . . . I will try . . . and distract . . . the others." He turned his head tiredly and faded away. His words lingered after him, as ghost words often do.

"And I shall guide you there and back," said the cat, looking her up and down, its tail twitching. Wynter jumped, startled to see it still there. The cat narrowed its eyes at her and sneered, shaking its head in disapproval. "Great Hunter, girl! Do try not to quail! It makes thee look like prey."

Make Merry, And Laugh While We May

". . . and they have done a good job?"

Wynter sighed, "Aye, Dad. They did a good job." She didn't lift her eyes from the sheet of paper in her hands. She knew that Lorcan's rasped question was just for the sake of saying something. Of course Pascal's boys had done a good job. They had done an *excellent* job. There had never been any question of them doing otherwise. That was why Lorcan had chosen them in the first place. However, it didn't escape Wynter's notice that Lorcan didn't ask for her opinion on how the library looked.

She sighed, folded the paper and dropped her hands to her lap.

The library looked awful. Particularly to Wynter's professional eye. All those blank spaces glaring out from the beautifully carved wood. Everywhere one looked, bare, naked patches jarred and caught the eye. She closed her eyes and shook her head to remove the images from her mind.

When she had turned up at the library this morning she had been genuinely surprised to find only Pascal waiting on her. He had been gazing thoughtfully out a window when she came in, and for a moment she had thought something terrible had happened to his boys. But the man had just smiled sadly at her and swept his hand around the room, "So," he had said. "And we are done."

Wynter had gaped around her in shock. She had not noticed how quickly the work had been progressing. It occurred to her that she had spent most of the last few days sitting on a windowsill staring into space while Pascal's crew had worked around her.

And now it was done, this shameless mutilation of her father's work, finished.

Wynter snapped her eyes open with a grimace. She looked at the paper in her hands again and unfolded it once more, scanning the page, as if its contents could some-how erase the memory of that awful destruction.

Lorcan eyed her from his pillows. She was sitting cross-legged, in her work clothes, at the bottom of his bed. She had come straight into his room after the library, left her tools by his door and climbed onto the foot of his bed without a word. She'd crossed her legs, leaned her head back against the footboard, and closed her eyes. She had stayed that way, silent and withdrawn, until poor Marcello had made his gentle, unobtrusive exit. Then, once she was sure they were alone, she'd opened her eyes and looked at her father. Lorcan had sighed heavily and smiled at her, and nodded.

Wynter glanced up from the paper again as her father slowly eased himself lower in the bed and settled back against the pillows with a hiss. He had tried to spend as much time as possible out of bed today and it had taken its toll. He closed his eyes. He had not seemed at all surprised when she told him that the library was done.

Wynter dropped her eyes to the paper, re-reading the careful, squared-off notations, the painstakingly executed staves. It had never occurred to her before, how difficult it would be for Christopher to use a quill, but of course, it must have been a very laborious procedure. *Designed to rob me of everything I am*, he had said, *a very effective revenge.*

It was a carefully ruled score, three repeating stanzas. A duet for recorders, one a deep register, one high. The lower register was a slow, stately, pulsing melody, beautiful in its simplicity, weighty and grand. And over the top of it, a tripping harmony, chuckling almost. It was like a bright stream running through the depths of a mighty forest, majesty and joy combined. It was called "Lorcan" and Christopher had left it folded under her father's tea-glass before he left that morning.

Wynter could not keep looking at it. If she did, she would begin to crack. She folded the paper for the last time and handed it to her father. He reached out without looking and slipped the sheet under his pillow, his eyes on the rapidly darkening sky outside his window.

They had tomorrow, that was all: tomorrow. The day after that, Wynter would have to leave him. There were so many things they should say to each other, but neither of them seemed to have the heart for words. Maybe tomorrow. Yes. Tomorrow she would be able to speak, and all the things she had to tell him would just flow from her.

"Perhaps tomorrow," said Lorcan quietly, speaking to the sky, "I might manage a walk in the orange garden." His words were a reflection of her own thoughts and Wynter nodded wordlessly, too filled up to reply.

The sky was like a bruise outside the window, Lorcan watched the clouds darken, the bright edges of them growing dim as the sun set. He closed his eyes in a small frown, pain perhaps, or an unhappy thought. He turned his head towards her, opened his green eyes and hesitated. He began to say something. Then they both froze, listened intently and grinned at another slight scratching on the secret panel. Razi! They blossomed in delight rousing to action.

Lorcan heaved himself into a sitting position. Nodding to Wynter that she should get the door, he happily smoothed down the covers and raked his fingers through his hair in grinning anticipation. Wynter leapt from the bed and ran to slide back the secret panel.

Razi stood uncertainly in the passageway, as if unsure of his welcome. He had a portfolio under his arm and was stooped to see under the doorframe. He smiled hesitantly, peering at her from the shadows.

"Hello, Wyn," he said. "May . . . may I come in?"

Her smile faltered at sight of the fresh bruises on his face, and then she stepped into the passageway and wrapped her arms around him in a gentle hug.

"Hello, Razi," she said softly. "We were worried for you." She tried not to squeeze too hard, but still he gasped and stiffened, and gently pried her arms from around his waist.

He kept hold of her hand and kissed her fingers with a gallant little bow. "No need to worry. I'm indispensable, remember?"

Lorcan sobered at the sight of Razi's face and the stiff hunched-over way in which the young man entered his room. But Razi only grinned at him, and no one made any comment when he winced and faltered before sitting down into the chair by Lorcan's bed.

Razi placed the portfolio onto Lorcan's covers, a little smile on his face. "I brought this for you, friend. I knew you would love it." He nudged the folder with his fingers, his eyes bright with expectancy, nodding for Lorcan to open it. "I had it copied while in the Moroccos. Though I say it myself, it's a very, very fine translation. I got one for Father's library, but this one . . ." he glanced shyly into Lorcan's face, "this one is yours."

Lorcan ran his hand over the plain leather folder, and he glanced at Wynter in obvious pleasure. She grinned at him and sat on the foot of the bed, intrigued. The big man bit his lip in pleased anticipation and undid the ties, opening the folio to reveal a beautifully bound book. His eyes widened in awe, and he sighed with amazement as he drew the book onto his knee and slowly turned the pages. It was entitled *The Book of Ingenious Mechanical Devices,* and as Lorcan became absorbed in the intricate drawings, Razi spoke quietly and pointed to this bit and that bit of text or illustration.

"The original is about three hundred years old, written by a fascinating man, Badi' al-Zaman al-Jazari. An engineer and an inventor . . ." Razi looked up at Lorcan, "Just like you." The two men smiled at each other, and Lorcan turned his attention back to the book.

"Incredible," he murmured, "Three hundred years?"

"Aye."

The three of them bent their heads to the pages and Wynter pointed to a lovely illustration of some Persian waterwheels. "This reminds me of the system you designed for Shirken, Dad. Remember?"

"Aye," breathed Lorcan absently, turning another page.

"Dad designed a wonderful system of plumbing for Shirken's palace, Razi. It brought water to every room in the complex, using something Dad called a pump."

Razi's eyes widened in fascination. He was about to ask a question, when Lorcan commented dryly, without looking up from the book. "I never saw it completed. Jon called me home before I had a chance to oversee construction. Look at this!" He tilted a page to Razi, pointing to some intricate system or another.

But Razi did not look at the page, instead he gazed at Lorcan. He seemed to consider something and then he said, "An interesting thing about al-Jazari, Lorcan: it is said that he suppressed many of his own inventions." Lorcan froze and glanced sharply at Razi. "It would appear he considered much of what he created too . . . destructive . . . for public consumption."

Lorcan straightened and closed the book. His face shuttered, his eyes suddenly cold. Razi held up his hand, his mouth curving into a smile. "Lorcan. I am not probing. I am just telling you. Al-Jazari was an interesting and intelligent man. A decent human being. Everything he has left for posterity was to the benefit of mankind. Men like him, men like *you*, they are few and far between in this world. That is all I wanted to say." He spread his hand, and tilted his head. "That is all."

Lorcan blinked and Wynter looked down at her hands. There was an uncomfortable, strained silence, during which Razi huffed out a little laugh and patted Lorcan's hand. "Why do we find it so hard to hear the *good* that people have to say about us?" he murmured.

Lorcan took Razi's hand and squeezed it. "Would you . . .?" he asked hoarsely, "Would you like to see the plans for Shirken's palace? And perhaps, this new idea I had for Tamarand, in the Midlands? Wherein I proposed he could hold back the water from his fields with a reinforced . . ."

"I'm leaving tomorrow, Lorcan."

Razi's blurted exclamation stopped Lorcan's words in his throat and had Wynter frozen in the act of slipping from the bed. She had intended to fetch her father's portfolio, anticipating Razi's interest in Lorcan's new inventions. Now she slid to the floor, horrified, her mouth open in disbelief. She looked across Razi's head and met Lorcan's panicked eyes. *Tomorrow! No!* She wasn't ready! She wasn't ready yet to leave! She'd thought they had at *least* tomorrow! Give her that much, just that much! Please!

Lorcan looked at her, eyes huge and liquid and despairing.

"Oh Razi," whispered Wynter. "Why? I thought . . ."

Razi turned stiffly to look around at her, winced, and wrapped his arm around his chest with a hiss.

"Razi," murmured Lorcan in concern. "What has happened you?" He reached across and put his hand on Razi's head. To Wynter's surprise, Razi chuckled but at the same time, he leaned wearily forward and rested his forehead on Lorcan's bed, still cradling his chest. Lorcan began to stroke his hair, running his big fingers through Razi's untidy curls, as if comforting a child.

"Oh, nothing too bad," said Razi lightly. "Father's men just got a touch over zealous in their search for Christopher's papers."

Wynter swallowed in fear. "Did they find them, Razi? Your father has men in the forest and . . ."

Razi turned his face to peer at her from under his hair. "Not any more he hasn't."

The cold certainty in Razi's voice sent a chill through Wynter. Razi shut his eyes again and turned his face back into the covers. Lorcan kept combing his fingers through the young man's hair. His eyes met Wynter's and she saw her own sorrow reflected there. This was so wrong, that Razi should need to be this person. So wrong.

"I will leave tomorrow," sighed Razi, "I cannot stay any longer. I cannot bear to stay any longer."

"It is pointless, I suppose, to ask once again, that you take my daughter with you?"

Wynter jerked at Lorcan's request and glared at him, but he stubbornly levelled his eyes at her, his face set.

Razi sighed and shook his head. "Please stop, friend. Please. I will only get her killed. Wynter is safer here, far from me. Far from my bloody, God-cursed company." Lorcan's eyes fluttered and he moved his hand to Razi's back, absently rubbing a circle between the poor man's shoulder blades.

Wynter squeezed her eyes shut in blessed relief. She was free of that complication at least. What a nightmare it would have been, had Razi agreed. Her eyes opened in anxiety for him, and for his safety, should the search for Christopher's papers continue. "Are Christopher's papers safe, Razi? Once you are on the road, it will be a lot harder for you to keep them hidden."

Razi chuckled again. He raised his head, shrugging Lorcan's hand off him and pushed himself carefully back in the chair. His face was creased with delicious mirth, and he grinned at the two of them as he settled against the cushions. "*I* don't have them!" He laughed, amused at their expressions. "Oh, come now! Do you really think that I would send my good friend into the world, unpapered? And he a branded slave? Please." He continued to grin at their confusion and spread his hands as if to say, *honestly now, are you really so dim?* "Christopher has them!" he exclaimed, when they still showed no signs of comprehension. "They're in his dressing trunk. He will find them when next he changes his clothes."

Lorcan gasped. It had been a bluff. A crazy, dangerous, heart-stopping bluff. And it had paid off. But now Razi had to take his father by surprise. Had to leave as soon as possible, before the wily King began to suspect that all Razi's power over him was nothing but smoke and mirrors.

And because of this, Wynter, too, would have to leave early. She sank despairingly to the edge of Lorcan's bed. Razi leant over and shook her knee, completely innocent of the implications of his early departure. "Come on, sis!" he said softly, "No long faces, eh? It's only one day less." He grinned at her and she raised her eyes to Lorcan. He was watching her, his face carefully neutral, his eyes sad. One day less.

"Well," rasped Lorcan, shaking himself. "Shall we have some wine? I know I'd like some!" He smiled at her then, and shrugged. *What can we do?* that shrug said, *What can we do? Make merry and laugh while we may. Tomorrow is another day.*

Razi pushed to his feet, smiling hopefully at Lorcan as he did. "I'll fetch your portfolio, Lorcan? If I may?" The big man nodded in agreement and waved his hand to his dressing trunk. Razi crouched to look Wynter in the eye, shaking her knee again. "Hello? Madonna of the Sorrows? Will you send a page for wine?" *Please, please*, his desperate smile said, *let us not grieve, not tonight.*

"Wynter?" he repeated. "Some wine?"

She snapped out of her gloomy reflection and focused on his pleading face, only inches from her own. Overcome with tenderness and pity, Wynter impulsively took Razi's face between her hands and kissed him, then she placed her forehead against his. She felt Razi's breath hitch with a suppressed sob, and he tried to pull away. She gently tightened her hands against his smoothly shaven cheeks, keeping him in place. "I suppose," she said. "That you'd like some cakes, too?" She looked up into his eyes without pulling away and his face creased up for a moment, his eyes full.

"Aye," he said unsteadily. "I'd like some cakes, too."

"Jam tarts!" rasped Lorcan from the top of the bed.

"Bah!" cried Wynter in mock irritation. "You men and your sweet things!" She pushed Razi from her and he rose to his feet, moving to kneel by Lorcan's dressing trunk, where he stayed motionless for a moment, his face hidden, before opening the lid to look for the manuscripts.

At the bedroom door, she paused to look back at them. Lorcan was surreptitiously pushing back the covers and reaching for his robe. He winked at her and mouthed, *I'll get up for a while.* She shook her head in exasperation, but made no move to stop him as he slipped his arms into the sleeves and laboriously pushed himself to his feet. With a look of utter concentration he took aim, and then launched himself at the fireplace. Razi yelled in shock and consternation when the big man plopped breathlessly down in the fireside chair, and Lorcan laughed in delight at the wonderfully startling effect he'd had on his young friend.

Big child! thought Wynter fondly and turned to leave.

They all froze at a quiet knock on the hall door.

"Oh, get rid of them!" cried Lorcan, "whoever the hell they are!"

Razi stared anxiously up at her, the folio on his knee. Wynter's face hardened. It didn't matter who it was – messenger, councilman, guard – she was determined they wouldn't get access tonight.

"Stay here," she whispered and crossed quietly to the hall door. Another knock, a little louder than before. "Who is there?" she queried, her voice cold. "It is *much* too late for callers."

Razi had followed her and was standing in the retiring room door, listening. The two of them shrank back at the familiar voice of the King.

"Open the door, Protector Lady. I would speak with your father." Jonathon spoke quietly, his face obviously very close to the other side of the door.

No! Wynter turned to Razi in despair. He had folded over on himself, utterly distraught. *No! No, no. Was he to be denied even this?* His last night. His farewell? He turned and staggered into Lorcan's room. He looked like a man who had been kicked by a horse.

Wynter panicked for a moment. How could she deny the King? "I . . . give me a moment, your Majesty . . . I am undressed."

"Make haste."

She ran from the door to Lorcan's room. Razi had fallen to his knees at Lorcan's feet, his arms wrapped around the big man's waist, his head buried in Lorcan's chest. Lorcan smoothed his hair, his cheek pressed to the top of the young man's head.

"Shhhhhh," whispered Lorcan helplessly, "Shhhhhhh . . ."

The King knocked on the door again. Insistently this time.

Razi," cried Wynter softly. She felt her tears, wet and hot on her cheeks as she tried to pull Razi from Lorcan's arms. "Razi!" she begged "*Please!*" Then she realised that Lorcan was also gripping tightly, refusing to let the young man go, and she gave in. She flung herself on Razi and rested her cheek against his heaving back.

Suddenly Razi threw them off. He literally shook himself out of their arms with a violent shrug and surged to his feet, his tear-stained face shining in the firelight. He turned immediately from them to stalk out of the room. While Razi was still in the doorway, Jonathon knocked once more and Razi spun in rage and glared at the hall door, his fists clenched. Wynter had never seen such utter hatred on his face.

"Razi," hissed Lorcan.

The young man turned to him at once. He spread his hands in helpless grief, his eyes lost.

That was Lorcan's last sight of Razi. Then he was gone.

No Way Back

As soon as Wynter unlatched the bolt, Jonathon slipped into the room and shut the door carefully behind him. He looked Wynter up and down, frowning slightly at her dishevelled hair and puffy eyes. He smelled strongly of wine and Wynter took a step back. She had an abiding distrust of drunkards.

But the King was only a little unsteady on his feet and his eyes, though red and heavy, were lucid. He stood swaying slightly, and peered past her to the retiring room.

"Is he awake?" he asked quietly, glancing at her.

Wynter nodded, keeping her distance. *What the hell do you want?* she thought. *On this night of all nights, couldn't you just have left us alone?*

Jonathon looked uncertain for a moment, and expelled a deep sigh. Then he ran his hands through his curls in a movement that was so *Razi* that it knocked Wynter sideways. She had expected impatience at being kept waiting, or rage at the fact that she had obviously *not* been getting herself dressed. But Jonathon seemed so diffident standing there, so unsure of himself, that she was uncertain of which way to act. Then he seemed to come to a decision, and to Wynter's shock, he actually patted her shoulder before passing into the retiring room and leaning in at her father's bedroom door.

"Lorcan," he said, hesitating on the threshold, his hand on the lintel.

"What do you *want*, Jonathon?" Lorcan's rasp came clear and cold.

The King dropped his head, the firelight crowning him in burning gold.

"Allow me enter, brother. I would speak to you."

The seemingly genuine request in Jonathon's voice had Wynter narrowing her eyes in suspicion. *I wonder*, she thought, *would you really leave, if my father refused you entrance?*

It seemed that Lorcan was considering the same question, because there was a long, heavy silence during which the King continued to lean at Lorcan's door, waiting. Finally she heard her father say, "I am tired, your Majesty. Another time perhaps."

The King straightened and stared in at Lorcan. Wynter held her breath, waiting for the explosion, anticipating the sudden rush of temper. But Jonathon just stood very still for a brief moment. Then he dropped his head, pushed himself from the doorframe and turned to leave.

Wynter stood, frozen and anxious, as the King approached her. But he simply made his heavy way past her and drew back the bolt to the hall door without comment. He had already crossed over the threshold when Lorcan called out.

"Jon!"

The King paused, his posture tense, listening. There was another long pause, then Lorcan said quietly, "Come back here."

Jonathon stepped back into the room and closed and bolted the door. As he passed through the receiving room, he picked up one of the heavy round chairs and carried into Lorcan's room.

Wynter loitered in the door for a moment, eyeing the King as he clumsily placed his chair in front of Lorcan and sat himself down. She raised her eyes to her father and awaited his instructions. Lorcan was slumped in his own chair, glowering. He had rubbed his face clean of tears and pushed his tangled hair back behind his shoulders; there was no softness in his eyes now. He glanced at his daughter, "Come in, Wynter," he said. "Sit down."

Jonathon looked over his massive shoulder at her, not pleased. But he didn't object when she crossed the room and perched at the end of the bed.

"I have not yet eaten, Father," she said. "I may eventually have to grab a bite in the kitchen."

Lorcan met her eye and understood immediately. She had business to do, business that he would assume had to do with her early departure. He nodded, "Whenever you feel hungry, dear, you go right ahead. Otherwise, stay as long as you wish."

"Thank you, Father."

Then Lorcan turned his full attention to the King, his face hard. Jonathon returned his gaze and, for a moment, the two men silently regarded each other across the remains of their tattered friendship.

Lorcan's face remained stony and Jonathon was the first

to look away. He shut his eyes and shook his head. He looked into the fire and seemed to consider something. Reluctantly, he reached into his shirt and withdrew a folded piece of paper. He clutched it for an instant, as if unwilling to part with it. Then he leant across the space between himself and Lorcan, and held it out in offering.

Lorcan frowned at it, as if it might bite him, and Jonathon gestured with it impatiently, thrusting it at his old friend. "For Christ's sake!" he growled eventually. "Take the bloody thing!"

Lorcan took the paper, his face tight. He snapped it open and scanned the contents. Wynter saw his face go slack, and she saw him read and reread and then once more read the entire document. His eyes lost their focus then, and he lowered the page, staring at nothing for a moment. Then he turned his gaze to Jonathon, scanning his face with renewed suspicion.

The King groaned in genuine distress and held his hand up as though to ward off an accusation. "Oh, brother . . ." he said, averting his eyes. "I fully deserve that look . . . but have some mercy on me, please. I *swear* to you, there are no demands attached. It is yours. It's all yours," he mumbled. "Too late, I know, but I wish you whatever joy is left of it."

Wynter could hear the effects of liquor in Jonathon's speech, and it made her nervous. Drunk men were always so unpredictable and strange. She straightened and slid warily from the bed, alarmed at the expression on Lorcan's face. She stood, watching him for a moment as a confusion of emotions fought for dominance. He looked as though he might cry, as though he might scream, as though he might rear up and strike Jonathon down. His breathing was just a touch too fast, his cheeks flaring red. Finally, his eyes on the King, his jaw working, Lorcan flung his arm out, offering her the paper. The fire illuminated it briefly in his outstretched hand, Jonathon's fluid script visible in shadow through the backlit parchment.

Wynter took it. It was, of course, her father's licence of work. Signed and sealed, all in order. Granted, free and willingly, and for what God-known reason, she couldn't tell. She read it, the paper trembling in her hand and she lifted her eyes to glare at Jonathon, who sat with his face averted still.

"We thank your Majesty," she hissed, "for your kindness and generosity in granting my father his licence of work. What a pity you could not have found it in your heart to trust him with it before you drove him into the ground."

"Does this mean, Jonathon, that you want me to leave?"

At Lorcan's dry whisper, Wynter bared her teeth in panic and clutched her father's shoulder. *Oh no, surely not! Surely you won't throw him out? Not in this state? Not when I am about to abandon him into your care?*

But Jonathon raised his eyes to stare at his old friend, and his face was so deeply distraught that Wynter had to blink to ensure it wasn't a trick of the light. He shook his head inarticulately, searching Lorcan's pale and shadowed face and finding only recrimination there.

"Friend," he managed finally, "have I become such a monster, that you would believe that of me?"

There was no reply from Lorcan, but Wynter felt his posture soften a little, and she wondered what it was that he was thinking. For herself she could not see past the man who had so cruelly mistreated Razi, who had almost cost

Christopher his life, and who had set Alberon fleeing like a fox from hounds. She looked into the soft pleading of Jonathon's wine-flushed face and saw only self-indulgence and a childish desire for absolution.

Jonathon tilted his head, wholly concentrating on Lorcan, his voice low and despairing. "Lorcan?" he said, as if asking her father a question. "Today, Razi beat five of my men out of their senses. Not just that . . . but I suspect he also had three of them *killed* . . . they were in the forest, and have yet to be found." Jonathon paused in disbelief, shaking his head and looking at nothing for a moment, trying to puzzle it out. "*Razi* did this," he murmured. "My Razi."

Lorcan was merciless. "You have always known, Jonathon, what that boy is capable of when protecting those he loves. What the hell did you expect? After you pushed him so hard?"

"But what choice had I!" cried the King, genuinely distressed "Tell me what I could have done differently, Lorcan? Tell me how it is possible to change anything, now that it's all in motion?"

"I cannot do that, friend," said Lorcan softly. "Because I still do not truly know what it is that you have done."

Jonathon laughed bitterly and flung up his hands. "Other than oppress my people and ruin my beautiful boys? Other than that?" He looked Lorcan up and down, and met his eyes, his throat working. "Other than drive my good friend almost to his grave because I did not trust him to have my back?" He bit his lip, his eyes bright. He made a helpless gesture with his hands. "I am sorry, brother. I have no idea how we can get through this. And I am sorry for it."

There was a moment's silence. Wynter felt Lorcan lean forward a little. He gazed into his old friend's face. Wynter did not like how shallowly he was breathing. She shifted her hand from his shoulder to his back. "Perhaps," Lorcan said hoarsely. "Perhaps it is not too late? If you forgive Alberon, if you revoke the *mortuus* . . ."

Jonathon sat back, ruefully shaking his head. "Lorcan, do you think I would have done all this, were I not certain of Alberon's intentions? The boy is set against me. He plans a coup. There is no doubt of it. As we speak, he and Oliver gather representatives to their camp. They are deep in negotiations with all the rival factions that nibble the edges of this fragile kingdom." The King looked into the fire, his eyes wide. "They will gather their allies, and, using your machine, they will attempt to wrest the kingdom from me." He shook his head again, sighed, and closed his eyes. "I am caught. I can think of no other options. Other than to kill Alberon and destroy poor Razi by putting him in his place."

"Using my . . ." Lorcan's muscles jerked under Wynter's hand. "They have the *machine*?" He gripped the arms of his chair, and Wynter could feel him trembling.

"Father," she murmured. "Calm yourself . . ."

"*No!*" cried the King impatiently, "they do not *have* the machine. There is only one left, and it is . . ." he glanced at Wynter, "in my care." He looked again at Lorcan and there was something new in his eyes now. A sulky kind of vindictiveness that put Wynter on alert.

"I used your machine to suppress the insurrection, Lorcan . . . Oliver was there . . . he was on the crew."

Lorcan groaned and covered his face with his hands,

and Wynter saw a bright moment of satisfaction flare in Jonathon's face.

"Oh, don't bloody worry," he sneered. "It wasn't in *battle*, there were no loose tongued survivors. It was just like before . . . an ambush. Every living man, dead in minutes." Lorcan groaned again and rocked gently to and fro. Jonathon watched him, his face cold.

"The crew," hissed Lorcan. "What became of the crew?"

"Besides Oliver and myself? All of them, my men . . ."

Lorcan raised his head to stare beseechingly at Jonathon, "Jon . . . Jon . . . did you?"

Jonathon tutted and flung his hand up, sitting back and turning his head away. "They still live. All nine of them, my personal guard. They would die rather than talk." He knotted his jaw and glared into the fire. "But Oliver," he snarled, "Oliver . . ."

Suddenly Lorcan leapt as if burned and turned his face to Wynter. He stared at her, appalled and pushed her away from him. "Out!" he hissed, "Out! You can't be here!"

Jonathon snorted from the other side of the fire. "Oh yes," he drawled, and Wynter and her father turned big eyes to him, both on alert at the cold disdain in his voice. "We cannot let the little Moorehawke child be tainted by any of this, can we? The Kingssons can hurl themselves on the flames for all you care. But your precious baby must stay free and blemishless."

"Jonathon," implored Lorcan, as he snaked his powerful arm around in front of Wynter and pushed her slowly behind his chair. "Oh, Jonathon . . . please. Don't . . ."

"Don't what?" Jonathon leant forward in his chair, glaring at his old friend. "Don't *what*, Lorcan? Oliver wants to use *your* machine to expand the kingdom. He wants to produce them in their dozens!" He scanned Lorcan's face for a reaction, and seemed gratified at the horror he saw there. "He has stolen your plans," he continued. "He has taken hundreds and hundreds of your *ingenious* little *paper-charges* and he is promising any of the factions who join him that they can have a machine of their own!"

Jonathon thumped his chest with a fist suddenly, his voice wavering. "I'm sacrificing my boys, Lorcan. Sometimes I think I'm sacrificing my bloody *soul* in trying to prevent this from happening." Tears began to roll down Jonathon's cheeks, but there was no softness in his face, only rage and bitter, bitter resentment against the man who sat before him. He jabbed a finger at Lorcan, his face scarlet, his teeth bared. "You *made* this bloody thing! You bloody *made* it! Don't sit there and tell me this isn't your fault! Don't you *dare* tell me that you're not to blame!"

"But Jon . . ." Lorcan held his hands out, his voice imploring "You said they were *destroyed*! You promised! We threw the paper-charges in the river! You let me burn the plans – the *only* plans, or so you told me. My God, Jon! Was it all one big lie? All the things we did . . . the men we . . . just to bury this! And it was a lie? But we swore, Jon . . . *we swore*. This is all meant to be over."

The King blinked at that. He looked confused. He sank back in his chair. "Well . . ." he mumbled, ". . . it's not."

There was a long, heavy silence. Wynter was afraid to move in case either man remembered her presence and decided to throw her from the room. Her father's protective arm had dropped to his side, and his hands lay corpse-pale in his lap. He seemed to have lost all his energy, and slumped motionless in his chair.

Jonathon might as well have been brooding by his own fireside for all the attention he was paying either of them. He watched the fire, his hands loosely resting on the arms of the chair, his eyes distant. When he finally spoke, he was very calm and thoughtful. There was no trace of his former bitterness or contempt in his voice.

"You did an excellent job up North, Lorcan. I would have been lost without you. You kept those hounds off my back all that long while." The King glanced at him, but his old friend did not raise his head. Jonathon turned to regard Lorcan closely, propping his cheek on his fist. "Without your machine, this bloody insurrection would have claimed more lives and resources than we could have afforded. You have saved my kingdom . . . again. You have been a true and loyal subject. And an invaluable friend." Lorcan still did not raise his head. Wynter felt him breathing slow and deep under her hand, as though he were asleep. She glanced down at him. His eyes were brightly reflecting the firelight as he looked down at the toes of Jonathon's boots. "I am sorry I doubted you," continued the King. "I wish I had never pushed you so hard on your return. I wish . . ."

"Take your wishes and burn them," growled Lorcan softly. "I have no desire to hear what you *wish*, or what you are grateful to me for, or how you feel about anything at all. I have no desire to even look upon your face. I wish only that you would leave me in peace."

Jonathon smiled and huffed a little breath out of his nose. "Well, you have always had the luxury of the noble sentiment, old friend." He pushed himself from the chair, steadying himself before straightening. "Whereas I?" He chuckled bitterly. "I must kill my friends and murder my principles and throw my sons on the funeral pyre of state." He swayed a moment, then turned unsteadily for the door. "Because I . . ." He spread his arms in an expansive gesture as he exited. "I am the goddamned King!"

They heard him stumble into the receiving room, then the bolt drew back and he left without closing the hall door.

Lorcan stayed as he was, staring at the floor. Wynter moved to kneel at his side and he spoke without looking at her. "Go shut the door, darling."

"Dad, I . . ."

"The door please, Wynter."

His hair had fallen forward, and from this angle she couldn't see his face. As she hesitated, Lorcan's hands slowly tightened into fists, and Wynter sighed and went to shut the hall door.

It had grown dark, and the receiving room was lit only by the sharp rectangle of light thrown in from the hall. As Wynter crossed the room, a flash of white caught the corner of her eye and she stuttered to a halt, her heart hammering in her chest. The orange cat was sitting in the shadows, its white chest and the tips of its paws glimmering like spectre-light in the gloom. Its paws were tucked neatly together, the tip of its tail switching incessantly to and fro. It said nothing, but it dipped its neat head to one side and widened its eyes expectantly.

Well? that look said, *I don't have all bloody night.*

Wynter took a steadying breath and held up a hand, *hush*, she indicated, *stay there.* She closed and bolted the hall door, then crossed to return to her father's room, glancing all the while at the cat. She paused at the retiring room door and gave the cat one more warning look. *Wait there!*

The cat tutted and rolled its eyes, and grizzled softly in complaint. Wynter took that as an agreement to wait.

Lorcan had not moved. He still stared grimly at nothing, his jaw tight, his hands fisted in his lap. Wynter longed to take the tangled curtain of his hair and brush it back into its usual, neatly contained plait. Instead she went and knelt at his feet. She was horribly aware of the cat in the next room, listening, impatiently waiting.

"Dad," she said softly. "Are you all right?"

Lorcan continued to stare at the floor, and she took his hand. He was very cold and she chafed his fingers as she gazed into his face. He didn't seem to notice.

Wynter couldn't really understand any of this. In her opinion this machine, whatever it was, sounded to be a godsend to a kingdom. Surely anything that could hasten the end of a conflict was a good thing? As it was, battles were fought at the expense of hundreds, sometimes thousands of men's lives. Men were battered with cannon, pierced with arrows, and hacked by swords and halberds. They were punctured by pike and lance, beaten, broken and mutilated, and left to scream and die under the trampling hooves of their horses. If her father had created something, some *weapon*, that brought all that to a rapid close . . . well, all to the good! Let Jonathon fashion them in the hundreds, and ring the kingdom with them! If it were up to Wynter, that is most certainly what *she* would do.

But peering up into Lorcan's face, she saw that her father was broken at the idea, hollowed out by it. This puzzled her. Lorcan, though no lover of war, had never shied away from the brutal necessity of physical conflict. He had gone to war himself, and when younger, he had been famous for his ferocious battle rage. In the early stages of this insurrection, before he was sent North, Lorcan had stood at the war table with Jonathon and devised strategies and battle plans that would surely have sent hundreds to their deaths. So why was he distraught by the possibility of his machine being used in defence of the kingdom he loved?

Now, Jonathon? Jonathon, Wynter understood better. He feared the machine being used against him . . . He had perhaps wanted to keep it for himself, and therefore wished to suppress the knowledge of it. But why had he agreed to destroy it in the first place? Such a powerful tool! None of it made any sense to her at all . . . It made her all the more determined to seek out Alberon, and get some answers.

Lorcan hissed and Wynter snapped back to herself with a start. He looked pained and gently extracted his hand from her grip. She realised that she had been grinding his fingers between hers, kneading them like dough in her anxiety.

"Oh Dad! I'm sorry."

He was distracted and upset. "He will regret this in the morning," he muttered. "When the wine wears off him."

"Well, he can't take it back now, Dad! It's in your possession!"

Lorcan looked at her blankly, then realised that she was referring to the licence. "No, darling. He will regret having spoken like that in front of you. It will eat at him . . . he will not feel safe. Knowing that he has revealed himself like that to you." He stared through her. "More than ever you must go. As soon as Razi has left, you must follow him. Do not hesitate, in case you lose him . . ." He looked into her eyes, shook her lightly, to emphasise the importance of his words. "Do . . . not . . . *hesitate*!"

"What of you, Dad?"

"What *of* me? I'm done, that's the end of it. But I will *not* have you burn in the fires of my making. Go! Follow Razi to Padua! Throw yourself under his protection, for he will never send you back here, I promise you that. Have a good life, baby-girl . . ." He raised his eyebrows and gave her a twisted smile. "Sure, has the King himself not just handed you the best licence of work ever granted man or woman in the history of his kingdom?" He stroked her hair again and tilted his head fondly. "With your talent, girl, you can't fail to thrive."

"Oh, Dad, please." She wouldn't look at him then, couldn't see the determined hope in his eyes and know that she would deceive him right up to the end. Her eyes slid past him in distress, and her face froze at the sight of the cat sitting on the windowsill. It bared its teeth in an impatient snarl and glared at her. She tore her eyes from it. *Oh Christ.*

"Wynter?" Lorcan touched her hand. "Darling?"

She met his gaze and her eyes welled up and overflowed He cupped her cheek in his hand, running his thumb under her eye to wipe away the tears. "Darling," he whispered. "Can . . . can we pretend?"

This brought more tears to her eyes and she dipped her head quickly to scrub them away. They weren't pretending type of people, the Moorehawkes, not pretending type of people at all. She lifted her face to him again, and took his hand.

"Yes, Dad. What would you like to pretend?"

He squeezed her hand. "Let's pretend that tomorrow is not our goodbye." Her breath caught in her chest with an audible hitch. Lorcan caught her eyes and held them hopefully with his. "Let's pretend that you're going to Helmsford to check a stand of timber. That you'll be back in a week. That we'll see each other in a week. Wynter, can we do that?"

It didn't matter how hard she clenched her jaw, her chin wouldn't stop trembling, and the tears were back, spilling down her face and dripping off her chin. Lorcan made a desperate little sound and put his hands on either side of her face and swiped her cheeks dry. He pushed her hair back off her forehead, with a determined tightening of his mouth and then wiped the tears off her face again. "Let's pretend, darling," he growled. "Please. Let's . . ."

"Yes, Dad!" She grabbed his hands and took them from her face, holding them tightly in her own, stilling his ever more frantic attempts to dry her tears. "Yes. Helmsford. Timber. A week. Yes."

His eyes got huge for a moment, and for a moment, she thought he wouldn't be able to do the very thing he asked of her. But in the end, he compressed his generous mouth to a thin white line, clenched his jaw to nearly snapping point and nodded tightly.

"I need to go to bed now, darling," he said. "I will send word to Marcello to come very early tomorrow, that I may get ready to have breakfast with you . . . before . . ."

She nodded. "You'll need your rest," she said. "And I need to go speak to Marni." Lorcan tensed, concern sharpening his face. Wynter patted his hand reassuringly. "I shall be careful, Dad. I will stick to the halls." She glanced significantly at the cat and it stalked haughtily out of sight, along the ledge back to the receiving room window, no doubt. "I promise, there will be no sneaking about, Dad. Nothing shall happen to me."

Lorcan nodded, and his implicit trust in her almost broke Wynter's heart.

With a fierce sniff, she shook herself and carefully pushed every feeling down to that roiling place in the pit of her belly. She set her jaw, shoved her shoulder in under Lorcan's arm, and helped him heave himself to his feet. With her support, Lorcan made his slow way to bed, stiff and agonised. He eased down onto his pillows, as heavy as a stone. He held her hand briefly, not looking at her, then pushed her gently away.

Wynter glanced back at him as she shut his door. He was staring into the fire, his hands clenched on his chest, his face haunted. Sleep was miles from him.

She delayed just a touch longer, going to her room to belt on her dagger and slip a candle and travel tinder-box into her belt-purse. On the point of leaving she added Christopher's map to the crackling reassurance of Razi's note against her heart. At the last minute, she shrugged Christopher's jacket on over her tunic and then she finally went to face the cat.

It was practically spitting with rage by the time she stepped into the receiving room.

"You certainly took your own sweet time, did you not?" it hissed. "I suspect that I have aged considerably in the course of your interminable congress with that man."

Wynter breathed deep and knotted her hands by her

sides. "Let us make haste, then," she ground out. "Before you slip into your dotage."

The cat growled and Wynter showed it the door. "You will have to find me another entrance to the passages. I cannot risk my father hearing me enter from here."

The cat led her through the halls, and it wasn't long before it paused and slipped smoothly behind a tapestry. Wynter followed. A quick search of the dim panelling revealed the ubiquitous cherub sconce, and she twisted it on its head. A small secret door slid open for them and they made their way into the dusty blackness of the passageways, carefully shutting the door behind them.

Almost immediately, Wynter felt the cat swarm up her legs and body, and curl itself onto her shoulders. The hissing instructions began at once and Wynter's heart hammered painfully against her throat as she began the winding journey through the dark.

Whispers in The Dark

"Stretch out your hand and push gently at the panel to your right."

Wynter did as the cat bade her and the panel slid forward and to the side. It remained impenetrably dark, but the air freshened slightly and chilled. Wynter slipped out of the passageway, still clinging to the doorframe. She was completely blind. Keeping her back pressed against the reassurance of the wall, she ran her hands over the stones on either side of her and lifted her arms to feel the low corbelled roof of an underground passage.

She knew instantly where they were. This was the low-ceilinged corridor where she had first heard the inquisitors torturing the assassin. She froze and strained her ears, expecting ghostly screams. But there was nothing, just the ragged sound of her own breathing and the wild hammering of her heart.

The darkness was a good sign; it meant that there were no torches lit, and no torches meant no activity. No human activity, at least. Wynter strained her ears again. She wished that she could manage to hold her breath, all the better to listen, but she was too frightened and could not pause her fearful panting. It had occurred to her on the journey through the passages, that the spirits of the inquisitors themselves might still be here. Their ghosts intent on causing pain. The thought made Wynter's knees unhinge, and she gripped the stones of the wall in panic

Ghosts don't tend to harm, she thought feverishly, *ghosts don't tend to harm*. Christopher's wry lilt came back to her, clear and bright in the blackness. *Tell that to the raw meat we left in the dungeon a few nights ago.* She squeezed her eyes tight: *Oh shut up, Christopher. Ghosts don't tend to harm. They don't . . .*

The cat hissed and squirmed impatiently on her shoulders. "Are you planning a nap, girl?" it asked sharply. "Shall I go grab a bite to eat, and return when you are ready?"

Its grizzled sarcasm forced Wynter to put some iron in her spine, and she pushed herself from the wall with a long, controlling breath. Sinking cautiously to her knees, she felt for her tinderbox and fumbled the candle from her purse. The cat tutted and leapt from her shoulders with a growl. The abrupt loss of its reassuring weight froze Wynter in mid action, and she suppressed a whimper of fear at the thought that it might have deserted her again. She listened for a moment, staring uselessly into the dark, her hands poised in the act of opening the tinderbox. There was no sound to indicate that the cat remained in her vicinity. It had left her.

Wynter felt her mouth tighten into a bitter little line. To hell with the damned creature, she certainly wouldn't give it the pleasure of hearing her cry out. She angrily turned her blind eyes to the task at hand, and struck the flint over the tinderbox. The ensuing spark lit the hall like a flash of lightning, but didn't catch the tinder. She bit her lip and struck again, and again. The bright flashes left light-scars on the backs of Wynter's eyes and she blinked rapidly, forcing the red trails away from her vision. *Come on*, she thought, poising to strike again, *please*.

The next spark caught the tinder, and Wynter bent her head and blew gently until the little pile of wood shavings blazed. She lit the candle with shaking hands, and lifted it over her head so as not to ruin her vision. The candle and the rapidly dying tinder-blaze threw a wavering circle of light.

To her relief and anger the cat stood just a foot away, eyeing her with undisguised contempt.

"Honestly," it hissed, showing all its needle teeth. "Your species! So utterly dependant on its *props*." It shook its head in disdain, and stalked into the darkness.

Wynter gritted her teeth, packed her stuff away and stamped out the last of the mostly dead fire. Then, lifting the candle even higher, she followed the cat's arrogantly twitching hindquarters to the top of the corridor.

The two of them stood at the head of the steps, looking uncertainly down at the door of the torture chamber. The air in the stairwell seemed to writhe under the unsteady illumination of the candlelight.

"I will await you here," murmured the cat, unusually quietly. "Whatever business you have in The Black Room, it's . . . it is no concern of mine." And it sat stiffly down on the flagstones, its eyes glued to the shifting darkness at the foot of the steps.

Thank you so much, thought Wynter, *thank you so, so very much for all of your great help.* Her feeble sarcasm warmed her not a jot as she descended the stairs.

She heard the whispering as soon as she neared the closed door, and it stopped her dead. It seemed to fill the bottom of the stairwell as a living presence. It did not so much inhabit the air, as attempt to inhabit Wynter. Hissing and slipping through her skin, it filtered into her brain. It crawled underneath her clothes and ran itself along her ribs. It twisted under her skin, and slid, cold and stealthy, up her spine

The memory of Christopher's voice rose, bright and clear against the gurgling terror of the whispered litany . . . *You ever seen an eye drawn from its socket?*

Wynter choked out a little sound and took a step back. She began to tremble and her wildly shaking candle spattered her upraised hand with gobs of hot wax.

Every whispered word was clear and distinct, though the voice that spoke was clogged with pain and guttural with fear. It was the Midlanders' prayer to their virgin. Wynter stood and listened to it, her eyes wide and staring. Fat drops of wax fell into her hair and spattered on her cheeks, as she tried to gather the courage to reach out and turn the handle.

"*Ave Maria,*" implored the desperate voice, "*gratia plena, Dominus tecum . . .*" The words gained speed, as if afraid of being stopped, "*. . . benedicta tu in mulieribus, et benedictus fructus ventris tui, Jesu.*" Surely no earthly person could speak so rapidly and so clearly. Wynter felt her head begin to spin. "*Sancta Maria,*" whispered the voice, its wretched pleading reaching new heights of despair "*Mater Dei ora pro nobis peccatoribus, nunc et in hora mortis nostrae. Amen.*"

Holy Mary, Mother of God, pray for us sinners, now and at the hour of our death. Amen.

There was no pause after the "amen", no ghostly inhale. The voice just continued on into another driving round of prayer, launching once again into "*Ave Maria, gratia plena, Dominus tecum . . .*" It rose in pitch and speed. Its desperation palpable "*Benedicta tu in mulieribus . . .*" it cried, as if the words themselves could save it, "*. . . et benedictus fructus ventris tui, Jesu.*"

Christopher's voice broke through again, calmly documenting this poor soul's terrible last hours . . . *Then they took hot pokers . . . have you ever smelled that? Hot metal on flesh?*

Wynter pressed her free hand to her ear and took another step backwards, shaking her head. She could not go in there. This was something she just could not face. Her heart was beating so rapidly that she felt in immediate danger of fainting. She couldn't face the source of this terrified prayer. She couldn't. She had not the nerve . . .

"Child . . ."

Wynter screamed and spun around, casting wax in a wide splattering arc. The candle guttered and darkened, and then flared to blessed life again as she stumbled back against the wall. Dark spots of fear and shock blossomed in her vision and she felt her legs begin to buckle for real. Terrified that she might be about to faint, she yelled out, to release the pent up horror from her chest and to clear the fear blossoms from her head.

Rory stood on the steps beside her, his translucent face heavy with concern. Wynter held the candle out against him like a weapon. It took several seconds for her to get enough control to allow her to lower her violently shaking hand, and straighten from her terrified crouch against the wall.

"Child," he repeated, his voice far less distinct than that of the pitiful soul trapped behind the door. "You must hurry . . . the others . . ." he looked behind him, every movement slow and laborious. Rory was barely standing, he slouched in place, his head low. Wynter thought that, were he not a spirit, he would be slumping against the wall.

She lifted her hand to him, moved by his terrible condition. The words, *we cannot do this*, were poised on her lips. But Rory turned wearily without looking at her, and waved a hand over the catch of the door. Wynter heard heavy mechanisms moving within the lock and the door swung open without a sound. Rory slipped into the darkness and, without a pause, almost against her own volition, Wynter followed.

Rory stood just inside the door, gazing towards the chair, his face suffused with pained compassion. The frantic prayers had subsided to a crooning repetitive mantra "*nunc et in hora mortis nostrae . . . nunc et in hora mortis nostrae . . .*" The sighing whispers echoed around the room. Every inch of Wynter's body was trembling and she could not bring herself to tear her eyes from Rory.

"I must go now . . ." he murmured, glancing at her, his eyes soft. "Be kind to him. He's had too much suffering and cannot leave it behind." Suddenly Rory gasped and looked sharply ahead of him. "I must go," he cried, turning quickly, his arm clutched round his waist. He jerked forwards into a jogging run towards the back of the room. "Don't forget, little Moorehawke . . . fast and far . . . as soon as I tell you . . . run . . ." and Rory was gone, passing effortlessly through the far wall of the torture chamber.

Wynter kept her eyes on the diminishing phosphorescence that marked the place of Rory's passage. She watched it until it disappeared completely, then reluctantly turned her eyes to the whispering man

He was nothing but a cloudy shape at first. A starry manshape, clutched, spread-eagle, in the black arms of the chair. But as Wynter focused her attention on him, he grew in definition and detail so that she had to look away for fear of being sick

"Mary . . .?" he whispered. "Mary . . .?" Wynter thought he was still praying. Then she realised that he was turning his head from side to side, seeking her out. "Mary?" he whispered again and Wynter saw the black holes in his gums where the inquisitors had removed his teeth. He must have heard her unwilling footsteps on the gritty floor because he turned his eyeless sockets to her and followed her movement across the room as she approached him. "Mary . . . they have hurt me . . ."

Wynter's hand was shaking so badly that she was in danger of extinguishing the flame, so she set the candle on the corner of a table. It illuminated all the terrible array of instruments that had been used against this poor man and Wynter averted her eyes and clutched her hands together in horror and despair. *Razi was here,* she thought, *Razi allowed this to happen. God help us.*

"MARY!" the spirit screamed suddenly, and Wynter leapt in shock. "*MARY! Oh please . . . darling, don't go . . .*"

Wynter couldn't stand the awful despair in his voice and she stepped closer, her hand up as though she could somehow touch him and give him comfort. "I am here," she lied. "It . . . it is all over now . . . you are . . . you . . ." she searched his tormented face and knew it was not over. Not for him. She dropped any pretence at being his Mary. "What is your name?" she asked softly.

He turned his head to her, straining his neck against the leather straps that no longer held him in place. His words should have been blurred and distorted by his cruelly punished mouth, but they were not. His voice was cultured and warm and thoroughly bereft of hope. "Mary . . .? Darling . . .? Am I so awful? Do you not know me?" His head lolled back, his mouth gaping in despair. "Oh release me," he begged. "Oh, Mother of Jesus, hear me. Release me. Release me . . ." He began to pray again. Rolling his had from side to side in desperation, his empty eye sockets wells of glistening darkness. He arched suddenly against his invisible bonds and shrieked. The smell of fire and burning flesh flared to life in the close room and Wynter pressed her hands to her mouth and nose, and sobbed.

Outside the walls a low wail began to sound and a barely perceptible vibration began to build in the soles of her boots. Wynter looked around in fear, but there was nothing to see. She was overcome with the understanding that she must be quick.

"What is your name?" she asked again, but the spirit rolled its head and bucked, bloody tracks streaming down its tormented face, like tears. "What is your name?" insisted Wynter, unsure of why she needed to know. "Tell me and I will take a message to Mary!"

"Mary!"

"Yes! Tell me how. Tell me how to get a message to Mary. Where is she? Is she at the camp? Is she with his Royal Highness? At the camp?"

"At the camp . . . aye . . . she is at the camp. She is with the others . . . Mary . . ."

The vibration was all around them now, raising the hair on Wynter's arms and on the back of her neck, buzzing against her eardrums and itching at the roots of her teeth. The wail outside the walls had begun to invade the room. Little runnels and sparks of phosphorescence outlined the stones of the walls.

The spirit gasped and began to shake, its heels and the backs of its broken hands drumming the wood of the awful chair.

Wynter forced her voice to stay soft. She did not want to sound like an inquisitor, though the urge to shout and grab and shake was almost uncontrollable.

"Tell me where she is and I will ensure she gets your . . ."

"She is in the camp . . ."

"Which camp? There are so many . . . *which* camp is Mary in?"

He tried to turn his face to her but he was jerking and shaking so violently now that the back of his head battered rhythmically against the chair. "Indirie Valley . . . in . . . Indirie Valley . . . with Oliver . . . with the Combermen . . . she . . . guhhhh." his words were lost in a bubbling gurgle and his mouth overflowed with black and glistening blood. Wynter scurried backwards.

The entire room was alive with phosphorescence now. It washed the walls in shimmering ghostly light. It spread greedy tendrils across the ceiling. The wail had become battle noise. Shouting, horses, there was the unmistakable sound of matchlocks firing, but so fast, unbelievably fast, that it resembled fireworks going off over the horizon.

The ghost arched up against his non-existent bonds, curving like a longbow, his head and heels the only contact between himself and the black chair. "MARY! he shrieked. Tell . . . MARY!" Blood sprayed up from his lips with each word. The smell of blood and gunpowder, smoke and burning flesh was unbearable

Wynter snatched her candle from the table and staggered backwards, her hand clamped over her mouth. *Indirie Valley*, she repeated, *Indirie Valley. Don't forget . . .*

Rory Shearing ran through the wall at the back of the room He stumbled towards her, clutching his belly, his face the picture of agony. His mouth was open in a silent yell and he flung his hand out to her. *Go! GO!*

The glowing mist surged from the wall behind him, filling the chamber from floor to ceiling in an immutable swirling mass. It advanced across the room in a slow wave, bringing with it the stinging reek of gunpowder and the heavy, continuous firing of matchlocks. Rory stumbled ahead of it, but he was weak and uncoordinated and it caught him in its advancing tide and lifted him from the ground. His head fell back in a howl of agony, and his arms and legs flung helplessly out. Rory was spread-eagled against the shimmering surface, like a man floating on a river of pain. It drew him across itself, suffusing him with dancing green light. Then, as Wynter watched, it slowly tore Rory Shearing apart.

"NO!" she screamed, "Rory!" But Rory was gone, destroyed by the glowing mass of advancing light, his despairing scream rapidly diminishing as the noise of battle grew louder.

The light continued to creep forward. It moved sparking fingers across the black chair, finding the edges of the tortured man. He cried out in fear as green witch-light ran into his eye sockets and sparked across his lips. It lifted him from his prison and raised him into the air, and he turned his head to Wynter, as she continued to back away.

"Tell her . . ." he wailed. "Tell Mary . . . tell her that Isaac stayed true. Tell her . . ." Then he, too, was drawn across the surface of the advancing tide and, screaming, torn slowly limb from limb.

Wynter choked and stumbled, the backs of her legs hitting the steps as she fell over. The tide continued to advance upon her, and she turned and sped up the stairs on her hands and knees.

Her candle guttered out, and Wynter scaled the rest of the steps in pitch darkness. She cleared the top like a salmon breasting a weir, missed her footing and crashed, sprawling, to the ground with a desperate yell. The breath was slammed from her and she grazed her chin and skinned her hands as she slid across the floor on her belly. Her feet were already scrabbling for purchase, her hands thrust out to feel her way in the dark. She got her legs under her, ran in a half-crouch for a yard or so and slammed face first into a wall. Bouncing back, stars and sparks filling her vision, Wynter staggered a few steps, then ran into the dark again.

Green ghost-fire blossomed behind her, and her path sprang into view as the mass of phosphorescence rolled up the steps and advanced down the corridor. The battle noise swelled, the continuous fizzing pop of the matchlocks agitating the air.

Wynter slipped and sprawled again, scampering on hands and knees for a few paces before getting her feet back under her. The corridor turned and she was in a narrow spiral stairwell in the pitch black, scrambling on all fours, climbing, climbing.

Green light illuminated the staircase and Wynter's way was clear. The steps were very steep. She clambered onwards, all the time on her hands and knees. Then the green light swelled, and Wynter cried out in breathless panic as she realised she wasn't going to outrun it. It was coming around the corner! It was on her!

A phosphorescent tendril wrapped around her ankle and Wynter's leg went dead.

She screamed and sprawled flat as her feet were pulled from under her. Her belly and chest slammed hard and painful into the sharp edge of the steps. The ghost-fire closed around her other leg and numbness shot up past her knees. Eyes bulging, mouth wide with terror, Wynter continued to haul herself desperately upwards, hand over hand. Her legs were dead and useless. She heard the toes of her boots bumping against the steps as she frantically pulled herself up the stairs.

She was too terrified to look down, but she felt her waist go cold and numb. Her spine cramped suddenly and a jolt went through her belly as though someone had driven an icicle into the small of her back. She scrabbled fruitlessly against the stone steps but couldn't pull herself any higher.

No! No!, she thought desperately, *I don't want to die! Dad! Dad! Help me!*

Green sparks traced the contours of her outstretched hands and danced at her fingertips. Wynter felt her breasts scrape and catch painfully against the steps as she slid backwards into the humming, nettle-sting embrace of the phosphorus light.

"*DAAAAAAD!*" she screamed.

Then the light blinked off, the battle noise ceased, and Wynter was dumped, face down and panting, on the gritty steps. She cringed, waiting for the assault to continue, her breath a ragged whimper in her throat. But the world stayed silent, black and cold.

Slowly, she turned her cheek against the stone, then lay perfectly still, her eyes open in the pitch black, listening. There was nothing. No ghost-light, no sound. The surge had run out of energy. Wynter had survived it after all.

For a while she just lay there, staring into the dark, and waiting for her legs to come back to life. Then she moved her fingers against the rough surface of the stone and was amazed to find the candle lying beside her. She closed her hand on it, taking reassurance in its warm solidity, and slowly she drew it to her, curling her arm inwards until she cradled it against her cheek. Her heartbeat gradually slowed. She tried to summon the energy to roll onto her side.

Something moved on the steps above her and Wynter was too drained even to be frightened. She felt, rather than heard, a soft movement on the step by her face and she opened her eyes to stare, once more, into the darkness.

"Cat?" she whispered.

"Aye." Its voice was more thready and shocked than any cat-voice Wynter had ever heard.

"Are you . . . harmed?" she asked.

The cat did not answer. Instead Wynter felt a warm rasping sensation on her face, not altogether pleasant, and she realised that the cat had licked her cheek. Then it butted its head in under her arm and squeezed itself into a tight, warm ball against her neck. Wynter curled her arm around it, and it fit its head up under her chin. It whimpered. They stayed like that for a while, pressed to each other, wordless and shaky, blinking sightlessly into the dark.

Eventually, the life returned to Wynter's legs, and she rose stiffly to her feet and began slowly to climb the stairs.

The cat stuck close to her for the long winding journey out of the pit, and then it abandoned her in the hallway of the middle gallery. It just slid into the night without a word of goodbye, there one minute, gone the next, and Wynter was left to stagger the rest of the way home alone.

Pretend

$\mathscr{W}$ynter woke to the clock tower bell sounding the hour.

"RORY!" she thought, opening her eyes, and jerking from sleep with a start. She was sprawled face down on her bed, arms and legs akimbo, fully dressed and filthy.

The bell sounded again. Three tolls in the darkness. The third quarter! Already? Razi was leaving at midday. *She* was leaving at midday. Wynter had less than six hours left with her father.

She scrabbled at the quilt in panic and tried to get her thoughts together. Six hours! Less than six hours, and then she would abandon him. Lorcan would be all alone without her, and she would be out in the world. Oh, Christ in heaven, she did not think she could do this.

Dazed and staring, every inch of her aching, Wynter pushed herself onto her hands and knees and slid from the bed. She stood for a moment, swaying and trying to get her balance, her vision distorting as the blood rushed from her head. She leant against the footboard and tried to get some coherent train of thought going. She would go in now and wake her dad, and the two of them would—

A sound from the retiring room stilled her and she paused and listened. Marcello Tutti was murmuring outside her closed door and Wynter's heart twisted as she heard Lorcan groan and then chuckle in reply. The two men were making their slow way past her door and into the receiving room. Wynter could hear her father's halting, deliberate footsteps as Marcello helped him across the room. What an effort it was for him, this simple journey from one room to another. Wynter knew at once that he was doing this for her, so that they could have a proper breakfast, without Lorcan seeming like an invalid, propped up in his bed.

If she had paused and thought for one brief minute, she would never have gone to the door without cleaning up. But she was completely exhausted, her mind buzzing like a jar of flies, and she threw the bolt and stumbled into the receiving room before she'd formed a thought any more coherent than just getting to see her father.

Marcello was helping Lorcan take his seat at the breakfast table when she came to the receiving room door. Lorcan was supporting himself against the edge of the table, while Marcello, one hand on Lorcan's back, was pulling out a chair for him. They paused when they noticed Wynter, and the two of them gasped, their faces falling as they took in her appearance.

Marcello exclaimed, "Oh! Signora!"

Lorcan's face drew down, black and dangerous as he looked at her filthy clothes, her scraped chin and bruised face. "Who the *hell* did that to you?" he snarled.

Their outrage was lost on Wynter for a second as she looked at the multitude of candles, the vase of yellow roses, the beautifully laid out breakfast things. Her dazed eyes turned to her father and she took in his crisp white shirt, his formal long-coat and britches, his highly polished boots. Lorcan's hair was brushed out loose and glossy, falling freely over his shoulders, as if dining at court. He was still corpse-pale, his eyes and cheeks hollow, and was leaning heavily against the table, his powerful arms shaking with the strain. But he was magnificent despite it. Wynter looked at the rage in her father's face and knew she was going to ruin this, this carefully planned farewell, if she did not snap to it. Now.

She took a shaking breath and straightened her spine. She blinked fiercely, forcing the hazy fog of exhaustion to loosen its grip on her mind. She cleared her throat and then forced herself to chuckle. She was very pleased at how convincing it sounded.

"You can hold off the white chargers for a little while yet, gentlemen," she said wryly. "I did this to myself." The two men regarded her uncertainly and she gave them a mock bow, gesturing to the torn knees of her britches, the sooty marks on her tunic. "My candle snuffed itself on the back-stairs and I came over all girlish in the dark." She sparkled a grin at them from under her dishevelled fringe of hair, "I'm afraid I fell down quite a few steps before I got a grip on myself. I'm lucky I didn't break my damned neck!"

Lorcan searched her face, his teeth bared, his breathing shallow. Marcello looked at him. He laid his hand on the big man's arm, and murmured softly in Italian that Lorcan's chair was ready.

Wynter licked her lips and met her father's eye. *Come on, Dad. We're pretending, remember? Let's pretend!*

"Why don't you take your seat, Dad?" she said lightly,

"And I'll go make myself presentable. I promise I won't be long."

Lorcan looked her up and down again. Wynter gazed at him pleadingly. He made a visible effort to control his anger. He released a long breath and forcibly relaxed his hands from their clenched fists. He nodded to himself. He straightened his spine he tilted his head in acquiescence. Then, turning purposely from her, he let Marcello help him into his chair.

By the time he had settled himself at the table, Lorcan was completely given over to the game. Pulling his napkin towards him, he grinned up at her. "You'd better hurry, girl," he said, "or you'll have naught but eggshells and butter-smears for breakfast."

Wynter gave him a narrow look and held a finger up to him, holding his eyes sternly as she left the room. "I will be but a moment! Touch nothing!"

As Wynter was passing through the retiring room, she heard Marcello excuse himself to Lorcan. She paused at her bedroom door, turning to look as the little man let himself out into the hall. Wynter suspected that Marcello was no fool, but nonetheless he was choosing to go along with whatever tale Lorcan had spun him about this highly unusual breakfast. Perhaps Lorcan had told him that it was her birthday, or some special anniversary. Whatever the truth, Wynter was immensely grateful for this discreet little Italian. He was a balm to her heart.

She leant against her doorframe, gazing at him and, just as he was shutting the door, Marcello raised his eyes and saw her. He paused. His face softened, his eyes shining in the blaze of candlelight. His mouth twisted, his brows drew together in gentle sympathy and he nodded. Wynter lifted her chin, tremendously moved, for some reason, at this shared look. Then Marcello gently shut the door and she passed into her room.

She shut the door behind her and gathered her resolve.

Coiling her hair on top of her head, Wynter stripped naked and groped her way forward in the gloom to fill her wash basin with tepid water. Lips compressed into a fierce little line, she lathered her sea-sponge and commenced to scrub herself from head to toe. Everything she did was precise and contained. Her mind, her face, her heart, empty of everything but determination.

She rinsed her body. She dried herself, rubbing hard all over, so that her skin tingled and glowed. She cleaned her nails. She scrubbed her teeth with tooth powder. She went to her mother's dressing trunk and selected the pale rose gown with the dark rose trim and shift. At the mirror she brushed out her hair, leaving it loose and free, a dark red curtain hanging beyond her shoulders, as though she, too, were about to dine with a king. *I will wash it later*, she thought, *before I leave*. God knows when she would get the chance to wash it again.

She regretted the raw patch on her chin, the vivid scratches on her hands. She regretted the dark bruise on her forehead where she had run into the wall. She did not like that her father would look at her across that beautifully laid table and see these stark reminders of the truth.

She closed her eyes, her lips trembling, her hands clenched. Then she turned abruptly, and made her way into the receiving room.

Lorcan smiled and made a gallant move to rise as she

entered the room. Wynter lifted her hand and graciously indicated that he might remain seated. Lorcan dipped his head in polite assent and sat back down, as if her raised hand was the only thing preventing him leaping to his feet and rushing to pull out her chair.

My God, we are good at this, Wynter thought. She surveyed the table as she settled into her place. She drew her napkin towards her and inhaled as appreciatively as she could. *Will I be able to eat? Please God let me be able to eat!* "How lovely this is, Dad!" She smiled, raising her eyes to her father, meaning every word. "Thank you so much." Lorcan smiled back at her and some small knot of tension released itself from the air.

They worked their way through the food, eating every bite. They spoke easily of music and of books. Lorcan retold amusing stories of his youth. It was gentle, it was pleasant, and the time ran through their fingers with imperceptible speed.

Eventually they were done and they dawdled, smiling, over the debris, until Wynter rose and cleared the table of everything but the coffee things. She left it all on a tray outside the hall door, and when she turned back to the room, Lorcan had pushed back from the table, shifting his chair sideways to stretch his long legs. He was carefully adding cream and sugar to their coffee bowls and Wynter realised that his hair was burnished with bright sunshine.

She pressed her back to the door, and turned to the look out the windows. Pretty little clouds were moving slowly across the pale blue sky, glowing in the full light of day. Her chin began to tremble, and she gritted her teeth and dug her nails into the palms of her hands. *Come on!* she scolded herself, *come on!* Her body obediently relaxed, the coil of knots in her stomach released themselves. *Good.*

Wynter unclenched her hands and began to move calmly about the room, quenching the candles. The air filled with the warm scent of snuffed wick and Lorcan looked up, suddenly aware of what she was doing. He glanced at the windows, and his eyes widened in disbelief.

Approaching the breakfast table, Wynter laid her hand on his big shoulder and leant to snuff the final flame. Lorcan put a hand on her arm. "Not that one, darling." Wynter paused. "Leave that one." His voice was unsteady and he did not let go of her arm.

Wynter leant her weight on the table then, her head down, suddenly unable to go on. Neither of them looked at each other. Lorcan squeezed her arm, his eyes on the candle flame. He shook his head. He looked away.

"I had thought . . ." he whispered. "I had thought that . . . I would be up to a walk . . . in . . ." his grip on her arm tightened.

In the grounds the clock-tower bell struck the fourth quarter. Four more hours. Lorcan looked around the room in despair. What could they say to each other? What could they do?

Wynter sank to the floor at his feet and laid her head on her father's knee. She snaked her arms around his waist, slipping them under his opened coat and knotted her fists into the fabric of his shirt. Lorcan rested his big hand on her hair and sat back, turning his head to look out the window. Wynter did the same, resting her cheek against his knee. He stroked her hair. Together, they watched the little clouds move across the morning sky and they simply did not feel the time passing. It went in silence, too quickly, and when the fifth quarter sounded, they still had not moved or spoken a word.

Lorcan leaned forwards and kissed her cheek. "Time for you to get ready, baby-girl." She twisted her grip on his shirt, tightening her arms around his waist. He rubbed her back. "Come on, darling. It's time. You have things to do." She did not move, so he gently pushed until she was compelled to sit up and release her grip on his shirt. He brushed the hair from her face. He winked, "Go on."

Wynter rose numbly to her feet and went into her room

Most of her provisions were waiting for her outside the palace wall. They had been slowly assembled and packed by Marni over the last few days. Her horse too awaited her, having come down with a mystery ailment that required quarantining from Razi's precious Arabians. He would be tacked up, and waiting, fully packed in the stables of a little inn half an hour's walk from the palace.

All Wynter needed to do now was pack her grooming kit, her travel belt, a change of clothes, supplies should her menses come upon her, and her maps. The maps most importantly of all. Up until last night, she had had no idea where she would be heading. She had a lot of work to do with those maps.

She stood heavily in the centre of her room, doing nothing. *The longer you stand here*, she told herself, *the longer you leave Dad sitting in there, alone.* That spurred her on.

By the time she stepped back into the receiving room, she was transformed. She had washed her hair and bound it tightly to her skull, containing it in a tight-fitting light-knit hood. She had her riding britches on, her riding boots and a long sleeved tunic over her undershirt. She wore Christopher's dark jacket, and a wide brimmed straw hat hung down her back. Razi's note crackled with each breath, snug against her heart, her guild pendant nestling beside it, its chain tucked under her shirt. All her belongings including her guild badges, were neatly stowed in the little knapsack on her back or distributed amongst the pouches and bags that adorned her travel belt. She was well coined, well armed and not at all ready to go.

Lorcan looked up from his chair and met her eyes. He did not indulge in his usual litany of exhortations. *Mind your purse in the crowd, girl. Are you well moneyed? Are you provisioned for the gripes? Make sure your dagger is easy to hand.* Instead he just gazed at her, his eyes stricken and huge, his hands white-knuckled on the arms of his chair. The two of them gazed at each other across the sunlit room.

The clock-tower bell struck the half quarter, and they were out of time.

Wynter's vision blurred, her eyes overflowed and tears ran down her face.

"You must go now, baby-girl."

She shook her head at his half-hearted whisper.

No. She shut her eyes. *No.*

No! She made up her mind. *No.* She could not do this. She began to fumble with the ties of her knapsack. She *wouldn't* do it! She wouldn't sacrifice this lovely man, and everything they meant to each other, all that he had given for her. She wouldn't sacrifice it all for the sake of politics. She would stay. She would damned well *stay*. What had she been thinking? She would be his comfort and his harbour as he had been for her. She would be with him, right to the very end.

She couldn't manage the God-cursed knots! She grunted in frustration and began scrabbling at the buckle of her travel belt.

Lorcan was rising slowly to his feet. She sensed him making his unsteady way around the table towards her.

"No, Dad!" she growled without looking at him. "No!" and she tugged clumsily at the buckle of her belt.

He was beside her then. He wrapped his arm around her shoulders, and, still leaning heavily on the table, he pulled her into him, squeezing her tightly against his chest. Wynter buried her face in his shirt. She could feel him trembling. He rested his cheek against the top of her head, and she knew he would let her stay.

"Oh Dad . . ." she began gratefully, snaking her hands up to wrap them around his neck. But his grip tightened even more and trapped her hands between them. With a groan, Lorcan pushed himself suddenly from the table, sending the two of them staggering sideways, toppling towards the door.

Wynter though they would fall, and cried out in panic. But Lorcan flung out his free hand and caught them both with one powerful arm against the hall door. He leant there for a moment, panting. Wynter, still clutched against his chest, as helpless as a doll, felt him shaking, his heart beating fast and unsteady.

"Dad!" she pleaded, "No!" She turned her face up against his shirt, trying to push out of his determined grip. "Dad! Please!" He was holding her too close to let her see his face. All that was visible when she finally managed to tilt her head, was his blood-red hair, falling into her face, and the clean-shaven set of his jaw.

"Dad! Dad! Please!"

She felt his breath hitch as he shifted to support himself with one shoulder against the wood, and Wynter heard the awful sound of metal against metal as, one-handed, Lorcan slid the bolt open.

"DAD!" she wailed. "*DAD!* Please!" A tear fell onto her upturned face, and then another one. They were sliding over the clean line of her father's jaw and they dropped into her eyes, onto her cheeks. She sobbed and Lorcan pushed the two of them away from the wood, almost losing his balance as he drew on the last reserve of his incredible strength to stand back and open the door.

He pulled it open a crack and shifted abruptly to hook his free hand over the top of it. Supporting himself on the door, Lorcan abruptly released Wynter from his powerful grip and pushed her through the narrow gap into the hall.

"No! No!" She clung desperately to him. But he was determined and had already started to close the door and withdraw his arm. Wynter's hands slipped from his shoulder to his elbow. He continued to pull his arm back, she clung to his powerful forearm, he pulled back. Their fingers squeezed for a moment. And then Lorcan pulled his hand free, and shut the door in her face.

He drew the bolt. He turned the key in the lock.

Wynter clung to the wood, tears streaming down her face. She listened. There was no sound from within.

"Dad," she whispered. "Dad."

"Please . . ." he said softly, his voice muffled as if his face was pressed to the other side of the door.

Wynter shut her eyes and sobbed.

"Please . . ." he said again. "Go . . ."

Wynter spread her hands against the wood and pressed her forehead to the door. Tears dripped from her face, dropping to the stones at her feet. She nodded.

"Goodbye, Dad," she whispered. "I love you."

There was no more sound from inside the room. She pressed her ear to the door and faintly, very faintly, she heard a long slow slide against the wood, as if her father had run his hand down the panel on the other side.

Slowly, every movement a supreme act of will, Wynter pushed herself back. She stood for one last moment, one hand still on the door. Then she dropped her head, let her hand fall to her side, and walked stiffly away.

The Uncharted Path

Wynter stood, staring at the jostling line of people as the gate guards meticulously checked each egress paper. The midday sun blasted down on her straw hat, throwing a stark shadow across her blank face. Her tell-tale hair was hidden beneath her dark hood; she had pulled the legs of her britches out to hid her expensive riding boots. She was just another whey-faced servant girl in travel clothes, patiently waiting in line. She was Madge Butterfield, to be precise, Under Pot-girl and Scour, fully papered, courtesy of Marni, and legitimately released from work to head home and tend her sickly mother.

The gates were unusually busy for midday in the summer. Dust rose in choking clouds from the shuffling feet and the restless horses and the wagons, and most people had their faces covered. It was Progress Day and people had been trickling from the complex all morning, heading into the town for the two day fair. Wynter suspected that Razi had specifically chosen this uncomfortable time to depart, so that he could do so in the relative safety of a big crowd. She knew he would travel with only a small band of men, probably in disguise, and once outside the complex they would simply melt into the eternal chaos of the Port Road.

A small band of Musulman boys and women strolled up the gravel path, chatting amiably amongst themselves. At first Wynter had thought that they had come to see Razi off, and it had puzzled her. Much like everyone else in Jonathon's kingdom, the Musulmen had no idea what to do with Razi. Like everyone else, they paid court to him for his position and power, but many of them thoroughly disapproved of the man they called The Prince Who Would Not Pray.

Wynter watched them as they took their places at the end of the queue, and realised that they were waiting their turn to leave. A pilgrimage then, or an extended family heading to some wedding or another. The women chattered happily, the men laughed and jostled, their faces covered against the appalling dust. One of their number hurried up the gravel path to join them, pulling his keffiyeh tight across his face. He got a gentle ribbing in Arabic for being late, and quietly joined the other men, his head ducking under the heavy tide of good-natured insults. Their happy, familial camaraderie filled Wynter's chest with black despair and she turned bleakly away as the line moved forward.

Everyone fell quiet at the sound of horses cantering up the drive, and the whole queue stepped back and turned as one. They watched silently as the royal travel party trotted up and stayed their horses under the gate-arch. Wynter shrank back into the crowd and peered up from under the brim of her hat.

Razi sat, remote and imperious at the heart of a small group of well armed men. He was dressed in the Bedouin robes that he had always preferred, and his head and face were protected from the sun and dust by a pale blue keffiyeh. Only his beautiful eyes were visible, hooded and reserved. His horse stamped and snorted and shook its magnificent head, and Razi gazed out into the middle distance as though none of this concerned him. One of his men leapt from his own mount and handed papers into the gatehouse. He pulled his keffiyeh from his face as the guard checked the papers and Wynter recognised Simon De Rochelle. She was filled with a mixture of nervousness and relief for her friend. Thank God he didn't have to travel under the dubious protection of Jonathon's hate-filled men, but at the same time, De Rochelle? He was as oily and as self-serving as a cat. She glanced at Razi, and her heart filled with fear for him.

De Rochelle accepted the papers from the satisfied guard and remounted. All the gate guards snapped a neat salute, and Razi paid them no more heed than he would a dog as he urged his horse forward through the open horse-gate and into the blistering sun. The party clattered unhurriedly over the drawbridge and set off uphill, allowing the thin stream of travellers to set the pace for their horses.

Wynter handed her papers to the guard, her eyes glued to the small knot of riders as they climbed the hill. The guard tossed the papers back at her and turned to the next in line. Wynter passed under the horse-gate and set off at a quick walk. She did not falter as she left the protective shadow of the gate-arch. She did not look back. But a small piece of her tore away as her feet left the bouncing timbers of the drawbridge, and she felt her heart begin to bleed as she took to the dust-laden road to town.

Razi was still in sight when she got to the inn, his party a good distance away, but easily discernible as the only group of men on horseback in the predominantly pedestrian and cart-filled road. She glanced at them as she entered the stable-yard, and then looked around for Marni's nephew. There was no mistaking him. He was Marni with a beard. She caught his eye as he wrestled a recalcitrant hog into a sty, and she made Marni's special hand signal to let him know who she was. He nodded almost imperceptibly and disappeared into the stable, returning moments later with Ozkar, who snorted and blew lippy kisses at the sight and smell of his mistress.

"Good lad," she murmured to the horse and thumped him on the neck and rubbed his whiskered nose. "Good boy." She checked him quickly, but he was in good condition and fresh, and he had obviously not been standing around full-saddled for more than ten minutes or so. She nodded gratefully at the big red-headed man and he gravely cupped his hands to give her a leg up into the saddle.

When she was seated and just clucking the horse forward, the man placed his hand on the horse's neck and murmured softly. "Tanty sayed to tell you, take care, Lady. She sayed to tell you, nort to be a bleddy fool." He blushed at the message, but Wynter smiled at him.

"Tell your aunt that I love her, Goodman, tell her that I am for ever in her debt . . ." she hesitated, "ask her please . . . ask her please, to take care of my father."

He nodded gravely again and stood back as Wynter urged Ozkar out onto the road.

She hesitated momentarily as the thin crowd flowed past her, and she watched Razi's distant figure as the gap between them grew. If she were to follow her father's carefully thought-out plan, she would fall in behind the slow-moving travel party, and trail them all the way to down the Port Road and then a good deal of the way to Padua. Three weeks into their journey, when they were halfway across the mountains, and there was no fear of Razi sending her back, Wynter would have thrown herself on his mercy and put herself under his wing, travelling the rest of the way with him to Padua and starting a new life there within his protection.

Wynter watched as Razi nudged his horse through the crowds, his pale blue keffiyeh a bright spot of colour above the hanging drifts of yellow dust. She was choked with fear for him, travelling, as he was, surrounded by men he did not trust, into a life so utterly beyond his control. She shut her eyes against the desire to go to him and turned her horse into the crowd, nudging against the main flow of the traffic and heading back in the direction of the palace.

Ten minutes later, Wynter paused at a small crossroads and looked at the thin ribbon of road that led away to her left. Barely populated with traffic, it wound off across a narrow belt of pasture before quickly rising up, climbing the hilly slope and disappearing into heavy forest. She could almost hear the bandits and purse-lifts coming to attention at the smell of a woman taking this path alone. She took a deep and terrified breath, and glanced back up the road to town. Razi was well out of sight, gone from her, perhaps for ever. Behind her the palace crouched over the horizon. Her father lay clutched in its poisonous heart, abandoned and deceived and ailing, completely at the mercy of his wilful and unpredictable royal friend. She turned her head in his direction, trying to imagine him, praying he was well.

It is not too late, her mind whispered temptingly. *You can turn back. Just urge the horse in either direction and you will be safe and protected and not alone.*

Wynter looked longingly towards the palace. The crowds were thinning now, as most of the travellers were well on their way to the fair. Soon she would be alone on this road, for the first time in her life, conspicuous and vulnerable, with no one but herself to rely on. She was the wrong sex for this task, she was the wrong age, she could not do this. She couldn't.

Blinking, Wynter dropped her head and looked at her trembling hands. *I cannot do this*, she repeated, *I want to go home*. Even as she was thinking it, she urged her horse forward and he obligingly nudged through the last of the stragglers and stepped from the main road and onto the rutted little tributary that led to the mountains.

A few people turned to glance at the dark-clad woman as she wound her solitary way down the track. Most that looked her way just turned back without even registering her. But some few, particularly the women, likely felt a twinge of sympathetic alarm. *What can that girl be thinking!* they might have gasped, *is she mad? And they would have crossed themselves or knocked their foreheads or made some other warding sign, that they might never find themselves in such a situation.*

For who would choose to be alone and without their men like that, heading away from the comfort of civil-folk and out into the cut-throat wilds? Some of them could not stop watching as the young woman trotted away from them. It was a morbid fascination that kept drawing their attention, so that they craned their necks back to keep track of her. She was travelling at a good pace, though, and it was not long before she disappeared up the winding path, to be swallowed into the treacherous depths of the bandit-laden forest and the company of wolves.

extras

www.orbitbooks.net

about the author

Born and raised in Dublin, Ireland, **Celine Kiernan** has spent the majority of her working life in the film business, and her career as a classical feature animator spanned over seventeen years. Celine wrote her first novel at the age of eleven, and hasn't stopped writing or drawing since. She also has a peculiar weakness for graphic novels as, like animation, they combine the two things she loves to do the most: drawing and storytelling. Now, having spent most of her time working between Germany, Ireland and the USA, Celine is married and the bemused mother of two entertaining teens. She lives a peaceful life in the blissful countryside of Cavan, Ireland.

Find out more about Celine Kiernan and other Orbit authors by registering for the free monthly newsletter at www.orbitbooks.net

interview

What was the inspiration to write?

I can't seem to come up with a satisfactory answer to that. It's the same as when people ask me "how did you come up with the idea for that drawing?" The idea is just there. It's as if the characters and situations are there already, as if they've actually happened, and I'm just reporting them. Sometimes a story is so "big" inside my head that if I don't write it down it feels like I will explode.

Where did the idea come from for the Moorehawke Trilogy?

Hee. I have this thing, this kind of visual in my head of a dark room with lots of boxes in it. Each box has a story in it, and they sit there till I'm ready to work on them. Inside the box, while they're waiting for my attention, they percolate, or they grow. Like coffee, or fungus.

Anyway, the Moorehawke Trilogy began while on holiday to the south of France. It was a little story about a carpenter's daughter, a missing prince, a ghost in an avenue and, perhaps, the mention of a talking cat. It was intended as a sun-soaked, bright, action adventure type thing. My kids like to tell me that it went into the box a happy, skipping child and shambled out the other end a drooling blood-soaked monster. I suppose they're not far wrong.

Do you have a favourite character in *The Poison Throne*?

No, I don't think so. They're all so different, and they all have their own motivations and their own ideas on how to deal with this very trying and extreme situation they find themselves in. I may not agree with how some of them handle themselves, but I feel for and sympathise with them all.

Is there a character that you really hated creating?

Gosh no! Even my bad guys are fascinating to me. I think it would be impossible to create a character towards whom I had no sympathy at all. There are some characters that I hate to let go – Rory, for example; I really wanted to put more of him into the story. But there was no place for him. Thankfully he plays a huge role in the prequel, so I get to hang out more with him then.

Are some of the characters based on historical people?

Badi' al-Zaman al-Jazari was a real person, as was his work *The Book of Ingenious Mechanical Devices*. I believe it was on tour in the Chester Beattie recently; I deeply regret not having seen it. But, of course, he's not a character in the book. So the answer is no, the main characters are not based on real people.

I've kept everything grounded in the realities of everyday life at the turn of the 1400s, though. Even the fact that Wynter is a guild-approved carpenter isn't too far off the wall, as records show that there were two female blacksmiths practising in London only a few decades later. Though there is an element of fantasy to the books (ghosts and talking cats and the like) I've kept the technology as accurate as possible. In regards to some things that come later in the series, I'm trying as much as possible to make sure that Lorcan would actually have been able to succeed in building The Bloody Machine.

I have greatly re-imagined Europe and Africa's political geography, not to mention its history. There never having been a Moorish invasion or any Crusades, political relationships are vastly different then in real life. It is also a fragmented, quarrelsome Europe, with many small powers rather than three or four big ones, and religious persecution and racial intolerance loom in the form of various "inquisitions". For a kingdom as economically fragile and militarily vulnerable as the Southlands, there are dark times ahead if things aren't handled properly. Though Jonathon has powerful allies in the Moroccos, and though he has control of the valued Port Road, he knows his kingdom is more and more vulnerable to the instability that surrounds him. As a man of conscience, Jonathon would not like some of the things he will be forced to do as king; they would eat at him as a man.

In your imagination, where precisely in Europe is *The Poison Throne* set?

In a small kingdom that takes up most of the south of France, stretching approximately from north of Lyon to

Marseilles, including the mountain ranges that flank that area of land and all of the coast.

Given that you were working full-time when you began the Moorehawke Trilogy how did you make time to write it?
It's not easy sometimes. The last few years, I found myself staying up till three and four in the morning most nights, and then getting up for work the next day. It nearly killed me. For the next year at least I can write during the day. That will be bliss.

Describe your writing routine, if you have one.
I have a very strong work ethic. I write four pages a day, regardless of the quality, and if I don't stick to that I get very anxious. Perhaps if I start biting my nails it will relieve the pressure.

Who inspires you?
In terms of what writers inspire me? I have an abiding love of John Steinbeck. I love Neil Gaiman, Patrick O'Brien and the great Shirley Jackson. I also adored Stephen King's early work; his early stuff is absolute genius.

I suppose, anyone who's work moves or intrigues me is an inspiration!

if you enjoyed
THE POISON THRONE

look out for

THE PRODIGAL MAGE

by

Karen Miller

CHAPTER ONE

It was a trivial dispute ... but that wasn't the point. The *point*, as he grew tired of saying, was that dragging a Doranen into Justice Hall, forcing him to defend his use of magic, was demeaning. It was an *insult*. Placing any Olken hedge-meddler on level footing with a Doranen mage was an insult. And that included the vaunted Asher of Restharven. His mongrel abilities were the greatest insult of all.

"Father . . ."

Rodyn Garrick looked down at his son. "What?"

Kept out of the schoolroom for this, the most important education a young Doranen could receive, Arlin wriggled on the bench beside him. And that was *another* insult. In Borne's day a Doranen councilor was afforded a place of respect in one of Justice Hall's gallery seats—but not any more. These days the gallery seats remained empty and even the most important Doranen of Lur were torced to bruise their bones on hard wooden pews, thrown amongst the general population.

"Arlin, *what?*" he said. "The hearing's about to begin. And I've told you I'll not tolerate disruption."

"It doesn't matter," Arlin whispered. "I'll ask later."

Rodyn stitled his temper. The boy was impossible. His mother's fault, that. One son and she'd coddled him beyond all bearing. A good thing she'd died, really. Undoing ten years of her damage was battle enough.

Justice Hall buzzed with the sound of muted conversations, its cool air heavy with a not-so-muted sense of anticipation. Not on his part, though. He felt only fury and dread. He'd chosen to sit himself and his son at the rear of the Hall, where they'd be least likely noticed. Aside from Ain Freidin, against whom these insulting and spurious charges were laid, and her family, he and Arlin were the only Doranen present. Well, aside from his fellow councilor Sarnia Marnagh, of course. Justice Hall's chief administrator and her Olken assistant conferred quietly over their parchments and papers, not once looking up.

Everyone was waiting for Asher.

When at last Lur's so-called saviour deigned to put in

an appearance, he entered through one of the doors in the Hall's rear wall instead of the way entrances had been made in Borne's day: slowly and with grave splendour descending from on high. So much for the majesty of law. Even Asher's attire lacked the appropriate richness—plain cotton and wool, with a dowdy bronze-brown brocade weskit. This was Justice Hall. Perhaps Council meetings did not require velvet and jewels, but surely this hallowed place did.

It was yet one more example of Olken contempt.

Even more irksome was Sarnia Marnagh's deferential nod to him, as though the Olken were somehow greater than she. How could the woman continue to work here? Continue undermining her own people's standing? *Greaaer?* Asher and his Olken brethren weren't even *equal.*

Arlin's breath caught. "Father?"

With a conscious effort Rodyn relaxed his clenched fists. This remade Lur was a fishbone stuck in his gullet, pinching and chafing and ruining all appetite—but he would serve no-one, save nothing, if he did not keep himself temperate. He was here today to bear witness, nothing more. There was nothing more he could do. The times were yet green. But when they were ripe . . . oh, when they were ripe . . .

I'll see a harvest gathered that's long overdue.

At the far end of the Hall, seated at the judicial table upon its imposing dais, Asher struck the ancient summons bell three times with its small hammer. The airy chamber fell silent.

"Right, then," he said, lounging negligent in his carved and padded chair. "What's all this about? You're the one complaining, Meister Tarne, so best you flap your lips first."

So that was the Olken's name, was it? He'd never bothered to enquire. Who the man was didn't matter. All that mattered was his decision to interfere with Doranen magic. Even now he found it hard to believe this could be happening. It was an affront to nature, to the proper order of things, that any Olken was in a position to challenge the rights of a Doranen.

The Olken stood, then stepped out to the speaker's square before the dais. Bloated with too much food and self importance, he cast a triumphant look at Ain Freidin then thrust his thumbs beneath his straining braces and rocked on his heels.

"Meister Tarne it is, sir. And I'm here to see you settle this matter with my neighbour. I'm not one to go looking for unpleasantness. I'm a man who likes to live and let live. But I won't be bullied, sir, and I won't be told to keep my place. Those days are done with. I know my place. I know my rights."

Asher scratched his nose. "Maybe you do, but that ain't what I asked."

"My apologies," said the Olken, stiff with outrage. "I was only setting the scene, sir. Giving you an idea of—"

"What you be giving me, Meister Tarne, is piles," said Asher. "Happens I ain't in the mood to be sitting here all day on a sore arse, so just you bide a moment while I see if you can write a complaint better than you speak one."

As the Olken oaf sucked air between his teeth, affronted, Asher took the paper Sarnia Marnagh's Olken assistant handed him. Started to read it, ignoring Tarne and the scattered whispering from the Olken who'd come to point and stare and sneer at their betters. Ignoring Ain Freidin too. Sarnia Marnagh sat passively, her only contribution to these proceedings the incant recording this travesty of justice. What a treacherous woman she was. What a sad disappointment.

Condemned to idleness, Rodyn folded his arms. It seemed Asher was in one of his moods. And what did that bode? Since Barl's Wall was destroyed this was the twelfth—no, the thirteenth—time he'd been called to rule on matters magical in Justice Hall. Five decisions had gone the way of the Doranen. The rest had been settled in an Olken's favour. Did that argue bias? Perhaps. But—to his great shame—Rodyn couldn't say for certain. He'd not attended any of those previous rulings. Only in the last year had he finally, *finally*, woken from his torpor to face a truth he'd been trying so hard—and too long—to deny.

Lur was no longer a satisfactory place to be Doranen.

"So," said Asher, handing back the written complaint. "Meister Tarne. You reckon your neighbour—Lady Freidin, there—be ruining your potato crop with her magework. Or did I read your complaint wrong?"

"No," said the Olken. "That's what she's doing. And I've asked her to stop it but she won't." He glared at Ain Freidin. "So I've come here for you to tell her these aren't the old days. I've come for you to tell her to leave off with her muddling. Olken magic's as good as hers, by law, and by law she can't interfere with me and mine."

Arlin, up till now obediently quiet, made a little scoffing sound in his throat. Not entirely displeased, Rodyn pinched the boy's knee in warning.

"How ezackly is Lady Freidin spoiling your spuds, Meister Tarne?" said Asher, negligently slouching again. "And have you got any proof of it?"

Another hissing gasp. "Is my word not enough?" the potato farmer demanded. "I'm an Olken. You're an Olken. Surely—"

Sighing, Asher shook his head. "Not in Justice Hall, I ain't. In Justice Hall I be a pair of eyes and a pair of ears and I don't get to take sides, Meister Tarne."

"There are sworn statements," the chastised Olken muttered. "You have them before you."

"Aye, I read 'em," said Asher. "Your wife and your sons sing the same tune, Meister Tarne. But that ain't proof."

"Sir, why are you so quick to disbelieve me?" said the Olken. "I'm no idle troublemaker! It's an expense, coming here. An expense I can't easily bear, but I'm bearing it because I'm on the right side of this dispute. I've lost two crops to Lady Freidin's selfishness and spite. And since she won't admit her fault and mend her ways, what choice do I have but to lay the matter before you?"

Asher frowned at the man's tone. "Never said you weren't within your rights, Meister Tarne. Law's plain on that. You are."

"I know full well I'm not counted the strongest in earth magic," said the Olken, still defiant. "I'm the first to admit it. But I do well enough. Now I've twice got good potatoes rotted to slime in the ground and the market price of them lost. That's my proof. And how do I feed and clothe my family when my purse is half empty thanks to her?"

The watching Olken stirred and muttered their support. Displeased, Asher raised a hand. "You lot keep your traps shut or go home. I don't much care which. But if you *don't* keep your traps shut I'll take the choice away from you, got that?"

Rodyn smiled. If he'd been wearing a dagger he could have stabbed the offended silence through its heart.

"Meister Tarne," said Asher, his gaze still sharp. "I ain't no farmer, but even I've heard of spud rot."

"Well, sir, I *am* a farmer and I tell you plain, I've lost no crops to rot or any other natural pestilence," said the Olken. "It's Doranen magic doing the mischief here."

"So you keep sayin'," said Asher. "But it don't seem to me you got a shred of evidence."

"Sir, there's no other explanation! My farm marches beside Lady Freidin's estate. She's got outbuildings near the fence dividing my potatoes from her fields. She spends a goodly time in those outbuildings, sir. What she does there I can't tell you, not from seeing it with my own eyes. But my ruined potato crops tell the story. There's something unwholesome going on, and that's the plain truth of it."

"Unwholesome?" said Asher, eyebrows raised, as the Olken onlookers risked banishment to whisper. "Now, there's a word."

Rodyn looked away from him, to Ain Freidin, but still all he could see was the back of her head. Silent and straight-spined, she sat without giving even a hint of what she thought about these accusations. Or if they carried any merit. For himself . . . he wasn't sure. Ain Freidin was an acquaintance, nothing more. He wasn't privy to her thoughts on the changes thrust so hard upon their people, or what magic she got up to behind closed doors.

"Before it was a Doranen estate, the land next door to mine was a farm belonging to Eby Nye, and when it was a farm my potatoes were the best in the district," said the Olken, fists planted on his broad hips. "Not a speck of slime in the crop, season after season. Two seasons ago Eby sold up and she moved in, and both seasons since, my crops are lost. You can't tell me there's no binding those facts." He pointed at Ain Freidin. "That woman's up to no good. She's—"

"*That woman?*" said Ain, leaping to her expensively shod feet. "You dare refer to me in such a manner? I am Lady Freidin to you, and to *any* Olken."

"You can sit down, Lady Freidin," said Asher. "Don't recall askin' you to add your piece just yet."

Young and headstrong, her patience apparently at an end, Ain Freidin was yet to learn the value of useful timing. She neither sat nor restrained herself. "You expect me to ignore this clod's disrespect?"

"Last time I looked there weren't a law on the books as said Meister Tarne can't call you *that woman*," said Asher. "I'm tolerable sure there ain't even a law as says he can't call you a *slumskumbledy wench* if that be what takes his fancy. What I *am* tolerable sure of is in here, when I tell a body to sit down and shut up, they do it."

"You *dare* say so?" said Ain Freidin, her golden hair bright in the Hall's window-filtered sunlight and caged glimfire. "To *me?*"

"Aye, Lady Freidin, to you," Asher retorted, all his Olken arrogance on bright display. "To you and to any fool as walks in here thinkin' they've got weight to throw around greater than mine. Out there'?" He jerked a thumb at the nearest window, and the square beyond it with its scattering of warmly dressed City dwellers. "Out there, you and me, we be ezackly the same. But in Justice Hall *I* speak for the law—and in this kingdom there ain't a spriggin as stands above it. Barl herself made that plain as pie. What's more, there's a way we go about things when it comes to the rules and how we follow 'em and you ain't the one to say no, we'll do this your way."

Enthralled, the watching Olken held their breaths to see what Ain Freidin would say next. So did Arlin. Glancing down at his rapt son, Rodyn saw in the boy's face a pleasing and uncompromising contempt. So he was learning this lesson, at least. Good.

Asher picked up the summons bell's small hammer. "If I use this, Lady Freidin," he said, mild as a spring day now, and as changeable, "the hearing'll be over without you get to say a word in your defence. D'you want that? Did you come all this way from Marling Vale to go home again a good deal lighter in your purse, without me knowin' from your own lips how Meister Tarne lost his spuds to rot?"

"I cannot be deprived of my right to speak," said Ain Freidin, her voice thin with rage. "You are *not* the law here, Asher of Restharven. One act of magical serendipity hardly grants you the right to silence me."

"I don't want to silence you, Lady Freidin," said Asher. "I want you to answer Meister Tarne's complaint. What are you up to in them outbuildings of yours?"

"That's none of your business," Ain Freidin snapped.

"Reckon it is, if what you're up to means Meister Tarne keeps losing his spuds," said Asher. Still mild, but with a glint in his eye. "Folks be partial to their spuds, Lady Freidin. Boiled, mashed or fried, folks don't like to be without. Last thing we need in Lur is a spud shortage."

"So *I'm* to be blamed for the man's incompetence? Is that your idea of Barl's Justice?"

Asher idled with the bell's hammer. "Answer the question, Lady Freidin."

"The question is impertinent! I am not answerable to you, Asher of Restharven!"

As the watching Olken burst into shocked muttering, and Ain Freidin's family plucked at her sleeve and whispered urgent entreaties, Arlin wriggled on the bench.

"Is she right, Father?" he said. "Does she not have to say?"

Rodyn hesitated. He'd told the boy to be quiet, so this was a disobedience. But the question was a fair one. "By the laws established after the Wall fell, Lady Freidin is wrong. We Doranen must account for our use of magic."

"To the *Olken?*"

He nodded. "For now."

"But—"

Rodyn pinched his son to silence.

Ain Freidin's family was still remonstrating with her, their voices an undertone, their alarm unmistakable. They seemed to think she could be brought to see reason. But Asher, clearly irritated, not inclined to give her any more leeway, smacked the flat of his hand on the table before him.

"Reckon you be tryin' my patience, Lady Freidin," he announced. "Impertinent or not, it's a question as needs your answer."

"I am a mage," said Ain Freidin, her voice still thin. "My mage work is complex, and important."

"There!" said the Olken farmer. "You admit it! You're up to no good!"

Ain Freidin eyed him with cold contempt. "I admit you've no hope of comprehending what I do. I suggest you keep your fingers in the dirt, man, and out of my affairs."

"You hear that, sir?" said the farmer, turning to Asher. "She says it herself. She's doing magic in those outbuildings."

"That ain't breaking the law, Meister Tarne," said Asher. "Not if the magic's in bounds."

"And how can it be in bounds if my potato crops are *dying*?" cried the Olken. "Meister Asher—"

With his hand raised to silence the farmer, Asher looked again to Ain Freidin. "Aye, well, that's the nub of this dispute, ain't it? Lady Freidin, Barl made it plain to you Doranen what magic was right and what magic weren't. So . . . what mischief are you gettin' up to, eh?"

"*You* can no more comprehend the complexities of my work than can this—this—*clodhopper* beside me," snapped Ain Freidin. "Olken magic, if one can even *call* it magic, is not—"

"I'll tell you what it ain't," said Asher. "It ain't why we're here. And I reckon I've heard more than enough." He struck the bell with the hammer, three times. "I declare tor Meister Tarne. Lady Ain Freidin is fined twice the cost of his lost potato crops to cover Justice Hall expenses, five times their cost in damages plus one more for disrespecting Lur's rule of law, payable to him direct.

And she's to pay a hundred trins to the City Chapel, seein' how Barl never was one for proud and haughty folk of any stripe. Also she'll be frontin' up to the Mage Council on account of there being a question raised of unwholesome magic. Unless—" Leaning forward, Asher favoured Ain Freidin with a bared-teeth smile. "She cares to have a friendly chat in private once the business of payin' fines and charitable donations is sorted?"

For a moment Rodyn thought the foolish woman was going to create an unfortunate scene. He found himself holding his breath, willing her to retain both dignity and self-control. Ain Freidin intrigued him. There was something about her, he could feel it. She had power. Potential. She was someone he'd do well to watch. But if she forced Asher's hand . . .

As though she could hear his thoughts, Ain's braced shoulders slumped. "A private discussion is agreeable," she said, her voice dull.

"Then we're done," said Asher. He sounded disgusted. "Lady Marnagh will see to the details, and bring you to me once you've arranged payment of your fines."

Rodyn stood. "Come, Arlin."

Leaving Ain Freidin to her fate, and the Olken rabble to cavort as they felt like, he led his son out of Justice Hall. Standing on its broad steps he took a deep breath, striving to banish his anger. A Doranen mage answerable to Asher of Restharven? The notion was repellent. Repugnant. An affront to every Doranen in Lur. But as things stood, there was nothing he could do about it.

As things stood.

It was past noon, but still enough of the late winter day

remained to send messengers to discreet friends, call a meeting, discuss what had happened here.

And it must be discussed. The situation grows less tolerable by the day. I know how I would like to address it. The question is, am I alone?

"He didn't know. But the time was ripe to find out.

"Come, Arlin," he said again, and started down the steps.

"We're walking back to the townhouse?" said Arlin, staying put. "But—"

He turned. "Are you *defying* me, Arlin?"

"No, Father," Arlin whispered, his eyes wide. "Of course not, Father."

"Good," he said, turning away. "That's wise of you, boy."

"Yes, Father," said Arlin, and followed him, obedient.

Sat at the desk in the corner of the townhouse library, tasked to an exercise he found so simple now it bored him to tears, Arlin listened to his father wrangle back and forth with his vistors over Lady Ain Freidin and her hearing in Justice Hall.

"There's no use in protesting her being called to account by an Olken, Rodyn," said Lord Baden, one of Father's closest friends. "The time to protest is ten years behind us. When Lur came crashing down around our ears, *then* we had the chance to mould the kingdom more to our liking. We didn't. And now we're forced to live with the consequences."

"Forever?" said Father. "Is that your contention, Sarle? That we meekly accept our portion without question until the last star in the firmament winks out?"

Arlin flinched, tumbling his exercise blocks to the carpet.

"What are you doing, boy?" Father demanded. "Must I interrupt my business to school you?"

On his hands and knees, scrabbling under the desk to retrieve the scattered blocks, he fought to keep his voice from trembling. "No, Father."

"Get off the floor, then. Do your exercises. And don't interrupt again or you'll be the sorrier for it."

"Yes, Father."

The training blocks cradled awkward to his chest, he caught a swift glimpse of sympathy in Sarle Baden's pale, narrow face. Father's other visitor, Lord Vail, eyed him with a vague, impatient dislike. Cheeks flushed with embarrassed heat he got his feet under himself and stood. In the library fireplace, the flames leaped and crackled.

Lord Baden cleared his throat. "Rodyn, my friend, I think you need to be a trifle less circumspect. Are you suggesting we foment social unrest? For I must be honest with you, I doubt the idea will be met with anything but distaste."

"I agree," said Lord Vail. "Lite is comfortable, Rodyn. What Morg broke is long since mended. The royal family's not missed. We've suffered no hardship with the fall of Barl's Wall. I strongly doubt you'll get anyone to agree with stirring trouble."

Arlin held his breath. Father *hated* to be contradicted. The blocks he held in his hands hummed with power, fighting against their proximity to each other. He subdued them, distracted, and waited to see what Father would do.

Father nodded. "True, Ennet," he said, with a surprising

lack of temper. "Nothing's changed in Lur. Unless of course you count the Olken and their magic."

"But I don't," said Lord Vail, sneering. "You can't say you do, surely? You can't even say it's magic, Rodyn. Calling what the Olken do magic is like calling a candle-flame a conflagration."

Contradicted again, and still Father did not snap and snarl. Bemused, Arlin set the blocks on the desk and sat once more in his straight-backed chair. The blocks jostled before him, their energies tugging fitfully at each other. With a thought he calmed them, smoothed them to amity. Then, picking up the foundation block, he let his gaze slide sideways, beneath his lowered lashes, to see what happened next.

Instead of challenging Lord Vail, Father looked at Lord Baden. "Sarle, what do you know of Ain Freidin? Didn't you court her cousin?"

Lord Baden laughed. "Years ago, without luck. And Ain was a child then."

"What did you make of her?"

"Make of her?" Lord Baden stared at Father, surprised. "She was a *child*, Rodyn. What does one make of a child?"

"Whatever one needs," Father murmured, smiling faintly. Then he frowned. "Was she precocious, when you knew her? Was she inclined to take risks?"

"Risks?" Lord Baden tapped a thoughtful finger to his lips. "I don't know, but now that you mention it, Rodyn . . . she was certainly *bold*."

"In the hearing she was accused of destructive magics."

Lord Vail grimaced. "You'd take the word of an Olken?"

"Never," said Father. "But I can't deny it's likely she was caught out in some mischief. She accepted the adverse ruling and the fines without fighting them and was quick to avoid explaining herself to the Mage Council. That says to me she had something to hide."

"It's your opinion she's been . . . experimenting?" said Lord Baden, after a moment. "If that's so, then she's grown more than bold." He glanced over. "But perhaps this isn't a fit topic of conversation. Young Arlin—"

"You needn't concern yourself with Arlin," said Father. "My son knows how to hold his tongue."

"It's not his discretion I'm concerned with, Rodyn. He's a boy, yet. I don't care to—"

"And *I* don't care to be lectured, Sarle," Father snapped. "Arlin cannot learn soon enough what it means to be Doranen in this new Lur of ours."

"For the life of me, Rodyn, I can't see what you're getting at," Lord Vail complained. "Lur hasn't changed. *We* haven't changed. All is as it was, aside from the Olken and their dabblings and as I keep telling you, they don't count. They weren't important before and they're not important now."

Father leaned torward in his comtortable leather armchair, elbows braced on his knees, his expression keenly hungry. "That's my point, Ennet. As Sarle so rightly has said, the destruction of Barl's Wall and the fall of House Torvig—the end of WeatherWorking—that was a moment when our lives could have changed. *Should* have changed. But we allowed ourselves to be overcome by the upheaval. We permitted ourselves to be paralyzed with guilt, over Morg, over Conroyd Jarralt, and Durm.

FOR THE LATEST NEWS AND THE HOTTEST EXCLUSIVES ON ALL
YOUR FAVOURITE SF AND FANTASY STARS, SIGN UP FOR:

ORBIT'S <u>FREE</u> MONTHLY E-ZINE

PACKED WITH

BREAKING NEWS
THE LATEST REVIEWS
EXCLUSIVE INTERVIEWS
STUNNING EXTRACTS
SPECIAL OFFERS
BRILLIANT COMPETITIONS

AND A GALAXY OF
NEW AND ESTABLISHED SFF STARS!

TO GET A DELICIOUS SLICE OF SFF IN <u>YOUR</u> INBOX EVERY MONTH, SEND YOUR
DETAILS BY EMAIL TO: <u>ORBIT@LITTLEBROWN.CO.UK</u> OR VISIT:

 WWW.ORBITBOOKS.NET

THE HOME OF SFF ONLINE